Modern Love

An anthology of
erotic fiction by women

Black lace novels are sexual fantasies.
In real life, make sure you practise safe sex.

First published in 1997 by
Black Lace
332 Ladbroke Grove
London W10 5AH

Extracts from the following works:

Aria Appassionata	© Juliet Hastings 1996
Crash Course	© Juliet Hastings 1995
The Tutor	© Portia Da Costa 1994
Healing Passion	© Sylvie Ouellette 1995
The Silken Cage	© Sophie Danson 1994
Cassandra's Conflict	© Fredrica Alleyn 1993
Black Orchid	© Roxanne Carr 1993
Eye of the Storm	© Georgina Brown 1995
Virtuoso	© Katrina Vincenzi 1994
The Devil and the Deep Blue Sea	© Cheryl Mildenhall 1995
Led on by Compulsion	© Leila James 1995
The House in New Orleans	© Fleur Reynolds 1994
Wicked Work	© Pamela Kyle 1994

Typeset by CentraCet Ltd, Cambridge
Printed and bound by Cox & Wyman Ltd, Reading

ISBN 0 352 33158 4

Contents

Introduction

*B*lack Lace is the first series of books to recognise women's erotic fiction as a genre. Before the series was launched in the UK in summer 1993, there was very little material of this nature which was designed with a female audience in mind. Nancy Friday, author of *My Secret Garden*, was one of the first people to recognise female sexual fantasy as a valid and exciting area for exploration and study. Her work was non-judgmental and legitimised no-holds-barred writing about sex from women's viewpoints. Despite this, erotic *fiction* remained the preserve of men. Friday's book was categorised as non-fiction/sexology and was first published in the early 1970s. Much writing about women and sex in the following two decades took a journalistic path; it was where women felt comfortable.

Of course, women writing explicit stories is nothing new; Anais Nin was working in this area 50 years ago and her work continues to sell long after her death. It has taken a long while for publishers to realise that women want to read erotic stories which aren't deliberately obscured by metaphorical or circum-spect writing and which only hint at sex. We have been told that women 'aren't interested in reading about such things' and 'prefer romantic novels'. The female erotic imagination is a storehouse of secret treasures whose diversity constitutes a genre in its own right. Men have always been able to access sexually explicit material and have controlled its production and distri-bution for centuries. At Black Lace, we think women have as much right as men to read blatantly arousing fiction which is their own. Our readers like the fact that Black Lace books guarantee female authorship.

Modern Love brings together extracts from some of the most popular and best-selling Black Lace titles which have contemporary settings. Whether set in the corridors of academia or a haunted mansion; on a river trip in New Orleans or in an opera house in London, each story is imbued with a rich and unashamed sense of erotic escapism. Some of our authors are fond of exploring the darker facets of the female imagination; places where 'sex and shopping' novels have feared to tread. It is important to remember that the free-flowing imagination is not censored by notions of political correctness; any imprint which gives a free rein to explore sexual fantasy is going to encounter writing in which characters challenge notions of 'acceptable' behaviour. Erotic fantasy is an exciting and endlessly fascinating subject. We've no shortage of manuscripts from women of all ages and walks of life, and we are confident that Black Lace books will continue to reflect the infinite diversity of the female erotic imagination.

Kerri Sharp October 1996

Aria Appassionata

Juliet Hastings

Tess Challoner is due to play Carmen in a new production of the opera which promises to be as passionate and explicit as it is intelligent. But Tess is inexperienced. To play Carmen convincingly she needs to know a lot more about physical desire than she does.

In the following extract from *Aria Appassionata*, Tess is reflecting on her life, her lovers and her future – and taking positive action to get herself into the role of opera's greatest femme fatale.

The second piece is from Juliet's first Black Lace story, *Crash Course*. Kate is a successful management consultant whose skill at teaching assertiveness and interpersonal dynamics to business employees is well respected. When she has to run a course at short notice, she is pleased to find that three of the four participants are attractive, powerful men and Kate takes the opportunity to bring out the best in them. In the chosen extract, Sophie, the only woman on the course, confronts Kate about her methodology but soon finds herself succumbing to her persuasive charm.

Juliet Hastings has written six books for Black Lace. Although comfortable with contemporary settings, her knowledge of history has provided the series with a wealth of meticulously researched and beautifully eroticised historical detail. Julia's other Black Lace novels are: *White Rose Ensnared* (15th-century England), *Forbidden Crusade* (set in the Holy Land in 1160) and *The Hand of Amun* (Ancient Egypt).

Aria Appassionata

*T*ess returned home alone and lowered her bag slowly to the floor inside the door, sighing heavily. Although it was late, the June light was still bright outside the flat, and green leaves stirred at the tops of the trees, level with her windows.

'I'm tired,' Tess told the flat. And she was, very tired. For a week she had worked hard at rehearsals, gone to movement and body workshops run by Adam, visited her teacher for technical coaching through the hardest parts of the score, worked with Julian at solos and ensembles so that she understood what the conductor wanted, and each night she had gone to Tony's flat and allowed herself to be drawn into his sexual world, which each night had become more and more strange, exotic and peculiarly satisfying. There were blue bruises on the white skin of her haunches where Tony's strong fingers had gripped her tightly and pulled her violently back onto his throbbing phallus, and her wrists and ankles were red and raw where he had tied her up. She knew that he behaved as if he owned her, but she could hardly decide whether he was in love with her and eager for her to experience the whole gamut of lust, or whether he hated her and simply wanted to degrade and humiliate her. Either way, he was opening her eyes to an entirely new sensual world. But sexual discovery was time and energy consuming. Tess had hardly been in her own flat all week, and now she was so exhausted that she could hardly see it.

She walked wearily into the kitchen, thinking with pleasant anticipation of a mug of hot chocolate, and opened the fridge.

An unmistakably cheesy smell told her that the milk had gone off. 'Bugger,' she said.

There wasn't much point in thinking about hot chocolate without milk, and Tess simply didn't feel up to going back into Hampstead to find some. So she slammed the fridge door, picked up an apple from the fruit bowl and stalked through to the bathroom, moodily munching.

She looked at herself in the bathroom mirror. There were rings under her eyes and her skin looked pasty. 'Early night for you,' she said to her reflection. 'Nice hot bath and an early night.'

Moving slowly, she turned on the taps and then pulled off her clothes and dumped them into the laundry basket. It was almost full, because she hadn't even had a chance to do the washing for about a week. I'll run out of clean knickers soon, she thought, and then where will I be? And then she reflected that Tony would probably approve heartily of her going without knickers, and the thought made her laugh.

Presently she was naked and the bath was almost full. Tess poured a little body oil into the water and added a few drops of tea tree oil, because her voice felt furry and she wanted to inhale the sharp, soothing steam while she soaked. She got into the bath and lay back, looking up at the ceiling.

After a while the clean, antiseptic smell of the oil cleared her head and made her feel able to sing a little. She closed her eyes and began to murmur to herself, very soft and low:

> *There's somebody here who's waiting for me,*
> *I hope that he turns out to be*
> *Someone who'll watch over me . . .*

Then she stopped and lay still, breathing deeply and frowning to herself. Why sing that song? What did it mean?

Every man Tess had known had been, in the physical sense, someone to watch over her. Leo had taught her how her body could give her pleasure and how she could give pleasure to a man. Dan had used her, but his extraordinary beauty had made her actively desire him. And Tony – Tony was possessive, physically affectionate, kinky, masterful. Certainly someone to watch over her. So why sing that song now, and why sing it in that tone of soft, aching longing?

Carmen wouldn't have wanted someone to watch over her.

4

Tess shifted a little in the bath, letting the warm, silky water play over her floating breasts and between her legs. She thought of Carmen, her character, as she would like to portray her. Strong, beautiful, callous, doomed. Doomed because she insisted upon her passionate independence, her freedom to love whom she chose, and a man's jealousy could not bear it.

Tess caught the chain with her toe and let a little of the water run out of the bath. Then, hardly knowing what she was doing, she picked up the shower head and turned on the shower. Hot water pulsed out on to her warm wet body. She let her head tilt back so that her hair floated around her and gently, slowly guided the spray between her legs.

She let out a long, blissful sigh as the tingling stream of water caressed her thighs, her labia, the entrance to her sex. The bobbing orbs of her breasts tensed and tautened with sudden arousal and her nipples erected, stiff symbols of desire. The beat of the water on her sensitive flesh was almost too much, and for a moment she drew the shower head away, letting the weight of the flow fall onto the furred mound of her pubis. But it wasn't enough, and after a moment she moved the spray infinitesimally, until one glittering thread of water sprang through the air and struck the swelling bud of her clitoris.

'Ah,' Tess breathed slowly. Her diaphragm rose and fell, drawing air deep into her lungs, and as she breathed her hips also lifted and fell, surging up towards the insistent touch of the spray.

She felt her body floating in the warm water as if she were the only living creature in the world, as if she were isolated and alone, seeking her solitary pleasure without compunction or shame. The ripples lapped across her breasts, stroking her tight nipples, and between her pale, parted thighs the shower beat down on to her quivering sex, pummelling the sensitive flesh with unbearable pleasure.

For a moment Tess thought of Tony, his smooth, olive skin and his dark eyes and hair; the way that when he prepared to take her his lips would curl with lustful anger as if he were the toreador and she the bull, run down, exhausted, helpless, waiting for him to plunge his spear into her shuddering body. But although she did not consciously know it, her body had had enough of being Tony's slave. She wanted variety, and of itself

5

her brain provided the image that would accompany her pleasure.

A mermaid on a rock, silver-green tail coiled over the slimy, cold stone. Her breasts are small and round and high and her body is white as a corpse's, starred with her coral lips and her rosy nipples like bright shells upon a beach of white sand. Her eyes are the colour of her tail, the colour of the sea, and her hair is dark red, like dried blood. It is long and thick and shining and she sits very calmly on the rock amid the foaming sea and combs her long tresses with a comb of pearl. She is beautiful, but with an unearthly beauty, a deadly beauty, and her eyes are cold as the waves and quite pitiless.

She lifts her head, never once interrupting the rhythm of her combing, like the rhythm of the waves that beat against her limpet-studded rock. In the distance she has seen a ship. It is a warriors' ship, brightly painted, and on its square sail is drawn the figure of a bull. She can see the men in it at their oars, naked for their labour, rowing with all their strength against the surging might of the contrary sea.

Men are her prey, she needs them as a beast needs meat to live. Her cold eyes brighten and she flickers her tail against the rock like a cat that sees the mouse. She combs and combs her heavy hair, and as she combs she opens her soft, red lips and begins to sing.

Her voice is like wine, like dark, soft fur, like a coil of smoke that seeps from the hearth fire to draw the man home from the hunt. She does not sing loudly, and yet that sweet dark voice carries over the crash and roar of the waves and flies straight to the ears of the young warriors rowing their ship. They hear it and stop their work, helpless, enchanted, dumbstruck and frozen by the promise of delight in the mermaid's song.

Still she sings, and now the young men tremble. Her song is wordless, and each of them hears what he wishes, and each of them hears her singing of the zenith of sensual delight. Each one hears her telling him how she longs for him, how her small snowy breasts are taut with yearning, how her nipples are tight and hard as rose-hips, how her soft white flesh aches for him to come to her and take her in his arms and possess her with his strong, male body, thrusting himself into her, making her sweet voice cry out in pleasure for him alone. They see her beautiful whiteness, her breasts stirring as she combs her hair, and they forget that she is a sea creature, that where a woman has a sex she has nothing but a fish's tail, and they cannot tell that her song is no more than the web a spider spins to catch a fly. They drop their oars and begin to fight among themselves for the privilege of flinging themselves over the side into the heaving surf to swim to her.

The mermaid watches them and sings still, and now her song is more urgent. The young men fight furiously upon their shuddering ship, drawing blood, for they can hear her singing, *Draw me on to ecstasy! Make me yours! Take your pleasure in my body, spill your seed within me, ravish me, possess me!*

At last one of them pushes another aside and leaps up on to the side of the ship, which is protected and bedecked with painted shields. For a moment he stands poised, splendidly naked, his beautiful body taut with eagerness, his face bright with anticipation as he hears the siren's song. He throws himself at last from the ship's gunwale and cleaves the foaming sea in a perfect dive, and the mermaid smiles and drops her pearly comb and slides from her rock to meet him in the tumbling waves.

Her song has ceased, and the other young men on the ship suddenly stop fighting and draw apart and look at each other with horror in their eyes. While she sang they were bewitched, and now they are freed they know their danger and run to their oars to try to save their foundering ship, unable to spare even a glance for their companion as he cuts through the surf towards the white body of the mermaid. But they are too late, they are doomed, the rocks are snapping their eager teeth at the ship's frail timbers and in moments they will be shivered into spars and flotsam.

In the sea the mermaid dives and circles once around the swimming youth. He is as strong and beautiful as her cold heart could wish. She swims up beside him and rubs her soft breasts against him. His body is muscular and warm and it pleases her to touch him, as it pleases a cat to rub itself against a stranger's hand. She laughs to see how his flesh reacts to her, his strange male sex stiffening despite the cold kiss of the fierce sea, and he laughs to see her laughing. She presses her chilly skin close to him and reaches up to kiss him with her mouth. Her tail locks around his thighs and her arms wrap around him, pinioning his hands to his sides, and with the tip of her tail she caresses that strange stiff rod of flesh, rubbing it, stroking the soft skin up and down until the young man groans into her open mouth and his body heaves against her and warm pearly liquid bursts from the end of his male organ and floats like froth on the surface of the waves.

He is limp in her arms, as if he has spurted his strength into the sea with his seed, and she smiles at him again and puts her lips over his. She pulls him down beneath the waves. He does not struggle, and as he drowns in her cold grasp she puts her tongue into his warm mouth and tastes his fleeing soul.

Tess arched in the warm water, her eyes tight shut, every muscle tense as the cascading liquid drew her into an orgasm that shuddered and rippled through her like the cold sea that was the mermaid's home. For an infinite second she hung there, not breathing, not thinking, a body of pure pleasure suspended in nothingness. Then she relaxed and lay back, her breath coming raggedly, her lips dry and aching.

As she made her way slowly to bed she thought about that strange fantasy. It was new to her. Where had it come from? Why should it arouse her to think of dragging a beautiful young man to his doom? That it had aroused her was clear: her climax had been tremendous. For a moment she was afraid that Tony's dominance was making her strange. Then she realised the meaning of it. The mermaid was another personification of the character she was trying to become; of Carmen, a callous, cold, beautiful creature, binding men to her with the powerful spell of her lovely voice, sucking the strength from them and then abandoning them, limp, lifeless husks.

Tess slid down below the duvet and shivered. Such power, such control, and all springing from that extraordinary gift – her own voice. For a moment she was almost afraid. But then, as sleep crept up on her, the sense of fear began to fade, and when she slipped into dreams they too were dreams of strength and erotic power.

She woke very late. Fuzzy with sleep she rolled over in bed and caught hold of her alarm clock. It was quarter to eleven, and she blinked and swayed as she sat up and pushed her hands through her hair.

A day to herself. She had nothing planned, and it felt quite odd to have time to do nothing if she wanted. She got up slowly, made herself tea, sorted out a wash, showered and then put her dressing gown back on and went and sat on the sofa, still half dozing. Outside the weather was gloomy, with heavy clouds threatening rain. Tess considered the dark sky for a few moments, then went to find warm clothes and her Wellington boots.

By the time she was ready to go out the rain was coming down in sheets. She pulled the hood of her Goretex jacket securely up round her ears, galumphed down the stairs and out into the rain. Within a few minutes she was on the Heath. There was nobody else about, even the most diligent dog walkers were waiting for the weather to improve, and she splashed across the soft leaf-mould under the great oaks, breathing in the fresh, wet air. There was something about the quality of the air when it was raining that she found irresistible, healing and soothing both to her vocal cords and to her mind. She stood in a little glade on a patch of new grass, pulled back her hood and tilted her face to the pouring rain. The cold drops stung her eyelids and her forehead, her cheeks and chin, and she stretched out her hands and breathed deeply.

She would remember how it had felt to be the mermaid. She would remember that sense of power and strength, of sexual desire and sexual desirability combined with absolute callousness. She would infuse her portrayal of Carmen with that feeling.

Jeannette had been right, she had needed time on her own. It was so easy to allow herself just to become an adjunct of Tony, someone who went along with whatever he wanted, acceding to all his demands. Not good enough.

As she turned for home another thought occurred to her. If research was what it took to play a part well, then perhaps she ought to do some research on the other point of Carmen's character that was giving her problems: her reliance on the cards.

Back at the flat Tess shed her soaking clothes and wrapped herself in a warm towel, then picked up the phone and dialled. She made a face when after three rings Emma's sweeter-than-honey voice said, 'Hello. You've reached the answering service of Emma Ridley, Catherine Gibbs and Jeannette Baldwin. Please leave a message after the beep. Thanks ever so much.' Awful woman, Tess thought. She even gushes at her answering machine.

'Jeannette,' she said after the beep, 'hi, it's Tess. It's Sunday morning and I – '

'Hi, Tess!' Jeannette's voice was breathless. Tess held the

receiver away from her ear. Talking to Jeannette on the phone was like talking to a sawmill. 'What's up?'

'How are you?' Tess asked. 'Did you have a good time last night?'

'Wow, did we! You were right about Julian, Tess. He's got a tongue like a corkscrew. Though I think the two of us must more or less have worn it out last night. And we stripped his thread, too.'

'He's not still there, is he?'

'Oh no, he went home in the small hours. He didn't want Emma to see him here this morning. Don't blame him, either. She sniffed around a bit before she went out, you could almost hear her thinking *I'm sure I smell a man*, like the witch in *Hansel and Gretel*. But Cath and I have kept quiet, so Julian's secret is safe with us.'

'Listen,' Tess said hesitantly, 'I was thinking about what you said. About research. And I wondered if you would give me the number of your friend, the one who reads the Tarot? I'd like to call her.'

'Why, sure!' Jeannette sounded surprised and pleased. 'Hang on while I get my organiser. Here you go. Her name's Sarah, Sarah Carter.'

'Very ordinary name,' said Tess, surprised.

'She's just a friend of mine,' said Jeannette. 'We met at a party, years ago. She's not a singer or anything, she works in an office. But she's a good reader.' She read out the number. 'Lives in Bow. Give her a call, go and see her. Say I sent you.'

'Is she expensive?'

'She does it for fun. I doubt she'd charge you anything.'

Early in the afternoon Tess found herself at Bow station, looking at the map of the local area on the station wall and trying to find out where Sarah Carter lived.

She had sounded almost absurdly normal over the telephone. Maybe a little older than Tess, in her thirties perhaps, and quite straightforward and pragmatic. Tess had explained that she was only doing research for a role and she really just wanted to talk in principle and Sarah had said, 'Well, why not? Why not come and have tea? I've got nothing particular to do this afternoon. I'd love to meet you.'

Tess found the house quite easily and stood in the street

outside, looking at it. It was a very ordinary Victorian terraced house, nicely kept. There were roses in the front garden, bowed down almost to the ground with the weight of raindrops in their tumbled flowers, and the door and the window frames were painted dark blue and white.

The door opened and a woman stood there, a nice-looking fair-haired woman. Yes, early thirties, tall and rather stately, with strong bones and deep-set grey eyes. She was smiling. 'You've found it,' she said. 'Come in. You must be Tess.'

Tess expected the house to be full of all sorts of arcane paraphernalia, but it wasn't. It was a perfectly normal house, tidy rather than not, comfortably furnished, with real fireplaces and what estate agents call 'original features'. Some of the pictures on the walls were rather odd, and the books in the drawing room bookcase revealed a very eclectic interest in all sorts of things – whale songs, folklore, herbalism, holistic remedies, aromatherapy, astrology and the occult – but there was nothing frightening about it.

Sarah brought a tray of tea and Digestive biscuits. The tea was Earl Grey, which Tess took as a good sign, and served in astrological mugs, dark blue with little golden star signs on them. It was excellent tea. Sarah smiled over her mug at Tess and said, 'So from what you told me, you're a sceptic and you want enough information to be convincing as Carmen.' Her voice was very reassuring, soft and pleasantly modulated.

'Well – ' Tess began to protest, but then she shrugged. 'No, you're right. That is right.'

'I would have thought', said Sarah, 'that the best way to proceed is for me to do a reading for you. Then you can see the style, and even if you aren't convinced you'll understand how it comes over.'

Tess shook her head. 'No,' she said, 'I don't think that would be a good idea.' She was filled with apprehension.

'Why not?' Sarah didn't seem offended, just interested.

'Because – ' because it might be true. Tess realised that she must be looking as if she was frightened, and she was angry with herself. If it was all rubbish, why be afraid of it? 'Well,' she said, trying to look casual, 'well, what the hell? Why not?'

Sarah looked quietly at her as if she were not the least convinced by this bravado. She said simply, 'I'll get the cards.'

* * *

When Tess left the house in Bow more than two hours later she was shaken. She had expected to hear nothing but platitudes, obvious statements which anyone with any sense of the dramatic could have concocted from what they already knew about her. But Sarah, in her calm, serious voice, had laid one pattern of cards, then another, and from them had drawn so much that she could not possibly have known.

She had said that Tess had worked hard to achieve her current position. Well, anyone who knew anything about singing could have said that. That she was now facing a challenge: fair guess. That in order to achieve what she now sought she would need to change herself, or at least to appear to others that she had changed herself.

By this stage Tess had felt uncomfortable. She had asked Sarah about her love life, making light of it, as if it were some sort of a joke, but Sarah had seemed equally serious on this question. She laid another pattern of cards and frowned, then said, 'You haven't had a great many lovers. Two or three, perhaps. And they have dominated you. The current man especially is jealous.' She looked up into Tess's eyes, perhaps seeking confirmation, but Tess looked hunted and unconvinced. Sarah could have learnt this from Jeannette. After a little pause Sarah laid an extra card and frowned again. 'Men dominate your work life as well as love. That's not surprising; men are in such a strong position. I suppose the person you are working for at present is male and you have to seek to please him. But the pattern is very strong for love, too. You allow your man to dominate you.' She looked concerned, and after a while she said, 'In the future perhaps – perhaps you will free yourself from this dominating influence and find your own way. If you are going to develop as much as you can, if you are going to achieve everything you want, then you have to do it. You have to free yourself. You can't go on relying on your lovers as you do. But, you should be careful.'

'Careful? Why?'

'I don't quite understand this,' said Sarah. 'It's as if – as if you are two people at present. And for both of them there may be – danger, conflict, but for one it is real, for the other – potential, or imaginary, I can't tell. But if you are to progress, if you are to succeed, you will have to face the conflict and brave the danger.'

Despite herself Tess was caught up. She leant forward, studying the cards Sarah held: the Chariot, the Knight of Swords. 'Will I succeed?' she asked in a low voice. 'In – in love, I mean?'

'Are you talking about love, or sex?' Sarah asked calmly.

'Sex,' said Tess, though she meant love.

Sarah turned another card. It was a Star. She said very slowly, 'If you come through the conflict, then there is great potential. But you must take control.' She looked up. 'I can't say yes or no. It depends on you.'

This was the sort of prevarication that Tess had expected. She refrained from curling her lip and asked in a cynical voice, 'Tell me, Sarah, can you ever see death in the cards? Can you tell if someone is going to die?'

Sarah's voice was very level. 'Sometimes, yes. But I would never tell them.'

Tess didn't want to go back to the flat with all of this rocketing around inside her head. At Tottenham Court Road she got off the Central line, intending to change to the Northern, and then on impulse left the station instead and walked down Charing Cross Road towards Trafalgar Square. Her head was buzzing with possibilities. It wasn't so much what she had been told as the way Sarah had spoken. It was clear not only that she believed what she said, but that in the past her observations and predictions had been confirmed as true. And Sarah seemed like an ordinary, sensible person, not a charlatan. She hadn't charged Tess anything, she didn't make her living from it, it was just something she did.

It's as if you are two people at present . . . Yes, two people. Herself, Tess Challoner, and Carmen, her character, the character she was trying to make her own. And unless she freed herself from the dominance of the men in her life, she would fail. It was horribly persuasive. Certainly she no longer had trouble in understanding why Carmen might believe what she saw in her own cards.

A savoury, delicious smell came to Tess's nose. She lifted her head, realising suddenly that she was starving. She hadn't eaten since the morning, and now it was nearly seven o'clock. She thought of her empty fridge and the smelly milk and turned without a second thought towards Soho and a bowl of pasta cooked by someone else.

Sunday evening, and the pasta bar she settled on was fairly quiet. A waiter showed her to a table in a corner and put a menu in front of her. She looked through it absent-mindedly, still thinking hard about what Sarah had told her. If this meant that she should not continue her affair with Tony, what would she do? And what would Tony do? It was true that he was jealous and possessive. How would he react if she ended it? Could this be the danger, the conflict that Sarah had foreseen?

What should she do? With Tony in charge she never had to think for herself, never had to worry. He took care of everything, deciding where they should go out to eat, when they should stay in, where they should make love, exactly how he intended that Tess would achieve orgasm that night. It wasn't always exactly the way she might have chosen if she had been left to herself, but it happened. What was she supposed to do without him? Take Julian home to Hampstead and keep him as a pet?

'Hi, good evening,' said a male voice. 'I'm Dean. Can I take your order, or are you waiting for someone?'

Tess looked up, her mouth open to speak. But she said nothing. The young man standing in front of her met her eyes, then slowly raised his brows and smiled at her.

There it was again, that audible click of sexual attraction that James had asked her for. It was even stronger now, when she was faced with a man she didn't even know, had never seen before. It was there, undeniable. She looked at the waiter for a long moment, committing the feeling to memory.

He was very handsome in a male model sort of way, fairly tall and broad shouldered, with very clean-cut features, bright blue eyes and light brown, thick hair which should have hung on his shoulders but was tied back for his work. Like all the staff he wore black trousers, a white, open-neck shirt and a long, white apron. His face was mischievous, with a deep dimple on one cheek. He looked into Tess's eyes and smiled slightly. The dimple deepened. His smile said, *You think I'm a hunk, and by God, you're right*.

Cocky sod, Tess thought. He was a hunk, but that wasn't the point. She shook back her hair and said coolly, 'I'm not waiting for anyone, and yes you may take my order.'

At that his expression changed. Now his eyes told her that he had enjoyed her little spark of temper and that he thought that she was very attractive too. He drew his order pad from the pocket of his apron and held his pen poised over it, looking attentive. 'What can I bring you?' he asked. He had a deep voice tinged with an East End accent, the voice of a bit of rough.

For one delicious moment Tess imagined herself saying, *Your cock on a plate, with a salad garnish.* She bit her lip and smiled to herself, then said, 'Spaghetti al pesto, please. And a bottle of sparkling mineral water.' She allowed herself to smile at him. *Yes,* her smile said, *I think you're a hunk.*

'Right away,' Dean said. He smiled back at her and then folded his pad and turned to go off to the kitchen. Tess watched him go. He had a really lovely bottom, high and taut, and it was framed by the ties of his white apron in a way that might have been designed to call attention to its pertness. Tess leant her chin on her folded hands and watched appreciatively as that athletic arse moved away from her, carried her order through the door and vanished into the kitchen.

A very good-looking young waiter indeed. And what, just what, did she propose to do about it?

Her mind shied away from the obvious suggestion. It made for a pleasant fantasy, but she couldn't make it reality. She moved her finger on the marble top of the small table, musing.

Somebody changed the background music from jazz to classical, the CD of the Three Tenors concert. The ringing voice of Pavarotti filled the restaurant, singing the most famous aria of all, the World Cup anthem from *Turandot. I shall conquer*, he sang, *I shall conquer.*

A movement by the table made Tess jump. She looked up and saw Dean looking down at her, smiling, a bottle of mineral water in his hand. He poured it into her glass and set down what was left on the table, then said, 'The pasta in just a few minutes.'

'Thank you,' Tess said. Their eyes met again. She thought, *He really is very good-looking indeed*, and she saw her attraction mirrored in his blue eyes. How old was he? 26, 27? He had an uncomplicated face and a splendid strong body under his waiter's uniform. She let her eyes follow him as he left the table, and before he went through into the kitchen he glanced over his shoulder at her.

She couldn't. She didn't dare. But as she sipped the cool water she imagined what she might do. She could lay her hand on top of his as he set her plate on the table or filled her glass. She could put her fingers on his thigh, on the back of his thigh where the apron did not cover him, where the skin was tender and sensitive below the fabric of his trousers. Any movement, one touch on her part would be enough. He would know what she meant – that she wanted him.

And then what? Ask him when he finished work, meet him outside, go for a drink, go back to his place or ask him back to hers? Oh come on, Tess, she thought. You're in a relationship, you don't want to start another. Why can't it just be a simple question of sexual satisfaction? You fancy him, he fancies you, you do something about it, you scratch the itch, no more to be said.

Because life's not like that, she told herself. She took a deep draught of her water and shook her head. Then she saw him coming towards her, her plate of spaghetti in his hand.

'Spaghetti al pesto,' he said, putting it in front of her. 'Enjoy it. Would you like some extra parmesan?' She shook her head mutely. 'Black pepper?'

'Yes please,' said Tess. Dean smiled and fetched the pepper mill, which was as long, thick and phallic as all its kind. He held it up and raised his eyebrows at her. 'All over?' he enquired archly.

'Please,' Tess managed to say, though she wanted to laugh.

'There you go,' said Dean, obliging. 'A couple of good screws is enough for most people.'

Tess couldn't resist it. 'Really? Only two?'

They had been joking, but suddenly he met her eyes and there was something more there, something hot and earnest. The pepper mill dangled unnoticed from his hand. For a moment they didn't move, didn't speak, just looked into each other's eyes and breathed shallowly. Then Dean shook himself and said, 'Excuse me. *Buon appetito,*' and turned to leave the table.

Tess slowly addressed herself to the plate of pasta. It was delicious, but she barely tasted it. Her heart was beating fast and between her legs her sex was clenching in the way that always signified a sudden swelling of desire.

She wasn't just imagining things. She really did want to taste Dean's body. She didn't care what sort of a man he was, she just thought that he was handsome and she lusted after him. Her hand covered her mouth as if she were afraid that the other people in the restaurant would be able to read her thoughts.

Research. Take control. *I want you to be amoral,* James had told her. *Self-centred. Just going after kicks.*

Why not?

She ate a little more of the pasta, but her appetite was gone. Presently she set down her fork and leant back in her chair, turning her head to look for Dean.

There he was. She caught his eye. Her face was serious, and he came at once over to the table. 'Is something wrong?' he asked her.

'No.'

'Have you finished?' he asked, gesturing at her half-eaten pasta.

Tess took a deep breath. She was excited and nervous, but her singing training allowed her to speak without a shake in her voice. 'Dean,' she said softly and clearly, 'where can we go?'

Dean's face changed at once. His attentive, well-trained waiter's expression changed, fading into a look of half suspicion, half shocked belief. 'Where can we go?' he repeated, speaking very quietly. He didn't have her control, and his voice was trembling.

Quickly Tess moistened her lips with her tongue and swallowed. 'Where can we go to make love?' she said. It wasn't as hard as she had feared. Startled lust flared in his eyes and she added quickly, 'Right now, Dean. Right now.'

His lips were parted and his chest rose and fell with his quick breathing. For a moment he didn't speak. Then he said, 'Are you joking?'

Tess shook her head. 'I'm serious. Try me.'

He was silent again. Then he said in a rush, 'The manager's office. At the bottom of the stairs, next to the Ladies' loo. It's open. You go first. I'll be there in a minute.'

Tess nodded quickly and got to her feet. He stepped back to let her go past him and as she did so she let her hand trail across the front of his apron, directly over his crotch. He drew in his breath quickly and pulled away from her. She smiled to herself and went to the stairs.

As she descended she felt her heart pounding, thumping as if it would leap from her chest. Her nerves, her caution, her sense of propriety said, *Go into the Ladies, hide in there, don't do it, you're an idiot, what will Tony think of you?*

But, inside her mind, the character of Carmen said, *I want him. Tony doesn't need to know. I want him, and for once, tonight, I am going to have what I want. I am going to tell him what I want, and he's going to do it to me.*

17

Tess put her hand on the door of the manager's office and pushed it open. Inside it was dark. She didn't turn on the light, just closed the door and stood in the darkness, waiting.

Footsteps on the stairs. She tensed, but the footsteps turned aside and went into one of the toilets. She began to breathe faster and faster, her desire fighting her better judgement. More footsteps, and then the door opened.

It was Dean, eyes wide and dark in the faint light. He saw her standing just inside the room and his eyebrows drew down tight over his blue eyes. Tess realised with a shock that he was afraid too; afraid of her. The knowledge filled her with eagerness. She glanced around the room, saw a light on the desk and switched it on.

Dean closed the door and turned the key in the lock, then stood by it with his hands opening and closing by his sides. 'I can't stay long,' he said, his voice no more than a clotted whisper. 'I just asked for – for ten minutes.'

Tess wanted to say that that would be long enough, but she couldn't make herself speak. She drew in a long, deep breath and took a single step towards him.

It was enough. In two strides he crossed the room to her, stood in front of her, staring down into her face. There was a second of silent tension, and then at the same moment she reached her arms up to him and he took her face in his hands and his mouth was on hers.

His lips were softer than Tony's and his kisses were not so demanding. It seemed as natural that Tess should put her tongue into his mouth as that he should taste hers. They stood for long seconds, gasping as they kissed. Then Tess reached behind him for the ties of his apron and unfastened them.

'Christ,' he hissed into her lips, and then his arms were around her, catching her under her haunches and lifting her. He pushed her back and up until her bottom was resting on the edge of the manager's desk and he was pressing against her, pushing her legs apart, reaching up under her skirt. She gave an urgent gasp of lust and heaved her hips up towards him, inviting him to touch her. His hand was shaking and his fingers fumbled before he got hold of her panties and pulled them aside, feeling inside them. Tess knew she was wet, but even so it was a delicious shock to feel his strong thick fingers sink without hesitation into her, penetrating her so firmly that her sex clenched around them as if to keep him there.

'God, you're wet,' Dean hissed. He felt with his other hand for his fly, unbuttoned it and unfastened the zip, and in one swift motion pulled his erect penis from his underpants and advanced upon her.

'No,' Tess said, pushing against him. He looked up into her face, scowling with anger and frustration. He looked as if he thought that she was about to change her mind. She gritted her teeth and said, 'No, not yet. I want you to make me come first. Then – then you can fuck me.'

'What?' said Dean, as if she hadn't spoken English.

Tess's hand was on his arm, holding him away from her. 'Make me come,' she said. She remembered Julian falling to his knees before her. Yes, that would be good. That was what she wanted. 'Use your mouth on me,' she said. She saw refusal beginning in his eyes and went on quickly, 'You'll get what you want, won't you? You get to have me. Well, I want to be sure I get my share. Use your mouth on me, Dean. Make me come.'

Still for a second it looked as if he would refuse. His face was set in lines of reluctance. Tess held his eyes and lay back a little on the table, spreading her thighs, waiting expectantly for him to obey her.

'Selfish bitch,' Dean said through his teeth.

Her expression didn't change. She said, 'Dean.' It was odd and powerful that she knew his name and he didn't know hers. 'Dean. Make me come.'

He stood still for a moment, then hissed, 'Shit.' But it was the protest of acquiescence. Even as he spoke he was dropping to his knees, moving up between her parted thighs, ready to serve her.

Tess let her head fall back and closed her eyes. She waited, every nerve tingling, for his first touch. She expected him to be rough, to devour her and try to drag her to sudden pleasure, but she was wrong. For long moments nothing happened. Then she felt his breath on her. His mouth was hovering over her open sex and he was breathing, warm steady breaths that quivered against her trembling flesh. She gasped in response and whimpered, and only then did he touch her.

He was very tentative, very hesitant, flickering the point of his tongue along her labia, first one side, then the other, gently poking it into her vagina, seeming to ignore her engorged clitoris

19

completely. My God, Tess thought, does he know what he's doing? Has he ever done this before? He touched her everywhere but there, teasing, drawing up her expectation to the limit. And then, just as she was about to cry out *Lick me there, for God's sake, lick me there*, his warm, wet mouth clamped down over her warm, wet sex and he began to suck, burrowing into her as if he were extracting the flesh from a juicy orange, using his teeth and his lips as well as his tongue, stimulating her so unbearably that she bit her arm to prevent herself from screaming aloud. He drew the whole of her sex into his mouth and thrust his tongue deep inside her and then withdrew and tormented her quivering clitoris, lapping at it with firm deliberate strokes, lifting her to a higher and higher plateau of pleasure. His hands gripped tightly at the soft flesh of her inner thighs, pulling them wider apart, opening her to him. Tess arched her back and strained up towards him, overcome with joy and amazement that it was really happening. Her climax began in the soles of her feet and climbed slowly, rippling through her loins, cold as ice in her spine and hot as fire in the pit of her belly, building and building until it soared to her brain and exploded there. She cried out and tensed against Dean's mouth as he thrust his tongue deep inside her and she gripped frantically at it as she gave herself up to spasms of delirious pleasure.

Then he let her go, quite roughly, and stood up. He wiped his hand hard across his glistening mouth. 'Good enough for you?' he demanded fiercely, leaning over her.

Tess almost laughed. She pushed herself up from the desk and shook her head. He was holding a condom, fumbling with it as he tried to tear it open. She said, 'Let me,' and took it from him. Her deft fingers quickly opened the packet and she leant forward to where his scarlet, swollen cock stood up from his trousers. She opened her mouth and quickly drew the smooth, shining head between her lips, flicked her tongue over it and heard him gasp. Then she rolled the condom down the straining shaft and ran her hands gently over his tight updrawn balls, feeling them heavy and turgid with the weight of his seed.

'All right,' she whispered, looking up into his face. 'All right, Dean. Now.'

He moved towards her and she lifted her thighs and hooked them over his hips, opening herself to him. He did not guide his thrusting penis but prodded blindly between her legs until he found the moist notch and then groaned as he pushed himself into her, all the way up her wet, hungry vagina in one strong stroke.

'God,' Tess moaned, locking her ankles in the small of his back and lifting her hips. She wanted to feel him even more deeply inside her, filling her, penetrating her. 'Oh God, that's it. That's it.'

But Dean didn't move. He held on to her tightly, clutching at her haunches, and pressed his body closely against her. Looking down into her face, he hissed, 'I'm going to fuck you so hard.'

'Yes,' Tess moaned. She tried to move against him and a pulse of urgent pleasure radiated from her throbbing clitoris and made her sex clench around him, gripping him so tightly that he gasped. 'Yes, do it.'

'I'm going to fuck you – now – ' And Dean withdrew his whole stiff length from her and plunged it back into her with all his strength, his hips meeting her open thighs with a sharp slap. The impact made Tess groan with pleasure. Dean snarled and pounded into her again and again, harder than she thought possible, grasping her hips tightly to hold her open to his determined, ravaging thrusts. Within a dozen strokes Tess was at the point of climax again and as he continued to shaft her she knotted her fingers in his hair and clamped her mouth against his to keep in her shuddering cries. There was no end to her response, it was as if every stroke drew her up to another level of sensation. Dean's tongue lashed against hers and his hands were slippery with sweat and he grunted as he took her. Not sex, not making love – fucking. Pure animal pleasure, direct and unadorned. He didn't even know her name. Gradually he built up speed until he was pumping into her like a great engine, until the blows of his hips bruised the tender skin inside her thighs and her whole body was juddering with the power of his thrusts and she was biting his lips in the intensity of her pleasure. With what was left of her mind she thought that he couldn't do it any harder, it wasn't possible, but even as she thought it he snarled against her devouring mouth and began to move even faster, working his iron-hard penis brutally to and fro with such savage strength that pleasure and pain merged into one and sparks burst behind her eyes. And then he groaned and pulled his mouth free of hers and flung back his head, baring his teeth as his whole body shuddered with the desperate ferocity of his climax.

Tess shut her eyes and revelled in the pure physical pleasure of feeling his cock buried deep inside her and throbbing urgently as he came. She wanted to remember this feeling, the sense of uncomplicated, amoral, remorseless lust. She pulled back a little and Dean staggered and put his hands on the desk to support himself. He withdrew from her with a jerk and turned away, covering his face.

For a moment Tess stayed where she was, eyes closed, regaining control. Then she slipped down off the desk and straightened her skirt. 'Thanks,' she said. 'I needed that.' And without another word she went to the door of the office and out into the lobby.

She left a ten pound note on the table and walked straight out of the restaurant before Dean reappeared. She didn't care about him now, she had had what she wanted. Her thighs and sex ached as if she had been beaten, but her whole body was quivering with the echoes of pleasure and she felt elevated, excited by what she had done and not in the least ashamed.

Well, she thought, two weeks into rehearsal and what have I achieved? I've got Tony Varguez as my lover, I've slept with two women, seduced a 22-year-old and screwed a total stranger on a restaurant desk. Carmen is certainly making some changes to my character.

Then she thought again about what Sarah had said. Other things faced her now, both in her own character and in Carmen's. Conflict, challenge. Danger. Was the danger to her, Tess, or to Carmen?

And what more could she do than she had already done?

Crash Course

Juliet Hastings

Crash Course

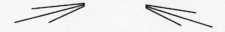

*K*ate stood naked before the mirror in her suite, examining her body and thinking about Edmond. A summer sunset glowed outside the window. She could hear from the grounds of the hotel outside cheerful shouts and the click of wooden balls: Edmond had discovered a croquet lawn in the grounds and had offered to teach the others how to play. Nick had initially derided the idea, saying pointedly that croquet was a game for tired old men, but Christopher had looked at him with a gentle smile and said, 'Do you know it's the managing director's favourite game, Nick? He played croquet for Oxford,' and Nick's expression had changed at once.

Apart from that one pointed exchange all three of the men seemed to be trying to pretend that the morning had never happened. When they met at coffee Nick had been silent and defensive for a while and then suddenly snapped back to his accustomed extrovert self, while Edmond and Christopher had behaved perfectly normally. Christopher seemed to have a glow about him, but he was so reserved that it was hard to be sure. Sophie had said hardly a word for the rest of the afternoon, but Kate had come to expect this of her and she was not concerned.

Edmond, Edmond ... the only one of the men Kate had not yet enjoyed. She thought of his slender, wiry body with pleasure and anticipation. She would make her interest clear over dinner and seduce him that night. He had long, delicate fingers, like a concert pianist; they would play her with skill, coaxing the music of her moans tenderly from her.

25

What would he like her to wear? A traditional young man, well brought up, aristocratic: he would like her to look feminine. Kate went through the clothes she had brought with her and pulled out a lacy Wonderbra and matching panties. She put the Wonderbra on and turned to admire herself in the mirror, running her fingers gently over the swelling twin moons of her breasts. Ignore those, Edmond, she thought with a smile, pulling on the tight lacy panties. There was a soft, floaty silk dress in her wardrobe, too smart for a course really but it would be just the thing. And high-heeled sandals to make her legs look long and appealing; and her hair up, with just one or two silken tendrils tumbling on to her shoulders. She went over to the dressing table to find the comb that she used to hold up her French plait.

There was a faint knock at the door. Kate frowned and glanced out of the window, seeing the three men still merrily playing croquet below her. She was not expecting room service. Puzzled, she caught up her cotton dressing gown and pulled it on and went through to her sitting room and answered the door.

Sophie stood there, her hands wrapped across her front in her normal defensive posture, her chin lifted nervously. 'Can I come in?' she asked.

'Sophie. Of course.' Kate stood back and gestured for Sophie to enter. 'Please.' She looked hard into Sophie's face. She looked as if she had been crying. 'Is something the matter? Would you like a drink?'

'I don't want a drink.' Sophie sat down on the chair nearest the door, then got to her feet again and paced across the room to the window. She looked out and saw the men below her at their game and turned away, a spasm of anger crossing her face. She was blinking rapidly and chewing at her lip and suddenly the tears came, blurring her dark eyes and trickling down her pale cheeks.

'Sophie,' Kate said in sudden real concern, 'what's wrong?'

She went hurriedly across the room to take Sophie's arm and comfort her. Sophie felt her touch and made an inarticulate sound of protest, flinging up her hand to shake Kate off. Kate withdrew, astonished, and Sophie stared at her wide-eyed, the tears still flowing. 'Don't you touch me,' Sophie sobbed. 'Don't try to pretend you care about me.' She drew in a deep breath and dashed her hand over her cheeks. 'I've had enough of this

26

course,' she said after a moment. 'I've packed my bags. I'm going to go home tonight.'

Kate had not expected this. She felt her stomach close and lurch with a sudden apprehension of failure. 'Sophie,' she said softly, 'I don't understand.'

'It's simple,' said Sophie, throwing back her head defiantly. 'I'm leaving. You don't need me anyway, you're only interested in the men. I'm just in your way, you'll have a much better time without me.'

Sudden guilt caught at Kate's conscience. 'No,' she said after a moment, 'no, Sophie, that's not right.'

'I'm going,' Sophie repeated stubbornly. She scowled at Kate and turned to the door. 'I don't know why I bothered coming to tell you. I might have known you'd try your horrible persuading tricks on me. I'm just going to go, and you can – you can sod off,' she said with emphasis.

'Sophie.' Kate reached out and caught Sophie by the arm, holding her back. Sophie swung round and stared at her angrily. 'Sophie, I just don't understand. You've made a real contribution during these two days and I thought, this morning, I thought you were really enjoying yourself. Was I wrong? Why have you decided to give up?'

For a moment Sophie still seemed to be considering walking out, but then she tightened her lips in determination. 'You want to know?' she demanded. 'All right. I'll tell you.' She pulled her wrist from Kate's hand and again folded her arms tightly across her stomach as she walked over to the window. 'I've had several – relationships,' she began, looking out on to the lovely summer evening outside. 'Three relationships with men, since I left school. I was even engaged to one once. They're all the same.' Her voice was chilled with a shadow of bitterness. 'They seem different at first, but they're all the same in the end. Every one of them just wanted me to do what he wanted, to be what he wanted. None of them wanted me to be me. They manipulated me and they bullied me.'

She stopped for breath. Kate said nothing: her mind was whirling as she tried to think of a way out of this situation. It would upset everything if Sophie decided to return to her office early; she would be sure to blow the whistle.

'It's just the same at work,' Sophie went on. 'They get me to do what they want, the men do, all the time. Oh, I don't mean

27

sexually.' She flung up one hand in an impatient gesture. 'I mean for whatever they want. Take my ideas, take my suggestions, present them as their own, take the credit. I've got twice the mind they have and they never give me the credit for it.'

'Your manager has a lot of admiration for your mind,' Kate said with simple truth. 'But he says that you never offer an opinion; he says he has to ask you for it, every time.'

'Is that what he says!' Sophie threw back her head, her thick curly hair bobbing. 'Bastard. He's the worst ideas thief of the lot. Let me do the research, let me write the report, he'll sign the covering letter. The bastard.' She swung to face Kate. 'I hoped for a lot from this course,' she said. 'I can't tell you what I hoped for. A friend of mine went on it a little while ago and you tutored her and she said it was brilliant. She said it would be just what I needed. I thought, she's a woman, she'll understand, she'll be able to help me. And then when we all arrived, and Nick was so bloody minded and awful and you didn't turn a hair! You were really cool; you just dealt with him and I admired you so much. I'd give anything to be like that.' Sophie's eyes were incredibly bright, glittering with anger and unshed tears. 'But now,' she burst out, 'now I know how you do it. You've just made yourself like a man. That's all you are. You're like a man: you're manipulative and exploitative and you don't care.'

Kate was really shocked now, shocked and distressed. Sophie's accusations went too close to the bone for her to ignore them. 'Sophie,' she said with real sincerity, 'Sophie, please tell me what has made you feel this way.'

'It was today,' Sophie said, 'this morning.' She was shivering, clutching at herself with her slender arms. 'I suppose yesterday I was so surprised, I didn't know what to expect, and after all we were only talking. But today, today, you – offered me to Nick! You offered me to him as if I was some sort of a whore!'

Kate shook her head, but she knew that denial would only make things worse. 'I'm sorry you feel that way,' she said softly.

'I do feel that way. I do! You told me to go off into the room with him and you knew that he would want to have me. You knew it! And if I hadn't been stubborn, if I hadn't been really stubborn, he might have ended up – having sex with me, and I didn't want him to!'

'What would you rather I had done?' asked Kate.

'You could have asked me. You could have asked me beforehand what I wanted. You didn't even ask me whether I would prefer anyone else. If you just wanted to watch two people having sex on that bloody TV screen, why didn't you let me go with Edmond? At least he'd have asked me nicely!' She clenched her fists in her anger. 'It was awful, it was inexcusable of you to take without asking. It was rude and vicious and I hated it.'

Kate took a deep breath. She had to meet this one head on; nothing else would work. She said, 'Sophie, I apologise. I am very sorry if what I did offended you.'

Sophie glared at her suspiciously, breathing hard. Her face was vivid and flushed with her anger and distress; she looked lovely.

'Sophie, you're very observant, said Kate. You're very intelligent. You could draw a lot from this course; it's just that the first two days were about things you can already do. You're a natural at bridging, I never saw anyone so good at it at a first attempt; and I'm sure that anyone as bright as you can persuade. But to do both of those things you have to be able to get people to listen to you, and for that you need tomorrow's session. It's all about getting what you want, it's about assertiveness. Sophie, what can I do that will persuade you to stay?'

Sophie took a deep breath and looked at Kate, a thoughtful appraising look. 'I don't know,' she said at last. 'Assertiveness. What is it about, really?'

'Just what I said,' replied Kate. 'It's about saying what you want. It's not about aggression or anger, just stating your rights.'

'Stating my rights,' Sophie repeated, her eyes widening.

'Your rights,' Kate said. 'So you might say, I have a right to sexual pleasure as well as you. I want to have an orgasm.' She saw Sophie's face change, a sudden softening, faint colour rising in her pale cheeks. 'And then you've stated your position and everyone knows where they are. You can use it to change people's behaviour, too.'

'You can't,' Sophie said softly.

'Yes, you can, if you know how to ask. You tell them some good news first, then you tell them what you don't like about them, then you tell them what you want them to do. You keep it practical, concrete, something they can correct. So I might say to you, Sophie: I really like the way you respond to erotic influences: I think you're a very sensual woman. I don't like the fact

29

that you won't join in our activities. I want you to tell me why that is.'

Sophie looked Kate in the eyes. 'Is that just an example,' she said, 'or do you really want me to?'

'I really want you to,' said Kate, and it was true.

Sophie was trembling. She came a little closer to Kate and licked her lips nervously. 'You see,' she said hesitantly, 'I really, I really haven't liked to think about sex. I mean, not even think about it, let alone do it. I always hoped I would enjoy it, but with every man it's been such a disappointment.

'Some people find it easier than others,' Kate said, 'but, Sophie, believe me, if you learn how to assert yourself, you'll be better at getting your own way than someone like Nick who falls back on aggression. You have all the other skills too; you just need to be able to be assertive.'

Sophie looked at her for a long time without speaking. Her dark eyes were very wide and her lips were parted. At last she said, 'Kate, don't lie to me. Do you really want me to stay?'

'Yes.' It was true. Kate felt a surge of sympathy and friendship for Sophie. She was desperately sorry for anyone who had closed herself completely off from sex rather than continue to be disappointed. 'Yes, I want you to stay. I want you to learn how to be assertive. I want to see you getting your own way tomorrow.'

'I want,' Sophie repeated softly. 'It sounds all right when you say it. When I say it it sounds rude, petulant, I don't know.'

'It's the way you're brought up,' Kate said reassuringly. 'It's a cultural thing. Women are supposed to be supportive and take a back seat, not come forward and say boldly what they want. But it helps so much, Sophie.'

'And I could really learn to be assertive? Even sexually?' Sophie sounded as if she could not believe it.

'Yes,' Kate said. 'What have you got to lose? The course is confidential; but if you go back to the office everyone there will know you've given up.'

Sophie looked up quickly, frowning. That touch of competitiveness had done the trick. 'All right,' she said. 'All right. I'll stay.'

'I'm so glad.' Kate was really pleased. She stepped forward and took Sophie's hands in hers and smiled at her. 'I know you won't regret it. Look, tomorrow is always hard work. Do you want to do a little preparation now?'

Sophie nodded eagerly. 'Yes. Very much. I would really like to be good at it.'

'All right. Look, let's have a drink. What would you like?' Kate went over to the mini bar and opened it. 'There's a bottle of champagne in here. How about some of that?'

'Champagne?' Sophie looked amazed. 'What for?'

'It's a great confidence builder. I'd like some. Shall we?'

After a moment Sophie shrugged helplessly. Kate found two suitable glasses, wrestled with the cork and finally poured the golden wine. She handed Sophie a glass and said, 'Your health.'

'And yours.' Sophie took a sip and giggled as the bubbles went up her nose.

'Now,' said Kate, sitting down on the sofa, 'let's think about what your objectives for tomorrow might be. A bit of planning, that's what we need.'

'*Sexual* objectives?' asked Sophie, looking apprehensive.

'Yes.'

Sophie shook her head. 'I can't. I told you, I try not to think about sex. I don't have any vocabulary, I don't have any images to fall back on.'

'Sophie,' Kate asked with sympathy, 'are you telling me that nothing has ever sexually aroused you? That you don't remember anything, that you've never seen anything that you'd like to try? What are your sexual fantasies, anyway?'

'Really, I didn't have any.' Sophie sipped her champagne, hesitating. Then she looked directly into Kate's eyes. 'But yesterday and today,' she whispered, 'I've been really aroused. I can't tell you. I mean, I never dreamed I could ever masturbate with someone else in the same room, but today I just had to. I didn't even care that you or Nick might see me. I had to touch myself.'

'What was it that aroused you so much?'

Sophie swallowed and put her hand to her throat. 'It was – it was seeing Christopher and Edmond,' she said. 'I never believed – I never knew. Did Christopher really have you last night? Or were you just saying that to defuse Nick?'

'He really did,' Kate confirmed. She remembered Christopher's huge strength and shivered. 'He was rough, too.'

'And today he let Edmond have him. He's so complicated. I think he's wonderful, but he scares me to death. Seeing him –

31

touching Edmond, touching his, his penis, taking it into his mouth, it made me feel so strange. And then, when Edmond was just about to take him and you were watching and letting Nick have you at just the same time, so they were moving in and out at the same time ... I've never been so turned on in my life. I had to touch myself. I had to.' Sophie was flushed and trembling slightly. 'I must be really weird,' she said at last.

'Weird? You're not weird, you're just broad-minded,' Kate said with a smile. She poured a little more champagne into Sophie's glass and watched her drink it. 'Look, Sophie,' she said, 'we don't really want to rerun yesterday or today; people wouldn't learn much from it. Perhaps you need some ideas. Would you like to look at some things that might give you ideas?'

Sophie's great eyes grew bigger and bigger. 'What sort of things?' she asked hesitantly.

'I've brought a sort of erotic library with me,' Kate said with a smile. 'It's in the bedroom. Would you like a look? There's books, toys, clothes, all sorts.' She got off the sofa and held out her hand and after a momentary reluctance Sophie got up too.

They walked together through to the bedroom. Sophie saw the great four-poster and said, 'Oh, what a lovely bed! What a lovely room!' She looked around like a child looking at a shop window full of toys.

Kate gestured that Sophie should sit down on the bed and lifted up her treasure box and put it on the covers so that they could sprawl side by side and examine the contents. 'Here,' she said, opening it. 'Here we are.'

Sophie looked into the box and drew in a long breath. After a second she put her hand in and drew out a leather garment and held it out between finger and thumb. 'What's this?' she asked gingerly.

'Oh, it's marvellous,' Kate said, taking the garment from her and showing her how it should be worn. 'Look, it's like a Victorian corset. It lifts your breasts right up as if they're on a plate and it leaves your nipples bare, and it pulls your waist in, but there's nothing to get in the way between your legs. I love it.'

Sophie looked both horrified and fascinated. 'Could I wear it?' she asked after a moment. 'Would it fit me?'

'You're slenderer than me,' said Kate. 'It laces up the back. Yes, you could wear it. Do you want to try it on?'

'No ...' Sophie turned her head away. Kate shrugged and put the corset down on the bed as Sophie put her hands again into the treasure box. When they emerged they were holding the polished wooden phallus with which Kate had pleasured herself on the evening of their arrival. She said, 'Oh, my God. Look how big it is.'

'It's wonderful,' Kate said softly. 'Look at the bumps at the bottom. When you push it in deeply it rubs all the outside of your lips.'

Sophie sat for a moment in silence. Then with her arms she pressed her small breasts closer together. Her erect nipples showed through her cotton shirt. She held the phallus in her hand and pressed it gently into the crease between her breasts, shifting her hips from side to side and breathing through parted lips. Her face was beginning to colour faintly as she became aroused. She looked so fragile and vulnerable that it took Kate's breath away. It would have been easy to seduce her; Kate knew that if she leant over now and kissed her Sophie would be unable to resist. But that was not the plan; the plan was to give her what she wanted. Perhaps she wouldn't want another woman to make love to her. Well, they would find out.

Sophie looked suddenly up at Kate. She said rather breathlessly, 'Kate, it's awfully hot in here.'

'It's the afternoon sun,' Kate said. She got up and went to the window to close the curtains. Outside in the glow of the evening the men were still playing croquet; Nick had become excited and was swearing at the others, and Christopher and Edmond were looking disapproving and shaking their heads. Kate smiled and lifted her arms to draw the curtains closed.

When she turned Sophie had taken off her shirt and trousers and was sitting on the bed in her underwear. She wore a very ordinary white bra and cotton panties, but her slender figure was so nubile and delicious that she could have posed as Lolita. She was still cradling the wooden phallus between her small breasts, moving it very gently up and down against her silky skin.

'There are some books in here,' Kate said, 'look.' She dug in the box and pulled out a large, glossy book, somewhat dog-eared. 'I like this one,' she said, offering it to Sophie. 'My lover bought it for me a couple of years ago. I like nearly all the pictures. Shall we look? Something might give you some ideas.'

Sophie looked brighter, as if she felt that a book could not possibly hurt her. 'All right,' she said. 'Yes, I'd like that.' She looked down at herself and gasped, as if surprised to see the thick wooden shaft still nestling in the crease of her breasts. She put the phallus hastily aside and shifted to sit beside Kate, both of them propped comfortably against the pillows in the warmth of the room. Kate held the book open on her lap and Sophie leant over to turn the pages and look at the pictures.

The first few pages showed nineteenth-century drawings of men and women coupling. They were well executed and artistic, but also highly explicit. The women were big-hipped and small-breasted, the men muscular and superbly equipped. In every picture the act of penetration was clearly shown, a thick, stiff penis sliding deeply into a moist, willing tunnel. Sophie shivered and reached out quickly, turning and turning, as if this representation of the act of love disturbed her. Then a page of watercolour sketches, obviously drawn from life, showing a pretty, voluptuous model servicing a handsome young man with hands and mouth. The pictures were beautifully drawn and slightly impressionistic, so that Sophie had to look more closely to understand the finely realised detail: the girl's hand gripping tightly just below the engorged red glans while her other hand stroked between her lover's legs; the way her breasts hung down like ripe fruit when she leant forward to take him in her mouth; his posture and expression, abandoned and ecstatic, his head thrown back as she sucked and fondled.

'They're lovely pictures, aren't they?' said Kate softly.

Sophie looked quickly up at her, passing her small pointed tongue over her lips. 'One of my boyfriends had a book of erotica,' she said, 'and he tried to make me look at it. But it was so crude, I thought it was horrible. These pictures are beautiful.'

'They're art,' said Kate. 'Erotic, but still art, not pornography.'

The picture on the next page caught Sophie's attention. It was a line drawing, superbly vivid, showing a woman straddling a man. Her white buttocks flared out from a slender waist and her vaginal lips were stretched wide to take in his rigid, thick shaft. She was just sliding down on it and her head was flung back in the bliss of feeling herself impaled. Her pubic hair and the man's mingled in a dark mass, the centre of the picture, calling the eye to the act of penetration.

The pages turned. A blonde girl, naked, her long hair tumbling down her back, struggling against a fully clothed man who stands between her parted thighs and thrusts himself firmly into her shrinking flesh; a woman with her hands bound, flung on to a bed with such violence that her shoulders hang off it and her back is arched, her breasts jutting towards the ceiling, gasping while the shadowy figure of a man drives himself deeply into the moist cleft between her wide-spread legs; a man prostrate on a bed, his head hidden beneath the thighs of a woman squatting over his face, while another holds his massive cock pointing skywards so that a third woman can sink down upon it.

Another page. A picture of two women, Twenties flappers by their clothes and hair. One lies on a bed, sprawled naked with her legs flung shamelessly wide and her fingers stroking her erect nipples, and her friend kneels over her, her skirt lifted to show the soft mound between the cheeks of her bottom. Her hands are on the naked girl's thighs, framing the tender lips of her sex, and she stares down at the shadowed cleft and her tongue is just visible between her parted lips.

Sophie sat leaning against Kate and looked at this picture for a long time. She said nothing, but she shivered. Kate looked at her face and saw it set in an expression of yearning desire. They did not speak.

The pages turned. Another picture: three women together, all naked but for their jewels and lipstick. One kneels over another's face, thighs spread, offering the moist lips of her sex to her prostrate friend's eager, probing tongue, and another stands between the thighs of the girl who is lying down, preparing to thrust into her vagina with a massive dildo strapped securely to her slender thighs. The head of the dildo is already hidden, the rest will follow.

Another page, another picture. A young man preparing to enter his lover, a voluptuous blonde. He is crouched over her, his lips about to fasten on the tiny pink peaks of her nipples, his hand guiding the shining head of his cock just between the damp, parting lips of her sex. Her head is thrown back, her mouth open so that her cry of pleasure as he slides himself into her is almost audible. Another: two men holding a woman down, spreadeagled on the ground, her eyes closed in desperate ecstasy as one thrusts his erect member into her body and the other places her hand on his stiff cock and encourages her to feel its thickness. One of them is dragging back her head to kiss her, exposing her white throat. The other is holding her breast in his hand, sucking hard at her nipple: the fingers are denting the white flesh that they grip.

Another: a couple copulating, seen from behind, starkly engraved in black and white. The girl's legs are wrapped around her lover's waist. His tight thrusting buttocks are visible and his massive cock, huge and thick, embedded deeply in her tender flesh. The light gleams off the hollows in his working buttocks and the round, smooth swell of her clasping thighs. All that can be seen of their faces is the girl's mouth, open, soft and gasping as he plunges into her.

Another. A beautiful girl lying on a bed, her head thrown back and her long hair sweeping against the floor. She seems to be almost fainting with pleasure. Kneeling above her is another girl; she presses against her and just flicks her tongue against the little erect cap of her breast. The recumbent girl's slender legs are spread wide and her friend is touching her between her white thighs, her fingers delicately resting on the just-visible stem of her clitoris. Although the girl is very still her head is flung back in ecstasy; the artist has chosen to paint the moment of crisis, the one split second at which she is motionless because her orgasm is just about to overwhelm her, and in a moment her back will arch and she will moan and thrust her breasts up into her friend's tormenting mouth and receive her fingers into her juicy flesh with cries of aching pleasure.

Sophie leant back into Kate's arms, closing her eyes and letting out a shuddering sigh. For a moment Kate did not move, just sat very still with her arms around Sophie as she sat in her lap like a child. Then she very gently brushed her lips against Sophie's soft curling hair and whispered, 'Sophie, Sophie, tell me what you want.'

Sophie's eyes opened and she turned her head and looked up at Kate. Her lips trembled. Beneath the thin cotton of her bra her nipples were tautly erect, asking to be touched. For a little while she seemed unable to speak. Then she said, softly but with precision, 'Kate, I want to make love with you.'

Without another word Kate leant forward and reached with her lips for Sophie's quivering mouth. Their lips met, touched, parted, touched again. Sophie relaxed against Kate's body and let her head fall back, turning up her face to Kate's caresses. Kate's mouth hovered above hers and Kate gently, gently touched Sophie's lips with her tongue, feeling their warmth and moistness, their delicious fullness. Sophie gave a shuddering moan and opened her mouth wide and Kate pressed her lips down hard and thrust her tongue deep into Sophie's mouth. Their tongues met and touched and tasted and all the time Sophie let out little trembling cries. Their kiss was so sweet, so sweet. The pictures had set Kate's juices flowing and she was already wet between her legs, but to kiss Sophie, to slide her tongue in and out between those quivering lips, filled Kate with a fierce protective tenderness, a desire to give pleasure, not to take it.

Her hands were on either side of Sophie's slender body. They kissed passionately, their mouths open to the darting thrust of their tongues, and slowly Kate's hands moved from the bedclothes on to Sophie's waist and up, feeling her ribs beneath her tender flesh and then the small subtle swell of her little breasts, cupped in cotton but tight with desire. She slipped one hand behind Sophie's narrow back and felt for the hooks of the bra, releasing it with a woman's ease. Sophie shivered as the straps slipped down her arms and the fabric peeled away, revealing her aching, distended nipples. Kate lifted her lips from Sophie's mouth for a moment to whisper, 'Your breasts are so beautiful, Sophie, so beautiful.' Then she kissed her again and put her hands on Sophie's arms and ran them up to her shoulders and then down on to the gentle roundness of those small breasts, cupping them in her hands, trapping the nipples between her fingers and squeezing them gently. The little peaks of flesh lengthened and swelled at her touch and Sophie cried out sharply into her mouth, her back arching, pressing her pelvis backwards into Kate's soft body.

It felt to Kate as if she were Sophie. She could feel the sharp pleasure, almost like a pain, arrowing down from breasts to loins as she caressed Sophie's erect nipples; she could feel the desire to be touched that made Sophie whimper and writhe in her lap. She whispered, 'Sophie, sweet Sophie, tell me what you want.'

Sophie lay with her head tilted back, her eyes closed, her tongue quivering in her open mouth as Kate touched and stroked and pinched the peaks of her small breasts. She did not open her eyes, only said softly, 'Touch me. Oh Kate, I want you to touch me.'

Obediently Kate released Sophie's breast with one hand and slipped her fingers slowly down the slender curves of Sophie's pale body, past the dimple of her navel, down to where the top of her cotton panties clung to her flesh. Her hand gently slid under the cotton, moving down and down until it felt the silky soft hair that fringed Sophie's delicate mount of Venus. She kissed Sophie again, her hot tongue filling her soft mouth, and her other hand working at her breast. Sophie moaned and lifted her hips hopelessly towards Kate's searching fingers.

So sweet, so soft, the opening flesh beneath her probing hand. Her fingers felt the beginning of the soft cleft, the tender lips, warm and moist. She sought delicately, gently, until her fingers found the little protruding morsel of flesh that was now swollen and proud with desire. She knew what she must do as clearly as if she were giving herself pleasure. Her fingers moved back a little, dipped into the slick juices that were seeping from Sophie's sex, and then returned to caress that tiny morsel of flesh with such infinite gentleness that Sophie opened her mouth wide to admit Kate's thrusting tongue and cried out as if she were being beaten.

Kate did not stop. Relentlessly her tongue probed Sophie's hot mouth, her fingers caressed her engorged nipples and the trembling bud of her clitoris. Sophie's cries became regular and her breathing came in pants and she writhed in Kate's arms, helpless, delirious with pleasure. Kate touched her more firmly now, stroking her as she liked herself to be stroked, one finger rubbing and rubbing against the peak of her pleasure while another dipped and dipped into the moist tunnel of her sex, stimulating the delicate lips. Sophie began to heave, thrusting her breasts and her loins towards Kate's working hands, and suddenly she tore her mouth away from Kate's and flung back her head, gasping, crying out, 'Oh yes, yes, Kate, I'm coming, don't stop, don't stop,' and then suddenly she stopped breathing and every muscle was rigid and quivering and her eyelids fluttered as her orgasm possessed her utterly.

After a long moment of ecstasy she slumped back into Kate's arms, trembling with the delicious echoes of her climax. She pressed her cheek against Kate's breasts, murmuring, 'That was wonderful, Kate, so wonderful. You knew exactly where I wanted to be touched.' Kate smiled and kissed her hair. Sophie sank down a little further, looking suddenly disconsolate. 'Is it because you're a woman?' she asked in a small voice.

'I wouldn't say that,' Kate said with a gentle smile. 'I have known men who had the knack.' Suddenly she thought of Edmond and without thinking she went on, 'Look at Edmond. He has such beautiful hands, long fingers. I'm sure he – '

She broke off: Sophie was looking up at her with a sad expression. She said in a little hopeless voice, 'Have you slept with him too?'

'With Edmond?' Kate smiled down into Sophie's lovely face. 'No, in fact. Why do you ask?'

'Oh,' said Sophie, wriggling uncomfortably in Kate's arms, 'it's just that I, I rather like him, and I was thinking, I was hoping, and I would rather – '

'Sophie,' Kate interrupted her gently. 'Sophie, remember to say what you want. I like, I don't like, I want.'

Sophie's dark eyes opened wide. She was silent, and then she said with a sort of timid firmness, 'Kate, I really like you, but I don't like the thought that you want to sleep with Edmond. I want you not to have sex with him unless I say so.'

'That was excellent,' Kate said, leaning forward to kiss Sophie on the lips. 'Well done. And if you want, Sophie, I won't touch Edmond without your specific order.'

'Thank you,' Sophie said earnestly, reaching up to catch Kate around the neck and pull her mouth down to kiss her again. 'Thank you.' She turned in Kate's arms and they were facing each other, kissing deeply. Sophie reached around Kate's shoulders to release the hooks of her bra and pulled it off. 'Oh,' she said, 'what lovely breasts. They're so big. I wish I had breasts like that.' And she leant forward and just touched her lips to Kate's swollen, sensitive nipple. Kate closed her eyes and gasped with pleasure and Sophie put her arms around her and held her tightly and they slid down on to the smooth covers with Sophie licking moistly at Kate's breasts, making her moan and writhe. Then she lifted her tousled head and looked into Kate's eyes and said, 'Kate, could we – I wonder if – '

'What do you want, Sophie?' Kate asked, gently and with a smile.

Sophie hesitated, but not quite so much this time. Then she

said, 'I want us to – to use our mouths on each other. I want to kiss you there.'

'All right,' Kate said in a whisper. 'Yes, Sophie, please, please do it.'

Sophie did not move for a moment and Kate realised that she was waiting to be led, waiting for Kate to guide her through what she should do. Rather than tell her Kate lay back on to the covers, looking at Sophie through half-closed eyes with an expectant smile. Sophie breathed quickly, then lowered her lips again to lick and suck at Kate's distended nipples, making her moan and shiver. Gradually she kissed further and further down Kate's sun-kissed skin and as she did so she turned her slender body so that they were lying with their lips close to each other's thighs. Kate was desperate to feel Sophie's small, soft tongue exploring her hidden flesh; she moaned and spread her legs apart, lifting her hips eagerly towards Sophie's face. Sophie gave a little whimper and reached forward, setting her lips to the delicate, secret place between Kate's legs. Kate felt her tongue, soft and warm, just touching her, licking, stroking, and she cried out with pleasure and reached out to catch hold of Sophie's white thighs. She dug her fingers into the taut moons of Sophie's buttocks and pulled her until they were lying pressed closely together, their mouths buried between each other's legs, licking and sucking avidly. Kate caught hold of Sophie's thighs and spread them wide apart and lifted her head from the bed cover, stabbing with her tongue at the soft folds of flesh, parting them, thrusting her tongue deep, deep into Sophie's sex at the same time as she felt Sophie's gentle caress sweeping across her clitoris, lapping at her secret heart, filling her with unbearable pleasure. Their bodies undulated, heaving like one creature, shining hair brushing against the soft flesh of thigh and vulva, tongues flickering, tugging, probing.

Kate felt her climax approaching, sweeping up inside her like a storm. She pulled Sophie's sex down harder on to her searching mouth and caught the delicate stem of her clitoris between her lips, flickering her tongue across it, and as the pleasure seized her and carried her into orgasm she heard Sophie crying out and the moist flesh beneath her lips clenched and spasmed with delight.

For a while they lay as they were, smelling the musky, delicious scents of their womanhood. Then Sophie suddenly sat up and turned around, lowering her lips to Kate's and kissing her with an eager directness that made her gasp.

Kate opened her eyes, looking up into Sophie's shining face. 'What is it?' she asked.

'Kate,' Sophie whispered, and her voice was trembling with excitement, 'Kate, I – I want to – ' She seemed to lose her impetus and stopped, turning her head away.

Sitting up hastily, Kate put her arms around Sophie's narrow shoulders, comforting her. 'What? What do you want, Sophie?'

Sophie hesitated, then swallowed hard. For a moment she did not move; then she reached out and picked up the wooden phallus where it lay on the bed. She licked her lips and looked into Kate's eyes. 'I want to – to – ' The words were hard for her. She took a deep breath, trying to calm herself. Then she said strongly, 'I want to fuck you with this, Kate. I want to push it inside your cunt and make you come.'

Those direct words, coming from Sophie's quivering lips, made Kate shiver with fulfilment. A day ago, an hour ago, Sophie could not have used those words. She leant forward and kissed Sophie deeply, touching the wooden phallus that she held, stroking it with her fingers. Then she lay back on the covers and the deep pillows and smiled up into Sophie's eyes, saying softly, 'Please, Sophie, do it to me. Put it in me. Make me come.'

Sophie knelt beside her, clutching the thick wooden shaft in her small hand, breathing quickly. At last she moved. She knelt over Kate and then lay on her, kissing her, her little tongue flickering deep into her mouth, her fingers squeezing at Kate's soft, full breasts. Kate slowly moved her legs apart and Sophie lay between them like a man, pressing her pubic bone into Kate's soft flesh so that she moaned and whimpered. Then she slowly wriggled down, down, her tongue lapping wetly over Kate's breasts and her round stomach and the soft downy curve of her abdomen, her fingers teasing and tweaking at the luxuriant curls of dark hair. Then she dug her fingers into the plump swell of Kate's thighs and pulled them apart and set the tip of the polished wooden shaft between the glistening fleshy lips that were the entrance to the silken tunnel of desire. Kate felt the cold head there, waiting, promising pleasure, and she moaned and softly lifted her hips, wanting to be filled.

Sophie lowered her dark head and licked Kate's clitoris, quickly, temptingly, just once, so that she cried out. Then she shook back her hair and looked up, teasing the broad smooth head of the phallus from side to side at the entrance. She said devilishly, 'Kate, tell me what you want me to do.'

'Oh,' Kate moaned, her head thrashing from side to side in her desperate need. 'Oh Sophie, please, do it to me.'

'No,' smiled Sophie, thrusting the thick shaft in a little way and then pulling it out, so that Kate cried out and arched her back. 'No, not good enough. Tell me what you want me to do.'

'Push it up me,' Kate whimpered. 'Please. Sophie. Please.'

'Say what you want,' Sophie whispered, her eyes glittering.

'I want you to push it in my cunt,' Kate gasped at last, and as she heard the words Sophie gripped the base of the phallus firmly and thrust it deep and Kate cried out as if she were being stabbed, feeling the thick smooth cold shaft sliding all the way up inside her, touching the neck of her womb, stretching her, filling her. She cried out, 'Oh God, yes! Yes!'

'I will fuck you so hard,' Sophie hissed, and she withdrew the phallus until only its tip remained within Kate's straining body and then pushed it back and Kate gasped and squirmed on the long thick rod that impaled her tender flesh. Sophie set her teeth and thrust and withdrew the wooden shaft again and again until Kate was crying aloud, sharp cries of agonised pleasure, desperate and drained. Then as Sophie thrust, driving the thick phallus deep into Kate's heaving loins, she leant forward and gently, very gently, lapped with her pointed tongue at the quivering bud of flesh that shuddered and ached to be touched. Kate felt her caress like a tongue of fire. Filled, fucked, wild with pleasure, she writhed and moaned as she felt her orgasm lapping through her with flame and ice, freezing her and burning her with ecstasy.

Sophie drove the phallus into Kate's body as far as it would go and held it there while she stiffened and arched in the throes of her climax. Then, gently, she withdrew the long thick rod, glistening and dewed with pearly moisture. She rubbed it against her breasts and between her thighs. Then she lay again on top of Kate and kissed her, and their deep searching kisses gradually grew more and more gentle.

'Now,' Sophie whispered, 'now I want to stay here with you.'

Kate's lips parted in a smile and she reached up and put her arms around Sophie and cradled her head against her breasts. They lay still and their breathing slowed.

Presently Sophie said, 'Did I really say that?'

'What?' asked Kate sleepily.

'C – cunt. Did I really say that?'

'It's just a word.' Kate kissed Sophie's hair and held her closely, feeling her slender body soft and relaxed with the bliss of fulfilment. 'It was the right word. It was what you meant. It's not a bad thing to say.'

There was a silence. Then Sophie said with soft determination, 'Tomorrow I am going to tell the men what I want. I wonder if I dare use that word to them?'

'If you want to.' Kate ran her fingers very gently down Sophie's slender back and she arched and pushed against her hand like a cat being stroked. 'Of course you will, if you want to. Sophie, tomorrow is about giving you what you want.'

'What I want,' Sophie repeated, gazing up at the canopy of the four-poster. Her dark eyes were wide with wonder and fulfilment. 'What I want.'

The Tutor

Portia Da Costa

In the following extract from *The Tutor*, we find librarian Rosalind Howard educating her employer's young cousin in the arts of erotic love. Having led a sheltered life, the young man in her care is simmering with youthful passion. As his confidence grows he is drawn into increasingly steamy scenarios with the spirited Rosalind.

Portia specialises in contemporary stories with a slightly fetishistic flavour. Apart from *The Tutor*, her other books for Black Lace are: *Gemini Heat*, featuring twins who compete with each other for the attentions of an enigmatic art dealer; *The Devil Inside*, a story of enhanced sexual perception, and *Continuum*, an exploration of games of punishment in a clandestine society.

The Tutor

DavId regarded Rosie steadily. 'Your shape is wonderful,' he murmured as he stepped towards her, his eyes bright and golden. Rosie sensed that he wanted to kiss her again – and not leave it at a kiss for that matter – and her insides quivered at his touch.

'Somebody might be watching,' she whispered when his arms folded all the way around her and his lips settled gently on her neck. She could feel him hard as stone against her belly, and marvelled at how quickly a young man could recover and be ready for another round of sex.

'I don't care!' he hissed, moving his hips suggestively.

'Well, I do!' she answered, fighting him yet failing to get free. His strength was unexpected, and his arms were like tempered steel binding. Rosie felt a lovely melting, yielding sensation start to pour through her loins like honey, and was profoundly tempted to encourage him. She imagined making love right here on the stone-flagged path in full view of the house; with Celeste and God alone knew who else watching from behind the curtains. It would be outrageous, but she longed to try it.

With obvious reluctance, David finally let her loose. 'I'm sorry,' he said quietly. 'I don't know what's got into me. I . . . I feel aroused all the time.' He looked down at his tell-tale bulge.

'Come on. Let's have a swim,' said Rosie with sudden inspiration. She'd seen the pool briefly on her first look around, and right now its cool, blue water seemed the perfect solution to their heat. They could dowse their unruly fires a bit, gain respite and

have time to think. 'And after that, I really must show my face
in the library.' She stuck out her tongue at David and his sceptical
'you're kidding!' look. 'Because no matter what you want to
believe, I *was* taken on to look after Julian's books!' David was
grinning now, trying not to laugh. 'As well as one or two other
little matters . . .'

The poolhouse, when they reached it, was a veritable tropical
paradise, part of a big, open plan conservatory that abutted onto
the side of the house. At one end of the pool was a lounging
area, complete with a selection of thoughtfully cushioned
wrought iron garden furniture; and at the other was a tiled deck
and changing complex – complete with showers, cubicles and
lockers. Tubs of flowers and flowering shrubs were dotted
around this area too, and the whole of the poolhouse was like
some kind of 'green' environmental bubble, filled with the fresh
scent of foliage and alive with the gentle, pervasive lapping of
the water. A door at the far end of the complex led – unsurpris-
ingly, given Julian's obsession with fitness – to a small but well-
equipped gym. There was also, Rosie noticed as they entered, a
full size leather-covered massage table in the changing area: a
fixture that reminded her of Ladybird, and the promise of
aromatherapy.

'What a gorgeous place,' whispered Rosie, then jumped when
her voice echoed off the high glass roof over the pool. 'It's like a
Caribbean holiday without the hassle of flying . . .' Her voice
petered out as a discouraging fact dawned on her. The water
was sparkling and deliciously tempting; but she had no swim-
suit. She could swim in her underwear, she supposed, but it was
all sweaty and sticky. Not a particularly inviting prospect.

'Celeste and Julian swim in the nude, apparently,' said David
from behind her, having obviously read her mind, 'although I've
never actually seen them myself.'

'But what about the staff?' Rosie queried, turning the idea
over and finding it dangerously appealing. All her body and her
clothing felt grubby, and she was sure there were shreds of grass
sticking to her bottom. The thought of plunging into all that
crystalline clarity was so alluring it almost made her ache. She
wanted to dive in and be renewed; made ready to do everything
again.

'They tend to stay out of the way most of the time.' David

quirked his fine dark brows. 'Well, you know what Julian and Celeste are like ... They're always doing *something*!'

'Too true,' murmured Rosie, deciding that the tendency towards exhibitionism must be catching. It wasn't more than half an hour ago that she and David had been putting on a performance – rolling around on the turf half-naked, making love in plain sight of the house.

'Shall we, then?' asked David, a touch of trepidation in his voice, in spite of his previous assurances.

'What ... Swim naked?' The water shimmered and danced and Rosie could no longer resist it. Without answering, except for a wink, she began pulling off her small amount of clothing. Trainers and socks, sweat top and shorts, pants and bra; she let them fall to the tiled floor around her. She caught her reflection in the glass of the opposite wall and saw a curvaceous wood-nymph about to descend into the water. As she half-twirled she realised she'd been right about her bottom. She was indeed festooned with stalks and grass, not to mention dark, earthy smears where she'd been slid along by David's strong thrusts.

Mindful of the purity of the water, she decided to shower before she went into the pool. She needed to urinate too, and slid discreetly into one of the several closed cubicles, set modestly out of the way around a corner. As she sighed with relief, she heard an adjacent door close quietly. Wild, plunging sex had obviously had the same bladder-stimulating effect on David, and the picture of him holding his penis and peeing had a powerful sexual resonance. Rosie had a sudden wish to be standing beside him, cradling him tenderly and kissing his neck as she directed his stream.

Banishing the bizarre thought, she finished, flushed, then made her way into the changing area. Beneath one of the open, Japanese-style showers, she began to sluice off the grime and greenery. The water heat was adjustable but she kept it cool; anything to zap herself into wakefulness and shake off her strange erotic cravings. She closed her eyes and let the water cascade over her face, her hair and her body, vaguely aware that David had stripped off too and had stepped into the shower beside her to wash off the grass on his body.

Wet and naked, they walked together to the water's edge then slid in. Rosie was intensely aware of the beauty of David's body, but somehow the feeling was more tender now than lustful. She knew she'd soon want him again, but for the moment it was nice to just swim together as friends, as companions, and to laugh and splash and frolic for the sheer, high-spirited fun of it.

The sensation of swimming naked was unusual but extremely pleasant. It was the first time Rosie had ever swum in the buff, but she decided that from now on she would take every opportunity to do so. There was a delicious but subtle excitement in the flow of water where it didn't usually flow; the silken rush as it slid over her breasts and buttocks, and the delicate tantalising drag as it filtered through her soft, pubic bush. Surreptitiously she took a sideways glance towards David, and wondered what effect nude swimming was having on his penis.

David was a strong swimmer, and he cut through the water very smoothly, his thick hair plastered dark against his scalp like the pelt of an otter or a seal. He appeared completely unperturbed by his naked state – at least until the tapping of footsteps sounded on the tiles of the conservatory, and Rosie saw his face start to colour with embarrassment.

She hardly dare look up herself, but when she did, she saw Ladybird. The fitness trainer was standing on the poolside, smiling and staring into the water, her green eyes bright with pure mischief. She looked wonderful; sleek and beautiful in form-fitting blue lycra leggings and matching skimpy top. Her red hair was loose on her shoulders, and her whole expression was one of devilment. It was obvious that she knew they were naked, and thoroughly approved of the state.

'Hi, you guys!' she called out cheerily. 'Mind if I join you?'

'No . . . Of course not,' said Rosie, treading water in the deep end. David closed his mouth where it had fallen open in surprise, and this caused him to splutter and cough.

Ladybird seemed to take that as a yes and began peeling off her clothes. In a trice, she was magnificently stripped and walking to the edge of the deep end, where she dived in neatly and cleanly. She was no paddler either, and didn't stop to chatter when she surfaced. Using a long, easy crawl, she powered cleanly from one end of the pool to the other at a speed that made Rosie feel distinctly hippopotamus-like.

Even so, Rosie couldn't find it in herself to resent Ladybird; and as she swam along at her own slower but respectable pace, her mind was filled with the striking but all too fleeting vision of the fitness trainer's perfect golden body.

David was obviously thinking of it too; from time to time he stared across the pool intently as if his unusual eyes could see clean through the light-distorting water to the superb female shape beneath. Rosie's thoughts drifted back to his penis, and its state as he swam. Was he hard again? Turned on by this streamlined, super-fit woman?

Taking the idea further, she wondered how David would react to being with *both* of them. Given this opportune gathering, it was the next logical step. She'd been shackled by conventions of one-on-oneness herself for far too long, but now she could see new ways to love. Could he? Or was it still too soon? Too early? Considering his progress so far, she thought not. He was quite a free-thinker in the making; an untrammelled, generous soul who could give himself joyously to many.

As if reading her mind, Ladybird suddenly broke out of her series of disciplined lengths and swam across to tread water at Rosie's side.

'Are you up for that massage then?' she asked, wiping the water from her face and grinning challengingly.

'Yes, I'd love it,' Rosie answered, feeling her heart skip wildly in her chest. 'And I think David would too.' She nodded over to where their companion was floating in a corner and watching them closely. 'Do you do men as well?'

'Try and stop me,' crowed Ladybird, striking out strongly for the side of the pool, then climbing from the water in all her glory, clearly proud of her fabulous shape.

Rosie was slightly less proud of *her* shape, but felt a hundred per cent better about it than she had a couple of weeks ago. And whatever doubts she had were quashed when both Ladybird's and David's eyes widened appreciatively at the sight of her.

Their scrutiny was like wine surging straight to her belly. She felt intoxicated and aroused, consumed by a rich sensuality that made her slow her steps and almost flaunt her nudity as she walked across to the leather-covered table.

'Ladybird's going to give me a massage,' she called across to David, who lingered in the water. 'Do you want to watch?'

His pale face looked flushed, and she saw him swallow. It made her smile. He was erect in the water, she guessed, and too embarrassed to emerge while they watched him.

'You can probably see from where you are,' she suggested, tacitly acknowledging his condition and making him blush even harder.

'Yes, I can,' he said quietly, then agitated the water around him as if to make sure they couldn't see his stiffness. 'I think I'll stay here a while . . .'

'No sweat,' she answered, feeling a lazy thrill of power. 'Just remember you've to come out eventually.'

David's face showed non-commitment, and he ducked under the water to avoid the issue.

'Don't worry,' whispered Ladybird, setting out an assortment of bottles and other nick-nacks on the tiled counter near the table. 'By the time I've finished with you, he'll be in such a state that he'll kill to get on this table!'

Rosie shivered. She'd never had a massage before, and the thought of Ladybird's long flexible hands working her over made her body feel hot and weak. What she'd said earlier to David was now more true than ever. She was suddenly ravenous for pleasure, and her sex felt moist and yearning for satisfaction. Even the smallest movement was uncomfortable, and the urge to touch her clitoris made her dizzy.

'Just lie on the couch and relax,' urged Ladybird, as if sensing her arousal. 'That's it. On your front first.' The trainer had covered the leather surface of the couch with a thick fluffy towel, and when Rosie settled gingerly down, the soft nubbly fabric seemed to caress every part of her it touched. Moaning under her breath, she flexed her hips and thighs luxuriantly then pressed her sex down hard against the couch.

She'd closed her eyes as she'd lain down, but after a second she opened them again and turned her face towards the pool. David had come to the water's edge and was staring back at her, his own eyes huge with wonder, as if he'd heard her tiny, hungering cry and correctly interpreted its cause. His gaze was so intense it was an embrace in itself, triggering heat in her vulva and her breasts. She was simmering, sizzling, at boiling point – and Ladybird hadn't even touched her. Unable to help herself, she wriggled again, holding David's almost agonised look as she rode her own surging desire.

As she began to gasp, her nostrils were suddenly assaulted by fragrance. A strong floral scent was drifting across from where Ladybird was concocting her magic – the sweet blend of aromatherapy oils that were intended for Rosie's bare body.

'Oh God, what's that? It smells beautiful,' Rosie murmured, drawing in the sumptuous vapours.

'Well, basically it's sweet almond oil, blended with a few stronger essential oils in a combination that both stimulates and soothes the senses,' said Ladybird authoritatively, drawing close. 'It's an aphrodisiac,' she whispered in Rosie's ear, moving her long hair carefully out of the way and tying it with a soft towelling cord. 'When I massage you, you'll come and come and come.' Her breathy voice sounded just as much threatening as it did promising. 'And I'll hardly even have to touch your pussy.'

'What ... what is it I can smell though?' gasped Rosie, knowing she barely needed touch now.

'Let's see,' said Ladybird, making slick, slurpy squishing sounds as she charged her fingers with oil, 'There's a mixture of jasmine, rose maroc, sandalwood and cumin... It's my own favourite blend. I use it when I want particularly strong orgasms.'

This time she didn't lower her voice at all, and as Rosie looked agains towards David, she saw him almost salivating with lust, his young face a taut, aroused mask. She couldn't see his hands, but she had no doubt at all that one of them was folded round his penis.

'Brace yourself,' purred Ladybird softly, then placed her slender hands on Rosie's shoulders and drew them slowly down the full length of her torso in one fluid, extenuated sweep.

The sensation of being oiled was so exquisite that Rosie trembled all over. The epicentre of the shivers was in her groin, but as Ladybird coated her scrupulously, the warm, slippery substance made every part of her tingle with pleasure.

Closing her eyes again, Rosie groaned without shame. Her yearning for genital contact seemed to double and treble as the oil sank into her skin, yet perversely she wanted the wait to be drawn out and prolonged. Ladybird began the real massage on the back of her neck for starters, humming a tune as her fingers skimmed and circled. As she went lower, along the shoulders and down the back, Rosie was possessed again by a massive need to touch herself, to slide her hand between the couch and her belly and drive her fingers onto the core of her sex. Just the thought created tension in her arm, which Ladybird was instantly aware of.

'Bad girl! Mustn't touch!' she hissed, as if Rosie's craving had been written on her flesh.

'Please... Oh God, I'm dying,' whimpered Rosie as her

masseuse moved on and began to concentrate on a small patch of skin just an inch above the crease of her buttocks.

Rosie cried out, louder this time. It was as if that minute area was a button – a switch – connected by a fine hot wire directly to the tip of her clitoris. She whined and wriggled, unable to stop herself, electrified by the giant wave of feeling. Her hands clenched automatically at her sides, shaking as she fought to control them.

'Very well then,' said Ladybird, her husky voice revealing that she too was affected by the odours. 'Here, David, make yourself useful!' she called out, and almost immediately there was a commotion in the water.

Half delirious, Rosie opened her eyes, and saw David moving towards her from the pool. His penis was sticking out before him, superbly erect, with a stream of water flowing lewdly from its tip. Rosie remembered her peculiar fancies in the lavatory, and moaned again at this new rush of yearning.

As he reached the side of the table, Rosie felt two sets of hands touch her body; Ladybird's guiding David's. She lifted her belly to give them access, then screamed out in an instantaneous climax when a wedge of laced fingers rubbed her clitoris. Dimly, she felt Ladybird withdraw and resume her uniquely skilled massage, while David's hand remained, and worked diligently in the chink of her sex. His narrow fingertips seemed to have absorbed Ladybird's talent somehow, and the masturbation he gave was slow and delicate, yet still sufficiently forceful to bring Rosie to peak after peak.

Amazed, she heard her own shouts and yells echoing off the glass roof of the poolhouse. Her crotch was a well of burning pleasure, and her whole body was alive with juddering swells of blissfulness that swept out from her vulva in circles and were stirred by Ladybird's kneading. She felt as if she were going to expire, orgasm herself into oblivion, and when she knew she could take no more, she begged her tormentors to cease.

Whimpering and snuffling into the couch, she was aware of them gently complying, then kissing her – one after the other – on the heavily oiled lobes of her bottom. In a brief lucid instant, she wondered where David had got the idea to do something so ritualistic, then surmised that he'd merely copied Ladybird. Whatever, the tender little gesture was beautiful.

For many minutes, Rosie floated in a spaced out, slack bodied haze. It was as if she'd been a bomb of sensation that had gone off with a bang then left perfect inner silence in its wake. She could hear the ripple of the water and small sounds of movement nearby, indistinct and unattributable. She could feel the diffuse heat of the sun on her back, filtered by the creeping vines that grew up the inside of the glass and also by the glass itself, that seemed to offset the fiercest of the rays and admit only beneficent light.

Pleasure such as she'd experienced wasn't easily gotten over, but at length, she pushed strongly with her hands and sat up as gracefully as she could.

A charming sight met her eyes. David and Ladybird were kneeling on a pile of towels – and she was slowly massaging his back. They were both still naked, and David still erect; yet there seemed nothing overtly sexual about their actions. David was stretching his shoulders from time to time, and making small sounds of contentment – but clearly only from the easing of knotted muscles.

'Ha! It lives!' said Ladybird pertly, pausing in her slow digital glide across David's scapulae.

Rosie managed a lopsided grin. Her body was fully satisfied now, but there was still a heart-tugging attractiveness about the couple before her. If she'd had the energy, she would have wanted one, or more probably both of them, but instead she accepted a temporary hiatus. There would be other days, and all just as delicious.

'Do you want this table now?' she asked, her voice coming out in a soft, almost mouselike squeak.

'Yes,' answered Ladybird, rising lithely. 'But only if you can stand, sweetheart.'

'I'll try,' Rosie said, then slid her feet cautiously to the floor. When she straightened her legs and tried to stand, her knees felt like water and she swayed. In a flash both David and Ladybird were beside her. David pulled up a nearby stool and helped her to sit down on it; while Ladybird draped her around the shoulders with another of the freshly laundered towels.

'Are you alright now?' the beautiful trainer asked, crouching down to touch Rosie's cheek. David just stood to one side, an expression of concern on his fine young face, while his erection was as solid as ever. It jutted out imposingly in front of him, pointing towards them, although David himself seemed barely aware of it as he looked worriedly in Rosie's direction.

'Believe me, I feel fabulous. Never better,' she replied, feeling her strength and vitality flood back. She fixed David with a long, steady look. 'And I seem to think it's your turn now, if I remember rightly.'

'Right, my boy, up on to that couch,' said Ladybird with a fair degree of authority. Whatever doubts she'd had about relating to David were now obviously gone. She looked strikingly confident and physically stunning. In the realm of the senses she was queen, supreme and empowered by her skills.

With a sure, natural elegance, David did as he was told, but then hesitated, kneeling on the couch. Rosie covered a smile with her hand, although really it wasn't funny. To squash a hard-on like that beneath him would be painful. Poor devil, she thought, watching him stare bemusedly at his own stiff manhood.

'On your back, Sunny Jim!' said Ladybird, reaching out to touch the offending member. 'We'll need full access to this . . .' She tapped his penis playfully and he gasped. Rosie saw his face contort, and his flanks quiver with effort. Slowly, and with extreme care, he lay down on his back, his splendid but unruly young cock pointing proudly at the distant glass roof. As he closed his eyes and settled back into stillness, Rosie could sit no longer, but rose to her feet and moved in closer to the table, knotting the towel around her waist as she walked.

Ladybird said nothing, but winked broadly, reaching into the sports holdall she'd placed on the counter earlier. From its depths she pulled out a bunch of the same soft towelling ties that she'd used for Rosie's hair. Her green eyes glittered like shards of emerald, and Rosie sensed a game beginning.

She bit down on her lip and held in a gasp, when Ladybird began arranging David's body on the couch – with his arms bent back above his head, and his legs widely parted. Rosie had noticed that there were metal rings bolted to the four corners of the couch, but she'd not really thought about their purpose. She'd supposed they were something to do with shifting the weighty contraption around, but realised now that they weren't.

They were for bondage. To secure some unwilling – or willing – subject to the table for the purposes of erotic stimulation. Even as the idea dawned, Ladybird nodded pointedly in the direction of David's feet, and handed Rosie two pieces of towelling, while taking two more for herself.

David had been strangely passive on the table, but as he felt their efforts to secure him, he began to struggle. 'What's happening?' he demanded, his right leg kicking and snaking in Rosie's grip.

'Keep still, David,' commanded Ladybird, her voice steely and strange.

Rosie was impressed, then suddenly realised that this role wasn't new to her friend. Ladybird had done this before, obviously, and her tangible aura of dominance – and the way she'd co-ordinated the restraints – suggested that she was intimately familiar with the more esoteric uses of this particular table.

I wonder who it was last time? thought Rosie as she fastened the ties around the ankles of a chastened and motionless David.

Julian? Very likely. He obviously liked that sort of thing. Or perhaps Celeste, who seemed quite catholic in her sexual tastes and probably loved anything slightly decadent.

Rosie's fingers faltered and she fumbled with a knot. What if Ladybird had chosen to tie *her* up? Then done exactly the same exquisitely arousing things that she'd done earlier? As she finally managed to make the tie safe, Rosie imagined it was her own body stretched helplessly on the couch. She could almost feel David's finger on her clitoris, rubbing it gently as she bucked and heaved in her bonds, torn apart by overpowering sensation.

And more shocking than even the fantasy of being tied was the realisatioin that she actually wanted it. Watching Ladybird scrupulously wash her hands then begin mixing her oils again, Rosie made a silent vow to sample these strange delights as soon as she was able – which in *this* household could be a matter of hours rather than days, she concluded wryly.

'Can you dry him off for me, please,' asked Ladybird as a new and equally delectable aroma-blend seemed to fill their immediate environment. This mix seemed more robust somehow, sharper in its top notes, and decidedly male. Combining oils and their perfumes was clearly an art form, and one that Ladybird excelled in. Picking up a fresh towel from the heap, Rosie made a second mental note. She'd like to learn this skill too, just as soon as she could think straight again.

David shuddered as she pressed the soft fabric to his skin. Instinct made her avoid his genitals though; mainly because his prick was so stiff and inflamed that the slightest of touches might trigger him. She'd come quickly herself under Ladybird's scented ministrations, and been glad of it, but she wanted David's experience to last longer. She wanted his pleasure to endure and be extended to its utmost limit. This was yet another whole new world for him, and she didn't want it rushed or hurried.

Smoothing the towel over David's body, she dried his face, his torso and his limbs. He kept his eyes tightly shut throughout the process, but his strong-featured face was revealing. His mouth narrowed with strain as she neared his groin, and he stirred restlessly, tugging at his bonds. On a whim, she leant over his prick and blew on it, and immediately he cried out, his hips bucking up towards her.

'Naughty!' said Ladybird chidingly, but to which of them, Rosie couldn't tell. The scent of the oil was overwhelming – it made her feel giddy and daring. It filled her head with smells that were hot and animal and spicy. She caught a citrus note somewhere in the blend, and found its bite both exciting and euphoric.

'Stand by ... He'll need you,' said Ladybird calmly as she poured the potion onto her hands, then moved closer to David's quaking body. With the lightest of strokes she began anointing his arms and shoulders, then worked smoothly across his chest and his ribcage.

The massage was brisk and businesslike, and it was hard to tell which element affected David most: the kneading or the pungent aromas. He began shifting around on the couch and moaning in a long, sub-vocal chunter. As Ladybird reached some particularly sensitive spot, he'd squirm like a wild thing and gasp; then relax again when she moved on to somewhere less critical.

Quite soon though, most parts of his anatomy seemed critical. Feet and forearms, shoulders and kneejoints – wherever Ladybird patted and circled and rubbed. His hips were in constant lifting motion and his penis swayed, jumped and ran freely with a clear, shiny fluid. Rosie felt her own resolve weakening too. She wanted to reach over, glove him gently in her fingers and bring ease to his rampant stiffness. She longed to hear him wail with rapture and gratitude, and see his grimacing face grow soft and calm. So focused was she on David, that Ladybird's sudden, faint cry, and the stilling of her deftly moving fingers came as a complete and rather piquant surprise.

'Oh God, Rosie, you're going to have to help me,' she whispered, leaning weakly against the table. David's eyes flew open as he absorbed the slight jolt, his face a picture of puzzlement and lust.

At a loss, Rosie glanced towards the bottles and the bowl with the oil in. Not quite sure what to do, she made a start towards it.

'Not that, *me*!' gasped Ladybird, swivelling around against the table, parting her long, sleek thighs and bracing her feet on the floor. 'Help me come, Rosie,' she begged. 'I know you're not sure about this, but please . . . just put your hand here and let me do the work.' On the word 'here' she flaunted her slim pelvis forward and made her moist sex open and pout between the delicate red curls of her motte.

Remembering how she'd felt in the gym back in London, Rosie didn't hesitate. She moved close and slid her hand between Ladybird's legs, gasping at her friend's heat and wetness. Instinctively, she waggled her fingers and rubbed them from side to side across Ladybird's large bud-like clitoris. The other woman groaned heavily, and true to her word began to work herself roughly and rhythmically on Rosie's rigid fingertips. Her slim hips rocked and swayed, then after only a few seconds she let out an uncouth gurgling grunt and jammed her hand in hard over Rosie's, almost hurting her.

'Yes! Yes! Yes!; chanted Ladybird, in the age old cliché of orgasm, her hot flesh rippling and her juices trickling and flowing. The spasms were deep and distinct to the touch, but as they faded she slumped forwards, her slender body finding momentary support against Rosie's. Then, just as quickly as she'd demanded her pleasure, it was over, and the trainer stood straight again, bouncing lightly on her toes and clearly ready to proceed.

Let's get on then, shall we?' she said, pouring fresh oil into the palm of her hand as if nothing unusual had happened.

Returning her attention to David again, Rosie saw a man tormented by need. His handsome face was a mask, his skin white and stretched, and there were great jagged spots of high colour daubed across his elegant cheekbones. His penis was vivid too, harder and more angry-looking than ever. Ladybird's casual climax had only exacerbated his lust, and he seemed only a couple of breaths away from coming.

'Please,' he entreated softly as Rosie leant across to stroke his sweaty brown hair off his face. As her fingers strayed, tempted by the beauty of his features, he craned up towards her and sucked her thumb into his mouth, pulling on it urgently, like a comforter. It was the first time a grown man had ever done such a thing to Rosie, and she felt a thin twist of pleasure between her legs, that seemed to flutter in time to his suction.

'I think he's ready,' said Ladybird suddenly, her fingers lying flat on David's belly. Rosie realised she was meant to do something. She drew her thumb out of David's mouth, moved behind his head, and pressed her hands against his tied-down wrists. Her hold on him was ineffectual really, but the gesture was primarily symbolic. She felt the muscles in his forearms tighten as Ladybird slowed her oily stroking, very delicately took hold of his cock, and at the same time – with her free hand – reached down between his legs to hold his balls.

'Dear God,' gasped David as Ladybird began handling him with the measured precision of a surgeon. Her grip – and her syncopated motions – remained constant even though he struggled; and within seconds he was shouting and groaning and jerking his body on the couch. Without his bonds Rosie couldn't have held him, and she expected them to snap any moment. Oil and his own thick fluids were squelching and squeaking through Ladybird's fingers; the noise revealing and graphic as she worked on his hard, red member. Rosie was utterly captivated, and felt her own sex drip and swell too; especially when Ladybird's fingers slid down to the cleft of David's botton.

'Kiss him,' she ordered curtly, nodding to Rosie and rotating her grip on David's prick. As she did so he screamed, his dark flesh leaping visibly and his rich creamy seed jetting out. Rosie wanted to watch, and to taste it, but obediently she dove around to his side and pressed her mouth down onto his.

As she pushed with her tongue, his lips yielded, even though he still tried to shout out and rave. Moulding his mouth with her lips, she drew his joyous cries inside her, absorbing the sound as if it were his very life itself. She felt like a vampire goddess, devouring his rapture and feeding on the essence of his orgasm. She wondered casually if Ladybird was sucking his penis, but found she didn't really care. His sweet young voice was born of his brain, his heart and his soul, while his semen came merely from his baser parts: his cock and his blind, aching balls.

As he finally grew still, she let her mouth rove over his face, kissing his chin, his cheeks and his eyes. With him quiet at last, she straightened up and watched Ladybird finish her ministrations. There were strings of silky whiteness on David's thighs and belly, and these she massaged into his skin like an unction. It was as if the product of his magical loins was the final ingredient in her spell.

Rosie moved to stand beside Ladybird, and stared downwards. Still bound to the couch, David looked angelic, his face and body both divine and wasted. His skin was slick and gleaming, and his hair – usually so neatly combed – was all tousled into spikes and points where he'd tossed and strained in his ecstasy. He seemed only semi-conscious, but he was smiling – a perfect, innocent, beautiful grin that turned Rosie's innards to fire all over again. His cock was flaccid now, but still held a marvellous promise – as if at any second it might stretch into the long, magnificent baton she'd felt move and swoop inside her as they'd squirmed and bucked on the grass. It seemed like a lifetime ago now, but as she glanced up towards the glass, and the sky beyond, she realised it was only an hour or two. If that.

As she remembered their sunlit frolic, she wanted it again. Wanted to be back there, kissing him, tasting his tongue, breathing his joy into her mouth as he came and she came too. She looked down at his soft, sticky cock and wished it a hard hot pole that she could mount and ride to glory. She thought of their first time, on the way to Stonehaven, and of how she'd taken exactly what she wanted back then.

But if David was too tired to perform now, wasn't there always Ladybird, whose sexual power was prodigious? The beautiful trainer had said Rosie wasn't ready, but what if she'd been wrong? Maybe now was the right time to experiment?

Then, suddenly, Rosie's anticipatory musings were shattered. She heard a high, clear voice calling her name. Someone was approaching, and looking for her. They weren't here yet, but they weren't far away either – probably in the passage that led to the main hall.

'Rosie? Are you there?' Celeste's bell-like tones rang out, much closer now. 'There's somebody here to see you!'

Rosie glanced desperately towards Ladybird, and then saw a truly extraordinary phenomenon.

It was like watching Wonderwoman, or Supergirl – naked. Rosie had simply never seen anyone move so fast or in such a highly co-ordinated fashion. In a flash, Ladybird had the ties off David's wrists and was handing him a terry-cloth robe from the selection piled nearby. To Rosie she just nodded significantly, and made folding and tucking motions.

Her heart beating wildly, Rosie picked up the cue and lashed her towel somewhat higher around her body in a makeshift but decent sarong.

By the time the double doors to the passage swung open, both she and David were clothed – although he still looked blank-eyed and dazed. Smiling broadly, Celeste swept into the room, preceding whoever the visitor was, and as she did so, Ladybird walked naked to the side of the pool and executed a smooth, almost world class dive straight into the water of the deep end.

Healing Passion

Sylvie Ouellette

Judith is fresh out of nursing college when she lands a job at the exclusive Dorchester Clinic specialising in cosmetic care for wealthy clients. It isn't long before Judith realises the staff are regularly engaging in recreational pursuits of a decidedly lascivious nature – with the patients and with each other. In the following extract, Judith has to bathe a very attractive male patient who has a broken leg and who is more than happy to allow Judith complete access to every part of his well-toned body. Her ministrations don't stop at the tub; when the time comes to put him to bed, Judith has a few ideas how to ensure her patient's complete comfort.

French-Canadian author Sylvie Ouellette has written three books for Black Lace. Her other titles are *The King's Girl*, set in North America in the early 1600s, and *Jasmine Blossoms*, a contemporary story of sexual intrigue set in Japan. *Jasmine Blossoms* is due for publication in June 1997.

Healing Passion

*T*he nursing attendant took Judith aside and looked around before bending down to speak in her ear.

'You've got to save my life,' he whined. 'It's almost midnight and I'm supposed to be off now. I really can't stay a minute longer. I was called to help on the third floor and it took longer than I had thought, so I fell behind in my list of tasks. All that's left to do is to help the guy in room 627 with his bath. I know it's not part of your duties, but if you have a minute could you take care of that? He says he doesn't mind waiting. Everybody else is asleep in their beds, so you shouldn't be too busy. Please?'

Judith looked around her, too. They were alone by the side of the nursing station; the other nurse who was assigned to work the night shift with Judith was nowhere to be seen.

She hesitated for a moment, knowing that when the attendants weren't finished with their tasks at the end of their shifts, they were expected to stay and work overtime. The nurses had more important things to do.

She glanced at him and was surprised by how young he looked. She decided he was rather cute. Then she glanced down again to read the name on the tag pinned to his breast pocket.

'Listen, Ray,' she began, 'you know that nurses are not supposed to do the attendants' work – '

'I know,' he interrupted impatiently, 'but my friends are waiting for me outside. We're off to this party and it's late already. I would have been finished by now if it hadn't been for that problem on the third floor. The guy in 627 is very cool; he won't say anything, I'm sure. Please?'

Judith hesitated, looking at him and trying to decide whether she should let him off. He seemed sincere and there would be no harm in helping him out. She knew he was about the same age as her yet he looked much younger; his cheeks seemed as soft as a baby's. His eyes were a pale brown, almost amber and, she thought, curiously, his hair was about the same colour.

He looked sweet and his voice sounded slightly worried, with a tinge of desperation. She felt her heart melt. He was right: there was hardly anything to do before her first round at one o'clock, and room 627 was one of hers. Besides, if anybody found out about it the blame would be on Ray, who left without finishing his tasks, not her.

'Where is the patient now?' she asked.

Ray smiled, knowing he was winning. 'I just put him in the tub; he's soaking now. All you need to do is scrub his back and then help him out of there. He's got a bad leg but other than that he's fine. He's in an island tub and he's on some kind of muscle relaxant: Desquel, I think. He shouldn't give you a hard time.'

Already he was pulling away, smiling at Judith. He winked before turning around. 'Thanks!' he whispered. 'I'll make it up to you.'

Judith went back to her station and sifted through the order sheets. The team who had just finished on the evening shift had left nothing to be done. All the medication had been distributed, the observation charts filled, and the patients tucked up, except, of course, for the patient in room 627.

PATIENT WAS PUT IN THE BATH TUB AT 23:50, the last nurse had written and put her initials in the next column.

Judith checked her watch and took out her pen. PATIENT WAS TAKEN OUT OF THE BATH TUB AT 00:30. She scribbled her initials. That would give her about 20 minutes to get him out of there.

The island tub Ray had mentioned was the kind installed in the middle of the bathroom, on a small pedestal, high enough and far away enough from the walls so the nursing staff could stand around it to help the patient, making things much easier for everyone. This would only take a few minutes, yet Judith didn't want to rush the patient.

The other nurse assigned to the station was checking on her

own patients, in rooms 600 to 615. Room 627 was the last one at the other end of the corridor, so chances were nobody would come and check up on Judith for a little while.

She re-arranged the papers on the desk and looked around quickly before heading down the corridor in a fast, silent pace. She had been assigned to this floor just last week, during the day shift, but she couldn't remember who was in 627 anymore. Besides, it wasn't unusual for patients to request a change after a couple of days, if a better room became available. This particular room was at the very corner of the building and had windows on two sides, offering a better view than the other rooms, and therefore making it quite popular with many patients.

When Judith entered, all the lights were out, even the tiny lamp above the head board. A pale triangle of light painted the wooden floor at the far end. It came from the bathroom door, which was only slightly ajar, and let faint splashing sounds escape. The lights in there had not been turned on to their full power and she concluded that the patient probably wanted to relax in semi-darkness. After all, it was after midnight already.

She walked over to the bathroom and glanced in. Just as Ray had told her, the patient was in an island tub, his back to the door. A thin cloud of steam was rising from the water and all she could see of its occupant was his broad shoulders and the back of his head. She didn't recognise him and concluded it must be a new patient. She knocked gently on the bathroom door, not wanting to startle him, and slowly entered.

'I'm coming to help you out of there...' she began. She swallowed the rest of her sentence when the patient turned his head and smiled at her.

'Very nice of you,' he replied with a smile. It was Mike Randall, laying in the bath tub with water up to his waist, covered by only a small towel over his loins. His left leg was still in a cast, wrapped in a plastic film and held a few inches above the bath tub by a thick rubber strap to prevent it from touching the water.

He looked comfortable, his arms dangling on either side of the tub, his upper back propped up by a rubber pillow. Judith approached him slowly, fascinated by the sight of his near-naked body, enthralled by the way his tanned skin contrasted against the whiteness of the enamel.

Mike was wide awake tonight and did not seem to remember her.

'I was just about done,' he said. 'Just relaxing now. Can you do my back?' He leant forward and handed Judith a large blue sponge.

Without a word, Judith grabbed the sponge and plunged it into the warm water, gently brushing the side of his ribcage with her wrist in the process. The moist heat of the steam rising from the water almost choked her for a minute, forcing her to breathe deeply.

As her hand hit the water she felt the heat rise up her arm and instantly radiate through her body. She didn't know whether it came from the water or from him. Slightly blushing, she looked at him. He looked at her, still smiling. He leant further forward to give her better access to his back, his chest now practically resting on his cast.

The fragrance of the soap assaulted her nostrils; a refined, distinct smell that hung in the room and which she would most probably associate with him from now on. She gently rubbed his back, working up and down the length of his spine and then across the width of his shoulders. She let her hand disappear under the waterline, pressing the sponge all the way down until her fingers came to hit the bottom of the tub, where she could feel the cleft of his buttocks.

He laughed softly. 'You are very daring,' he said. 'We've only just met!'

'No, you're wrong,' she replied. 'I was with you when you came out of surgery.'

'That was you? I thought I had been dreaming about angels . . .'

He let out a sigh of satisfaction as she slowly squeezed the sponge over his shoulders, making the water trickle to rinse off the soap. His voice grew soft as he continued talking to her in the flirtatious tone she had heard him use in one of his films.

However, she wasn't really paying attention to his words. Still holding the sponge in a light grip she traced the line of his muscles with her fingertips. She was fascinated by the way his wet skin felt, and somehow hoped she could drop the sponge and simply let her hands run over him.

A few days ago she had taken advantage of his sedated state to caress his chest. Now she was pretending to wash him to continue her discovery of his body. She brushed his shoulder, lost in thought, desperately wishing that the sponge could miraculously vanish.

His hand came up suddenly and seized her wrist. She let out a small cry and dropped the sponge, which splashed soapy water around as it fell back in the tub.

Still holding her hand he leant back and brought her wet fingers to his lips. 'Now I remember you,' he said before kissing them gently. 'You're the nurse with the nice touch. I thought you only existed in my dreams . . .'

Judith started to tremble as she felt his lips nibbling at her fingers. Once again she marvelled at the sight of his naked chest, the taut muscles, and the tight skin now glistening and bringing even more definition to the ripples of his flat stomach.

Her eyes wandered to the small towel which barely covered his genitals. His leg held high caused the towel to run up his thigh. If he tried moving his other leg at all there would be a strong possibility that his maleness would be revealed in its entirety.

She couldn't stop looking at the slight bump in the middle of the towel, and wondering what lay underneath. He followed her gaze.

'Good old Desquel,' he laughed softly. 'Always available when it's not really needed.'

At first Judith couldn't understand what he was talking about but then she remembered the attendant had mentioned the patient was still on medication. Desquel was popular in surgery, a powerful, non-addictive painkiller but with a slightly inconvenient side-effect: certain men were unable to achieve an erection whilst they were taking it. Obviously, Mike also had been told about this possibility.

So that's what Ray had meant when he said the patient wouldn't give her any problems. Somehow Judith felt relieved, knowing Mike wouldn't feel at all tempted to make a pass at her under these conditions. Therefore she could easily resist temptation. But suddenly she noticed a twitch in the fabric and the towel began to rise above the water line.

'But then again,' Mike continued, 'they stopped giving it to me a couple of days ago.'

Judith pretended not to notice anything and pulled her hand away from his to quickly reach down and pull the plug out. The water spiralled down the drain with a gurgling sound and she turned around to grab a large towel, throwing it across her shoulder.

Despite her efforts to keep calm, a storm was now raging within her. She had to help him out of the tub, dry him off and then get him to bed. That meant close contact with his naked body and his glistening skin. Just standing near him was enough to feel the heat of his body, compounded by the lingering warmth of the bath water.

How would she react to the moist touch of his arm around her shoulders? Perhaps she would also have to slip her own arm around his waist. She would most probably be tempted to touch more of him . . . Would she be able to restrain herself? Now she wished she hadn't let Ray go. That was all his fault; she shouldn't have agreed to this. If only she had known, she could have avoided finding herself in such a compromising position.

On the other hand, she was probably nothing to a man like Mike Randall. He most probably saw her as a nurse just like any other; one of those horrible women who like nothing better than to stick needles in people's behinds and force them to swallow all sorts of foul-tasting medications.

Yet his behaviour was quite revealing; the way he had kissed her fingers, and then blatantly directed her attention to his aroused genitals. She might have to fight off his advances, and this would require enormous strength from her, both physically and mentally.

He waited for the water to drain completely then braced himself with his arms on either side of the tub. Bending his good leg underneath him, he raised himself up until he came to rest his buttocks on the edge of the bath tub. Judith helped him by unhooking his cast from its support, slowly lowering his leg until his foot touched the floor.

He now sat astride the side of the tub, the towel around his waist soaked and dripping, threatening to come loose as the bulge of his erection kept straining the fabric, continually sending trickles of water down his thighs.

Judith came to him and held him whilst he swung his right leg over the side. Her arms were too short to encircle him completely and she felt his wet skin slipping under her fingers. She let him lean against the tub and handed him the towel whilst she went searching for his bathrobe. So far, so good, she thought.

The worst part was over and, on the whole, it had gone quite well. She had felt a vague fluttering in her loins as she watched him emerge from the tub, and saw his muscles playing under his skin. But at this moment she figured all she had to do was to cover his body. Then, at least her attention wouldn't be diverted by the sight of his bare flesh.

She found his robe hanging on the inside of the bathroom door and took it to him. When she turned around, however, she saw him pulling at the wet towel impatiently, tossing it back in the tub in a wet bundle.

She froze in surprise for a second as she saw his turgid phallus pointing in her direction and looked up at him, rather puzzled.

'The towel was dripping,' he explained in a childish tone. 'I can't get my cast wet, can I? I can't bend down with that cast. Could you please dry my leg?'

He handed her the towel with a smile. Judith licked her lips nervously and sensed her breath becoming shallow in excitement. Now he stood completely naked in front of her, except for the cast. He was asking her to touch him, to bend down in front of him and pat his leg dry.

She knew that by doing what he asked she would have to bring her face just a few inches from his erect member – which was still getting bigger. She felt her crotch grow wet at the thought of getting this close to his luscious body, and having to run her hands all over his muscular leg, albeit through the thickness of the bath towel. She had to think fast to find a way to avoid this contact or else she would not be able to resist such sweet temptation.

Stirred by a flash of inspiration, she stepped forward and almost forced him to put the bathrobe on, even fastening it for him at the waist. He let her cover him without uttering a word, an amused smile on his lips, perfectly aware of her confusion.

The robe came down to mid-thigh and Judith was somewhat relieved. She could still see his phallus pointing through the cloth but the rest of his body was almost completely hidden, making it less compromising for her if she had to offer her shoulder as a support.

She bent down briefly to pat him dry, starting with his foot and working her way up his calf, stopping slightly above the knee. But, although she tried to look casual and professional, all the while she sensed her breath quickening. She felt his hard

71

MODERN LOVE

muscles under her fingers, and almost wished she could touch him directly. But even more disturbing was the motion of his hips as she knelt in front of him.

She could feel his erection brush the side of her head repeatedly, as if he was doing it on purpose, and she desperately tried to retain her composure, not to move her head away too quickly, pretending she hadn't noticed anything. As his hips swayed next to her face she thought she heard him moan but quickly willed the impression away.

All her efforts seemed in vain. If he hadn't moved his hips so suggestively on purpose, then her imagination was once again getting the best of her. What if he really tried to make a pass at her? Would she be able to refuse him? There were hundreds of women out there who would probably want nothing better ...

Once she stood up he threw his arm around her, supporting himself on her shoulders and they got out of the bathroom to laboriously make their way to his bed. He moved forward in short hops, his left leg trailing behind, pressing his body against hers to keep his balance. The knot of his bathrobe belt came loose and as the robe fell open his cock slowly appeared, gradually getting harder with each step he took.

The bathroom door closed behind them, and soon Judith found herself trying to guide her patient in the dark. The only light came from the lamppost outside the window, which cast a pale blue light on the bed. They approached it inch by inch, his weight now heavy on her shoulder.

She could feel the moist heat of his body through the cloth of his robe. Because of the way he held on to her, she had no choice but to bend forward slightly, keeping her head lowered, thus watching his thick shaft bob up and down, the purplish head slowly emerging from beneath his foreskin, gradually coming alive.

Her own arousal began to mount as well, as she watched the glistening plum jump towards her lips time and time again, almost begging to be kissed. In the light of the lamppost she thought she could see a fine drop pearling from the tiny mouth. By the time they reached the bed his bathrobe was completely opened, and his member stood fully erect. Judith helped him climb into bed and lifted his cast up to lay it next to the other leg.

Although the trek from the bathroom had gone rather well, he seemed relieved to finally reach his bed and lay down quietly, his bathrobe spread underneath him, his taut body once again revealed. Judith took one last look at him. Outside the room the wind blew through the branches of a nearby tree and the light from the lamppost cast their moving shadows all over his smooth skin.

The effect was cinematic and captivating. He just lay there, still smiling, his eyes half-shut. Judith knew she had to leave. Not only was she afraid she wouldn't be able to fight the temptation to run her hands all over this gorgeous body for much longer, but she had been away from the nursing station for quite a while now and her colleague might start looking for her at any minute.

She turned around to leave but at the very last moment she felt his fingers grabbing hold of her arm and she was gently pulled back towards the bed.

'Do you remember your promise?' he asked in a whisper, his eyes still half-shut and staring at the ceiling.

'What promise?'

'That morning, when I came out of surgery, I asked you if you would take good care of me, and you promised you would.'

Judith didn't reply. Obviously he remembered more about that day than she would have expected. But exactly how much?

'I remember your hand caressing my chest,' he said as if reading her mind. 'I felt your touch soft and warm . . .'

Judith remembered as well, of course, but was that his way of asking her to do it again? She looked down to his engorged phallus and saw it twitch slightly in the blue light.

'You promised,' he repeated. 'You can't leave me like this now.'

Of course she couldn't, but she had to. She was so confused, remembering how warm and soft his skin felt in the palm of her hand, and how she had wanted him that day. Yet she knew perfectly well that he was a patient, and that she had to go back to her desk immediately.

He loosened his grip on her but his fingers continued to caress her arm. She felt a tingling sensation at the surface of her skin and let out a faint sob. Only then did she notice a large mirror on the wall by the foot of the bed. She looked up and stared at their reflections, a tiny white figure standing next to his gorgeous, naked male flesh.

'You want me, I know you do,' Mike continued. 'Besides, aren't you supposed to do everything your patients ask you?'

'I ... don't know,' she stammered. 'This wouldn't be right. You are my patient.'

'You must be new here, then. I heard it's a policy of this Clinic to offer special care to clients who ask for it. That means giving them everything they ask for.'

Judith was disappointed by this sad excuse, thinking it was indeed a strange way of trying to get to her. Yet at the same time she wished it were true, so she could let herself yield to the force of her desire. She began to tremble and immediately sensed his fingers growing insistent on her skin, travelling up and down the length of her arm, the bone of his wrist brushing the peak of her erect nipple each time.

He must have felt the confusion within her, for his tone grew even softer and his invitation more open. 'I want you, Judith. I want you to undress for me, to show me that gorgeous body of yours. I am hot for you. Wouldn't you want to feel my skin against yours?' He reached up and gently seized her neck in his fingers, slowly pulling her head down toward his.

She didn't offer any resistance as her lips came to meet his and she felt his tongue invade her mouth, its softness sending a shiver from her breasts to her loins. She had to put her hand on the bed to stop herself from falling on top of him, but he anticipated her move, grabbed her wrist, and brought her hand to his chest instead. She slowly bent her elbow until she came to gently rest against him, pressing her chest against his, once again letting the heat of his body radiate through her.

He let go of her mouth after a brief moment and pulled his head back slightly. 'Undress for me, I want to see all of you.' His voice was still soft but his tone was more authoritative. In the darkness she saw his eyes sparkle, and read his desire. He wanted her.

She hesitated a moment, but suddenly realised how good it would be to feel her bare skin on his, if only for a moment. There was no doubt in her mind that it wasn't right, mainly because he was her patient. But if no one ever found out about it, what harm would there be? Besides, when she had been hired to work at the Dorchester Clinic, there was absolutely no mention in her contract of what to do in such a situation.

Closing her eyes, she also realised she was now trying to find excuses, however futile they may be, to justify this desire that was growing within her. She also knew it was useless; she was vanquished.

She stood back and undressed quickly, her fingers trembling but precise. Her dress fell to the floor and her bra and panties followed right after. She couldn't fight her desire any longer, it was pointless. Right now he wanted her, and she wanted him. All she had to worry about was that somebody might see them.

Standing completely naked, she quickly drew the curtain around the bed, making sure that if someone entered the room they would think the patient was asleep. The bed was contained in a small space formed by the window on one side, the curtain on the other, a blank wall at the head of the bed, and the wall with the large mirror at the other end.

She took some sort of wicked pleasure out of walking around naked in the blue light, knowing his eyes were studying her every move. Coming over to the other side of the bed, by the window, she climbed and knelt on the it.

She watched her own shadow rise on the curtain and felt her arousal bloom. All she needed to do was to turn her head slightly and she could also watch herself in the mirror; she could see her now-naked body bending down to worship his.

By now her excitement was such that she practically fell on top of him, covering his chest with hers, pressing her swollen breasts against his hot skin, then straddling his right leg with her leg.

She knew he couldn't move because of his cast, and the thought of being in control of the situation excited her even more. She grabbed his mouth within hers forcefully, now wanting to taste all of him, her hips thrusting up and down rhythmically, grinding her wet pussy on to his hard thigh.

He couldn't do anything but yield to this passionate embrace, and he gently caressed the side of her hips, letting his fingertips wander over the swell of her bottom, his nails grazing at her delicate skin, just stopping short of her swollen love-lips.

Judith groaned with every breath, now slightly pulling away from him, her hands sliding between her body and his, caressing both his chest and her own breasts simultaneously.

She kissed, licked and sucked his mouth, his jaw, his neck, his chest. She heard herself gasping and moaning loudly, no longer in control of her own breathing, as she writhed on top of him.

From the moment she had climbed on to the bed she had been given a certain power over him; he was at her mercy. If she wanted to get off and go back to her station, leaving him alone and frustrated, she could do just that. Even if she chose to stay, because he couldn't move unassisted, she was in charge of both her own pleasure and his.

She sat up on his thigh and let her own weight crush her wet vulva against him, her hips never ceasing their thrusting motion. He reached up and grabbed her breasts, feeling their fluid weight in turn, letting his fingertips gently worry her erect nipples. She sighed.

This was better than she could ever have imagined. Of course he was at her mercy, but it was also up to her to satisfy him. 'Ask me anything,' she announced in a whisper.

'Sit on my face,' came the reply.

She smiled and looked at him. She hadn't expected that. Rather, she would have thought he would ask her to pleasure him first. Changing position, she slowly crawled along his chest and turned around to straddle his face. He reached up, grabbed her hips and eased them down gently until her moistness met his mouth.

His tongue on her flesh was a revelation. Judith felt herself melt on to him, his lips studying her methodically, his tongue reaching deep inside her. Her hips resumed their dance, using his mouth as a soft surface against which to grind.

His hands kept surveying her thighs, his fingernails gently scratching at her soft skin, sending tingling hot waves all the way up to her pussy.

Judith looked up and was almost surprised to see herself in the mirror on the opposite wall. She saw his body, hard and tense lying on the white sheet, brushed by the blue light, the shadows of the branches playing against the curves of his muscles. His stiff prick stood up against his belly, twitching sporadically.

But most impressive was the sight of her own body, straddling his face, writhing incessantly. She didn't recognise herself, not tonight. It was another woman she saw tilting her head sideways, her eyes half-shut, her face betraying the storm of pleasure that ravaged her.

She watched the woman bring her hands up to caress her own breasts, as her face began to contract in repeated spasms of pleasure, the eyes barely able to remain open, the mouth gaping open in successive ohs and ahs.

Her gaze came back to the statuesque body that lay underneath hers, and to the stiff cock that still remained untouched but now craved its reward. She bent down and grasped it delicately, gently pulling the foreskin back to completely expose the swollen plum. At first she bathed it in long licks, from the base of the shaft all the way to the tip of the head, inserting the tip of her tongue at the entrance of the tiny mouth, feeling her man's hips jerk smoothly every time.

Her hair fell forward and covered his hips. At the same time she took him in her mouth, completely, to the hilt, and began sucking gently. She heard him moan under her and his mouth grew impatient on her vulva.

In reply she lowered her hips even more, almost choking him, now grinding her pussy forcefully against his face. Yet she didn't increase the intensity of her ministrations of him. He had to earn his reward. He had to make her come first.

She let go of him for a while, sitting up again in order to concentrate on the wave of pleasure that was being born deep inside her at this very moment. Once again she looked up to the mirror. She wanted to see herself come.

She smiled at her reflection. Yes, it was her. How beautiful she looked on the verge of her climax, her hips now swaying rhythmically, her hands clasped on her breasts, kneading them furiously, her fingers pinching her engorged nipples.

She opened her mouth to scream her joy but no sound came out. Instead, her whole body arched under the strength of her pleasure and she leapt forward in an ultimate spasm, falling against the hard rock of his flat stomach.

Her vulva lay half-way down his chest, her thighs now straddling his shoulders. He inserted his finger in the gaping entrance which lay just a few inches from his chin. The moist flesh sucked at it readily, in successive spasms, as Judith's body shook under the intensity of her climax.

At the same time she was highly aware of it all, her limbs numb but her mind still very much alive. With great effort she lifted her head and looked in the mirror again, somehow fascinated by its presence, unable to find a reason for this attraction.

She saw the woman sprawled over the man's body, her face almost hidden behind the curtain of her own hair, her smile still betraying her pleasure. At the same time she felt the thick prick stir between her breasts. Now it was time to reward the man.

First she rolled on to her side, sliding off him. Then she stood up next to the bed, the cold floor assaulting her naked feet. She stared at the body that lay on the white sheets, once again wanting to force it into submission.

She walked over to the other side and opened the door of the bedside cupboard. Fumbling in the dark she managed to locate the leather restraints.

There was a chance he might object to what she had in mind but she remembered the procedure she had been taught at nursing school: first she had to grab the wrists quickly and secure the strap around them, then use her own weight if necessary to pull the other extremity and tie it to the head of the bed.

She acted swiftly and precisely, and by the time he realised what she was up to it was already too late. He whined in complaint but she ignored him, quickly picking her bra off the floor and gagging him with it. She thought of tying his feet as well but it was not really necessary, as once she sat on him he wouldn't be in a position to go anywhere.

She climbed back on the bed and knelt next to him again, amused by the worried expression in his eyes. This time he was all hers. Once again she straddled him, this time setting her knees on either side of him, her inner thighs rubbing against his hips, and she bent down until she came to completely lie on top of him. She gently nibbled at his chin whilst her hands caressed the strong muscles of his biceps.

She could feel his heart pounding heavily in his chest. What was he feeling? Fear? Arousal? Anticipation? A strange mixture of all three? At least she knew he wasn't indifferent.

Her foot grazed the side of his cast and a series of weird associations sprung in her mind. When the cast would come off he would most certainly need extensive physiotherapy.

She caressed his chest and his stomach lovingly, using only her fingertips, surveying every inch of his smooth skin. He was hot under her, and seemingly still getting hotter, his skin now exuding a moist, fresh aroma.

Against her belly his prick pressed harder and harder, trying to throb its way inside her. The engorged head seeped at the mouth. He was more than ready. But it was still too early for Judith; he would have to wait.

She could see his eyes sparkle in the dark, at times worried, at times lustful, and she took a wicked pleasure out of torturing him like this.

Her hands increased the intensity of their caresses on his skin, and little by little she began using her whole body to discover his, stroking the entire length of her arms against his, rubbing and pressing her erect nipples across his chest.

Her tongue also danced along his neck, travelling from one ear to the other, gently sucking on his earlobes for a moment before continuing its journey. She bathed him thus, remembering how she had felt when Edouard had done it to her, hoping it would have the same effect.

After a while her mouth worked its way down his chest, nibbling at his pectoral muscles in a succession of wet kisses until she came to suck on his nipples. They were already stiff and engorged, but grew even bigger in Judith's mouth. She sucked on them greedily, flicking the tip of her tongue over them at a maddening speed, teasing them incessantly whilst her hands massaged his hard muscles.

He began to writhe under her, moaning loudly despite his gag, as if surprised at his own reaction. He lifted his head briefly. Judith stopped her ministrations and looked up at him.

His eyes were begging her to untie him, his maleness now growing impatient on her belly. She smiled wickedly.

'You asked for it,' she whispered. 'Now let me have my way.'

She went back to concentrate on his nipples, satisfied that he was getting impatient, quite determined not to let him loose for a while still. Yet at the same time the engorged cock that throbbed against her chest was calling to her. It wanted her, and she decided she wanted it too.

Putting her hands flat on his stomach to support herself, she sat up and rocked her pelvis back and forth a few times, feeling his thickness brush her moist vulva, covering him with her dew. She heard him moan again. Now she was happy to have tied him up, she could take him on her own terms.

Soon her clitoris quivered against his hardness and she longed to feel him inside her. She grabbed hold of his shaft and presented the swollen head to her entrance.

She lowered herself upon him, slowly, feeling him stretch her gradually, but not letting him enter her completely, before lifting herself up again. Her entrance teased his rigid member, never giving it the satisfaction of total penetration.

His hips jerked up in a vain effort to impale her but she lifted herself up even more, pressing hard on his stomach to prevent him from moving again. This was an uneven fight however, his range of movements limited by the weight of the plaster cast around his leg. Yet Judith still wanted to show him she had the upper hand.

'Stop this,' she warned, 'it's no use.'

But as she glided up and down upon his length she gradually conceded. Soon she began to ride him, at first by simply rocking back and forth, then increasing the movement of her hips as she felt him growing bigger inside her, her arousal now mounting quickly. She was becoming a victim to her own game, having meant to hold out as long as possible to torture him, but realising she was the one who could no longer wait.

But, by now, she was acting solely with the intention of reaching her own climax. It didn't really matter if he came as well in the process; he had earned this reward. She heard herself panting, the muscles of her thighs soon tied in a burning knot as she rapidly moved up and down upon his shaft, her knees locking under the strain.

Her vulva was melting on to his member and quivering with delight, as Judith willed herself to continue her assault despite the pain in her exhausted legs. The swollen head stroked her inside, probing at the smooth walls of her tunnel, triggering that sensation which would soon take her to the point of no return. Her stiff clitoris rubbed itself on the hard shaft as well, only enhancing the pleasure she could already feel was about to explode.

She was breathless, highly aware of the pressure building up within her, yet her climax almost took her by surprise. Her head jerked back and forth a few times as successive sobs escaped from her mouth.

Her vulva contracted around his member and provoked his own climax. She hardly felt him quiver inside her, but she recognised the spasm that shook him, as if escaping from her own body to transport him right after.

She let herself collapse on top of him once more, this time recoiling on his chest and nestling her face in the groove of his neck. She listened to his heartbeat slowly returning to its normal rate, as was hers.

Although she would have liked to stay a little longer, she knew she had to shake herself from the cloud that now surrounded her, and fight the temptation to stay with him any longer.

His regular breathing told her he was completely relaxed now, and probably falling asleep. She rose with difficulty and felt his limp phallus slide out of her, falling back with a flop on his stomach.

Her patient was now in bed; she had done her duty. She undid the restraints and stored them back in the bedside cupboard, then took her bra from his mouth and began to dress.

The back panel was soaked and felt cold against her warm skin, right between her shoulder blades; a silent reminder of the daring way she had treated him. She laughed softly. She wasn't sorry for what she had done.

She finished dressing and pulled the blanket on top of him, looking at him one more time, still bathed by the blue light coming from the window, before making her way to the bathroom. Her hair needed to be tamed before she returned to her nursing station.

In the bath tub the wet towel still lay in a bundle, and its sight gave a smile to Judith's lips. This was something she wasn't going to forget for some time. She quickly gathered her hair up and checked her image in the mirror: prim and proper, who would have thought it? Glancing at her watch she suddenly realised she had been gone for over an hour.

She turned off the light and almost ran out of the room, desperately trying to think of a good excuse in case her colleague started asking questions. The best she could do was to tell the truth: she had to assist a patient out of the bath tub and help him settle for the night. The rest didn't matter.

Once she got to the station, however, the other nurse was busy preparing an injection. Judith quickly grabbed the order chart and pretended to absorb herself in it. For a second she felt this crazy urge to turn to her colleague and tell her all about what she had just been up to.

She could still smell him, feel him inside her, and her sore knees were still complaining about the way she had abused them.

It wasn't easy keeping a straight face.

The Silken Cage

Sophie Danson

In *The Silken Cage*, University lecturer Maria Treharne inherits her aunt's mansion on the windswept Brackwell Tor, Cornwall, and it isn't long before she finds herself the subject of strange and unexpected attention. Some say her new dwelling resides on sacred land. The mysterious Anthony Pendorran has waited a long time for an ancient promise to be fulfilled: for the true mistress of Brackwell Tor to take up residence. Maria senses strange forces are at work but cannot resist the powerful sexual magnetism of the dark-haired Pendorran.

Sophie Danson has written four Black Lace books. They are: *Avalon Nights*: bawdy stories from the time of King Arthur; *Web of Desire*: dark sexual intrigue via computer, *The Silken Cage* and *Pleasure Hunt*: the sexual initiation of a young Frenchwoman into an exclusive society of libertines.

The Silken Cage

Maria glanced at the clock on the marble mantelpiece in her bedroom. Its heavy brass hands clicked on inexorably towards seven o'clock, when Anthony had said he would send someone for her. It was a bind not having a car; she'd have to see about that – find out if Geraint knew anyone who had an old banger going cheap. If there was one thing Maria really disliked, it was being robbed of her independence – even by a man as desirable as Anthony Pendorran.

After their brief acquaintance yesterday, Pendoran remained a complete enigma to Maria. As she undressed, she reviewed what she knew about him – that he was a pagan, and that he lived in a house overlooking the sea at Polmadoc. Add to this that he was certainly an individualist, and more than a little arrogant, too, and you had the sum total of her knowledge. When she tried to think about him, she even found it difficult to picture his face in any detail. all she could remember were those compelling sea-grey eyes, and the feeling of frantic excitement that had overwhelmed her at the first touch of their fingers.

She went through into the adjoining bathroom and turned on the shower. When she'd first moved in, the plumbing had seemed dodgy to say the least – you never knew whether the water would come out ice-cold or raging hot, and sometimes it didn't come out at all. She'd been on the point of calling in a plumber when, as if by some miracle, the problem had righted itself. She sincerely hoped it would stay righted – until her solicitors came up with the precise details of this alleged private income, she was forced to live on her own resources; and St Alcuin's did not believe in paying its assistant lecturers any more than it absolutely had to. The sooner that fellowship came through the better.

Although she had become inordinately fond of this cosy little private bathroom. The Hall boasted three other bathrooms – or was it four? – but of all of them, this was Maria's favourite. She loved the antique feel of the room: the thick, syrupy glaze on the Victorian tiles that surrounded an old cast-iron bath with elegant lion's-paw feet and gleaming brass fittings; the pretty mosaic floor; the roomy shower-cabinet with doors of antique etched glass.

She stepped inside. Today, the water was just right: an even warmth that spread over her bare skin in high-pressure jets that tingled where they touched. Maria moved slowly round, allowing the water to caress her in new and secret places; offering herself up to the inquisitive jets that explored her every fold and swell. She reached up to push the wet hair back from her forehead, and the warm water fell like tropical rain on her upturned face, cascading down her cheeks and neck, running down into the deep valley between her breasts, and falling in huge, slow drops from the swelling crests of her nipples.

She reached out for the shower-gel and squeezed a little into the palm of her hand. The sharp, piny fragrance of horse chestnut wafted around her as she smoothed the cool gel over her shoulders, back and breasts, which had grown pink with the warm, tingling massage.

With slow, luxurious, circular movements she worked the gel into a foamy lather which mingled with the trickles of steaming water coursing down over her belly and flanks. The touch awakened new reserves of desire that even Geraint's enthusiastic love-making had neither reached nor satisfied, and her fingers slid inexorably downwards, towards the plump swell of her pubis.

Maria could not recall a time when she had felt so sexually aroused over such a long period. She had always enjoyed an active sex-life of course, but since she had arrived in Lynmoor, it was as though a dam had burst, releasing great floods of sexual desire that had been pent up inside her since ... for ever. Her whole body had become hypersensitive, each nerve-ending crying out for a touch, a kiss, a caress.

The reason was probably nothing more unusual than a release of tension, after a long and tense academic year that had left her strung up tighter than a steel wire. But all the same, there was definitely something about this place, this house in particular, that was uniquely conducive to the sweet, seductive warmth of lust, and the pleasures of the flesh.

Take this afternoon, for example. She had been talking to Geraint whilst he swung a scythe over the chaotic tangle of brambles and woodbine just outside the back wall of the Hall gardens. She'd initially intended leaving this part of the land until the formal gardens were properly cleared, but out walking yesterday evening she'd discovered a couple of small, apparently carved, stones peeping through the tight-knit vegetation.

On closer investigation, when they'd scythed away the long grass and brambles around them, Geraint and Maria had gradually uncovered not two, but seven small stones, some broken, and all cracked and worn, but arranged in a perfect circle, about six feet across.

She'd known instantly that this was something very special; it wasn't until she'd stepped into the circle that Maria had felt the power – like a hot wind blowing over her skin, dragging at her clothes and hair, caressing her like lewd fingers intent on exploring every nook and cranny of her body.

Could she possibly have imagined it, or had she really got in touch with some immense spiritual truth, hidden for years beneath an impenetrable carpet of bramble and woodbine? The initial exhilaration had lasted only a few seconds at most, and then it was gone from her, leaving a hot, sensual glow. Gone, leaving her standing alone in the circle, whilst Geraint watched her with a curious look in his eyes, not understanding, yet wanting – wanting so badly to share what Maria was experiencing.

'You all right, Maria? Thought you was goin' to faint just then.'

'I ... I'm fine, Geraint. Why don't you come and join me? Come on, come and stand here next to me.'

'Whatever you say.'

With a shrug of his broad shoulders, he took two long strides which brought him into the centre of the circle.

'What happens now, then?'

Could he not feel it? Could he not feel the hot, trembling lust running through her body to her very fingertips as she reached out and touched his cheek? As if reading her thoughts he caught her hand and kissed it, and she felt a new electricity tingle through her, raising gooseflesh on her bare arms.

'This. This is what happens, Geraint. If you want it to happen.'

She sank to her knees on the rough-cut grass, paying no heed to the sharp bramble twigs which stuck up out of the ground and dug into her bare flesh. Pressing her face against the crotch of Geraint's jeans, she breathed in the bitter tang of his sweat, and let her teeth bite gently along the hard, smooth outline of his cock; a swollen, slanting baton beneath the tight fabric. Geraint shuddered with excitement, his fingers gripping her shoulders and winding her hair into corkscrew tendrils as her hot, moist breath soaked through the skin-tight denim, exciting the flesh beneath.

Geraint's cock was so swollen that the flies of his 501s bulged, pushing out the material so that the buttons were clearly visible, and straining fit to burst. Maria tasted them with the tip of her tongue; the metal was cold and slightly rough to the touch, but it excited her. She wished she had the teeth of a wild she-cat, sharp enough and strong enough to slice through thick fabric and bite away the buttons and free her lover's cock from the prison of its covering.

She looked up at Geraint. His eyes were fixed on her, watchful and excited. She could sense how it was turning him on, just watching her playing the harlot with his arrogant young body. And she was incredibly turned on, too. She smiled, and she saw Geraint's eyes glitter with mischievous complicity.

'Unbutton yourself,' she whispered. 'Please. For me.'

She took his hand and placed it on his flies, kissing his fingers one by one as they unfastened the fly-buttons, baring the tight white cotton briefs underneath.

'Now take out your beautiful cock for me,' she urged him, his eyes following every movement as he slid his fingers under the waistband of his briefs. 'I want to taste you.'

His fingers lingered for a little while, teasing her as they curled about the turgid flesh. Perhaps he was showing her that he did not need her to give him pleasure. Then, in a single rapid movement, he pulled on his cock and it sprang out like a flick-knife, wickedly hard and so tempting that she could not resist opening her lips and taking it into her mouth in a single greedy thrust of her head.

Standing under the shower, massing the creamy lather over her belly, Maria recalled the salty taste of Geraint's cock. She remembered the divine slipperiness of the sex-fluid that oozed from the tip as she ran her tongue over it again and again, closing her lips very tight about the shaft so that each movement of her mouth became an unforgiving caress.

The remembered taste of Geraint's hot, white sperm on her tongue made Maria shudder with delicious excitement. There had been floods of it – great, creamy jets with a bitter aftertaste that only served to renew her thirst for more and yet more. And when she had swallowed every last drop, she had forced her lips against Geraint's, so that he too could enjoy the taste of their shared lust.

Smiling at the recollection of their joining, there in the sunshine amid the broken stones, Maria let her fingers wander slowly down over the soapy-smooth skin to the dripping-wet curls that adorned her pubis, their auburn glow now darkened by the water. She shifted her position slightly so that her feet moved further apart, and her love-lips parted gently, revealing the path to the hidden heart of her sex. As they opened, a trickle of warm, soapy water coursed down her belly and found its way into the interior, teasing and tickling as it ran, like an infinitely long, infinitely playful tongue.

Why hold out any longer against the sensual hunger that was gnawing away at her? Maria unhooked the shower-head and directed it between her sex-lips, shuddering with the explosion of sudden, brutal pleasure as the hot water-jets made contact with the hard rosebud of her desire.

She knew it would not last long; the need was too urgent, the hunger too immediate, the touch too brutal. But the pleasure was immense and all-consuming. Leaning back against the tiled wall, trickles of water from her wet hair still running over her neck and breasts, she began moving the shower-head over the inner lips of her sex, at first quite slowly and languidly, then with increasing rapidity, so that the water-jets flicked over her clitoris like a hundred needle-sharp tongues.

Images of her most skilful lovers flickered on the dark screen of her mind: Jonathan and Geraint – and another man: the dark and enigmatic figure of Anthony Pendorran. Which of them was running his tongue-tip over her pussy? Which of these imagined lovers was here with her now, manipulating her desire, summoning her to the heights of orgasm? All of their faces were blurring into one . . .

Jerking and moaning with pleasure, she abandoned herself to a climax that left her gasping. Her head reeled as she put a hand out to steady herself and as the last delicious spasms died away, the honeydew of her sex mingled with the hot, soapy water spiralling around her feet.

Drying herself with a fluffy pink towel, Maria padded across the tiled floor towards the bedroom. She glanced at the clock as she put on her stockings and suspenders: half-past six, and she'd only just showered. Only half an hour to get herself ready – for what? For a big dinner-date; or just a neighbourly get-together? Even on their short acquaintance, Maria had the feeling that there would be more to it than that.

Opening the door of the massive wardrobe, Maria scanned the row of clothes with growing dismay. The red dress with the embroidered yoke? No, no, far too gauche and unsophisticated. The dark green then? The one that everone said brought out the green in her hazel eyes? She ran the fabric between her fingers, but it felt coarse and alien. Nothing pleased her, not one of the dresses and blouses and skirts she had always felt happy in before. It was as though a change had come over her, as though this place belonged to a different Maria Treharne, with different tastes and different needs.

Well, she would have to choose something – she could hardly go out to dinner stark naked, though the idea was a diverting one. On a whim, she pulled open one of the drawers inside the wardrobe. Empty of course, except . . .

Except for a dress in an opulent purple silk; a dress which, frankly, Maria had never seen before in her life. She unfolded it carefully from its layers of tissue-paper and a few dried rose-petals fluttered out, still full of their rich, musky perfume.

She held the dress up against herself and admired the effect in the mirror. It must be very old – the quality of the workmanship and styling placed it way back some time in the thirties or forties – yet it was in near-perfect condition, as though it had been worn no more than once or twice, then put away in the drawer and forgotten. Which was probably exactly what had happened, reflected Maria, turning sideways to get a different perspective.

Had this once been one of the mysterious Clara Megawne's favourite evening gowns? It was lovely, but no, she couldn't. It wasn't a colour she could wear, not ever. Surely not.

It seemed impossibly small, impossibly fragile, but curiosity got the better of her and she slipped the dress over her head, astonished to feel her body slide easily into the narrow shape, her breasts swelling the tight bodice so that a deep cleavage showed above the sweetheart neckline. She tugged the heavy, old-fashioned zipper up and turned slowly round, so that the full, calf-length skirt swirled round her legs.

She felt good in the dress; surprisingly good. The fit wasn't quite perfect, but it was better than she could possibly have imagined, and the colour seemed to complement rather than clash with her tumbling red hair. The sleeves, full at the shoulders but tapering to three neat buttons at a tight wrist, flattered her hands, making the fingers look longer and more slender. Her breasts, which she had always thought a little too heavy for her tall, spare frame, seemed perfectly balanced by the full skirt, flaring out from a yoke which moulded tightly to her rounded hips and flat belly.

It might do. It might just do, at that. She rummaged in the bottom of the wardrobe for a pair of shoes and took out her favourites – a pair of thirties-style bar shoes with a Louis heel. Why not? And there was that dragon brooch she'd found the other day . . .

By the time the doorbell rang, she was downstairs in the hallway, gazing into the mirror at a red-haired woman in a violet dress, her eyes sparkling with anticipation. She was ready now; ready for anything – even the enigmatic Mr Pendorran.

'But Anthony . . . a horse and carriage!'

Maria allowed Joseph, Pendorran's manservant, to take her coat, then followed Pendorran along a rather dark corridor into a spacious but sparsely-furnished dining hall. He walked very close to her but without touching, without even looking at her so that in the end she almost willed him to turn his head so that she could gaze once more into those wild grey eyes.

At last he turned, his lips twisted by that curious half-smile that made him look just a little demonic in the dancing light cast by the candles arranged along the length of the heavy oak dining table.

'You must think me very old-fashioned,' he observed, ushering Maria to her seat at one end of the long table. 'But you see, I have always infinitely preferred horses to cars. And of course, I make a great deal of my income from breeding thoroughbreds, so horses are my livelihood as well as my transport.'

He sat himself down at the other end of the table, a good ten feet away, and nodded to his manservant to pour the wine. When he spoke again, there was a slight quavering in his sonorous voice, as though he were trying not to laugh.

'However, I do also own a 1200cc Harley-Davidson and a 1932 Velocette. Perhaps they would be more to your taste?'

Maria wasn't sure whether to laugh or squirm. This guy was like no one she'd ever met in her life before. He seemed to have the power to make her feel at once insignificant and important, beautiful and impossibly gauche.

She blushed.

'I'm sorry. I didn't mean to be rude. It was just rather a surprise, that's all.'

Pendorran raised his hand to silence her.

'Please I understand. No offence was intended and none is taken. I realise that I am a somewhat ... unusual man; but then you are an unusual woman, Maria Treharne.' He raised his glass in a toast and the red wine glittered like rubies in the candlelight. 'Welcome to Polmadoc, Maria. I trust we shall none of us disappoint you.'

The first course arrived – a cold watercress soup elegantly swirled with cream. It was delicious, but seemed slightly out of place in the vastness of this essentially primitive building. The roughness of the stone walls was barely softened by a coat of whitewash, and the ceiling of the hall rose a good thirty feet to a vault of ancient timbers, blackened and bowed like the ribs of some ancient ship.

'You have a very interesting house,' observed Maria.

Even as she spoke the words sounded idiotic, embarrassingly meaningless, but this man had the ability to regress her to the quivering sixteen-year-old she had been twelve years ago; tongue-tied and dry-mouthed in the presence of her oh-so-cool, oh-so-sarcastic music master. She had those same feelings now – the head-spinning intoxication, the inability to string two words together sensibly, the throbbing ache between her thighs that made her want to writhe on her seat, hotter than a bitch in season.

But Pendorran seemed not to have noticed her confusion; or, if he had, he chose to ignore it. Instead, he followed her gaze up to the ceiling.

'This used to be a Celtic longhouse,' he explained. 'No one is quite sure of its precise history before then, but its origins certainly lie far back in antiquity. The rest of the house was added on later, mostly in the sixteenth century, when my family was favoured with money by the Crown.'

Maria glanced up at him in surprise.

'Your family has been here all that time?'

Pendorran raised his glass and gazed into the ruby depths, as though he could perceive something fascinating within the clear, blood-red liquid.

'There has always been a Pendorran at Polmadoc,' he replied simply. 'And, if the Goddess wills it, there always will be.'

A breeze rolled in from the sea and ruffled the curtains, making the candles flicker and striking a shower of sparkling lights from the cut facets of the glass he was rolling slowly between finger and thumb. Half-mesmerised, Maria lifted her own glass to her lips and drank deeply, savouring the sharp aftertaste of the full-bodied, velvety wine as it slipped down her throat. And all the time her eyes were locked to Pendorran's gaze, his grey eyes steady and compelling in the ebb and flow of the orange-yellow light.

Out of the silence he spoke again, his words unexpected and, for a few seconds, inexplicable.

'They will destroy Lynmoor.'

Maria paused, a forkful of food halfway between her plate and her lips.

'I'm sorry?'

'The property developers, Maria.' Pendorran's voice was quiet but very distinct, a note of urgency hardening the soft tones into an insistent hiss. 'You must understand. They will destroy all that is ancient and good in this place. Will you stand by and see it happen?'

Maria laid down her fork on the plate. Pendorran's almost aggressive insistence disturbed her, but not as much as the steady gaze of those eyes, deep and grey and wild as the ocean breakers that crashed on the rocky coastline, two hundred feet below in Polmadoc Cove.

'I don't see what I can do. It disturbs me, of course it does, but what can I do to stop it happening? I've hardly been in Lynmoor five minutes.'

Pendorran got to his feet, pushing back his carved wooden chair with a sudden grating noise that filled the vast dining hall with a cacophony of echoes.

'What can you do? By all that is sacred, Maria, use what is within you! Stop fighting it, accept the Goddess's command.'

She stared at him in astonishment as he walked towards her, the steel-tipped heels of his heavy riding-boots striking out a staccato rhythm on the polished wooden floor. He was beautiful in the half-light, but his beauty frightened her. He seemed to threaten her with some secret knowledge he demanded she must share.

He towered over her, his face pale and his eyes grey shadows against the soft blackness of his glossy, swept-back hair, and the midnight darkness of his clothes. Only his silver belt buckle gleamed amid the black linen and leather, the raven's one crystal eye flashing fire as it caught the light from the seven-branched candelabrum, its bronze frame curiously gnarled and twisted like the trunk and branches of some ancient forest giant.

Maria's whole body trembled as Pendorran's fingers skimmed her cheek, tracing the soft white curves of her face, and the slight pout of her full, red lips.

'Accept the goddess,' he whispered. 'Accept me.'

In spite of her apprehension she found herself responding to his touch, her body calling out to his; but her response was instinctive, totally independent of her will, and its intensity stunned and alarmed her.

'What is it that you're asking of me?' she murmured. 'I don't understand, I really don't think I *want* to understand any of this.'

But Anthony's hands were on her shoulders now, coaxing her, drawing her to her feet; and suddenly she was obeying the call of his need, the need that was also hers, and was flooding through her like a fast-moving stream. Outside the thick stone walls, the Atlantic breakers were crashing against the rocky shoreline, the sound no less elemental than the thundering of Maria's heart; the pounding, surging pulse of the blood rushing through her head making her dizzy and disorientated.

They stood together, Pendorran's hand still on her shoulders, holding her close, whilst the other slid the silver pin from her hair, so that it came tumbling down about her shoulders in a mad disarray of russet waves.

'This is how I want you to come to me, Maria. Wild and untamed as your own heart.'

He let his hand fall from her hair and slide smoothly down her back to the firm roundness of her buttock, pressing her even more closely to him, so that she could not fail to be aware of his erection; a bold, pointing finger of swollen flesh beneath his leather trousers. It seemed huge, self-confident, insolent even – infinitely desirable yet flawed by its own arrogance, just like its master.

She tilted her head slightly back, so that she was looking up into Pendorran's wild grey eyes. They seemed filled with a yearning intensity, and the depth of his need was intoxicating. His kiss on her throat burned with a flame of passion so strong it seemed to sear her flesh with an exquisite pain. Could a man really want her this much; so much that his desire maddened him, turning gentle lust into a savage, unstoppable hunger? And was this what she wanted?

He massaged her backside gently but firmly, with broad circular movements that forced her whole body to move, sliding her belly up and down the front of his trousers. Part of her wanted to resist him, but she could not. Her pubis, perfectly bare beneath the purple silk dress save for the tangled thicket of her maiden curls, responded eagerly to the rough caress; and it seemed to Maria that she was thrusting herself against him instinctively, her body making the decision that her mind was much too afraid to make.

Afraid? But why on earth should anyone be afraid of Anthony Pendorran? He was just a man; a handsome, desirable, self-possessed man who was accustomed to getting exactly what he wanted. And her body was telling her, more strongly than she could have believed possible, that this was what she wanted, too.

The sounds of wind-blown ocean spray driving against the windows of the house filled Maria's mind with images of foam-white semen, bubbling and seething and spitting like magma in the belly of some great volcano, waiting only for the moment when it would boil and overflow, engulfing all in its path.

She felt a deep, burning warmth spreading through her belly, making her prickle with need. Pendorran's arms slid round her and he lowered his face to hers, planting kisses on her upturned lips, her brow, her cheeks.

'Give yourself to me, Maria. Here and now. The need is so, so strong.'

'But Anthony . . .'

He pushed her gently backwards, and she felt the hard edge of the table against her backside. She put out a hand to steady herself as he lowered her towards the smooth, polished surface, and a silver salt-cellar overturned, rolling slowly away from her towards the far end of the table. She turned her head and watched it go, mesmerised for a moment by the way the light caught the silver cylinder as it rolled over and over and then was lost in the shadows. It was like watching her own free will disappearing before her eyes, escaping from her grasp and rolling away, to be lost in the darkness of Pendorran's uncompromising desire.

In a daze of need, she heard Pendorran's low whisper:

'Maria, the power. Reach out for the power . . .'

His hand ruched up the skirt of the purple silk gown, exposing the lacy top of her black-stockinged thigh, and the margin of milk-white flesh beyond it. A cool draught of air swirled around Maria's bare skin, caressing her responsive flesh as though it were the strings of an Aeolian harp, playing the music of her desire. Smooth and slow, Pendorran's fingers slid up towards the naked secret of her sex, and she writhed at his touch, her body at once hiding from him and offering itself to his need.

'Anthony, please, I'm not ready.'

'Do not be afraid, Maria. All is as it must be.'

'No. Please . . .'

'Maria. What the goddess wills, no one must deny.'

His voice was hoarse and heavy with sex, and suddenly Anthony Pendorran was no longer the magical seducer, the master of her sexual enchantment. He was breathing heavily as he lay across her, and Maria smelt the spicy tang of wine on his breath. This was a man – an ordinary man with ordinary desires – and she was a fool. All this talk of obeying the goddess's will was just insincere rubbish, designed to make her fall obligingly into his arms. Well, if Anthony Pendorran thought she was so easily deceived, he had another think coming.

With a suddenness that caught Pendorran unawares, she pushed him hard and he staggered backwards, leaving her sprawled over the table-top with her dress-skirt pushed high up her thighs. His eyes widened in astonishment, and then clouded a moment later with the unmistakable thunder of annoyance.

'What the hell was that for?'

Maria rolled sideways and got up, tugging down her skirt with little irritated movements of her fingers.

'For pity's sake, Anthony – did you really think I was so naïve?'

'Stubborn certainly; naïve, no.'

Anthony leaned back against the whitewashed wall, the heavy curtain over the window billowing round him like a cape as the wind rolled in off the ocean. He looked more demonic than ever, thought Maria as she smoothed the creases out of her dress. More demonic, yet more potently attractive than ever. She forced herself to be angry with him, but in all honesty she was angry with herself. Angry for the weakness that made her desire this beautiful but insensitive man.

'Oh come on Anthony. You didn't bring me here to talk about the goddess, did you? You brought me here because you fancied your chances of getting me into bed.'

Maria paused, waiting for Pendorran to retaliate or defend himself; but to her annoyance he said nothing at all. His own initial anger seemed completely under control now, his hawk's face settling into its habitual expression of faintly cynical composure. She looked at him and hated him for being so impossibly cool, so nearly the master of her desire. Hated herself, too, for the lust that still pulsed through her, demanding to be satisfied.

Maria picked up the silver pin that Pendorran had pulled from her hair, and slipped into the pocket of her evening jacket, which she slung round her shoulders.

'Take me home. Now, this minute.'

When Pendorran finally spoke, she wondered if he had even heard her demand.

'What I have told you is no lie, Maria. Without you, Lynmoor will die – and with it, Brackwater Hall.' Pendorran shifted his position slightly, and Maria could not help noticing the fat, swollen line of his cock, and the kiss of his glossy black hair on his tanned throat. His beauty made her half-mad with desire for him, but she defied him with a scornful sneer.

'Do you honestly expect me to believe that?'

Pendorran's grey eyes gazed unblinkingly into hers as he walked slowly back towards her.

'You are a seer of spirits, Maria, an unlocker of souls. I understood that the first moment I saw you. Belief is natural to you, though the truth may be a stranger and more frightening than the lie.'

Maria hesitated, disconcerted by the excitement that refused to die down inside her.

'Just who do you think you are?'

'I know who I am, Maria. Can you say that much about yourself?'

Maria walked down the village high-street in a dream. She was still trying to figure out the previous night, trying to get to the heart of what had happened and work out exactly what game Pendorran was playing.

It was all very odd. One moment she had been on the point of giving herself to him, the next she was pushing him away, spitting venom at him as she ordered him to take her home. She still didn't quite understand why she'd reacted so violently to his advances, or refused quite so resolutely to listen to any of his explanations.

Not that they had made any sense. Nothing Anthony Pendorran said made sense. He spoke in hints and riddles, like a man at the far edge of a dream. Perhaps that was what both attracted and frightened her about him – he seemed to have only the most tenuous of links with reality.

Reality hit her full in the face as she approached the CA Developments marketing suite, where a group of dishevelled young men and women were chanting protests under the watchful eye of the village constable and a one-eyed mongrel dog.

'HANDS OFF OUR HISTORY. PLANNERS GO HOME.' The words bounced into her brain with an insolent energy, refusing to be ignored. She stopped and turned back.'

'Sign our petition, lady?' A shaven-headed young man with a spider tattoo indicated a much-fingered sheet of paper, attached to a piece of board with a bull-dog clip. 'Keep the fascist developers out of Lynmoor.'

She hesitated, then picked up the pen and scrawled her name across the sheet. Anthony Pendorran might be faintly unhinged, but he was right about one thing, at least: Lynmoor must not be abandoned to men who wanted to tear the very guts out of the place.

'You're from the travellers' camp?' she enquired.

'That's right.' She turned to face the new arrival; a bearded man with dull brown hair and eyes that twinkled like two brown diamonds. 'And you're the young lady from the Hall, am I right?'

'Yes, you are – how did you know?'

He chuckled.

'Folk round here may not like passing the time of day with us, but we get to hear a lot of things. We keep our eyes and ears open, see.

His accent held residual hints of a faint brogue – Scottish perhaps, or southern Irish. Maria found it quite pleasantly lyrical, though its owner looked more like a down-at-heel young tinker than a Celtic bard. She guessed that the amiable smile might conceal a wealth of secrets, by no means all respectable or pleasant. Nevertheless, there was something fascinating about the man – an intangible, dynamic quality that marked him out as a leader.

'Let me see – your name's Maria, and you're from Cambridge, though that's a Liverpool accent if I'm not much mistaken. Your auntie left you that great big house, and now you're wondering what to do with it. I'm right, aren't I?'

Maria laughed.

'In every detail. But how – ?'

The traveller silenced her with a shake of the head, wiped his right hand on his waistcoat and extended it in greeting.

'Let's just say we have our ways. Carolan's the name.' He carefully omitted to mention that, as far as the East Midlands Constabulary were concerned, he was still plain old Benjamin Tarrant. Maria slid her hand into his; its grip was vice-like. So this was the legendary New Age hellraiser she'd heard about from Geraint. At last he released her fingers. 'I've been waiting for a chance to get to talk to you.'

'Really?'

'Just come over here a little way, where we can talk without the whole world listening.' Carolan led her a few yards down the street, and sat down on the steps of the old museum. He lowered his voice to a conspiratorial whisper. 'I hear you are ... of the ancient faith.'

Maria nodded.

'I worship the goddess.' A faint irritation mingled with her surprise. Were there no secrets at all in this place? Did the whole of Lynmoor know who and what she was?

'We too try to live our lives in harmony with nature,' continued Carolan, an edge of bitterness entering his voice. 'But the establishment's only too happy to let men like Allardyce ruin it for us – and our kids.

'The thing is, we're doing our damnedest to get this Lynmoor Development scrapped, but alone, we're not strong enough. We need help.'

'I don't see what I can do,' chipped in Maria quickly, her mind suddenly filled with uncomfortable recollections of the previous night. 'I've no more power than you, and I've only just come to stay here. I don't even belong to Lynmoor.'

Carolan seized hold of her wrist with an unexpected energy that demanded her undivided attention.

'We must get in touch with the power,' he hissed. 'The ancient spirit. You can help us, you have the knowledge and the skill.'

'I think you're over-estimating my abilities,' protested Maria. But Carolan was not easily put off.

'A ritual, that's what we're planning,' he continued. 'Up among the old standing stones on Hilltop Tor – the ones Allardyce wants to move halfway to bloody Barncastle. A rite of conjuration, using sensual and sexual power; but we need your help.'

Maria released her wrist from Carolan's grip.

'Let me get this straight. You're asking me to take part in this . . . sexual rite?'

She saw Carolan's eyes gleam – with triumph? – and wondered just how far she could trust him. Was he really the Robin Hood of Lynmoor, or just a tatty little man with an eye for the main chance? As though in a sudden gesture of supplication, he took hold of her hand and pressed his lips against it.

'Think of the power you would bring to the ritual,' he urged. 'Join with us. In two weeks from now, on the night of the new moon.'

She gave no promise, but walked slowly away, painfully aware of Carolan's bright, bird-like eyes boring holes in the back of her thin cotton dress. First Pendorran, and now Carolan. Why did she have the uneasy feeling that – given half a chance – both of them would lead her into disaster?

Cassandra's Conflict

Fredrica Alleyn

Fredrica Alleyn's Black Lace stories are laced with dark eroticism. They go beyond the boundaries of commonplace sexual experience and enter a world where games of pleasure and perversity go hand in hand and where lust feeds on the erotic charge of fear and submission. Her first book, *Cassandra's Conflict*, set the tone of many subsequent Black Lace novels. Behind a façade of cultured respectability, there often lurks something sinister or exciting. The Baron von Ritter is both these things. Cassandra's sheltered life is transformed when she becomes governess in his household. He's playing games with her; games where only he knows the rules and where Cassandra is pitted against the manipulative Katya – the baron's wife.

Other Black Lace titles by Fredrica are: *Fiona's Fate, Deborah's Discovery, Cassandra's Chateau, Dark Obsession, The Bracelet* and – to be published in April 1997 – *The Gallery*. All of her stories have contemporary settings, and all deal with erotic power games.

Cassandra's Conflict

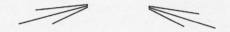

'*I* hate that girl,' Katya confessed quietly to Françoise as they watched Cassandra through the French windows. She was wandering round the garden chatting to a workman about the new rockery the baron was having built. 'He's changed since she arrived. Nothing's the same any more.'

Françoise smiled. 'Nothing ever remains the same; isn't that why we're with the men we are? Neither of us could survive a routine life.'

'That's not what I meant,' Katya retorted impatiently. 'Of course I'm not pining for domesticity and sex every Wednesday and Saturday night, but I sometimes think Dieter is. He's got the same look in his eyes that he had when he met Marietta.'

'Well she didn't last long!' Françoise laughed.

Katya, trying to suppress a dark memory that had to remain hidden if she was to keep sane, turned to her friend. 'This one would, Françoise. She's made of sterner stuff than Marietta, and there'll never be children to distract her either. I can't afford to have her remain here much longer.'

Françoise watched with interest as her own husband joined Cassandra by the rockery. She saw him put an arm round the girl's waist as they spoke, and noticed how Cassandra moved away at the first opportunity, by bending down to point to some plants she cleverly disguised her rejection.

'She certainly has something special about her. I confess to finding her very attractive myself. Not like Clara, of course, she's just a wonderful toy, whereas Cassandra would be a challenge.'

Katya scowled, then remembered what her beautician had said and quickly erased the lines from her forehead. 'I don't need you to admire her, too. What I want to know is what can I do about her? Dieter would never have humiliated me the way he did last night before Cassandra came.'

'For myself,' Françoise said with a smile, 'I enjoy the enemas. They are an acquired taste, but most pleasurable in moderation.'

'Last night wasn't at all pleasurable because I wasn't expecting it, and he had no right to do it to me.'

Françoise looked at Katya in surprise. 'He has the right to do anything he likes to you. It isn't as though you've ever persuaded him into marriage; you're only here because he lets you stay.'

Katya moved closer to the tall Brazilian girl. 'Help me, Françoise. How can I make sure she loses?'

'Loses what?'

Katya knew that the game was a secret and tried to cover her mistake. 'Loses out to me, of course.'

'I think all you can do is wait. Eventually Dieter will push her too far, and she will make a scene or irritate him. Rupert always says that Dieter's tolerance level is the lowest of any man he's met! Also, as a friend, I think I should give you a word of warning.'

'What is it?' Katya asked shortly; she hated taking advice even when she'd requested it.

'Your desire to inflict pain is not to Dieter's liking.'

'Of course it is! He's always been more than happy to accommodate me in that direction,' Katya said smugly.

'Yes, because you choose it; he does not care very much to inflict real pain on those who do not take pleasure from it, and when you hurt others he is not entertained.'

Katya knew that her friend was right, but it only irritated her all the more. 'What am I meant to do then? Give her nothing but orgasms? The whole idea of having her here was to teach her self-discipline.'

'There are limits surely,' Françoise murmured, surprised to see that Rupert was still following Cassandra round the garden.

'If there are, it's for the first time.'

'My advice to you,' Françoise said, deciding to go into the garden herself, 'is to bide your time. I have no doubt that Dieter has plenty of ideas up his sleeve to test Cassandra's true worth, and I would have thought it would take more than a withdrawn

Englishwoman to hold his attention for any length of time. One can scarcely imagine her at one of his magnificent parties!'

'I suppose you're right, but it isn't easy,' Katya muttered, wishing for once that there weren't so many cameras and microphones dotted round the house.

'Where's the fun if life's easy? Compared to my childhood, any problems Rupert and I encounter are nothing at all. Now I shall go and talk to my husband and then join Clara for a little more instruction in the joys of the flesh. She has a passion for Dieter that is really touching. I must try and persuade him to take her again before we leave.'

The conversation did nothing to soothe Katya's ruffled temper. She realised that she had to be sensible, and that Françoise was almost certainly right when she said Cassandra wouldn't last for long, and yet at the back of her mind there was always the spectre of Marietta. If Dieter's wife hadn't become so clinging and feeble after the birth of Christina, then she would have lasted and no one could have called Marietta adventurous. When she had joined in her husband's parties, it was always with the greatest of reluctance and he used to accept her token appearances with apparent equanimity. Once she was dead he reverted, hurling himself hedonistically into every possible sexual challenge, but there had been that moment of danger when Katya had sensed the possibility of an end to their relationship, and this was another such moment. Somehow she had to make sure that Cassandra lost without physically harming her herself.

In the middle of the afternoon, when they were all lying around in the garden enjoying the heat of the sun, the baron stood up and clapped his hands. 'I'm bored,' he announced. 'I think it's time for our competition.'

'What competition?' asked Françoise, who had Clara stretched out beside her and was continually fondling the girl's large breasts while making her eat pieces of truffle from her own mouth and ensuring that every time she did, it ended in a warm fusion of their lips and tongues, a fusion that excited Clara as much as it shamed her.

'You will see,' the baron said with his most boyish grin.

Cassandra, who was sitting in the swing seat reading a book, glanced up and saw the dimple in his cheek. As always it was irresistible to her, and she felt an instant tug of physical attraction. To her delight he looked directly at her. 'Cassandra, come with me. You are to take a leading role in the contest. Katya, bring Françoise, Rupert, Clara and Peter up to the top floor in fifteen minutes.'

'What about Lucy?' asked Rupert, who always enjoyed the little maid's company.

'Lucy has the other leading role. She will be with us. Come, Cassandra.' Holding out a hand he pulled her to her feet. She stood, but reluctantly, suddenly aware of the predatory way the others were eyeing her and beginning to suspect that the competition might not be to her liking.

The baron clicked his tongue impatiently. 'What's the matter with you? Are you already tired of us?'

She shook her head, managed to flash a smile at him, and put her hand in his. His fingers closed tightly round hers, but for once Katya didn't look in the least put out, in fact she smiled at Cassandra and this worried the younger girl even more.

Inside, the house seemed dark after the bright sunlight of the garden and she almost stumbled over the second flight of stairs. The baron's hands caught her round the waist and he could feel her tension. He smiled to himself.

Cassandra had been terrified that he was taking her to the room where Lucy had been disciplined, but this one was far larger and just as luxurious as those on the first floor.

It seemed to be some kind of a bedroom, but two beds were set in the middle of the large room, and they weren't normal beds but the kind of couches found in Victorian drawing rooms with a rounded curve at one end where the head could rest.

Lucy was already waiting in the room, standing by the window in her uniform. She smiled and bobbed a curtsy to the baron. He didn't smile back, but pointed towards one of the couches. 'Take off your clothes, except for your stockings and suspender belt, and then lie there. Cassandra, do the same and lie on the other couch.'

'I'm not wearing stockings,' Cassandra said nervously.

He pointed to a nearby stool. 'All that you need is there. Hurry, the others will be here soon and you must both be ready.'

'What's going to happen?' Cassandra asked.

'We are going to see how well you have learnt to control yourself since you joined us. See that clock on the wall there?' Both girls looked up to where a large clock had been fixed to the wall opposite their heads. 'Once the game begins the clock will be started. It will run for an hour. During that time we will all take turns to try and bring you both to as many climaxes as possible, but I shall be extremely disappointed if either of you has more than two and I am hoping that one of you will manage to last through the hour without having even one.' He glanced at their faces and allowed himself a small smile. 'But perhaps I am over-optimistic, yes?'

Cassandra was beginning to feel hot with embarrassed anticipation. 'What if we have more than two?' she whispered.

'It will show me how much more training you need. I shall make an allowance insofar as Lucy has been with us nearly a year, and her body has had longer to learn the ways of postponing her pleasure.'

'Is there a prize for the winner?' Lucy asked, climbing onto the couch.

'No, only a punishment for the loser.'

'What kind of punishment?' Cassandra asked, keeping her eyes fixed on his and searching for some suggestion of emotion or feeling in them.

'I have yet to decide! Ah, here are the others at last. I have just been telling the girls about the competition, now I will explain the rules to you.' He did, and Katya began to feel much happier. Lucy was well trained. She had suffered a great deal during her early weeks in the house, and her body was used to obeying whatever strictures either Katya or the baron placed on it. Cassandra had hardly been trained at all, except in pleasure, and her body would rush to welcome the sensations it had so quickly learnt to enjoy. She was quite certain that Lucy would win easily.

'Can we do anything we want to bring them to a climax?' Rupert asked, his eyes already on Cassandra as he remembered the previous night.

'The only rules are that you have to start slowly, and each of us can only spend ten minutes at a time on the same person.

'Peter, you, Françoise and I will start on Lucy while Rupert, Katya and Clara begin with Cassandra. After ten minutes we will change round. Does everyone understand?'

They did, and for once even Clara's eyes were bright. She knew only too well what it was like to be continually stimulated and here at last was a chance to do it to someone else. She could hardly wait to begin. The baron looked at all their faces, flushed with anticipation, and he was delighted with his little idea. With a quick movement of his hand he started the clock and the competition began.

Cassandra watched as Rupert, Clara and Katya approached her and her insides seemed to curl up with terror. They were all so skilled, and had seen her in the throes of excitement often enough to know how to bring about the release she now had to delay indefinitely.

Rupert, remembering that they had to start slowly, gently unfastened the suspenders and began to peel off the black stockings Cassandra had just put on. He rolled the first one down her leg inch by inch, his fingers lingering at each turn. Then he told her to lift her leg so that he could roll it off her foot, and his fingers brushed the soft pads of flesh at the base of her toes, tickling very gently and making her catch her breath. Then he repeated the process with the other leg, and this time she knew what was coming and her slim foot arched in advance so that his fingers had to stretch further to touch the soft flesh pads. This time he chose to rotate them and shivers of delight ran up her leg.

Once her stockings had been removed, Rupert sat at the foot of the couch and put her left foot in his lap, letting it brush against the tight bulge in his trousers so that she was aware of his excitement. Then he began to suck and lick at each of the toes in turn, and she gave little moans of pleasure at the delicious feelings that ran the entire length of her leg and up higher, into the join of her thighs.

As Rupert worked, Katya took a bolster from one of the cupboards in the room and slid this beneath Cassandra's hips, so that her stomach was pushed up. Tight extended flesh was always more susceptible to even the lightest pressure and anyway she wanted to see the frantic ripples of the stomach muscles when Cassandra began to fight off her first orgasm.

Clara, who at first had found herself unable to touch the pale, slim body lying on the couch, finally found the courage to take a long carefully pointed feather from a table at the head of the couch and she stroked this over Cassandra's small breasts, watching with fascination as the tightly puckered nipples began to swell and rise from the surrounding areolae. Intrigued, she held the feather point down and let the tip rest in the tiny hollow at the crest of the nipple, in the place where milk would flow if Cassandra should ever give birth, and this touch by the inexperienced Clara made Cassandra groan through clenched teeth as waves of pleasure flooded through her breasts.

With her belly raised by the bolster, Katya couldn't help but let her hand reach out and draw the backs of her fingers across the susceptible flesh, moving her hand down towards the pubic hair and then back up again to the narrow waist. Cassandra's body trembled, and all at once Katya remembered seeing Dieter's hands on the sides of the girl's body and she let her fingers drift to the hollows at each side of her waist and on down over the clearly visible hipbones. This time Cassandra's stomach leapt and her breath caught in her throat.

Rupert regretfully ceased his attentions to her toes and began to flick his tongue up her legs, paying particular attention to the insides of her knees before reaching the silken skin of her thighs. Once there he couldn't resist nipping lightly with his teeth, and while he was doing that, Clara was swirling the feather in the crest of her nipples and Katya was teasing the stretched skin over her hips so that Cassandra could feel herself becoming moist, and Rupert saw the first drops of liquid gleaming on her thick pubic hair.

Cassandra was going mad with the delicious torment they were inflicting on her. She knew that not even ten minutes could have passed because there had been no changeover in the people tormenting her, but already her body felt close to explosion and she could hear her own smothered moans and cries whereas there had been no sound from Lucy, who was only three feet away from her.

She felt Rupert's hands tenderly grasp her outer sex lips. Very slowly he began to part them and her legs went rigid as she tried to steel herself against his touch. He lowered his head and his long dark hair brushed against her lower stomach and upper thighs, a sensation entirely new to her body and highly stimulating. With amazing delicacy he continued to part her sex lips higher up so that he could see for himself her rapidly swelling clitoris and the damp moistness of the surrounding tissue that was such indisputable evidence of her excitement.

As he bent his head lower, Katya's fingers rubbed almost as lightly over her hips as the fiendish feather was moving over her tumescent breasts but, just before Rupert's tongue could begin its explorations, the baron's voice interrupted him.

'Time to change!' he called firmly. Rupert was tempted to let his tongue have just one stab at the frantic flesh beneath it, but he knew it wouldn't be fair to the girl and reluctantly stood up while Katya had to grab the feather from Clara's hand and push her over to where Lucy's shaking body was trying to recover from the manipulations of the other three participants.

As soon as Rupert moved, Cassandra let her knees fall apart and breathed through her mouth. She knew that she must not press her legs together or the pressure could trigger the climax she had to repress and breathing through her mouth seemed to calm the thrills of leaping pleasure in her breasts and belly.

The baron looked at Cassandra's upthrust abdomen, noted the swelling tightness of the flesh and the rigid nipples on the tiny breasts and knew that she was already struggling to survive. He wasn't surprised. This was an area of weakness that was to be expected so early on. Pleasure had become a part of her life; delaying it was new to her. She was bound to lose the game, what he wanted to know was by how much she would lose and how many more lessons she needed before her control was good enough to satisfy him and let her become an instructor of others.

Françoise immediately turned Cassandra across the bed and then made her turn over, so that she was lying with her stomach pressed against the bolster which was near the side of the couch, forcing her head and breasts to hang down towards the floor.

She felt the baron's tongue begin to lick the arch of her foot, and his tongue moved more slowly than Rupert's had, in long, lazy lines that followed the nerve paths with unerring accuracy until her toes curled with coiled pleasure. Just when the pleasure was becoming painful through repetition, he removed his tongue, and instead his mouth edged its way up the back of her legs, sucking on her flesh as it went and leaving tiny red marks of passion in its wake.

Cassandra wriggled against the bolster with the excitement, but quickly desisted as the pressure only increased the stimulation and blood coursed even more quickly through her hanging breasts. It was those breasts that were interesting Peter, who had taken a tiny piece of cotton thread, licked it and then shaped it into a loop which he eased over the already swollen nipple, moving it firmly down on to the surface of the breast. He repeated this exercise with another piece of thread until both Cassandra's nipples were encircled, and then began to suck steadily on the dangling tips which promptly swelled even more until the tight, moist thread began to cut into the incredibly tender flesh and further expansion became impossible. Yet still Peter continued to suck and Cassandra groaned at the streaks of pain that began to mix with the pleasure, arousing the red-hot heat of pain-edged flames to which Katya and Françoise had introduced her, and reminding her body of the flood of shuddering release such sensations could trigger.

Cassandra's breath quickened and she lifted her head, hoping to catch a glimpse of the clock and see how far into her second ten minutes she was, but Peter was in her way and now Françoise was busy pushing and pulling at Cassandra's body again until she was once more lying lengthways on the couch and the bolster was pushed up against her distended breasts so that the baron and Françoise could concentrate their attentions on the lower half of her body.

The baron spread her thighs wide and slid his hand up beneath her, feeling the slick of moisture between her thighs. He turned his hand, palm uppermost, and inserted the top of his thumb into the entrance to her vagina and let his other fingers beat out a rhythmic tattoo on the surrounding flesh, which was rapidly becoming slippery with her own secretions.

The cotton threads were tight round her fiery nipples, her swollen breasts were pressing into the feathers of the bolster and now at last someone was attending to the diabolically aching flesh between her thighs. Cassandra's hips twitched as the clever fingers danced across the leaping tissue and it felt as though something was sending currents of electricity through her body as the sensations flashed in jagged lines up from her thighs to her breasts.

Cassandra's legs began to stiffen, and then she felt Françoise's tongue licking the tender cleft at the base of her spine, in that special place where the baron had aroused her to such heights, and for a moment she thought that she was going to spasm immediately because the pleasure was simply uncontainable.

'Not yet!' the baron said harshly, and whilst his fingers didn't pause in their tantalising arousal, his words broke through the thick curtain of sensuality and reminded her of the penalty she would pay if she lost out to Lucy. She groaned with frustration, trying to lift her swollen breasts from the bolster to ease their arousal, but Peter pushed her firmly back, at the same time

111

letting his hands go beneath her and pinching the nipples firmly to keep them rigid.

Her whole body was swelling with the sensations, and the knowledge that she mustn't climax made it all worse. Suddenly she heard a groan from Lucy, and the maid's voice cried out, 'No! Please, don't! Not yet, please!' There was such despair in her voice that it gave Cassandra a boost of confidence. At least Lucy was finding it difficult too.

'Time to change!' the baron repeated, abruptly removing his fingers, and Cassandra collapsed in relief, pressing up on her knees so that there was a gap between her pulsating vulva and the couch.

Katya and Rupert were with her in seconds, though, their hands still warm and moist from inflicting the bittersweet torture on Lucy. Again Cassandra was turned, now on to her back with the bolster beneath her hips, once more putting her in the position that Katya knew was the most arousing for what was to follow.

Carefully, Rupert parted the outer sex lips of the trembling, passion-filled body, and the lips were so sticky they were reluctant to separate. Once they had, he held them spread wide while Katya pressed a long thin plastic rod along the exposed crease, making sure that as it moulded to Cassandra's innermost delicate places the tip of it pressed lightly against the tight little bud that was pulsating with its need for attention.

Cassandra gasped at the feel of the thin cool plastic against her, and then had to bite her lip to stop herself from crying out when she felt Rupert closing her outer lips around the rod so that there was now continual, relentless pressure against the whole length of her vulva, and then he made her cross her legs at the knees so that the rod pressed even more firmly against her, causing a constant steady stimulation that made her body almost cramp with the throbbing ache of thwarted need which aroused her sufficiently to engorge her entire pelvic area with blood without giving her enough stimulation to climax. But she knew that she would now explode instantly if that stimulation were to be applied.

Clara had returned to her favourite feather, only this time she tickled Cassandra lightly beneath the armpits and down the sides of her neck where the pulse of passion was throbbing wildly. She also ran it down between the breasts, the nipples still ringed by Peter's threads, and then round in the hollow of the belly button. This last movement made the distended belly leap and the plastic rod was pulled against her more tightly by her own contraction.

Katya looked down into the eyes of her hated rival. 'How does it feel, Cassandra? Isn't it wonderful? Don't you long for that one final touch to let the pleasure come? How much longer can you hold back? Lucy is still well in control, you know, but you're very near. Look at her, Rupert, it won't take much now.'

Rupert knew that Katya was right. Cassandra's stomach muscles were so tight it looked painful, her breasts more swollen with passion than he'd ever seen them and between her wickedly closed thighs the plastic rod had to be exciting her unbearably. 'Then make her come,' he said lightly.

'No, not yet!' Cassandra pleaded. 'It's too soon.'

'Of course it's too soon,' Katya laughed, 'but then you're only a beginner in this game. Your body still has a lot to learn.'

She leant down, and let one tiny hand begin to massage the distended stomach, pressing her outspread fingers as wide as she could so that the skin was pulled in all directions, and the gentle tugging motion could be felt between Cassandra's thighs as the rod moved with every tug.

It was almost beyond bearing, and Cassandra knew that she couldn't control herself against such experts. When Rupert finally let her uncross her knees and her legs fell apart, she knew better than to expect any lessening of their excited experiments on her, and she was proved right when Rupert pressed his strong hand between her thighs and then moved it round and round, not opening the outer lips but knowing that with each of his movements her clitoris was being rotated as well, and that the pressure of the plastic rod combined with the pressure of his hand should force Cassandra into her first climax.

She felt the bunching sensation in the pit of her stomach that always signalled the beginning of her release. Her toes curled in an involuntary movement and a pink flush covered her breasts and throat as her arousal reached its peak, and then Katya's busy little hand moved a fraction lower so that it was over the pubic bone. It seemed that her hand and Rupert's were one as the whole area of Cassandra's sex was so cleverly manipulated, rolled and rotated so that the plastic rod's pressure grew and grew and, without meaning to, Cassandra actually pushed up

113

against Katya's hand to hurry the explosion that she could no longer deny herself.

Katya laughed, the rod moved one final time against the delicate stem of the clitoris, Clara's feather dipped into the tiny belly button and there was a huge explosion of white light inside Cassandra's head as her entire body leapt off the bed and she screamed with a mixture of ecstatic relief and an agonised sense of failure.

Next to her, Lucy heard Cassandra's scream and strained to keep her sweating body from following suit. The baron was being diabolically clever with his tongue while Françoise was busy between her parted buttocks, and Lucy too was hideously near the edge but hearing Cassandra distracted her at the vital moment and she managed to slow her breathing. Out of the corner of her eye she could see the other girl's slim body still thrashing around on the bed.

'Time to change,' the baron called, apparently unperturbed by the sounds of Cassandra's failure, although he did pause long enough to make a note against her chart which was beneath the clock.

Now that she'd actually climaxed, Cassandra thought that it should be easier to hold out against another orgasm for some time. Half an hour had already passed, and she thought it unlikely she would be forced into another failure before the hour was up. Lucy's breathing had become quite audible now, and if they both had one climax in the hour there would be no loser. She would have shown the baron that she had gained more control over her body than he'd expected.

However, the baron knew that once fully aroused, Cassandra would be easy to bring to further peaks of passion, although different methods would be necessary. He and Françoise left her on her back at first, watching as Peter carefully sat between her carelessly spread thighs and began to insert the smaller set of Japanese loveballs into her opening. Cassandra was still coming down from her orgasmic glow and much to her relief the insertion irritated rather than stimulated her, but the baron knew that soon she would begin to feel the pressure in a more constructive way.

After they'd been inserted she was turned on her stomach, but first Françoise removed the pieces of thread from the now detumescent nipples, removing them with her teeth so that her

114

saliva covered the tips of the breasts and the skin began to rise as the moisture cooled in the air.

This time the bolster was left below Cassandra's hips and she was quite surprised when Françoise came to the head of the couch and began to play with her long dark hair, letting her fingers run through it and carefully massaging round her temples and hair line so that Cassandra's body relaxed even more.

As she relaxed, the baron and Peter were busy lower down her body. To begin with, the baron ran his strong hands round the tight buttocks, cupping them carefully and enjoying the feel of the smooth flesh. He was careful not to alarm her, his hands wandering up and down her spine and straying down the backs of her legs as well so that she didn't realise where his attention was really concentrated.

Then, when she was thoroughly disarmed, he got Peter to separate the warm globes of flesh and very carefully eased a pointed nozzle into the tight dark hole which immediately contracted against the invasion. Quickly he kissed the erogenous spot at the base of her spine which was her weakness, and automatically her body opened more to him, even there, where she was still unhappy with any intrusion. Once the nozzle was inside he pressed on a button and released a thick jet of mousse inside her. 'Don't try and push it out, contain it,' he instructed her. Françoise was still stroking her hair and head, and it didn't really hurt, so Cassandra obeyed, partly because she felt quite certain that whatever he was doing there it wouldn't give her an orgasm, and this was now her one objective.

The baron waited until her protesting muscles had accepted the mousse, and then Peter, whose erection had been paining him ever since he'd first set eyes on Cassandra's naked body, climbed on to the couch and slowly slid the swollen head of his penis into the tight opening which was now so well lubricated by the mousse, he caused no pain at all. Once he was inside he nearly came himself at the unaccustomed sensation of the foam around him, but such a look of fury crossed the baron's face that fear made the imminent climax swiftly fade, leaving him able to gyrate his hips, moving his throbbing glans around inside Cassandra and pressing through the mousse to touch the thin walls of her rectum.

Every time that he touched them, Cassandra's muscles tightened reflexively. He would then be lost to her again in the sea of foam, and she would relax until the next touch until eventually the continuing sequence of contractions began to trigger off a pulsing need in her that she'd never experienced before. She ached deep inside her stomach, not at the pit of her belly where desire usually grew in her, but higher up and so deep down that it was almost as though it was against her spine. She didn't understand the ache, didn't know how to end it, but she began to thrust her buttocks out against Peter's shaft, quickly learning that as she increased the friction the ache grew more pleasurable and assumed a sharper edge.

Françoise moved Cassandra until she was crouched on all fours, resting on elbows and knees, and then the baron stood in front of Cassandra and unzipped his trousers, letting his own erection thrust free. Putting out a hand he traced a line round her already parting lips. She was greedy for him, he could see it in her eyes, and when he thrust forward she encircled him hungrily with her velvet lips, letting her tongue flick at the ridge of his glans while she sucked carefully and steadily.

Cassandra saw the excitement and pleasure in the baron's eyes and her own excitement grew. Peter's skilled movements between her buttocks were having more effect than she realised, and the deep ache was spreading dangerously now but Cassandra was too busy licking and sucking on the baron's erection to really appreciate it. Then, as Peter's cock touched a particularly sensitive spot inside her back passage, her abdominal muscles contracted sharply and the Japanese loveballs, which she'd completely forgotten about, moved within her. At the same moment, the baron thrust his hips forward forcefully and she had to relax the muscles of her throat to accommodate him as the first drops of his semen began to trickle out of the tiny split at the end of the glans. She could visualise it all, and went almost wild with excitement as he moaned softly. It was his moan of pleasure that was her undoing. The thrill of pleasing him so much combined with the unexpectedly arousing feel of Peter in that forbidden part of her body and the rolling loveballs gave her only a split second's moment of tightness that served as an insufficient warning to allow her any chance of preventing the second climax that crashed down on her, and her body bucked so violently that the baron was very grateful he managed to withdraw safely. Peter was held tight by the spasms of her second orgasm, and her muscles tightened around him so that he couldn't withdraw and couldn't control himself but instead spilled his seed into the highly erotic mixture of her tightness and the dissolving mousse.

Finally both Peter and Cassandra were still. Peter, somewhat shamefaced, withdrew and carefully mopped at her with a towel to remove the now melted foam that was trickling from her while Cassandra collapsed onto her arms in exhausted despair.

'Two climaxes,' the baron said in a level voice. 'I hope there won't be any more. You still have twenty minutes to go.'

'I couldn't help it,' Cassandra gasped. 'I hadn't realised . . .' He turned away, totally disinterested in her explanation, and marked her chart for a second time.

'Ten minutes,' he called, and just as he did so, Lucy gave a shrill scream and then wailed with distress as her legs thrashed wildly in the air where they were imprisoned over Rupert's shoulders while Katya worked between the exposed thighs. 'One for Lucy,' the baron added, but Cassandra didn't feel any the better for the knowledge.

Although Katya, Rupert and Clara worked as skilfully as they could on her for their next ten-minute session, they were unable to arouse her to anywhere near the level needed for another orgasm, and when they changed over Cassandra hoped they would be all the more determined to force one from Lucy while she herself battled one final time against the baron and his accomplices.

At first there seemed little danger of her failing again. The baron and Françoise simply caressed her body in a gentle way with their hands and tongues while Rupert concentrated on her breasts, but then they all stopped their attentions at the same time and Cassandra looked at the clock, wondering if the time could possibly be up. In the brief moment of silence she could hear Lucy's ragged breathing and knew that the maid was very close to a second orgasm. Her spirits lifted.

'Sit up, Cassandra,' the baron said quietly. She moved up the couch, obediently lifting her upper torso from its previously reclining position. Peter removed the bolster and threw it to the floor. 'Now lick your middle finger,' continued the baron. Her mouth went suddenly dry and although she tried to force some moisture into it she couldn't. He smiled, and let Françoise bend down and suck on Cassandra's finger for her, swirling her tongue round it in such a suggestive way that to her horror Cassandra felt her legs twitch.

The baron saw the movement. He'd been certain that Cassandra wouldn't be able to avoid having three orgasms and this confirmed his suspicion. 'Now touch your nipples with it,' he said. Tentatively she let the fingertip rest against each pink shell. 'Harder than that, my darling! Françoise, lick her finger again. It seems to be rather too dry.' Again Françoise swirled her tongue round the digit and again Cassandra's legs twitched. This time Cassandra touched her nipples more firmly, moving the finger round so that the shells began to open and swell.

The baron smiled. 'Good. Now touch yourself between your legs. Did the others remove the loveballs?' She nodded. 'Excellent, then we can go all the way. Hurry now, we're waiting.' Trembling with a mixture of shame and desire, Cassandra moved her hand between her thighs and then hesitated. Peter quickly parted her outer lips to enable her easy access to the part the baron was determined she should arouse herself.

The baron thought that the joy of making her give herself the final climax would be immense. She would want to cry and yet not dare to show her feelings, and once again he would see the delicious confusion in her eyes that so entranced him as she tried to come to terms with all the different facets of herself he was forcing into the open.

'Now slide your finger around, my darling,' he whispered. 'Let me see you giving yourself pleasure. Run it up and down between the inner lips, dip it into the entrance and spread your own moistness around. It will feel wonderful, Cassandra, and I shall be able to see the rising desire in your eyes. Do it, Cassandra. You know you want to do it for me.'

And she did. She wanted to please him more than anything else, but she didn't want to lose the contest. She stared at him, her eyes pleading, but it was a fatal mistake because his eyes could drown her and she became hypnotised by them so that almost in a trance her finger began to slide over the hot damp flesh. She obeyed his instructions to the letter, until her clitoris emerged from its protective hood and rose up proudly, waiting for the finger to touch it and bring the sensations to a peak; but Cassandra didn't touch it. Instead her finger strayed round it, teasing the inner lips, entering the vagina and even moving around inside but never quite touching the tight bud of nerve endings that gave her body such ecstasy.

The baron watched her shining pink flesh and the way it darkened as her finger made the blood rush in and suffuse the tissue so that it swelled and expanded beneath her. His own breathing quickened and he wrenched his gaze away to see what Françoise was doing. She was licking round Cassandra's ears, dipping her tongue inside to swirl patterns inside the delicate entrance, adding further stimulation to that caused by Cassandra's own finger.

Cassandra's eyes flicked to the clock and she saw that she only had three more minutes to endure. Three more minutes, in which Lucy must climax again and she must not.

'Now touch your core,' the baron murmured huskily. 'Touch yourself there, where you ache to be touched, where I can see you throbbing with need. Touch it, Cassandra, and very lightly. Just flick it as you pass.'

Cassandra swallowed hard as she obeyed him. For a moment she thought her body would betray her, but although her breasts and stomach tightened and darts of passion lanced her body, the wrenching spasm was avoided.

The baron was surprised, and his eyebrows arched. 'Again, my love,' he whispered, glancing at the clock. There were two minutes left. 'This time touch it on the stem, beneath the very tip.' Cassandra wanted to refuse, although then she would have forfeited the game, but she knew that what he was telling her to do was fiendish because it always triggered an orgasm for her and her body was now so finely tuned that it would instantly respond. He looked steadily into her eyes and, almost crying with despair and the knowledge of defeat, Cassandra finally let her finger do as he had intended right from the start, but at the same time she opened her mouth and exhaled, thereby releasing some of her pent-up tension.

He realised what she'd done and knew that it would probably work and although disappointed he was impressed by her control, but at the very last moment Lucy cried out 'Yes! Oh, please yes!' as her own tormented nerve endings were triggered into such pleasure that she actually welcomed it after all the frustration. Ironically this orgasmic cry of pleasure coming at the same time as Cassandra's final touch, forced her third climax from her when she had only needed to last three more seconds in order to force a tie.

The baron's eyes remained locked on to hers as she gasped, her pert little breasts shuddering while her belly heaved and rippled for the last time and sweat trickled slowly down it from between the breasts.

'Three.' The baron's voice was totally dispassionate, but his eyes were soft and Cassandra was certain she could see a kind of amused sympathy in them as he marked her chart again, and also put Lucy's second release below her name. 'A close contest,' he remarked with satisfaction.

'But one which Lucy won,' Katya pointed out.

'Yes indeed. As I would have expected considering the hours of tuition she's had from you, Katya. In fact, it should not have been such a close-run thing.'

'A brilliant game!' Rupert said with satisfaction, watching Lucy begin to dress while Cassandra remained slumped on the couch, her head hanging down so that her hair hid her face from them all. 'You've got a great imagination, Dieter. We'll need that tomorrow, when Clara's stepfather pays us a visit.'

At that, Clara gave a cry of dismay while Françoise too looked far from happy. 'Does he have to interfere already?'

'It's just a quick visit, Françoise. To make sure she's learning something from us.'

'I will certainly try to make his visit agreeable,' the baron said with a thin smile. 'For Clara also of course. Now, let us all get ready for dinner and then I think some bridge. A quiet evening will probably suit us all.'

He lingered behind as the others left until only he and Cassandra were in the room. She lifted an exhausted, tear-stained face to his. 'I lost,' she said brokenly. 'If Lucy hadn't come, then I could have lasted.'

'You'd still have lost,' he pointed out. 'She had to come while you could not in order to draw. Besides, while you lost this little competition, in the overall game I think this could be considered a win.'

'What overall game?' Cassandra asked.

'Now that, my dear girl, would be telling,' he said softly, and then ran a hand gently through her tousled hair before leaving her to dress and return to her room to prepare for dinner.

Black Orchid

Roxanne Carr

Black Orchid was the first Black Lace book from Roxanne Carr and begins the adventures of Maggie, whose introduction to the world of carefree sex begins when she joins the Black Orchid club: an exclusive health spa for women who don't have the time to form meaningful relationships but who want the thrill of rewarding erotic encounters. Maggie likes the place so much that the owners ask her to interview some male candidates who have applied for a job at the club. The job is to satisfy the female clients and Maggie has a great time sorting the men out from the boys. It isn't long before she's a fully employed member of staff, enjoying the many benefits of her privileged position. Her adventures continue in *A Bouquet of Black Orchids* and *The Black Orchid Hotel*.

Roxanne's other books for Black Lace are: *Western Star*, set in the wild west of America; *Jewel of Xanadu*, set in the times of Marco Polo at the palace of the Kublai Khan, and *Avenging Angels*, which is published in April 1997.

Black Orchid

Maggie lay back in the warm, bubbling water and closed her eyes. Bliss! Seven a.m. and there wasn't a soul in the club to disturb her. She had exclusive rights to the jacuzzi and she revelled in the unaccustomed pleasure of her own company.

She had been living at the club with Antony and Alexander for six weeks now and she was beginning to wonder if she was losing her sense of reality. Today she was taking over from Jackie and a new batch of trainers were coming in for her to interview.

Each man had been personally selected by Alexander and Antony; they had conducted the preliminary interviews and weeded out those who were obviously unsuitable. It was her job to decide which of the five shortlisted would be most popular with the other women.

Judd was leaving after spending almost a year at the Black Orchid and Dean was being released after breaking the 'no outside relationships' rule. In addition, Antony had decided that the club membership had grown sufficiently large to consider employing more trainers. So that meant that Maggie could set on all five candidates she was to put through their paces if she so desired.

She smiled to herself and sank deeper into the jacuzzi. The bubbles gurgled and fizzed around her legs, tickling the inside of her thighs as they rose upward. She was naked, her dark hair piled up on the top of her head and secured carelessly with a cotton scrunchy. She never bothered with make-up this early in the morning, so she didn't have to worry about the warm water splashing her face, trickling down her cheeks with a lover's caress.

Maggie closed her eyes and, taking a deep breath, submerged herself in the warm water. As she resurfaced, she gripped the padded bar which ran around the circular pool and allowed her naked body to float on the surface of the water.

It was so peaceful with only the light chatter of the watery bubbles and the gentle hum of the air conditioning around her. Slowly, Maggie parted her legs, revelling in the controlled pull of her well-toned muscles. She had never been so fit, her body so trim and toned as she was now. And her skin – so soft and blemish free.

Since she had moved in with Antony and Alexander she was rarely allowed to bathe herself. Invariably, she would find the water had been run for her and one or other of them would appear, arms full of perfumed soaps and lotions and talcum. All that was required of her was that she lay back in the water and submit to their gentle ministrations.

Alexander was the best, lingering over every process, polishing her skin as if it were the finest, most valuable porcelain. Yet there was never any sexual contact, even though he was often visibly aroused by touching her. And Maggie ... Maggie had learned never to make overtures to him for fear of making him angry. No, not angry exactly, she mused. She opened and closed her legs in a scissor-like action which forced the bubbles to travel between them with more force, languidly enjoying the way they bumped and popped, unobstructed, against her sex.

Angry wasn't quite the right word to describe Alexander's reaction to the few times she had tried to initiate sex with him. Disappointed in her, perhaps. Certainly, she always felt contrite, like a child who has tried to take one more cookie from the jar.

The most unsatisfactory thing about living with Antony and Alexander was that she was only ever allowed to make love with Antony. They didn't seem to mind if she stayed while they made love to each other; she had, on occasion, even joined in. But she was never intimately alone with Alex.

Maggie sighed as she switched off the jacuzzi and wrapped herself in a huge white towel. Snuggling into its luxuriously soft warmth, she padded back to her private bathroom, part of her office, which adjoined the pool room. Antony was waiting for her when she went back upstairs to the apartment.

'Ready for the interviews, Maggie?'

'Do I get to eat breakfast first?'

'Only a light one, darling – I wouldn't recommend you have sex with five men in a row on a full stomach.'

He poured them both a coffee and Maggie frowned at him. His tone had been ever so slightly cutting and she sensed an air of resentment about him that she had noticed a couple of times before.

'Is everything all right, Antony?' she asked as he handed her a mug.

He looked up and smiled, somewhat ruefully.

'Don't mind me. I got out the wrong side of the bed this morning.'

He left her alone and Maggie reflected that Alexander had not returned home the previous evening. She had a shrewd idea that that was what had put Antony in such a prickly mood. The lounge door opened at that moment and Alexander appeared, as if her thinking about him had conjured him up. As was often the case when he disappeared on one of what Maggie privately termed his French Leave, he was in high spirits, kissing her exuberantly before sinking down beside her on the sofa.

'Phew, I'm exhausted!' he exclaimed.

Maggie slanted a look at him sideways through her lashes as he helped himself to coffee. He never seemed to feel the need to explain himself or his actions. Didn't he see how his behaviour upset Antony? She could feel the tension emanating from him as he came back into the room, and could feel the effort it cost him not to question Alexander about his movements. Yet Alex merely smiled at him before turning to her.

'I want you to try out each of the guys I've selected for you and mark them on a scale of one to ten. Their general attractiveness, their attitude towards you, their confidence and general level of skill, etc. Remember, you've got to bear in mind the needs of our members – don't judge the guys purely on *your* reaction to them. OK?'

'I think so. What about if one of them gets out of hand?' She blushed as Alexander raised an ironic eyebrow at her. 'I mean, if I don't want to and he . . . well, you know.'

'Antony and I will be behind a two-way mirror. Any problems, give a signal and we'll rescue you.'

Maggie raised her eyes heavenward. She might have known!

125

'Won't you two get bored, watching me all morning?' she teased gently.

'We'll find something to do if it gets too monotonous, won't we Antony?'

There was a slight challenge in Alexander's voice as he turned to the other man, but Antony just shrugged. Maggie had no doubt that Alex would talk him round – he always did.

Later, in the large, luxuriously appointed 'office' she had been given, Maggie began to feel nervous. She leaped up from the comfortable leather chair which sat behind the heavy, masculine-looking old oak desk and paced to the other end of the room, her high-heeled mules soundless on the cream carpeted floor

By the second-floor window which overlooked the city, there were two rattan chairs and a glass-topped table on which she had placed an assortment of drinks and crockery. A coffee percolator hissed and fizzed on the small counter in the corner, filling the room with the aroma of coffee beans.

Nervously, she drew the butter-yellow silk curtains and walked round switching on the softly shaded lamps placed strategically round the room. The large, comfortable, lemon chintz-covered couch faced the two-way mirror on the opposite wall and she went over to it and flicked off the privacy switch so that Antony and Alexander could see the room.

Glancing at the grandfather clock, ticking sonorously in the corner by the desk, Maggie saw that it was time to begin. Yet still she procrastinated. It all seemed so cold, so clinical, preparing to make love with five men she had never seen!

She was wearing a cream silk robe, belted at the waist, which brushed the floor as she walked. She was naked underneath and she suddenly felt vulnerable.

'What's the matter, Maggie?' Alexander's voice over the intercom made her jump.

'I . . . I just feel a bit awkward, that's all. Er . . . maybe this isn't quite such a good idea.'

'You knew what the job would entail, Maggie. Are you having second thoughts?'

Alexander's tone was cutting and Maggie stopped her pacing and took a deep breath. He was right, she knew what she was taking on. She trusted him to help her if she couldn't handle anything, and there wasn't much she felt she couldn't cope with. And she really didn't want to lose this job – apart from anything else, she loved living with Antony and Alexander. She wanted to please Alex and the idea that he was becoming impatient with her made her reply hastily,

'Of course not.'

'Just get on with it, then, Maggie, there's a good girl.'

Maggie pressed the buzzer on her desk and the heavy oak door opened silently on its well-oiled hinges. Maggie's eyes widened in surprise as the open doorway was filled by an enormous, broad-shouldered hulk. His skin shone like well-polished ebony, his shaven head as smooth and well shaped as the rest of him. The whites of his eyes showed up in startling contrast to the blackness of his skin and as he treated her to a slow, confident smile, her eyes were drawn to the perfection of his strong white teeth.

He closed the door behind him and Maggie's eyes were drawn to the way his shoulder muscles rippled under the tight-fitting black T-shirt. There was a glint of gold in one earlobe and around his thick, strong neck. As he walked slowly towards her, Maggie noticed the thigh muscles which bulged in the tight blue jeans and the unmistakable fullness at his crotch.

Her eyes snapped up as he stopped, standing in front of her, waiting. She swallowed, wetting her unaccountably dry throat, her former nervousness forgotten. This was one hell of a guy.

'Hello,' she smiled, holding out her hand, 'and you are?'

'Constantine G. Winchester the third,' he said, his smile flashing at her look of astonishment, 'but my friends call me Con.'

His voice was beautiful, rich as dark treacle, yet as smooth as a good brandy. Maggie felt the compulsion to make him talk more, just for the pleasure of hearing that strong, well-modulated voice. As he enclosed her soft, well-manicured hand in his larger, stronger one, though, the attractions of his voice faded into insignificance.

Maggie allowed him to pull her slowly towards him until they stood breast to breast. Even in her high-heels, she had to crane her neck to look up at him and she was glad when he lowered his head to hers and covered her mouth with his.

His kiss took her breath away, his tongue wrapping itself around hers and drawing it into the hot wet cavern of his mouth. His chest was solid, immovable as her soft breasts were crushed against it and she felt herself being lifted up, off her feet. His sheer bulk made her feel tiny, powerless in his arms as he held her to him with one hand while he opened her robe with the other.

He balanced one trainer-clad foot on her desk and literally sat her on his bent knee, cradling her with one arm as he covered one quivering breast with his hand. Maggie sucked in her breath as she contemplated the erotic contrast of his dark hand on her white flesh as he knowingly coaxed her nipple to hardness.

She ran her hand tentatively over the smooth dome of his stubble-free skull as he bent his head to her breast. The skin felt warm and velvet soft under her fingertips. Maggie closed her eyes as his lips tugged at her responsive nipple, sending little shocks of reaction along the nerves connecting it to her innermost centre of pleasure.

Con pushed the robe off her shoulders and she shivered as it fell to the floor in a silky heap, leaving her skin exposed to the air. It was comfortably warm in the room, yet she felt little goosebumps form all over as he ran the palm of his hand down her side from her armpit to her hip. The rough skin of his palm lightly snagged her skin as he polished her hip bone before gripping her thigh, lifting it up so that her leg was bent at the knee.

Smiling slightly at Maggie, Con used his free hand to unbutton his fly and release his tumescent penis from the constriction of his jeans. Maggie unconsciously licked her lips as the monster reared up and pointed its succulent tip at her. Her mouth watered as she contemplated savouring the musky, salty tear-drop which had appeared in its centre, but Con was holding her fast and she had no chance to move.

Easing his jeans over his taut buttocks, he left them stretched around his thighs as he sat her on the edge of the desk and positioned himself between her thighs, feet planted firmly apart. His large hands parted her sex and he framed the tender, moist pink fold of flesh with his two hands, touching her almost reverently.

Maggie watched with bated breath as he ran his two fore-fingers along the insides of the outer lips, exposing the glistening flesh leaves within. As he reached the most sensitive point, he squeezed the labia firmly together, making her pleasure-bud tingle in anticipation.

She was disappointed when he removed his fingers, though

not for long. His large hands slipped under her bottom and cradled each buttock, forming a warm cushion between her and the cold, hard wood of the desk. Then he was lifting her up, balancing her entire weight in his palms as he held her, poised, the entrance to her body opening above his swaying shaft.

Maggie gasped as he lowered her slowly and she was impaled on the hard rod which filled and stretched her to capacity. Her arms flew around his neck as he took her entire weight on his hands and moved her pelvis up and down, rubbing her clitoris firmly against the fine line of black hair on his lower belly as he did so.

He was so strong, so solid, he seemed immovable as Maggie clung helplessly to him, powerless to resist his determined manipulation of her body. His eyes were closed now, his lips slightly parted. A fine line of perspiration glistened on his smooth upper lip and the cords in his thick neck stood out as he neared his release.

The relentless, ticklish pressure of his belly against her clitoris was driving her wild, her well-lubricated sheath throbbing and burning as the huge cock slid in and out of her. She closed her eyes and concentrated on the sensations building deep within her.

A kaleidoscope of colours exploded behind her eyelids as the rhythmic rubbing brought her to orgasm, her ankles linking behind Con's back as she sought to meld herself further with him. A deep, guttural groan sounded deep in his throat, emerging as a triumphant shout as his seed burst from him and shot upward into her sex, still convulsing strongly around him.

Even in the throes of orgasm, Con stood, feet planted firmly shoulder-width apart, steady as a rock. He held Maggie firmly until the waves had subsided and she clung weakly to him, spent. Then he carefully lifted her up and off his still partially erect penis and put her gently onto her feet in front of him.

Maggie leaned weakly against the desk and watched him as he calmly pulled his jeans back up, tucking his formidable member inside before rebuttoning the fly. He smiled at her, cocking his head slightly to one side as if expecting her to say something.

'Th-thank you, Con,' she said shakily, 'we'll be in touch.'

He seemed to be about to say something then, thinking better of it, he grinned and nodded, striding away from her with the same jaunty coinfidence as when he approached her. Maggie watched him go, admiring the neatness of his muscular behind in the tight-fitting jeans. As the door swung to behind him, she slumped slightly, running her fingers distractedly through her dishevelled hair.

She jumped as the door opened again and another man came through. She hadn't buzzed to say she was ready yet – surely she had time to wash?

'One moment I . . .' she trailed off as she surveyed the man who hovered uncertainly in the doorway.

The contrast between this one and Con was so marked it was almost laughable. It was almost as if they were from a different species. This one was a good foot shorter, about equal to Maggie's own five feet six inches with a skinny, almost weedy build. His shoulders were rounded, his chest even more so, virtually concave. The white T-shirt he was wearing should have clung to his pectorals, instead it hung loosely across his chest and disappeared into his baggy grey slacks. Maggie guessed he must be here for maintenance, or some other thing that would have to wait until later.

'Sorry,' Maggie smiled politely, pulling her robe more closely around her, 'could you come back later?'

He blinked uncertainly and shuffled his feet. Maggie tried to conceal her impatience. She had an increasingly urgent need to pee.

'I'm rather busy at the moment,' she explained, 'you see, I'm in the middle of interviewing.'

If he thought it odd that Maggie was conducting job interviews dressed in nothing but a silk robe, he did not show it. He virtually wrang his hands together as if gathering his courage to speak to her. When, finally, he did dare to address her, his voice was shrill with nerves.

'Excuse me, but I'm next, madam.'

Maggie stared at him, fighting with the urge to laugh.

'Um, well, I'm sorry, but I think there's been a mistake. You do know what the job entails?'

'Oh yes, madam. I think I'm well suited to it, begging your pardon for being so bold.'

His ingratiating manner was beginning to get on Maggie's nerves. Her tone was abrupt as she asked him, 'What's your name?'

'Malcolm, madam.'

Well, it would be, wouldn't it? Maggie's lips twitched. He had virtually bobbed a curtsey as he introduced himself.

'Pleased to meet you, Malcolm, but I don't think you're quite what I had in mind for the job.'

She expected him to give up at that point, but he was still gazing at her hopefully with his wide, brown, lost puppy dog eyes. She sighed. He really was a most uninspiring specimen. Not only was he nauseatingly self-deprecating but his mousy brown hair stuck up in alarmed tufts on top of his head, reminding her of a toilet brush. Losing patience, she abandoned all pretence of charm and snapped.

'Look, Malcolm, I need a shower and a pee and I don't have time to stand here and argue with you. Do you understand?'

His face took on an expression of adoration.

'Oh yes, madam, but if you'd just allow me . . . may I?'

Maggie frowned. Maybe if she humoured him, he'd go away. She nodded, raising her eyebrows in surprise as Malcolm dropped to his knees and shuffled towards her. She stood stock still as he reached her and pressed his lips against each of her feet in turn.

Glancing uncomfortably at the two-way mirror, she imagined Antony and Alexander watching them. It was a new angle to her to find herself in charge of a man as submissive as this, and she was not sure if she liked it. Malcolm reverently lifted the hem of her robe and began to lick his way up her inner thigh.

Maggie tensed as a droplet of juice seeped out of her and ran down her leg. Malcolm lapped it up, sucking at the soft, damp skin as if the combined juices of her coupling with Con were the sweetest nectar. Whatever his deficiencies as a man in her eyes, Malcolm definitely had a skilful tongue. Maggie relaxed against the desk and obligingly parted her thighs, granting him access to the sticky curls between them.

Closing her eyes on the unattractive sight of Malcolm's hair between her legs, Maggie concentrated instead on the pleasant sensations of his respectful, wet tongue lapping its way along her moist folds. After the punishing encounter she had enjoyed with Con, Malcolm's attentions were soothing against her swollen sex.

He nibbled on her resting bud until it began to spasm, not with the furious, all-consuming tremors Con had evoked, but in a gentle, mild climax which was pleasant rather than mind blowing. Maggie smiled, glad that Malcolm had some talent.

Unfortunately the orgasm caused the muscles of her over-full bladder to relax and when Malcolm very deliberately pressed the tip of his tongue firmly against her urethra, Maggie was powerless to prevent a small trickle of urine from escaping.

Mortified, she clenched her pelvic floor muscles to stop the leakage, but Malcolm seemed determined not to let her go. The urge to pee grew stronger as he teased the tiny hole, probing with his tongue until she could hold back no longer.

Maggie looked down in horror as the steady stream of golden liquid flowed over Malcolm's face and down his neck. His eyes were closed, his mouth open, the expression on his face rapturous. He had unzipped his flies and was masturbating himself furiously. As Maggie finished, his orgasm overtook him and his semen spurted out, mingling with the steaming urine on the front of his trousers.

Repulsed, Maggie lifted her foot and pushed his shoulder with the toe of her mule. Malcolm toppled over, writhing about on the floor in a paroxysm of ecstasy.

'You filthy creature! Make sure you're out of here when I get back!'

She flounced into her private bathroom and locked the door behind her. Her angry, flushed face stared back at her in the mirror over the basin. Suddenly, she began to laugh. The little man was priceless! How many of their clients, probably stuck with a boorish, domineering partner, would like to get their own back on mankind? And Malcolm had obviously loved every minute of the humiliation to which she had unwittingly subjected him.

Taking the time for a quick, rejuvenating shower, Maggie changed into a clean robe, identical to the first, and ventured back into the office. To her relief, Malcolm had disappeared. Someone had been in to clean up for there was a damp patch on the carpet and the sharp antiseptic scent of cleaning fluid hung in the air. Maggie pressed the button on the intercom.

'Next, please.'

The next candidate virtually bounced into the room. He was fit, exuding good health in his casual, dark-red sweat top and baggy black track pants, and he was young. Very young.

'I'm Jason,' he introduced himself eagerly, trying not to make it obvious that he was eyeing her up.

Maggie hid a smile as she noticed he already had a hard-on and that the track pants could barely contain his enthusiasm.

'How old are you, Jason.' she asked him, resisting the urge to ask if his mother knew he was here.

Jason's cherubic, boyish face split into a cheeky grin.

'Everyone asks me that. I'm twenty ... well, all right, I'm eighteen – honestly,' he laughed as he saw her disbelief, 'I could show you my driver's licence?'

'No need,' she said quickly. She was sure that such basic, mundane matters would have been checked out long before he got to this stage. Briefly, she wondered if eighteen was old enough. But there was eighteen, and there was eighteen!

'Do you like women, Jason?'

'You bet!'

'*All* women?'

'Tall, short, fat, thin, blonde, brunette, redhead—'

'OK, OK!' she laughed, 'I get the picture.'

She walked slowly towards him, watching his reaction as she deliberately allowed her hips to sway. It wasn't difficult to adopt the exaggerated roll of the pelvis in the high-heeled mules. Jason stood still, only his eyes following her as she circled him, looking him up and down appraisingly.

He had an open, honest sort of face, smooth jawed, blue eyed with a smartly barbered crop of shiny, clean blond hair. There was a deep cleft in the centre of his chin which hinted at more craggy looks as he aged. His body was well sculpted, his legs long and lean, and his chest pleasingly broad. Maggie could smell the faintest trace of fresh, lemony soap as she stood closer to him, noting the way his cock leapt in his trousers in reaction to her proximity.

'Do you like to fuck, Jason?' she enquired, dropping her voice an octave.

His colour rose slightly, but he met her teasing gaze without flinching and grinned.

'You bet!' he said again.

'Hmm. And does your skill match your enthusiasm?'

'Want to try me?'

Maggie smiled and reached up to run her forefinger down the side of his smooth-skinned cheek.

'You bet!' she whispered.

Jason's lips were unexpectedly demanding as they moved on hers and Maggie felt her blood quicken. So he looked young – she certainly didn't feel in the least bit maternal towards him now! Taking him by the hand, she led him over to the lemon chintz couch and pulled him down on to it, on top of her.

Briefly, she wondered if Antony and Alexander were enjoying themselves behind the two-way mirror as she contented herself with savouring the kiss. Drawing Jason's tongue into her mouth, she sucked at it gently, encouraging him to relinquish the self-control she could sense he was struggling to retain.

She lifted her shoulders up off the couch to help him as he eased her robe down, exposing her soft-tipped breasts. His eyes were hot, warming her skin as he gazed down on her with a mixture of admiration and lust.

'God, you're beautiful!' he breathed.

Maggie hid a smile at the conviction in his voice. In anyone else she might have dismissed the comment as a stock line, but from Jason it sounded fresh and new. As he lowered his head to kiss her breasts, Maggie tangled her fingers in his thick, glossy hair, massaging his scalp as he drew one swelling nipple into his hot mouth.

Tiny shivers of pleasure coursed down her spine and she felt the moisture begin to gather between her thighs in response to the feel of his lean young body pressing against her silk-covered mound. Jason's hands were roaming at will all over her upper body, his mouth planting tiny butterfly kisses along the tender skin of her inner arm from her wrist to her armpit before tracing the line of her collar-bone and running back down the other arm from shoulder to hand.

Maggie helped him remove his trousers and briefs, her mouth curving into a pleased smile as his penis sprang into view. Like the rest of him, it was well formed and hard, the soft protective foreskin already drawing back to reveal the purple-headed glans beneath. Maggie would have liked to have tasted that magnificent specimen, but she was aware that time was short.

Her brief was to try out each candidate's satisfaction quotient from a woman's point of view. Any pleasure they derived from the exercise should be purely coincidental, not arrived at through any direct action from her.

With that in mind, she pushed his head gently lower. He

needed no further encouragement to open her robe completely and spread her softly quivering thighs.

Maggie gasped at the first contact of his tongue on her swollen vulva. This sensation was completely different from Malcolm's tentative, nervous licks. Jason ran his tongue around the tender folds in bold, confident strokes, as if he were settling down to a particularly delicious meal.

As the centre of her pleasure zone responded, she arched her back and bore down, inviting him to deepen his exploration. He did not disappoint her. She groaned as his hard, seeking tongue found the straining nub and flicked hungrily back and forth over it.

A delicious warmth slowly radiated out from that tiny point, suffusing her with a sense of well being that only truly good sex could imbue. Jason had found her blossoming opening with one finger and he gently moved it in and out as he continued to diligently stroke her outer sex with his tongue.

Maggie wrapped her long legs around his neck, holding him to her as the familiar waves began to break and the heat rose up and consumed her. All her attention was focused on that small core of her femininity as it pulsed and throbbed against the pressure of Jason's eager tongue.

She smiled at him as he raised his head. His eyes were glazed, his chin smeared with her feminine secretions and he was smiling. Dipping his head, he blazed a trail of kisses in a line from her pubis to her throat before claiming her mouth.

Maggie wrapped her legs around his waist and urged him to possess her. He leant his forehead against hers for a moment as the tip of his swollen cock nudged against the entrance to her welcoming sex. He slipped inside her with a sigh, resting there for a few seconds before beginning to slowly withdraw.

Gradually, he built up his rhythm, exquisitely slowly at first, then gaining momentum. Maggie matched his movements, bringing her bottom up from the sofa to meet him, drawing him into her and tightening her intimate muscles as he withdrew.

His smooth skin grew hot under her palms as he began to quicken his pace, building to a crescendo. They rolled together, slipping off the couch and on to the soft carpet. For a moment, Maggie was on top, then he rolled her over again on to her back, holding her buttocks in his hands as he thrust into her.

Maggie could feel little thrills of sensation rippling through

her as the movement of his thick, hard shaft stimulated the walls
of the silky sheath which enclosed him. She closed her eyes and
concentrated on the delicious friction, digging her fingernails
into his shoulders as his breathing became faster and more
shallow and his movement became frenzied. He cried out as he
came, collapsing on top of her and covering her face with kisses.

'God, you're fantastic!' he gasped, his voice quavering.

Maggie cradled his head against her breast as she waited for
his breathing to slow and his temperature to return to normal.
She was touched by his gratitude, moved by his innocence. His
sexual style owed more to enthusiasm than finesse, but it was
energetic and honest and she knew this was an experience she
would look forward to repeating.

At last, they peeled apart and he used her bathroom to freshen
up while she called for a cold drink. He took a coke from her
gratefully and drank it quickly. Maggie sipped at hers, watching
the muscles in his throat contract as he swallowed.

He grinned at her as he handed her his empty glass. 'Thanks –
I needed that! Have I got the job?'

Maggie smiled.

'We'll be in touch,' she told him.

His face fell, a picture of disappointment.

'Oh.'

Maggie could not let him leave like that. She stepped forward
and kissed him on the cheek.

'I'm sure we'll meet again,' she murmured, her face turned
away from the two-way mirror so that only he could hear.

Jason's face split into its usual happy grin and he hugged her.

'Be seeing you, then,' he said, and he left with as much spring
in his step as there had been when he first came in.

Maggie took a few minutes to compose herself. She knew now
why Alexander had decided to watch the proceedings. No doubt
it gave him a kick to see her take five men one after the other.
She shivered. If only she knew what went on in his mind!

After she had washed, she buzzed the intercom and took a
seat by the curtained window so that she would have time to
appraise the next candidate before he saw her. The door opened
and a young, long-haired man swaggered through it. His hair
was a dirty blond colour, his eyes, when he turned them on her,
a faded blue. He was wearing tight, brown leather trousers and

a white, wide-sleeved cotton shirt, unbuttoned at the front to his navel.

'Hi babe, I'm Darren,' he drawled.

Maggie winced. He looked and sounded like a parody of a seventies rock star. A complete turn-off.

'Hello. Won't you sit down?'

She indicated the other rattan chair and he strolled over and perched awkwardly on its edge. His eyes skittered from her face to the window and round the room. He linked his hands loosely in front of him, brought them up to his chin, then dropped them again. Finally, he seemed to be able to bear the silence no longer.

'Well, are we goin' to get it on or what?'

Maggie considered telling him to get lost and go and do 'or what'. She didn't have the energy. Standing up, she raised her eyes heavenward at the two-way mirror before turning back to Darren, unbelting her robe and letting it fall to the ground. Then she stepped out of her shoes and waited.

His faded blue eyes grew rounder, fixed on her naked breasts as he leapt to his feet and tore off his clothes. He had a good body, Maggie noted dispassionately, probably better than young Jason's. So why didn't the sight of him, naked and erect, do anything for her?

Darren's hands on her bare skin were cool and knowing. As if following a tried and tested ritual he had learnt off by heart, he smoothed the skin of her neck and squeezed her breast, kissed her half-heartedly and stared soulfully into her eyes as he led her over to the sofa and slowly laid her on her back.

Maggie's mind wandered to the meal Alexander had promised to cook that evening: one of her favourites. She frowned slightly as Darren thrust one hand between her closed thighs and twiddled about for a minute. Satisfied that she was wet – he wasn't to know that she had already been with two men and could hardly be otherwise – he bent her legs at the knees and thrust into her, making her wince.

His face was intent as he drove in and out of her and Maggie realised he had probably forgotten who she was. So intent was he on reaching his own climax, he didn't notice her grimacing frantically at the two-way mirror.

'Yes! Oh yes!' he yelled as he reached the peak.

Maggie fought the urge to giggle. He rolled off her and they both dressed in silence. There was a bubble of smug self-satisfaction about Darren which she was longing to burst. Her chance came soon enough.

'When do I start work, then, darlin'?' he asked her casually as he zipped his leather trousers.

'You don't.'

'Huh?'

'I think you have been labouring under a misconception, *darling*. This is an exclusive club for very discerning ladies. Not a knocking shop set up for the benefit of our male employees.'

'Whaddaya mean?'

Maggie ignored the belligerent scowl and continued. 'You're not up to it, my dear.'

'I've never had any complaints before.'

'No, but then sheep can't speak, can they?'

They both jumped as Antony's voice came from behind them.

'What's that supposed to mean, then?' Darren took a step towards Antony then, eyeing his superior physique, then obviously thinking better of it.

'It means it's time for you to leave. And try to learn a few manners before you next approach a lady.'

Darren swung towards the door, his high colour signalling he was offended. As he reached the door, he turned back to Maggie and spluttered, 'I'll tell you what your trouble is, darlin' – you're frigid!'

'Get out,' Antony said, his voice dripping boredom.

'I didn't enjoy it anyway, bleedin' lesbian!' was Darren's parting shot as he slammed out of the door.

Antony turned to Maggie and raised an eyebrow at her.

'Are you all right?'

She nodded, then couldn't keep back the laughter bubbling in her throat. Antony joined in.

'Frigid!' he said.

They put their arms round each other and laughed until the tears were running down their cheeks. When they had recovered, Antony brushed the hair out of her eyes tenderly. Holding her gaze, he asked, 'I'm sorry, I don't know how that boor got through.'

Maggie shrugged. 'Don't worry – I've dealt with far worse than him on the outside. It was probably Alexander's idea of a joke.'

'You could be right. If you're OK, do you feel up to the last interview?'

'Is this one civilised?'

'I'd say he is.'

Maggie laughed.

'Fancy him yourself, do you?'

Antony let her go and wandered back to the door.

'Mind your own business,' he replied good naturedly.

'Well, so long as he *is* half way decent, perhaps he could join me for some lunch – I'm starving!'

'That shouldn't be a problem. I'll have something sent up.'

Maggie went to brush her hair and thought longingly of the jacuzzi. She felt grubby and wished there was time to freshen up before she met the final candidate, but already she could hear the door opening and the sounds of heavy male footsteps coming into the room. For the first time in a long time, she wondered if she would be able to muster the enthusiasm required to put him through his paces. Laying down her brush with a sigh, she went back into the office to greet him.

'Hello, sorry to keep you waiting, I . . .'

She trailed off as she saw the man who had come in and was looking out of the window. He had pulled back the curtains and bright sunlight streamed in, outshining the lamps. He turned slowly at the sound of her voice and all Maggie's tiredness fled as she was caught by his dark eyes.

He was wearing clean, but well-worn denims with heavy-soled tan leather boots and a wide belt. His denim shirt looked soft from many launderings. It clung lovingly to the breadth of his strong shoulders and was open at the neck, revealing the merest hint of crisp, dark chest hair.

Raising her eyes to his face, Maggie saw that he was smiling at her and she felt the heat rise in her cheeks. He had a firm, well-shaped mouth which lifted slightly more on the left than the right when he smiled. His nose was slightly hooked, but perfectly proportioned, his eyes, so dark they were almost black, widely spaced and framed by thick, black lashes.

His skin was tanned, the tiny laughter lines radiating out from the corners of his eyes looked paler, as if he had spent a lot of time squinting in the sun. And his hair was as black and glossy as a Native American's, falling in a thick widow's peak over his forehead and curling wildly round his ears.

Recovering herself slightly, Maggie moved towards him and offered him her hand.

'How do you do? I'm Maggie.'

'Brett,' he said, clasping her slender hand in his capable fingers.

Maggie felt the tremors tingling up her arm and swallowed, hard.

'I hope you don't mind, but I've ordered lunch. It's been a hectic morning.'

She blushed as she realised what she had said and he smiled at her again. Maggie warmed to him and indicated with a wave of the hand that he should sit on one of the rattan chairs. As he did so, she thought of Antony and Alexander snooping behind the two-way mirror and knew *this* time, she wanted some privacy.

Casually wandering over to the two-way mirror, she blew a kiss at its opaque surface and flicked the privacy switch. Alexander was going to be furious! Serve him right for letting Darren slip through the net. She smiled to herself as she thought how she had outwitted him for once. Just then there was a knock at the door and one of the kitchen staff appeared with a hostess trolley. Thanking her, Maggie wheeled it into the room and locked the door behind her.

'It's just salad and baked potatoes, I'm afraid,' she apologised as she lifted the covers off the trays.

'Looks good to me,' Brett responded, relieving her of one tray.

Maggie couldn't take her eyes off him as he took a hearty forkful of fat, juicy prawns, dripping in mayonnaise and put it in his mouth. He chewed slowly, as if savouring every bite, his eyes never leaving Maggie's. She felt as if she could be eating sawdust, her mouth and throat were so dry, her heart beating irregularly. Despite her frequent escapades, it had been a while since she had felt this much desire for a man.

'How did you find out about the Black Orchid Club?' she broke the tense silence, wetting her lips with the cool, clear mineral water which had been sent up in a jug.

'A mate of mine worked here before he came out to Australia.'

'Australia?' That explained the deep suntan. 'What were you doing out there?'

Brett shrugged.

'This and that. Cattle herding, mostly.'

140

A vivid picture of him astride a horse, yielding a lasso like an old-fashioned cowboy pushed its way into Maggie's head and she smiled. The image suited him.

'What is it?'

'Nothing. Just that you struck me as being the outdoor type.'

'Really? And is that a good thing?'

His voice was thick, like double-cream. It trickled over her senses, affecting her concentration, drowning her in sensuality.

They had finished eating. Brett seemed to be waiting for her to make a move, but, for once, she didn't know the best place to start. She felt sticky, unclean, and she knew she wanted to come to this man fresh.

'Look,' she began, 'I feel awfully hot and sweaty. I'd really like to take a bath – would you mind?'

She hoped he wouldn't think she was rejecting him, would be happy to come back later. He smiled slowly at her.

'Sure. Would you mind if I joined you?'

Maggie's eyebrows flew up in surprise. She thought of the jacuzzi. There'd be plenty of hot water and there was a lock on the inside of the door. It would be the perfect place to be alone. Her lips curved into a smile of delicious anticipation.

'Be my guest,' she murmured huskily.

Maggie switched on the jacuzzi and poured a thimbleful of her favourite, scented bubble-bath into the swirling water. The taciturn maintenance man would not be pleased with her when he had to drain the system, she thought wryly. Too bad!

Taking out a large box of matches, she lit the scented candles which were held in glass-fronted iron sconces screwed to the walls and extinguished the harsh electric light. She looked around her with satisfaction.

The water in the jacuzzi was frothing gently, large, iridescent bubbles rising up and disappearing with a soft 'pop' the minute they touched a hard surface. A subtle, musky scent filled the room, laying heavily on the still air. The candlelight flickered as the door to her bathroom opened and Brett stepped through.

He had taken off his boots and the belt of his jeans and he stood, barefoot, looking round him. His expression was inscrutable and Maggie felt her heart quicken. She watched silently as he slowly unbuttoned the denim shirt and shrugged it off.

His chest was broad, carpeted in a light covering of curly black hair which arrowed down the line of his belly and disappeared

141

into his jeans. He held her eye as she stood across the pool from him and began to slip the buttons of his jeans through the stiff buttonholes. He was wearing plain black cotton boxer shorts underneath and he made no move to remove them, merely staring quietly back at her.

The tension in the room was palpable as Maggie slowly slipped her robe off her shoulders and kicked it aside. Brett's eyes flickered briefly over her naked, candlelit body, before returning to her face. Maggie was aware that her nipples had grown hard, her legs weak as she anticipated the feel of his strong, hair-roughened arms around her, longed for the touch of his cool, firm lips on her skin.

Very slowly, she walked to the edge of the jacuzzi and sat down on the edge. He watched her as she slipped into the water with one graceful, fluid movement, closing her eyes for an instant as she sank up to her neck into the warm, bubbling water.

When she opened them again, she saw that he had dispensed with his boxer shorts and was moving towards her. Proudly naked, his erect penis swayed invitingly as he plunged feet first into the pool, submerging his entire body under the water.

Maggie giggled as she felt him brush against her ankle as he resurfaced, water streaming down his face, his black hair plastered against his skull. Without feeling the need to speak, they relaxed against the padded side of the pool, wet shoulders touching, both enjoying the sensation of the bubbles burbling around them.

The illicit bubble-bath had caused the jacuzzi to overflow, huge, frothy masses of white bubbles rising up into the air so that soon only their heads were above it. Maggie could feel the constantly moving water washing away the remains of her encounters with Con and Malcolm and Jason and Darren. She felt clean again, renewed.

She jumped as Brett's wet hands slithered around her equally wet waist, lifting her up and towards him. His naked body pressed against hers, the wet skin slippery and soft. She could feel his hardness nudging at her outer thigh as he turned her and crushed her foam-covered breasts against the hard, hairy wall of his chest.

Maggie welcomed his kiss, tasting the warm, sweet water on his lips and tangling her fingers in the damp curls at the nape of his neck. His tongue probed against her teeth and she drew it in, liking the taste of him and eager for more.

They were almost completely submerged now, mountainous walls of white foam climbing around them. The candlelight shone dully through the bubbles, enclosing them in a wet, frothy cocoon, a secret world inhabited only by their seeking, hungry bodies.

Maggie allowed the water to buoy her up so that Brett's head was level with her hard-tipped breasts. She sucked in her breath as his lips touched first one, then the other, suckling gently until she felt the erotic pull deep inside her. His teeth grazed her nipples as he pulled away and lifted her, his large hands spanning her waist as he pressed his face against her navel, delving into it with his tongue.

Looking down, Maggie could see the crisp, dark hair between her legs, almost entirely obscured by the clinging foam, inches away from his busy tongue. She parted her legs slightly in invitation, imagining how the soft pink folds of her inner flesh, streaming with warm water from the jacuzzi, would now peek out at him.

She braced herself against the padded bar as he tilted her pelvis, one strong hand supporting her buttocks. With the fingers of his free hand, he gently parted the pouting lips of her vulva and spent a long moment gazing at the intricately formed flower within.

Maggie felt her cheeks grow warm as his scrutiny continued, sighing in a mixture of relief and ecstasy as he gently entered her with two fingers. She sank down on them, grinding her hips against his, searching for his lips with her own.

Brett hooked one of her legs around his waist and she brought the other up to join it, crossing her ankles behind his back. The foamy bubbles hissed and popped against her skin as she lay back in the water, her shoulders resting against the padded bar. Then she welcomed Brett into her body.

They made love slowly, almost lazily, indulging in long, hungry kisses. Maggie loved the feel of him moving inside her, filling her up, his strong arms supporting her in the water. As his tempo gradually increased, she closed her eyes, laying back her head in the water. She could feel her hair floating like a halo around her head. Her ears filled with water and the bubbles crept up, over her face, splashing her nose and mouth.

She sensed the moment that Brett reached the point of no return and she opened her eyes. He was staring straight at her, his mouth set in a grim line. Gathering together all his will power, he waited until the deep ripples of delight had begun to course through her body before allowing himself to join her. They both reached the peak together, clinging to each other as each was overcome and they sank, slowly, into the warm water.

Maggie held her breath, holding tightly to Brett's reassuringly bulky shoulders as they resurfaced. He lifted her up, away from the foam and she felt the water course down her face and drip off the ends of her hair.

'I think we'd better get out of here before we drown in this stuff!' he murmured against her ear.

Maggie laughed.

'OK, can you reach that switch?'

He looked in the direction in which she was pointing and waded over to it. Immediately, the bubbles stopped and the foam which had been stirred up by the activity in the water began to pop and hiss.

As they both climbed out of the pool, they were covered in foam. Laughing, Maggie handed Brett a large, white towel before rubbing herself down with an identical one.

'Allow me.'

Brett took the towel from her and began to pat her shoulders gently. He had wound his own towel around his waist. Maggie sighed as he began to blot the water running in rivulets between her breasts, obligingly shifting her weight so that he could press the soft towelling against her streaming sex.

When he had finished, Brett wrapped the towel under her arms, sarong style, pulling her to him as he tucked it in. His kiss was warm, friendly even, and Maggie returned it in full measure. She felt pleasantly tired and leant against him, grateful for his strength. 'Shall we go back to my office?' she whispered.

He nodded and they meandered slowly through the foam-filled room to the relative normality of the office beyond.

Eye of the Storm

Georgina Brown

In Georgina Brown's *Eye of the Storm*, Antonia Yardley discovers that the globe-trotting bachelor with whom she is in a long-term relationship is in fact a married man. She can barely contain her rage and disappointment. Seething with the anger of the deceived, she runs away to sea, having accepted a crewing job on a yacht. Her employers include Emira, who isn't all she seems, and the handsome and wealthy Philippe Salvatore. The vessel is in constant turmoil as rivalry, family feuding and bizarre sex parties interfere with what should be a smooth-running craft. This extract is from Toni's arrival at the airport, where she meets the beautiful and beguiling Emira for the first time.

Georgina loves writing contemporary erotic stories and her other Black Lace novels are *The Stallion* and *Runners and Riders* – both set in the competitive and kinky world of British showjumping.

Eye of the Storm

*I*n Rome, the sky was grey and slanting rain drummed against the steamy windows that enclosed the warmth of the airport arrivals lounge. Today, Italy, that supposedly warm, inviting place full of sunshine, was sticky, a little off-colour and very noisy.

Through the double doors that opened and closed between her and the Eternal City, Antonia Yardley caught the whiff of petrol fumes, and heard the honking of a thousand car horns, the animated shouts of baggage handlers, taxi drivers and irate mammas with screaming children. Rome, she decided, held no attraction for her. Too busy, too noisy and very wet.

Once her baggage was safely beside her, she eyed the bustling crowd for the promised courier. It seemed a pointless task really, considering he would know her name and had a vague description of what she looked like. She, on the other hand, would not know him.

The fact that she was waiting and looked as though she was waiting deterred those who believed she might be lost and alone and therefore easy pickings. All the same, it did not deter the admiring glances or the suggestive words that a few more determined souls threw her way.

So she waited patiently and passed the time thinking first about Julian, his good looks and his wife. She also thought about his inhibitions: the way he automatically adopted the missionary position, and always in bed.

The inhibitions were not hers, she was sure of that. Much as

147

she had loved him, she had also harboured a yearning for more adventurous sex, and more exciting places in which to have it.

Everything that had happened, like his wife coming to see her, had happened for a reason. She convinced herself of that. It only needed the merest spark from a kindred spirit for her to prove it.

Then she thought about adventure. This was the first step to a new life, and she would allow nothing to spoil it, including regretful memories.

Thinking made time fly. Before long, a message in English came over the loud-speaker that told her to go to the Inland Carriers desk. Coat over one arm, suitcase handle digging into her fingers and her shoulder sloping to one side, she did as requested.

Beneath the sign for Inland Carriers, was a very tall woman wearing a very smart navy uniform. She was rangy, her shoulders broad, her hips narrow. Her skin was as brown as a conker, her eyes and hair very dark. She was beautiful in a strangely exotic way: her nose straight and slightly hooked, her cheekbones high as though carved from solid mahogany. Full and sensuous lips, the kind only seen on the most rare and prized African carvings, smiled politely at her. Her eyes seemed suddenly to dance as though they had just been waiting for the right moment, the right note.

She held out her hand, palm white, skin glistening. Toni took it. It was cool, soft yet oddly firm.

'Antonia Yardley? My name is Emira. I work for the Salvatore family. I will be taking you to Mister Salvatore's private island and his yacht, *Sea Witch*. We will be travelling in the Salvatores' private jet. Your interview will take place promptly. It is now one o'clock. Can I suggest we proceed without delay?'

Toni looked at the woman in surprise. Back in England, the voice that had asked her about her hair, her eyes and her experience had been dark brown and, she had believed, definitely masculine. Not for a moment had she expected it to belong to a woman.

She barely had time to smile, and only vaguely managed to confirm that she was indeed Antonia Yardley who had been sailing yachts since she was about twelve years old. Emira left her breathless. Without asking if she needed help, Emira took her case from her aching fingers, lifting it as though it only held a quarter of the clothes that bulged against its sides.

'Come along, please,' she said in a no-nonsense way. 'I have a take-off slot already booked. I must not miss it.'

Abruptly, she turned and marched off. Toni followed, half-running, half-skipping to keep up with her.

The Lear jet was emblazoned on the outside with a snaking S in a vibrant red script. Once inside, Emira ushered Toni to a seat. 'I think this one will suit you. You don't mind sitting by the window, do you?' Emira smiled without showing her teeth as she asked.

'No, not at all.' Toni was filling up with excitement. She was also aware that Emira seemed more relaxed than she had been at first, as if the jet was an oasis amid the hustle and bustle of the rain-soaked city.

'Unless *you* want to sit here,' she added. 'I don't mind sitting elsewhere.' She smiled herself, thinking her offer might help her gain Emira's friendship. Loneliness was something she no longer wanted to experience, regardless of any man. Friends were something that had been sadly lacking in the last few months.

Emira still smiled in that Mona Lisa way, though her eyes flashed with amusement. 'I do not think so,' she said, her voice as thick as honey and tinged with an accent Toni couldn't quite place. 'Somebody has got to fly this bloody thing!'

'You're the pilot?' Suddenly Toni felt a fool, but then, how was she to know that this incredibly sophisticated woman who moved with outstanding grace could also fly a modern jet? 'I'm sorry. I didn't realise.'

'Do not be.'

As she spoke, Emira leant over her and her long fingers reached out to check her seatbelt. A mix of heady perfumes escaped from her hair and her flesh as she came close. Toni breathed in the rich mixture, aware of the fragrance of her hair near her face, her anointed body near her own. Something tangible about that smell would not go away. It loitered in Toni's mind like half-remembered memories, and spread eerie tremors of excitement throughout her body. What was there in this woman's perfume that could arouse such feelings more commonly reserved for a man?

She was aware of a tightening in her stomach muscles and a tingling in that moist valley at the top of her thighs. Such feelings, such erotic tremblings, quelled any resistance to what happened next.

Almost casually, Emira's long fingers, with their red-painted nails, strayed across her vision to her breasts. She watched, mesmerised, unable to do anything. The fingers, flexible beyond belief, traced the curving outline of her flesh through the crispness of her cotton tunic blouse. This, she knew, was no accidental touch.

Emira's lips moved inexplicably as though she were hungry and contemplating eating something. They opened and she spoke. 'You have a firm bosom. They are a very good shape. I would like a bosom like that. It is so unfair that I do not.' She said it very thoughtfully, turning her head to one side as though contemplating swapping what she had for those of her passenger. Her very dark eyelashes swept across her high cheekbones. Toni felt the warmth of her breath; the sweet honeydew freshness of it coupled with the perfume and that special something else that aroused rather than repelled her.

It was a strange feeling to watch Emira's face and feel her fingers running over her breasts. There was admiration in her eyes, even desire. Toni's own breathing increased and she half-closed her eyes. A small moan escaped her throat, but she did manage to speak and remind herself that this was a woman.

'Thank you. That's very kind of you to say so.' She said it all in a rushed breath.

'See,' said Emira suddenly. 'Feel your own breast, then feel mine.'

Aroused feelings replaced any inhibition Toni might previously have felt. At first, her own hand moving inside her own blouse and covering her own breast felt uncannily alien. But the feeling did not last. Her flesh felt pleasant beneath her fingertips – like satin. And cool, firm, perfectly formed. How strange it felt, and how exciting that her hand covered one breast, and Emira's covered the other.

She looked into Emira's big, dark eyes, studying the beautiful face that was so squarely cut, so sharply defined, yet so incredibly beautiful. Black liner edged the dark eyes, a blush of rose rouge adorned the strong cheekbones, and lipstick the colour of ripe plums coated the plush richness of her lips. She saw a pink tongue flick out from between those lips. Almost as if she'd been willed to do so, she found herself imitating the same action.

'Now,' said Emira, 'feel my breast.'

Slowly, Toni unfurled her fingers, reached out her hand, and felt the hard thrust of Emira's breast through the clean-cut lines of her jacket. The jacket itself had a cool sharpness about it. The style and cut looked to be nothing less than Armani.

Toni's own hand was still on her own breast. So was one of Emira's. There was a contrast between the feel of each woman's breast: Toni's was firm, Emira's had a hardness about it she could not describe.

For a moment, her fingers hesitated as she considered the difference.

'What's the matter?' asked Emira. 'Haven't you ever seen or felt transplants before?'

Surprised by her open declaration, Toni stared, then shook her head. 'No,' she said, and tried to smile. 'I haven't.'

With a widening smile and the unbuttoning of her jacket and silk blouse, Emira firmly guided Toni's hand inside the lace that spanned her breasts.

Toni gasped as her fingertips gently touched the firm brown flesh. She shivered, wanted more; not just because she was curious, but because she was aroused.

'It feels – very good,' she said. Thoughtfully, she paused as she searched for the right words. 'Quite incredible.'

Emira's smile was big and brazen. 'Do you mean it?' she asked in that nut-brown voice of hers.

'Honestly,' replied Toni. 'I mean it. I'm sure there's nothing else like them.'

Suddenly, Emira threw back her head and laughed long and loud. She only stopped when she saw Toni staring at her Adam's apple which was cruising rapidly up and down her throat.

A little perturbed by Emira's laugh, Toni concentrated on Emira's bosom. With the hardening of Emira's nipple between her finger and thumb, a wetness invaded Toni's thighs and any words she might have wanted to say seemed to stick in her throat.

Emira's own hand eclipsed the breast that was not covered. Now each of them held one of their own breasts, and one of each other's.

Emira's nipples stood purple and proud from between one set of white fingers, and one set of dark brown. The top few buttons on Toni's shirt were undone, and her own nipples showed pink from between a matching set of fingers.

'Does that feel good?' Emira asked.

'Very good,' Toni replied. 'Very good indeed.'

'Taste them,' said Emira. 'Go on. Taste them.'

It might have been an order or it might have been an invitation, but whatever it was, the sensations running through Toni's body urged her to respond. 'I've never done this before,' she said softly. But her eyes were fixed on Emira's nipples, and her mouth was open and moving forward.

'Then now is the time to try it,' said Emira. Her teeth flashed like polished ivory against the deep purple of her lips.

'I will,' murmured Toni. 'I most certainly will.'

Memories of London fell away from her the moment that her lips encompassed the rose-like nubs. She sucked the first one into her mouth as her other hand moved to Emira's twin breast.

As she sucked and nibbled, her own arousal was heightened, invigorated by the heady scents of Emira's body: that odd mix of exotic perfumes, and that intangible something that was there, smelt, yet not quite recognised.

Dark lashes closed over her own green eyes. Red hair escaped from the black velvet band that held it at the nape of her neck. In her mind, she was falling, flying away from everything, from Rome and from herself. She was stepping into uncharted territory, and, so far, she was enjoying the experience.

'That's it, my darling Antonia. Keep sucking my breasts. Play with them for all you are worth, and I will make you remember this moment, this first time.'

Engrossed in the feel of the breasts against her face, in her hands, and in her mouth, Toni was only vaguely aware of the fingers unfastening her waistband, of the sound of her zip being undone. She felt the long fingers slide down inside her white lace underwear, felt the nails catch in her pubic hair as they travelled further and divided her lips.

She opened her legs, and moaned in gratitude as Emira's fingers slid over and around her most passionate bud and its surrounding petals of sensitive flesh. Slippery with juices, her sex opened wider to accommodate the advancing fingers that slid onwards to her most secret portal. They slid in, and as they did so, Emira's other hand held Toni's head more tightly against the hard round breasts.

Toni was smothered by them, enveloped in their warmth and their scent. Her tongue explored the silky skin, her teeth nibbled the hard nipples. Her own breath was hot and quick against the dark flesh, and her moans were lost in ecstasy as Emira's fingers withdrew from her vagina and concentrated on her swollen clitoris.

At first, each of Emira's fingers tapped at it before just finger and thumb tightened, rolled, tapped, touched and dug. She could not move from where she was. Her head was held tight against Emira's breasts. Yet she did not want to move. She was lost in her own ecstasy, her new adventure.

Soon, her thighs trembled. Her hips rose, again and again and again, until she was bucking hard against the hand and the knowing fingers. Holding it firmly in her hand, Toni held Emira's breast tightly against her mouth. She gripped the other breast with her free hand until spasm upon spasm of climax washed over her in diminishing waves. One wave of sensation followed another, until the latter spasms were nothing more than mere echoes of the first, the second and the third.

Emira was smiling when at last Toni opened her eyes. She smiled back, and knew her eyes must be sparkling. A new awareness made her flesh tingle. Something had erupted deep inside: it had been dormant, but now it had come to the surface. She was beginning a new chapter in her life, a more lively one than the episodes that had gone before.

'That was incredible,' she said breathlessly as she tossed her wild hair away from her face. 'I never knew it could be like that with a woman. I've never done anything like it before.'

There was a hint of mockery in Emira's smile that Toni could not understand, so she ignored it. 'Well, you have now, my darling,' said Emira, before kissing her on the lips. They tasted like honey. Her smell dominated Toni's senses and she could not help but respond. She felt grateful, and she had a need for more exploration. More adventure. She sighed and ran her hands down Emira's body. To her surprise, Emira caught her hands before they got below waist-level. 'Later,' she said in a strangely conspiratorial tone. 'There is time for that later.'

Toni frowned at the tightness of Emira's hands around her wrists. She clenched her fists and tried not to sound childish as she spoke. 'I thought you might need it too.'

'Not as much as you evidently did,' Emira returned as she

stroked Toni's Titian-red hair away from her face. 'Care to tell me about it?'

It hadn't occurred to Toni to tell anyone about it, certainly not until she had had time to completely banish Julian and her own stupidity to the past. After all, it was early days yet and time would make things easier and make her feel less stupid.

But there was something in Emira's eyes and the soft, deepness of her voice that gave her comfort and trust. So she told her. 'What an idiot I was,' said Toni, when she'd finished recounting her sad tale. 'What a stupid little cow!'

'Yes,' said Emira, with a laugh. 'Yes. You certainly were. But now,' she said, her long fingers caressing Toni's face, 'everything will be different. There will be adventure, Antonia Yardley. There will be many adventures and new experiences before your time here is through.'

Again, she caressed Toni's hair, and as she did so, pulled the velvet band from her head so that her hair fell to her shoulders. As one hand slid the band into the pocket of her jacket, Emira refastened the pearl buttons of her own so white, so silky shirt.

'I hope there will be. I really do,' murmured Toni, her voice sparkling like her eyes.

Emira looked into those eyes that were so green and so bright. She reached out and touched the hair that was as red as sunset. Antonia Yardley was everything she had said she was, and that was enormously pleasing.

Emira stood up and ran her hands over her own breasts and down over her stomach. With a wry and secret look on her face, she patted her palm against her crotch and murmured something that Toni could not catch. Then she went, and before long, the hustle and bustle, rain and honking car horns of Rome were behind them and the plane was slicing through the clouds.

Soon the marbled grey of the sky turned to clear blue. From the window, Toni looked down on the sea which looked no more than a reflection of the sky. Sunlight kissed her face as the plane banked and turned towards the island of the mysterious Madame and Mister Salvatore.

From where she was, it appeared that his island was really a group of islands; four or five in fact. They were small, with only five miles or so between each one. They were yellow, except for dotted greenery and the sprawling expanse of whiteness which she assumed to be buildings.

She pushed her breasts back inside her shirt that had started out so crisp and was now slightly crumpled. Thoughtfully, she ran her own hand over her golden-haired sex and briefly touched her clitoris with the tip of one finger. It was still tingling from her recent climax. Soon, it would lose that last tingle, and again it would be as ready for adventure and new experiences as she was.

As though it were a hidden treasure, she smiled down at her crotch, did up her zip, and waited to land on Philippe Salvatore's private island.

They landed at Melita's private airport where a car awaited them. The car was black, sleek as a panther, and shiny as a newly minted coin. It had cost big money, Toni thought to herself, and was as much a statement as a mode of transport.

Silent and as solid as a colossus, the driver held open the car door for her. He was a thick-set man with broad shoulders and a shaved head, a gold ring in one ear and a scar down his right cheek. His skin was the colour of cast bronze. Although it glistened with sweat, he still had the appearance of being made of metal.

Intrigued, Toni eyed him. Like Emira, he was unusual, even exotic. She thanked him before she slid into the back seat of the car, then let her eyes run downwards from his immobile face and over his wide chest and thick thighs. His whole body seemed to be bulging in protest against the cut of his white jacket and the pencil-sharp seams of his linen trousers. Her look was provocative. She knew it was, and felt a delicious thrill that she could get away with looking at him like that.

Julian would not have approved. But Julian was behind her. She was in a new place with, hopefully, a new job in the offing and, if recent experiences were anything to go by, she could indulge herself.

Anyway, the man gave no indication that he had heard her speak or seen her brazen gaze. He did not blink. Did not move. But just for a moment, she fancied his eyes had stayed with her. It was brief, half-imagined perhaps, but she thought she saw a glint in his eyes and a swelling in his trousers. Both disappeared once Emira came into view.

Now higher in the cloudless sky, the sun was getting hotter.

The car smelt of warm leather, and she could feel it through her clothes.

Emira's shadow cooled her body as she slid in beside her.

'Welcome to Melita.'

There was sincere warmth in Emira's voice, and even more in the lips that kissed her cheek. Her smile was wide and obviously welcoming.

Toni responded with reciprocal warmth and an excited smile. 'I'm glad to be here. Very glad.' She meant it. She really did. She carried on expressing what she truly felt. 'I was trapped, and now I'm free.' She filled her lungs with the sea-fresh air that wafted into the car, and looked out at the passing white and yellow of the landscape, the odd clutch of greenery, the black-clothed men working in the fields. Her hair blew freely around her face. 'I will never allow myself to be trapped again,' she said in a voice that rose little above a whisper. 'Never!'

Because she was looking out of the window, she didn't see Emira's frown, couldn't know how Emira was trying to discern exactly what she meant by 'trap'. She only saw the passing scene, the blue sky, the patches of gold sunlight and black shadows thrown by square houses and conical trees. Emira was interested in this young woman, not just because she was beautiful, but also because of what she might achieve.

She reached out and gently touched Toni's shoulder. 'Let me see your breasts again.'

Surprised from her daydreaming and sightseeing, Toni turned to look at her. Just doing that reawakened the sublime sensations she had experienced earlier. What was it about Emira's looks, her presence, and that more subtle scent beneath the expensively glorious perfume she wore?

For a moment, Toni did not answer, though her lips were half-open, and her breathing quickened as her mind and body responded. But that something she sensed in Emira got through to her and took her over. With slow deliberation, and still not quite knowing why she did it, she undid the top buttons of her shirt.

Without waiting for further invitation, Emira's fingers slid up beneath Toni's shirt and caused her breath to flutter in her throat. Not with uncertainty; more with apprehension. Eyes glinting beneath half-closed lids, she moaned as she lay against the warmth of the car seat.

Like a woman drowning, a certain light-headedness erased any inhibitions she might have felt about what this woman was doing. Instead of protesting, she moaned and shivered as the advancing fingers ran over her skin and gently caressed the lower outline of her right breast.

Her breasts were firm and stood proud of their own accord. It was rare for her to wear a bra and, even when she did, it was worn more as a pretty lace garnish than for necessity. As a result of Emira's earlier caresses, her nipples strained outwards pressing against the crisp cotton she was wearing. Once they were exposed, they grew to even more fruitful proportions.

Toni was all desire, all listless feelings of wanting to drown in the touch of Emira's hands. But her attention was suddenly drawn to the black eyes watching her via the car's rear-view mirror. The driver was of necessity paying attention to the road. But he was also watching her.

'But what about him?' asked Toni. She nodded in the direction of the broad-shouldered man who sat on the other side of a sheet of clear glass.

'Does it worry you?' asked Emira, her eyebrows arching high on her forehead, her voice flowing in a long and sluggish way.

Toni's green eyes met Emira's bitter chocolate ones. In one way, she thought, they were a mirror image of each other. Both women had eyes that looked as though they were outlined in black, as though some artist had decided to accentuate the feature. Such eyes could haunt a man's dreams, could follow you round a room. That was where all similarity ended: Emira was the reflection in a dark mirror, Toni's was that in a lighter one.

Toni looked from Emira's dark eyes to the jet-black ones of the man driving. Poor man, she thought. He could only give her body *some* of his attention. Emira gave all of hers.

'No. It doesn't worry me,' she said. Serenely, she smiled as she pulled her shirt away from her breasts. To tease him more, she arched her back away from the warmth of the seat so that her breasts thrust forward before Emira's hands covered them.

'Let him look,' breathed Toni, her green eyes half-closed and her breath quickening, 'Let him see what he can't have.'

She writhed and moaned and closed her eyes completely as Emira's fingers squeezed and tapped at her nipples. Her palms covered, then cupped her breasts as if assessing their worth.

All the time, she was aware of the driver watching, his face immobile, his eyes darting like a panther's. She enjoyed that, enjoyed the feeling of power it gave her; the power to tantalise, to tease. There was an other-worldliness about this whole episode, almost as though she were standing apart from it and the exploring fingers were cool and arousing on someone else's body and not her own. It was like she was only watching, but unlike him she could feel the thrill of sexual desire emanate from those fingers.

Emira kissed each swollen nipple before bringing her face close to Toni's own, her breath mingling with hers, hot and rapidly intense.

'Are you enjoying this, my darling? Are you enjoying what I am doing to you? Do you like Emilio watching what I am doing to you?'

'Yee-es.' Her reply was a long hush of a drawn-out sigh, as much half-said as her eyes were half-closed. Like them, she was only partly aware of the outer world, yet slave to the inner world.

The long fingers of the hand that had caressed her breasts now cupped her face. Despite the heat, Emira's fingers were still cool, smooth yet strong.

As the gap between their lips lessened, their breath mingled, a sweet and spicy perfume in the air between them. Eyes met eyes. Emira's lips met hers, and the warm wetness of her tongue stabbed against Toni's teeth.

Unable to resist, she gave it entry, sucked on it, and raised her own to meet it. Emira took hold of her hands, raised them and spread her arms along the back of the car seat. Her fingers tightened around her wrists and her lips pressed more firmly, more determinedly on Toni's mouth.

Then Emira's lips left hers, but her face was still close, her breath still sweetly near. She smiled and her teeth flashed white. 'My dear,' she said in that deep-sea voice. 'You did say you wanted adventure, and in the service of Madame Salvatore and your duties for her son, it is adventure you shall have. This,' she said, nodding towards the driver, 'is your first adventure. By virtue of this first adventure, you will gain entry to many more. Tread where you have not been before, my dear Antonia, enjoy what you have never tasted. The sweet fruits of your own sexuality will wither and wilt if you leave them hanging on the tree. Pluck that sexuality. Lick, nibble and bite it; eat it whole until you are satiated, until your appetite is in tune with its many flavours, its many diversities.'

'Yee-es.' Toni's reply was as lost on her breath as before. Her eyes sparkled like jade and the world and her surroundings seemed to disappear as she looked into Emira's eyes. In those eyes, she felt she was melting.

Was it the smell of this strange woman, or was it her honeyed words that made her feel she was swimming in the warmest of waters and could only go on, go forward and believe everything she said? The question was unanswerable, but the heat of her own arousal was hot in her veins yet tingling like dry ice all over her body.

A fire burned in her loins. Her legs opened in response. She could do no more than obey. No, not obey – go with the flow; enter the adventure.

Beyond control, her breasts rose and fell as her ardour and breathing quickened. Her flesh tingled in response to the exploring fingers. Emira's touch was languorous, her fingers soft and cool.

Toni glanced towards the eyes of the driver. He was still watching intently, his eyes glowing with excitement. In that split second, she felt desire and power all rolled into one. She wanted this man who watched to respond to her body, yet not touch it. She wanted him to desire, to feel his pulse quickening, his cock hardening as he drove and watched, but did not have. Just as Emira had suggested, she was entering adventure, truly savouring the first bite of the apple. She was enjoying, and this man was watching.

And how deliciously did Emira play with her breasts, the path of her fingers leaving tingles of anticipation in their wake.

Toni closed her eyes and savoured the rapture, the sheer ecstasy of her sensations. When she opened them, Emira's gaze was fixed on the breasts she was kneading beneath the firmness of her soft palms.

Her own desires put words in her mouth, on her tongue. 'Kiss them,' she pleaded. 'Please kiss them.'

Emira's eyes met hers before she licked her generous lips, opened her mouth, then bent her head.

Toni moaned long and deep, her eyes closing as she savoured the effect of the long tongue that flicked over each hard nipple.

Moans of pleasure deepened as the licking ceased and her nipples were sucked into Emira's generous mouth. She flexed her fingers, wanting to hug Emira to her. But her wrists were held tightly against the back of the seat. Emira was in control, and Toni was enjoying it.

Dark hair brushed roughly against her collar-bone, its smell sweet, its texture as black and soft as velvet. But it was her warm lips and tongue that made Toni moan. Her nipples stretched to the point of pain as Emira sucked each of them into her mouth in turn. With her teeth, she held them there, nibbling them at their root and tip whilst her tongue probed and circled again and again and again, until Toni felt she could scream.

All the time, when driving allowed, the man whose skin glistened like metal eyed the action in his mirrors. But he was forgotten. This pleasure of being done to – of being watched – was Toni's alone. Her breasts ached from Emira's treatment of them. Her sex was damp again, but this time there was to be no satisfaction.

The car came to a standstill, and Emira kissed her breasts one last time before she released them and her wrists and sat bolt upright.

'We are here,' she said in a brisk and businesslike fashion, and reached for the car door.

'That's a shame. A little more time would have been very useful,' said Toni as she re-buttoned her blouse. Emira's hand covered hers. 'Adventure, Toni. Remember, you have come here for adventure, for more bites of the fruit of passion. You have plenty of time for more. Plenty of days to enjoy many new experiences, many new adventures.

Toni slid across the seat after her.

The sun was bright yellow amidst a clear blue sky. The air was warm, and feeling its warmth on her body gave birth to sensations she could not describe. She was happy, and that was enough.

Full of new confidence, she slid across the car seat. The driver held the car door open; as she got out, she glanced up at his face.

He did not return her glance. He looked beyond her, over her head to some point near the rocky headland where white-crested waves smashed against jagged rocks. She smiled smugly to herself. This, she decided, was fun. For once, she had enjoyed herself at the expense of a man. It made a very nice change.

The sun hit her body and her eyes. Even though it was only spring, its warmth gave a taste of what was to come. She squinted and looked about her. This was the private quay where Mister Salvatore kept his yacht. From the quay, white marble steps rose to an expansive sun terrace on which she could just see the tips of waving palms, the legs of tables and sun loungers. The perfume of spring flowers mingled with the smell of the sea. She heard the splash of someone diving into a pool and the rattle and clink of ice against glass. Beyond the terrace were the white balconies and façade of the main house; a villa in true Mediterranean style, shining white as a wedding cake in the sun, its balconies shaded and facing seawards. Just like them, she turned her gaze to the water.

Bobbing gently at anchor, the water throwing diamonds of moving sunlight against its sides, a yacht was moored. This was the yacht she had come to crew. Its sheer symmetry of design and pure elegance took her breath away. She could not help but be impressed.

Sea Witch was ketch-rigged and eighty feet or more from stem to stern. Her whiteness shone like glass in the climbing warmth of the sun, and her rigging tinkled like bells in the soft breeze that blew up from the Sahara.

Admiring the trim lines of the long, white yacht, Emira reminded Toni why she was there.

'Come. You need to freshen up and rest before your interview with Madame Salvatore.'

'Will I have time?' she asked, after glancing at her watch. It was almost three and she was impatient. 'When will I meet Mister Salvatore?'

'Your interview will be soon enough. First, I will evaluate you myself. Only when I am satisfied that you are suitable will you meet Madame Salvatore, and only when she is satisfied, will you meet her son.'

'What about my luggage?' she called out, and turned back to the quay. The driver, who had his back turned to her, was handing her luggage to two young men with blonde hair, bronze skin and uniforms that were white and smacked of navy smartness and navy discipline.

Politely, and in perfect time one with the other, they turned and smiled at her. 'After you,' said one.

She thanked them, smiled at them both, and both smiled back.

She saw admiration in their eyes, a desire to please, but also a desire to savour.

Not only were these young men worth more than a second look, but the way they were dressed caused her to stare longer than she should have; she tripped over a piece of anchor chain. Only Emira's quick action saved her from falling. Emira's hands were strong. Her smile was almost mocking.

'Easy does it, my dear Antonia,' she said with a knowing look towards the bronze young men. 'All appetites must be controlled, even the most hungry. One bite at a time, my sweet lady, one bite at a time.'

It was noticeable that Emira's voice was deeper than it had been earlier. Even then it had been deep enough. Something about its sound echoed the smell that Toni had found so intriguing when they had first come close.

On board, Emira turned and waited for Toni and the two young men to come to her side.

'Antonia. This is Mark. This is Martin.'

The two young men nodded and smiled. 'Pleased to meet you,' they each said. 'Welcome aboard.'

Toni's breasts rose with her sigh of pleasure, and her hair caught in the breeze as she responded. 'Nice to be here,' she said, and meant it.

'Take Antonia to her cabin. She has a need,' said Emira, her lush lips smiling suggestively. 'Make sure that need is fulfilled – within reason.'

The two young men, who now held only Toni's coat and over-stuffed suitcase, saluted smartly.

Their smiles were wide, teeth white, their skin a well-weathered bronze. Their blonde hair curled over the crisp neat collars of their white shirts. The effect of their appearance was vaguely naval and tropical, except that, as this was a sailing yacht and agility was needed, they wore white trousers made of some stretchy material which accentuated the muscles of their thighs and calves. It also accentuated the rising bulges that pressed against the square naval flap where trouser flies would normally be. Their deck shoes were white too. The only relief to the whiteness was the red insignia of the snaking 'S' on the epaulettes of their shirts, the gold trim in two stripes along them, and the brass buttons that ran from the deep 'V' of their open necks to the gold-braided belts around their waists.

The whiteness of their uniforms and the tawny healthiness of their skins was further relieved by the gold bands around their wrists and matching chokers around their necks which drew attention to their handsome faces. A few links of loose chain hung from the glistening bands and nestled in the groove of their collar-bones. A few also fell from their bracelets and tinkled like laughter when they moved.

There was no mistaking what the bracelets and necklets were made of. They could only be gold.

'I am glad to be back, but I am very tired, my darlings,' Emira said. 'I will go and take a bath and then lie down. I will see you all later.'

Below decks was cool and dark compared to the brilliance of the sunshine outside. For a moment, Antonia had trouble seeing until the sunspots before her eyes had disappeared.

Toni entered the cabin, followed by Mark and Martin.

Their presence and what they might have to offer were enough to dispel any insecurities Toni might have had. What they might have to offer was very much on her mind.

Even before she turned to face the two young men, an enticing and very masculine smell filled the whole cabin. It was an intoxicating mixture reminiscent of sea spray and indelible youth.

Mark put her luggage down, and Martin followed.

'Welcome aboard *Sea Witch*,' said Mark, whose eyes were brown. His smile was still bright, his teeth as white as his uniform. They were both handsome and almost a mirror image of each other except for their eyes.

Toni looked from Mark to Martin. She felt like a child in a sweet shop. Toffee fudge or coffee cream. What a choice!

'As I understand it, you are to take care of my needs – all my needs. Is that correct?'

Brown eyes looked to blue and back again to her. Their mouths smiled, their teeth sparkled. 'That's exactly right,' said Mark.

'Exactly,' echoed Martin.

'But we will help you unpack first,' said Mark.

'Be my guest.'

The door closed and the porthole was opened. A breeze carried in a hint of salt and fish and the screams of circling gulls.

No time was wasted in unpacking, though both Martin and Mark did take some time to lovingly finger her more beautiful bras, pants, stockings and lacy suspender belts before they put them carefully away.

She let her silk wrap fall like a wave on to her bed in a shock of azure blue. 'I'd like to take a shower now,' she pronounced, and raised her fingers to her shirt front.

'We'd like to help you.'

Just the sound of their voices and the look in their eyes was enough to make her tingle. She tried to speak, yet only little jerky noises escaped from her mouth. She made an effort to form them into words. 'I thought you might,' she said. Then she smiled. Slowly she began to unbutton her blouse. Again her breasts were free to the air and to someone else's sight. She let the blouse fall to the floor and tossed her fiery hair. She kept her head tilted backwards so that she could continue to feel her hair brushing against the small of her back. As she wetted her lips and made them glisten, she narrowed her eyes.

Ripples of pleasure made her body tingle. She tingled even more when she saw the tightening of their jaws, the glint in their eyes and the growing bulges in their trousers. Slowly, for their pleasure and her own, she cupped her breasts, and fingered her well-used and, by now, bright red nipples.

Martin and Mark did not wait for her to say anything else. Martin reached out and began to unfasten her faded but high-quality jeans. Mark went behind her and helped Martin pull them down to her ankles.

They ran their hands down over her hips, her thighs, her knees, her calves.

Above them, she moaned, reached down to touch the head in front of her and the head behind.

'No. Leave us to service you, to take care of your needs. Put your hands on your head. Relax,' ordered Martin.

'Leave it to us,' added Mark. 'We'll take care of you.'

Hesitantly, then decidedly, Toni did as ordered. Tremors of nagging desire began to re-stir throughout her body. In the mirror opposite, she saw herself, graceful arms raised, hands on head, breasts proudly thrusting forward. Her eyes sparkled, her mouth was slightly open, alive to quickening breath and quickening pulse.

Like a rich, red veil, her hair framed her creamy flesh. She was beautiful, an epitome of autumn, a fire goddess whose hair was of flame and whose eyes were made of emeralds. Classic and

Grecian, she thought to herself, sure of her beauty, her free-roaming sexuality.

But all the time, she could almost hear the pounding of her heart as two pairs of obviously male and powerful hands ran over her naked thighs, down her legs, and pulled off her jeans from around her ankles and her sandals from her feet.

She blinked, seeing the pinkness of her face in the mirror, and fingers other than her own hitching into the band of her underwear and pulling them slowly down over her hips.

Like a burst of flowers, her pubic hairs sprouted into view.

She felt a pair of hands run down over her behind and take each perfect orb in hand, divide them and run thumbs down in her most secret crease.

In the mirror she watched Martin's thumbs play over her pubic hair as his fingers pulled her knickers down further. Without urging, she opened her legs a little wider and gasped in sweet delight as his thumbs returned to pull aside her lips. She heard him gasp as her budding clitoris sprang from in between them.

Just as she had hoped – in fact, what she had always dreamed Julian would do – Martin dropped to his knees and pressed his mouth against her pussy.

His lips were firm and demanding. His tongue was wet, strong and gratifying. With strident flicks and probings, he divided those willing lips and licked her growing bud with loving abandonment. She moved slightly. Her legs opened more to give him that bit of extra room to manoeuvre so his tongue could journey more easily through the silky hair and the velvety folds of her labia.

So light and so gentle was his touch, she wanted to expose her rosebud to his tongue even more than if he had been forceful.

She moaned as she undulated against his mouth, burying his nose in her nest of hair. Behind her, she felt her buttocks being opened wider by forceful fingers and thumbs. Another tongue ran slow and wet down her glossy cleft and prodded at her tightest orifice.

Her first instinct was to clench her buttocks together. She resisted the urge, and caught the gasp of surprise in her throat. This tongue was not violent in its quest to enter the puckered opening of her anus: it was tentative, speculative even, as though it were politely asking whether she would accept his intrusion.

All tenseness in her buttocks vanished, and the sliding tongue invaded further. All virginity that area might have held dear was untouched no more.

The reflection in the mirror beckoned her eyes to look, to behold what was happening to her. There in its glassy gaze she could see herself, see these golden-haired men, one at the front, and one at the back, probing into her.

Like slaves, they knelt before and behind her. In the mirror, her body glistened and trembled with pleasure as she wove her pelvis forward to one man, and back to the other. It was hard not to moan, not to respond to their pleasure-giving. In time, that sweeping crescendo of orgasm would envelop her as if eating her whole. She let it rise, waited for it to take her. With the clearest detail, she imagined their hardness invading her hair-covered cleft, dividing it like the prow of a boat slicing through a wave.

Her orgasm was unrestrained and washed over her in a torrid and unstoppable wave. She moaned, writhing on the twin tongues that wrenched this climax from her. Through narrowed eyes, she saw herself come. Rapturous and undulating against these twin worshippers, she rode as though riding the waves.

Her hands were still on her head. She moved like a tree in a gale until the storm had passed, her climax over. The young men who had knelt around her thighs now got to their feet.

'It's time for your shower,' said Martin. Gently, he kissed her cheek.

Mark did the same before going to switch it on.

Toni, with breathless anticipation, eyed Martin's crotch for any sign of a rampant member rising against his so white trousers. There was none.

How could he be that controlled? she asked herself.

The question could not go unanswered. 'What about you? Don't you want to come, too?'

Martin smiled at her as though she were nothing more than a child. 'It's not part of my timetable for today.'

Mark joined him, and sorrowfully shook his head. 'Nor mine.'

Aware that her cheeks were turning pink, Toni looked from one to the other. Was she reading what they were saying correctly? 'Do you mean to say that you were ordered to do that? To bring me to climax, but not to climax yourself?'

There was no attempt to lie and spare her blushes. It was Mark who answered. 'We were. And a very nice task it was, too.'

'It was just to make sure that you really were suited to seek adventure. Emira ordered us to do it. Some people say it, but don't really mean it. They only think they do. You, I can see – we both can see – really *are* ready for adventure.'

Toni was speechless and still as pink-faced as before. On top of that, her mouth hung open. But she rallied. If the happening in the car with Emira was one adventure, and this was another, what others were in the offing, and would they all be just as pleasant, just as exciting?

It was Mark who spoke again, giving her what sounded like orders, but no clues. 'You'll be sent for later,' he said. 'Madame Salvatore wishes to see you personally. She wishes to explain the rules. Emira will come for you, tell you what to wear, what to expect.'

'But I thought I had to satisfy Emira's evaluation first?' she said.

Mark shrugged. There was a smile on his lips, almost, she thought, as though he was having a joke at her expense. 'I don't know anything about that. Ask Emira. Emira knows all the little secrets around here.'

She shrugged it off. Perhaps Emira didn't tell everybody everything.

'Your shower is ready for you now,' Martin added. 'You haven't got much time. We'll be sailing shortly. Your help up top would be appreciated. Wear your own clothes for now – until your employment is confirmed.'

'Right.' Her voice faded into disappointment as they opened the door to leave.

They left her there, though she had half-expected them to stay and help her wash and wipe herself dry. The door closed, she was alone, and the shower was running. Water is a precious commodity on any boat, so she did not let it go to waste.

The water washed away the smell of sex and male bodies, but it did nothing to quell her curiosity. It also did nothing to assuage the lingering sexual demand in her loins. Although recently satisfied, it was smouldering like a dormant volcano and would readily spring back to life given the right circumstances.

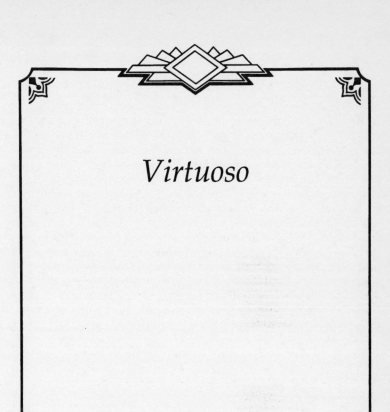

Virtuoso

Katrina Vincenzi

In Katrina Vincenzi's *Virtuoso*, Mika and Serena inhabit a world of secluded passion and privilege. Since Mika's tragic injury which halted his meteoric rise to fame as a solo violinist, he has become a recluse and cannot face the world which brought him the prestige he desired. Serena is a dedicated sensualist and is determined to change the situation. She misses the jet-set lifestyle they used to share. When she invites Franca, a young and talented musician, to meet with Mika, her intention is to rekindle his zest for love and life through unexpected means. This extract describes Franca's first meeting with the once virtuoso performer and explores the allegorical nature of music and lovemaking.

Katrina's other books for Black Lace are *Dream Lover* and *Odyssey*: both have contemporary settings and link the worlds of art and creativity with sexual sophistication and discovery.

Virtuoso

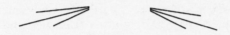

Mika had agreed to meet her. A car would be sent for her that evening. She would stay at the villa, for a few days at least. The woman's voice had been soft and smoky, but with a barely concealed edge to it. It was a voice accustomed to immediate acquiescence.

Franca glanced around the tiny room. She hadn't unpacked the night before, so there was little to be done. She dressed quickly: slim black trousers, a thin black silk sleeveless top and over-sized matching jacket and black leather boots. An indirect compliment to Mika, who always wore black, she knew how well it set off her pale skin and flaming hair. Taming her hair into a twist, she leant closer to the mirror.

Her eyes seemed huge, her skin too pale. She was nervous, she realised, as she carefully applied some mascara. She hadn't expected things to move this quickly and had been anticipating a few days alone in the village to get her bearings; prepare some version of herself that Mika would find desirable.

Sheer nerve and deliberate bravado had carried her thus far. Eve and Sally, the two scouts from Disc-O, had been easy enough to deal with, and she'd impressed Max Schiller, consciously and deliberately projecting a heated sensuality she was far from feeling. But Mika . . . Mika was a different story. And Serena, the dark-haired, voluptuous siren never far from his side. Everyone knew they were long-time lovers. How would she react to Franca's presence? Jealous? Suspicious?

She picked up a book and put it down; prowled over to the

window and gazed with unseeing eyes at the picturesque landscape; changed her clothes twice, once into a white cocktail dress
which she rapidly discarded, struck by a sudden and irrational
dislike for her legs, and then into a long skirt in dull purple. It
looked ugly and old-fashioned, and in despair she reverted to
her original choice. Eyeshadow might help.

A knock on the door interrupted her. Opening it, she discovered a tall, blond, bullish man in a uniform.

'I'm your driver, Sergei,' he said, entering the room before she
could say a word. 'Your bags?' gesturing to the cases on the bed,
but never taking his eyes from her body. She had the fleeting
impression that the room was suddenly smaller. Under his air of
deference, there was something . . . she shook her head.

'Yes, please, no, not that one, I'll take the violin myself,' she
managed to reply.

In the plush grey embrace of the limousine's luxurious uphol-
stery, she tried to relax, tried to summon the confident, assured,
even arrogant air that she had learnt to wear in the competitive,
cut-throat arena of the musical world. But she was conscious
only of a growing, thrilling anxiety mixed with budding excitement. At last, at long last, she was going to meet him.

Mika.

The superstar of the violin.

The sensual genius of the strings.

The teacher she craved. He would become her master, her
maestro, her conductor, would teach her how to summon the
passion from the strings that still eluded her.

'If you would care to follow me?' said Sergei. Engrossed in her
thoughts, she hadn't noticed that the car had stopped, that he'd
opened her door and was waiting for her to get out. She slid out,
looked around and received a confused impression of a massive,
brick-fronted exterior, soaring turrets, acres of velvety green
grass, and then she saw him.

He was standing in the curved archway, leaning nonchalantly
against a pillar, a massive yellow blur heaped on his shoulder
that, as she ascended the steps, resolved itself into the outlines
of a cat.

'Miss Tonelli.' He nodded a formal greeting, did not attempt
to take her hand. 'Sergei, thank you. Maddie has put her in the
Green Room. You'll take care of things?'

His voice was beautiful – a deep, rich baritone, clear and

beautifully modulated, like honey-coated crystal. It was a voice that could tempt saints to sin or lure sinners to virtue. She felt a sudden surge of pleasure at the sound and wondered, irrelevantly, if he knew the power of that voice, knew how it caressed the ears.

His physical presence was somehow shocking, like an unexpected blow. His face, familiar to her from countless album covers, was subtly different in person; the eyes deeper set, the mouth fuller, more sensual. And his eyes were more forceful by far, a blazing electric blue that seemed to pierce beneath one's skin and search through the skull beneath.

'I thought we should listen to you together,' he said, motioning her inside.

'Yes,' she said, swallowing quickly, grimly aware that she must have been staring. Wordlessly, she followed him into the huge entrance hall, heels clicking on the pale marble floor, eyes darting here and there to the carved Corinthian columns embedded in the walls, the huge chandelier, the spindly grace of stray chairs and tiny tables scattered at seemingly random intervals, the massive arrangements of cut flowers.

Opening a pair of huge carved double doors to one side of a spiralling staircase, he stepped aside, allowing her to enter. From the corner of one eye she saw a slim figure dressed in white lingering at the top of the stairs but, when she turned, it had vanished.

The room was huge, a shining expanse of marble interrupted by the jewel tones of scattered Persian rugs, antique glass-fronted cabinets containing leather cases, and a complicated sound system occupying one entire wall.

He walked over to it and inserted a CD. With a thrill of surprise and disquiet she recognised Mozart, the A major recording she had done for Deutsche Grammophon. She waited uncertainly, awkwardly, watching him as he stood motionless, listening to the music, caressing the cat who was fixing her with an evil, yellow stare.

She let the magic of Mozart calm her, mentally approving the purity of her sound in the first movement, appreciating the skill of the orchestra in developing the sonata-form movement in the second. Nerves tightening, she waited for the third ... Yes, here it was, *The Seraglio*. She'd never quite captured the exotic colouring demanded by the Turkish Allegro theme, never quite evoked the mysterious flavour of the East.

'You recorded that last year, I believe.'

'Yes,' she agreed, pleased to hear her voice was cool and clear.

He played it again. And again. And again. Time passed. When he finally spoke, his words surprised her.

'Come, let's have dinner. We'll be dining alone,' he said, stooping to drop the protesting cat to the floor and gesturing to her to follow him.

'Oh? But I thought perhaps Max and—' She stopped, halted by the force of a withering glance from those magnificent, electric-blue eyes.

Wordlessly she stood, then hastened to catch up with him, their footsteps echoing on the marble floor. Glancing at her watch, she was amazed to see that it was eight o'clock. So much seemed to have happened already. He made time somehow irrelevant, stretched it, compressed it, changed it.

Dinner was simple and beautifully prepared. A roast of lamb, delicately seasoned with fresh rosemary, new potatoes glistening with butter, and a fresh green salad followed by fruit and cheese. He spoke little, said nothing beyond the polite commonplaces of dining together, commenting on the wine, passing the bread and then, after a brief, disparaging remark about the local brandy, had fallen silent.

She was disappointed.

She found her eyes returning again and again to his hands. Encased in soft black leather, the fingers seemed long, shapely and elegant, offering no clue to the disabling injury that had forced his premature retirement.

He used his hands with the unconscious, precise grace of the true musician, idly balancing the heavy silver tableware as though testing the weight of a bow, skimming the faceted bowl of the crystal wineglass as thoughtfully as if it were the varnish of some priceless violin. With his thumb and forefinger he traced the crystal curves in a repeated caress, meeting the ruby level of the wine, then drifting down to the stem, again and again in an hypnotic, almost erotic appreciation of the fine contours of the glass.

He looked at her thoughtfully. Unaccustomed to the company of strangers, he was mildly surprised to find her an almost comfortable companion. Hers was not the sweet, sinuous silence of Serena, which accompanied him effortlessly, but still it seemed she had some appreciation of sound, didn't seek to clutter the air mindlessly.

Suddenly full, she toyed with the food on her plate, drank more wine, and was conscious of feeling lightheaded. A stray breeze stirred the candlelight, casting his face into sharp relief.

He watched her in the warm glow of the candles. Objectively he admired her face, the pale skin, the unusual, slanting eyebrows. She was beautiful, of course, but he had long ago become sated with beauty.

Idly he wondered about her life, the private, intimate, intrinsic details that could never have found their way into the potted biography prepared by Max's staff. And he wondered about Max and Serena, now dining alone in another part of the villa, the two arch mainipulators who had engineered this meeting. On second thoughts, he decided that he might possibly acquit Max.

Suddenly he felt sorry for this flame-haired girl, tool for so many ambitions. 'So they've brought you here to me, Miss Tonelli. You're a pawn, you know that? We both are. But you're the sacrifice to a dying god Serena will never let rest. Doesn't that trouble you?' he said.

For a moment she couldn't believe that she had heard him correctly, but the words refused to disappear. A sacrifice? A dying god? What melodrama was this?

'It's not a bad parallel,' he said calmly, as though reading her mind. 'But I forget, you don't know Serena. Have you ever considered the relationship between master and pupil?' he asked, apparently changing tack.

'Frequently,' she said, striving to remain as calm as he appeared. 'But I sometimes wonder if my teachers have. They have all been singularly stupid.' She stared at him challengingly, with a fair assumption of her usual arrogant bravado.

So, she was not a passive tool. Better that way. 'It rests on power,' he explained, ignoring her remark. 'But it rests on power that is not simply imposed. It must be a relationship in which the pupil is willing to trust the teacher's instinct, give him or herself over to the dominance of greater experience. It's a relationship like that between parent and child, but more intimate than that of lovers.' Across the table his eyes were fixed on hers. She felt drawn by them, unable to look away.

'If,' he paused then, drawing out the silence, 'if by some

chance you were to interest me sufficiently, I might be willing to teach you.' He heard himself say the words with some surprise. 'But you should understand the nature of the relationship. You would have to be willing to suspend your critical faculties at first, and obey me without question.'

He lounged back in his chair, sipped more wine, wondering whether he was actually contemplating teaching her or merely toying with the idea to please Serena. The Mozart, though, had moved him; gifted as she was, she had failed to etch *The Seraglio* with the sensuous, forbidden incense of the East. He knew how frustrating that could be.

'Read my reviews,' she challenged. 'Technically, I'm flawless. Your natural successor, the critics say. That should interest you, at least a little.'

To her surprise, he laughed. 'The critics say?' he mocked gently.

'Well, one critic,' she admitted. And he hadn't said exactly that.

'You are an innocent. That A major was played by a virginal talent. You're still playing the score, the notes – in an exceptionally brilliant way, I agree – but you are not a channel for the music,' replied Mika.

'Virginal,' she repeated, confused. 'What do you mean?'

'Music starts deep inside you. It's not governed by the mind, by slavish devotion to the score. It is a primitive, primal urge, or even instinct, deep in the bowels of your soul. From there it radiates out, expands to your heart, your breasts, down to your groin, encompasses your most sensual imaginings. You become the violin and it becomes you. It's a consummation.' He stopped then, aware he had come too close to revealing the secret that had fed his genius.

If she had spoken then, even a single word, he would have left the room, had her briskly and unceremoniously removed from the villa, wiped her from his memory.

But she said nothing, sat motionless, head bowed, slanting dark brows drawn together in thought.

When she finally lifted her head, her eyes were bright with unshed tears. 'It was the third movement, wasn't it?' she acknowledged softly.

He nodded, disarmed a little by her perception, disarmed by

the tears now coursing unheeded down her cheeks. She hardly seemed aware that she was crying.

Quietly he rose from his chair and stood behind her. 'An audition, perhaps,' he said softly, as though to himself. 'Why not? We'll test your instrument, see if it has any resonance at all. Put your hands on your breasts.'

'What?' she asked, startled, and felt his hands on her shoulders poised and waiting.

'Trust me. Do as I say.' The tone of command was unmistakable, edging the dark honey of his voice.

He demanded a willing submission to his dominance, a blind faith in his genius, obedience without question. She was intensely aware of the warmth of his hands through the supple black leather gloves; intensely aware of the hard column of his body standing behind her; could almost feel the electric waves of energy pulsing from him. To be so near to such musical genius, to find it allied with such a sensual presence, was intoxicating, and in that moment she knew this was a man who could do anything with her, that she would submit blindly to his voice, his hands.

'Yes,' she murmured, lifting her hands to her breasts, unsurprised to feel them trembling.

'Good,' he said more softly. 'You must be in tune with your body, in touch with your real instrument. Focus on the idea that your body is a violin, your fingers a bow. Every instrument has its vibrator and its resonator. The strings are the violin's vibrator. Make your nipples the strings of your body.' And so she brushed her hands against her nipples, feeling them tighten against the black silk.

'Good,' he approved. 'Brush them up and down, feel them.'

She felt the heat rising to her face; felt the tingling sensation that coursed from her fingers to her breasts; felt his hands gently cup the back of her neck, then search through her hair and come to rest at her temples.

'Don't stop until I tell you you may,' he said. 'Concentrate on your body.'

Closing her eyes she brushed her nipples with her thumb, up and down as he commanded, feeling the softness of the silk like an irritation. Sensitised to touch now, her nipples were erect, quivering with life. There was something profoundly erotic in touching herself, arousing herself as he stood behind her, his long fingers cradling her head.

He must be watching, seeing how her nipples were standing out firmly, confidently, challenging him to warm and suck them.

Standing behind her, he could feel the betraying pulse at her temples, sense her arousal.

'Tell me what you feel.'

'Heat,' she said softly. And she was hot, burning almost. The most delicious, searing heat, soaring through her body, knowing that he was watching her, his eyes fixed on her hands, her breasts.

'Harder,' he said. 'Pluck the string, pizzicato.'

Pizzicato. She tightened her fingers, pinching her nipples as firmly as if plucking the strings and felt the electric jolt ripple through her body, radiating from her breasts to her groin, thrilling her spine.

'Again,' he said, his hands moving gently to her shoulders. 'And again.'

Her nipples felt like twin circles of fire, hot and unbearably sensitive, her breasts heavy and swollen. Closing her eyes, she leant back in her chair, resting her head gently against his midriff. Through the silk, her nipples were distending, growing, and without his urging she pinched them harder, rolling them between her fingers. She felt the burgeoning moistness between her thighs, the swelling of her lower lips, the first, greedy stirrings of her clitoris. Caught in the sensations coursing through her, she twisted in the chair, would have turned to face him but he tightened his grip on her shoulders, forcing her to stay still.

'Tell me.'

'Still hot,' she murmured. 'But fuller now.'

'And wet?' he suggested, feathering her ear with his breath.

'Yes, wet.' She felt the lips between her legs growing warm and swollen, mimicking her nipples, the hot wet liquid of arousal bathing her groin.

'*Water Music*,' he said softly. 'Think of wet and water and the strings.' She felt his hands slip from her shoulders to cup the curve of her breasts, support the lush fullness that her fingers had plucked to swollen warmth.

'Arco,' he said softly, using the term that directs string players to resume the bow after a passage of pizzicato. 'Arco.'

Almost gratefully she slid her hands over his, relishing the supple coolness of the leather, relishing the sensation of both their hands enfolding her breasts.

'Now find the strings. Touch yourself wherever you feel the strings. Your body is the sound box. Make it vibrate.'

Caught by his voice, hypnotised by the flickering candles, her hands dawdled. And then she gasped as his gloved hands tightened just a fraction on her breasts, causing a frisson of shuddering delight.

'Your hand,' she whispered and then felt it trailing gently down to her belly. Her nerve endings tightened, rippled in an arpeggio of anticipation. She was harp now, as well as violin, meant to be plucked and played, and felt herself moisten, growing hotter and more liquid. Through the silk she felt the warmth of his gloved hand gently pressuring her pubic hair. She could feel the juice seeping out of her, knew that she was now not moist, not wet, but sopping, soaking the flimsy silk panties she wore. She was flooding in a blush-pink tide, flooding and flowing.

'Yes?' he prompted.

'Tides,' she said, the words coming from nowhere. She felt strangely disembodied, hazy, conscious now only of a slow burning sensation stealing over her body. Her breasts were full and hot, and she felt her clitoris stirring like some nipple wanting too to be fondled, plucked and sucked. Beneath the silk she was heating, perspiring, felt the drops trickling down her neck. The air was closer now, like velvet.

'Tell me,' he said, amused, and felt her push against his hand. Watching her from behind hooded eyes, he saw the flushed cheeks, her lashes fanning them, breasts rising and falling. Her ready passion surprised him. He meant only to test her a little, find her resonance, watch the flames lick like a slow movement and dry her tears, but already this girl was rushing to the edge.

Deliberately he slowed the movement of his hand and, extending a finger, felt for her clitoris through the silk, brushing gently, feather soft, searching between the folds of fabric to find the erect little core.

'Red. Red and silky and bitter, like roses and salt,' she murmured and felt his finger stiffen, press hard against her.

She'd used the very words he had used long ago to his women when his face was buried between their thighs, licking, sucking,

179

tasting and teasing. Salt and roses. Caught off guard, he felt himself stiffening.

'Enough,' he said abruptly, releasing her and turning away.

'But why ... what?' Confused, disorientated, she opened her eyes.

'Enough. You're losing the flow. Handel isn't roses, not the *Water Music* at any rate. Spring flowers, perhaps, but never roses.' He stood with his back to her, apparently intent on examining the painting on the wall in front of him.

Dumbly she stared at him, feeling the unfulfilled pulse between her legs like a second heartbeat, hearing his words as though from far away.

'So, have you learnt anything? One can learn even from an audition. Especially from an audition, in fact,' he said casually.

Frantically she cast her mind back, struggling to find something that made sense, words he'd said only moments before, struggling to subdue the aching void left by the imprint of his fingers. 'My body is the violin,' she said slowly.

'And your hands?'

She knew the answer he wanted; knew also it wasn't the right one. It had been his hands touching her, plucking her that became the bow; his hands that made her the violin.

'Hands are the bow,' she said, dissembling a little. He nodded, apparently satisfied.

'And Handel?'

She thought furiously. Handel's *Water Music*. Published 1740, probably composed for a royal trip on the Thames. What did it have to do with the receding tides of her body, that wet, hot flood denied release?

'Handel isn't roses,' she replied.

'Yes. I'll make my decision tonight. You should go to bed, get some sleep. You're in the Green Room at the top of the stairs. Ring for Maddie if you need anything.'

'But I—' she managed, but too late. He'd already gone. Unsteadily she rose to her feet, clutching the table for support. Her body felt disordered, confused. The waves of sensation that had washed through her so violently only moments before were slackening now, leaving her weary but elated.

Carefully she walked across the room into the hall, felt for the balustrade on the staircase, grateful for its support. Her room

180

seemed terribly far away. Finally she reached it, closed the door with trembling fingers and collapsed on the bed.

'Well?'

Surprisingly, Mika started at the sound of her voice. A few drops of Calvados marred the mahogany sideboard. He mopped them up, then finished pouring his drink. With a sigh, he selected another goblet.

'Drink, Serena?' he asked.

'I'd love one, darling. So?' Her voice rose invitingly.

Deliberately he kept his back to her, pouring out the Calvados with the concentration of a scientist mixing a particularly difficult formula.

From the buttery depths of the leather sofa, she smiled to herself. 'So?' she repeated.

'Serena.' Her name was enough to calm him. He repeated it softly under his breath. The disquiet that had flooded through him at his body's unexpected response was receding. 'Serena . . . perhaps you were right.'

'Of course I was, my love. Why are you surprised?' Some basic instinct cautioned her against pressing for the details she was dying to learn. She would find out in her own time, in her own way.

'She's locked much of it away,' he mused. 'You can sense it suppressed in the A major. But she can respond. You must listen to the CD.'

'I will,' Serena answered, a smile hovering on her lips. 'But do you have any plan, any theme?'

'*Water Music*,' he said, finally turning to her and crossing the room with her drink. 'She needs to be receptive, uninhibited. Perhaps some sleep therapy . . . would you send Maddie up with something?'

'Of course,' she said softly. Their fingers met as she took the glass from him. 'Shall I conduct?'

'No, I'll do it.'

'But Mika, you've never—'

'Allow me, Serena. I'm . . . I'm experimenting tonight. It's what you wanted, isn't it? Isn't it?'

Was it? Sipping her Calvados, she scrutinised him closely as she considered her reply.

* * *

181

She was asleep. No, not exactly asleep ... dreaming perhaps? She had woken, she thought, saw him looming over her, this fair-haired god dressed in black, but then everything swam out of focus again. And now she was naked, nude. She'd felt the whisper of her night-dress leaving her skin, the cool air caressing her body; felt exposed somehow as the silk drifted down her arms, her breasts, soft swathes pooling along her belly, settling momentarily in the juncture of her thighs, then whisked along her legs.

And now there was music. She recognised it at once as Handel's *Water Music*, that stately, joyous, sensuously flowing passage. It seemed very close, almost as though she were in the front row of an audience. And then she was moving, being carried as though in a barque along the Thames, in strong arms, to the flowing source of the river. There was water running. Carefully, reverently, as though she was one of the royal princesses in that stately procession, she felt herself lowered to the cool marble of her seat. But she was naked, she knew, and could feel the veins of the marble against her own skin. And then her arms, again ever so delicately, ever so reverently, were lifted from her sides, entwined with silken cords. If she were to be bound, it must be in silk, she thought, a little confused. And then those same hands were spreading her legs, opening her thighs, encircling her ankles with thick silken cords. Instinctively she knew they were white. She should, perhaps, be embarrassed, naked as she was in front of her courtiers, but she knew her skin was as white as the cords, knew herself to be as sensuous and voluptuous and open and flowing as the very water they sailed on.

He stood back, breathing a little heavily. She was so slender, it was hard to believe she was so heavy to carry. Her eyes were closed, and her breathing regular. He was sure she had woken when he lifted her, but she seemed completely given over to the sleep-inducing drink Maddie had given her before she retired for the night. How fortunate that Maddie had put her in the Green Room, which had its own en suite jacuzzi. Against the black marble of the cavernously deep tub, her skin glowed like a pearl. Spreadeagled on its surface, her long white legs spread wide, her flaming hair in disarray, she resembled the sacrifice he'd likened her to earlier. Something to devour. Recalling himself, he concentrated on the music and turned on the taps, testing the water to make sure it was neither too cold nor too hot, then took the showerhead in his hand. The more powerful jets from the jacuzzi would come later.

Oh God, yes, that was it, bliss, those warm summer showers moistening her skin, flowing around her, warming her. The touch of the cool marble contrasting with the warm, pulsing jets of the spray. But what a strange shower it was. It moved leisurely, slowly, starting from the soles of her feet, pulsing intimately between her toes, then tracing the curves of her calf, her thigh, then pressing against her apex, pulsing, swirling, dancing with her lips, her labia, flirting with her clitoris. Again and again the path was repeated, sometimes slowly, sometimes in sharp little thrilling, trilling, bursts ... it followed the strings. *Water Music*, she realised, and arching toward the shower tried to capture it, summon it to the centre of her pleasure, but found her wrists bound, her legs immobile. Only her torso could move, wave towards the waves. Like some sea creature caught in the tide, a flowing anemone, she was at the mercy of the water, its creature, sucked into its dark roiling depths, then spat out and cast forth in an unrelenting rhythm.

Leaning over the tub, he was entranced with the picture she made. The water level was rising, and her red-gold hair was fanning out as though it were alive. And she was ready; he could sense it from her skin, knew it from the rocking of her hips, questing toward the jets spurting from the showerhead he held in his black-gloved hand. Swaying a little to the music, he realised that he was now the conductor and she was the orchestra. This crude instrument in his hand was the baton with which he would call forth the entire symphony. Her body now was almost submerged, only the tips of her breasts peaking above the water. He felt the tension in his wrist returning, almost as though he were playing again. Delicately, deftly, with a mathematician's precision, he positioned the showerhead between her thighs and waved it gently, fanning it across her pubic hair.

It was humming, she could feel it, hear it, sense it, like a bee coming to drink the honey of her juices. Warm wet waves, pulsing towards her, stirring her hair, ruffling through it to the tender skin beneath. Her groin felt heavy, as though all her blood was rushing and coursing to settle between her legs. Under the hypnotic rhythm of that fanning warm tide, her lips were growing, engorging, plump and red and slick. Her clitoris was stirring, hard and greedy, desperate to reach that humming, pulsing jet. It had caught the rhythm, was humming and pulsing too, pushing through the swollen folds of her labia. The tides were ebbing and flowing, washing now against the inside of her thighs, now swirling through her hair. She could feel the pulsing jet coming closer, tantalising her clitoris with the faintest watery caress before swirling to lick the plump leaves enfolding it. Lightheaded, disembodied, she was at the mercy of the tide, desperate for that pounding, crashing wave to slam into her, slam through her. It was coming closer and closer, she could feel it coursing through her.

Mika saw her body tense, and could almost feel the first tremor of her response.

And so he stopped.

Carefully, with long, slow strokes, he moved the showerhead under the water, tracing the long line of her legs, moving from her thighs to her knees, finding the sensitive flesh of the inner curve of her knee, then down to her feet, positioning the pulsing head between her toes.

With his free hand, he reached behind him and turned up the volume of the CD.

Just poised on the crest, she felt the wave recede. Moaning, she tried to rock towards it, follow it, but it ebbed away, settled between her toes, found the little hollow between her baby toe and its mate and throbbed against the sensitive skin. Warm and pulsing, thrumming, it was the symphony of sensation she needed between her legs. Her clitoris was quivering, trembling with need, suffused with aching. And the tide understood, because it was flowing towards her again, leaving that tiny hollow between her toes, washing up along her calves, her thighs, coming closer, fluttering against the swollen lips encircling her clitoris, then receding along the path of her other leg, tracing the curve of her thigh, the swell of her calves, then settling between her toes again.

Again and again, with infinite patience, he waved the showerhead under the water, following the contours of her legs, his leather gloves sodden with water. Her torso was rocking frantically, with water sloshing against the sides of the black marble tub. This was the moment to prolong to infinity, to turn greed to need to imperious desire, so that the final explosion was a shuddering flourish.

Throbbing, aching, pulsing, all of her, every part. Drowning, submerging in the warm wet want, her toes were her clitoris, her clitoris her toes, ten, no eleven, erect little mounds of flesh dancing and palpitating for release. Her breath was coming faster and faster, she could feel the salty sweat of the sea on her brow. The waves were pounding now, dashing her against the hard black shore.

He could hear the music coming to its end now, the stately barge preparing to dock, throwing out the lines to the shore. It really wasn't long enough for his purposes, he decided; probably wasn't even the right music for this one. She deserved something from *Tristan and Isolde*, perhaps, something from the post-Classical period. Still, for the sake of symmetry . . . He smiled a little tensely, and moved the showerhead between her legs.

Crashing closer and closer and now, the warm jets were pulsing towards her, dashing against her clitoris in a surging tide and, as it throbbed in response, she could feel her inner walls throbbing too. The water was beating against her faster and faster, sucking away then flashing back, sucking and flashing, sucking and crashing.

The final notes were sounding. Firmly he placed the black plastic head, still spewing the pulsing jets of warm water, against her lower lips, then turned the taps on full force.

Tense, straining for release so long denied, with the streaming pressure of the jets thrashing her clitoris, she came in a rushing, screaming frenzy, a torrent of suppressed sensation, a fury of ecstasy unlike anything she had ever experienced.

He knew she could come again and again, was almost tempted to make her, but the tape had finished. Leaning over the tub to replace the showerhead he was aware of a sudden tingling in the tips of his fingers. Accustomed to the phantoms of sensation that still sometimes haunted his sleep, he ignored it and reached for a large, fluffy white towel. Bending down he flicked the mechanism that drained the tub and waited while the water flowed away. Her skin was flushed from the warmth of the water and the force of her orgasm, and she was still breathing rapidly. For a moment, watching the fronds of her water-darkened hair wave in the draining water, her taut, milky breasts still heaving, the muscles in her perfectly formed calves still trembling, he was almost tempted.

Briskly he shoved the thought aside, unbound her wrists and ankles and, wrapping her in the towel, carried her back to her bed. She roused a little then, he was sure, because her eyes opened for a moment. It didn't matter. Because of the draught she would not know what was dream and what was reality, would retain, only, he hoped, the physical memory of sensations. Already she was snuggling beneath the blankets, drifting into sleep.

A cool gust of air stirred the draperies and, walking to the window he peered out. Storm clouds, thick and gravid with rain, were gathering over one of the mountain peaks faintly visible in the distance. How very appropriate, he decided.

He returned to the bathroom, hastily wiping down the wet surface of the tub, and pocketed the four silken coils with which he'd bound her. Finally he unplugged the CD player and, returning to the bedroom, hesitated. She had clasped a pillow close to her breast, cuddling it close like a lover, looking for the security and warmth of another body. Her fingers, long and graceful, were clasping it close to her, drawing it into the warm, dark embrace of her body. Unthinkingly, he bent down, kissed her cheek and left the room.

The heavy carpet muffled his steps as he walked down the hall. He hesitated outside the door to Serena's suite, then moved on. He wasn't quite ready to tell her.

Tell her what?

She could respond, this girl, this violinist; she had a reservoir of sensuality that could be unleashed on the music, if she learned how to draw on it, sustain it. Did it matter?

He felt edgy, unsettled. The unusual energy, the almost clinical sense of purpose that had driven him to her room had deserted him, leaving him tired but restless, irritable and weary.

In the old days he would have had a woman, taken one almost automatically, to relieve the tension, the music shivers shuddering his fingers. Unconsciously he flexed his fingers, extending them and then balling them into fists. It was a simple reflex now. He knew, despite early hopes, early promises, that his hands would never recover.

The Devil and the Deep Blue Sea

Cheryl Mildenhall

The Devil and the Deep Blue Sea has been a very popular Black Lace title. Many readers could identify with Hillary and her friends as they rent a country house for a summer holiday and set about devoting their time to sun, sea and sex. It is a pleasant surprise for Hillary when she discovers the owner of the estate is the most fanciable man in the locale. That is until she meets Haldane, the gorgeous blond Norwegian sailor who works nearby. Attracted to the charms of two very different men, Hillary wastes no time in exploring the possibilities on offer. However, by the end of the vacation, she has a difficult decision to make. In this extract, Hillary and her friends plan to spend the afternoon relaxing on the beach, but plans go awry when Haldane makes an appearance and whisks Hillary off to the sand dunes.

Cheryl Mildenhall has written four other books for Black Lace. They are: *Summer of Enlightenment*, which explores a young woman's new-found sexual freedom; *The Lure of Satyria*, which is set in a mythical principality; *A Sense of Enlightenment*: a story about inheritance and kinky goings-on in a hotel, and *Pulling Power* – about one woman's ambition in the competitive, sexy world of motor racing.

The Devil and the
Deep Blue Sea

Hillary glanced around, hoping to catch a glimpse of Torran, then remembered he had gone to the village. With a sigh of disappointment she lay down on the sun lounger, rolled on to her stomach and unhooked her bikini top, then with an air of bravado removed it completely and dropped it on the flagstones. When Torran finally returned, he found her prostrate, struggling to coat her back with suntan oil.

'Here, let me do that for you.'

Hillary almost sat up in surprise, then remembered that she was topless and sank down into the mattress as far as she could. She sensed him approach her, then he took the bottle from her trembling hand, poured a little of the oil into his palm and began rubbing it into her sun-soaked skin.

For an uncultivated country boy he certainly had a gentle, rhythmic touch, she thought to herself dreamily, almost moaning aloud as he inadvertently brushed his fingertips over a particularly erogenous zone. As he moved up her back he lifted her hair; she raised her arms and held it over her head, exposing the full length of her neck. Inexplicably, she felt as though she had just revealed an extremely intimate part of her body to him.

Eventually she found her voice. 'Have you done this before by any chance?'

'What? Covered a beautiful woman in suntan oil? No, I have not, I'm afraid.'

She noticed that his accent was very pronounced today and wondered if he was more nervous than he appeared.

'Don't worry, you're doing a wonderful job.'

She squirmed luxuriously as he massaged the oil into her shoulders and turned her head to one side so that she could see him. Unlike the dark, almost austere trousers and jacket that he'd been wearing the day before, he was now dressed in a pair of black denim jeans and a white cotton vest. As he poured a little more oil on to his palm she noticed that he wore a silver ring on the middle finger of his right hand bearing a design of a coiled serpent.

'I noticed your friends were all at home today.' His tone was light and conversational. She marvelled at the change in him overnight.

'Yes, I mean, no.' She, on the other hand, seemed to be having a little more difficulty organising her thought processes.

'Which is it to be then, yes or no?' He kneaded the tightly clenched muscles at the base of her neck and the last vestiges of her hangover disappeared as if by magic.

'Oh, God, that's better,' she groaned, then added, 'In answer to your question, they were here earlier but they're not here now.'

'I see.'

He continued to massage her in silence for a few more minutes, then replaced the lid on the bottle with a decisive snap. She couldn't help feeling a little disappointed that he'd finished so soon.

'Would you like a drink?' She gestured toward the table which bore the jug of Pimms.

He noticed there were two glasses but said nothing and simply poured out a drink for each of them. Now she was in a quandary. She wanted to take a sip of her drink but couldn't do so without sitting up. For a moment or two she groped around surreptitiously for her bikini top then, to her horror, noticed that it was hanging on the back of his chair. He must have picked it up when he arrived, she thought, her mind whirling. She had no choice but to sit up.

Hoping that she was exuding an air of graceful ease she pushed herself up with her arms, then turned over and stared him straight in the eye. There was no doubt that her sudden movement had an impact upon him – his face flushed and she could tell he was trying desperately to keep his eyes trained above her shoulders. Reaching across to the table to take her glass, she noticed his eyes follow her and thought she heard him inhale deeply. She sipped her drink and searched her mind for something innocuous to say.

'Darius, I mean, Mr Harwood, stopped by here again last night. He's invited us all to a party. Will you be there?'

'He fancies you, y'know.' Torran spoke matter of factly.

'What?' His words took Hillary completely by surprise. In her confusion she took a large swallow of her Pimms and almost choked, her breasts shuddering as she struggled for breath. She had to give Torran credit for pretending not to notice.

With a totally inscrutable expression on his face he repeated his statement. 'Darius. He fancies you, anyone can see that.'

Hillary blushed. Feeling extraordinarily pleased and excited, she could sense the familiar tingling sensation deep in her belly.

'Mind you, I can't blame him,' Torran continued, obviously feeling a little bolder. 'You're a fine-looking woman.' At last he allowed his eyes to travel across the bronzed, naked globes of her breasts, then continue on their journey.

She glanced down her body, seeing herself as he saw her; tanned, slim, with long athletic legs. Nevertheless, she couldn't help noticing that he referred to her as a woman rather than a girl.

For the second time in as many days, she felt as though she were sitting opposite a man, not a boy, and she desired him as a man. She opened her mouth to speak but Fearn's lilting call carried over the short expanse between the two wings of the house.

Torran jumped up hurriedly, almost spilling his drink in the process. 'I'd better be going.'

Hillary nodded, watching him thoughtfully until he reached the far side of the kitchen garden, then he disappeared from view. Although she expected him all day, he didn't reappear. Eventually she went inside the house, desperate for another shower to cool her down and wash the oil and perspiration from her sun-soaked flesh. She padded into her bathroom and stepped out of her bikini bottoms. When she turned on the shower nothing happened. Cursing quietly under her breath she turned it off and on again a couple of times but still nothing happened.

'That's all I need,' she muttered to herself angrily.

Wrapping herself in a short white towel she tried Alicia's shower, then Chloe's and finally Odile's. None of them were working.

'Damn!' She surveyed her surroundings for a few seconds, tapping her foot and wondering what she should do next.

She picked up the telephone and dialled the number Darius had given them for such eventualities. Although he wasn't there she spoke to his secretary who assured her that it was probably just a case of temperamental plumbing.

'It's probably working perfectly okay everywhere else,' the woman added brightly.

Hillary thanked her, put down the receiver and thought about her words for a few minutes – if what she said was right there was a chance that the showers were working perfectly in the main house. Pausing only to collect her washbag, she walked decisively down the hallway and pushed open the swing doors that connected the two parts of the building. She had expected to hear some sounds, possibly of music or Fearn's vacuum cleaner, but everything was bathed in total silence. She opened the first door she came to but the room was completely empty, as were many of the others she tried.

'Hello!' She called quietly, then a little more loudly, 'Torran! Fearn! Anybody!'

She marched on down the hallway trying door handles until she came to a room similar in layout to the sitting room in her own quarters where she found Torran sitting alone watching a tennis match on TV.

If he was surprised to see her standing there clad only in a short towel, he didn't show it. 'Are you looking for someone in particular?'

'Where is everyone?'

Torran stood up and faced her, his palms turned towards her in a gesture of friendliness. 'What's the matter, Hillary? Can I help?'

It was the first time he had actually used her name and it sounded strange coming from his lips. Suddenly feeling self-conscious she struggled to maintain her equilibrium. With a falsely casual air, she waved the washbag in front of her. 'The showers in our wing have packed up and I was wondering if yours were still working.'

He smiled, his hazel eyes forming deep creases at the corners. 'Let's see.'

He led the way to the nearest en-suite room and she looked quickly around. From the few masculine bits and pieces scattered about it looked as though he had chosen his own room. He reached into the shower cubicle and it immediately gushed into life.

'No problem here,' he said, shaking water droplets from his arm.

'Do you mind?' Hillary gestured toward the shower, the fall of clear water looked so inviting she forgot all about her reservations.

He stepped back. 'No, feel free.'

She waited but he seemed in no hurry to leave. Finally, she raised her eyebrows and looked directly at him. 'Do you mind?' she said again.

He backed out of the room, embarrassed. As soon as he had left she looked around again. Damn! She might have known the lock on the door would be broken. After a few moments' hesitation she dropped the towel on the floor and stepped into the cubicle, the breath catching in her throat as the sharp jets of water hit her naked body.

As she soaped herself she hummed quietly, thinking once again how glad she was that she had decided to come on this holiday. She thought about school but it all seemed far away, as though teaching and London were part of a different life altogether. Just then her thoughts were interrupted by a loud rap on the bathroom door, and she quickly turned off the water and held her arms protectively around herself. She didn't need to ask who it was.

'Would you like anything to drink?' Torran's voice called to her through the closed door.

'Yes, please,' she called back. 'A little white wine if you have it.'

'I think so,' he mumbled.

It was several minutes later when she heard him return just as she had finished showering and was rinsing conditioner from her hair. The shower had invigorated her. Now she felt relaxed and happy, positively glowing and more than a little aroused.

'Why don't you bring my drink to me?' she called provocatively as Torran rapped on the door a second time.

She could sense him hesitating, struggling to amass all his powers of control before entering. It wasn't vanity on her part as Torran had made it quite clear how he felt about her, although she suspected that it wasn't her that interested him in particular, but rather women in general. Briefly she wondered if he was a virgin – that could be interesting, she thought.

She stayed under the shower as the door opened slowly, listening intently to his footsteps as he walked across the bathroom and then the sound of a glass being placed on the window ledge. She opened the cubicle door a fraction and looked at him over her naked shoulder. He was just standing there, a mixture of anticipation and fear upon his young face. Suddenly she felt very grown up, a woman of the world. She took a deep breath and smiled. 'Come here, Torran.'

He stepped forward and as he did so she turned around and opened the cubicle door completely, revealing her naked body to him as it glistened, still slick and steamy from the shower. He sucked in his breath and stared at her, looking her up and down with long, sweeping strokes, his eyes taking in every inch of her as she stood proudly before him. He started to speak but she put a finger to his lips, enjoying her role. 'Ssh, don't say anything.'

With one swift movement she grasped his T-shirt and pulled it over his head, then she knelt down in the shower tray and unbuttoned his jeans, holding his gaze with her own as she pulled down the zip. She rubbed a hand over his crotch, feeling the bulge swelling and growing beneath the thick black denim. Now it was her turn to catch her breath as there was no mistaking his desire for her. She pulled the material over his hips and clasped his buttocks using her forearms to ease his jeans further down his legs. She was slightly surprised to find that he wore nothing underneath.

He helped her then, kicking off his jeans and moving closer still. Fortunately he was barefoot and was able to step into the shower straight away. She closed the door once again but still didn't rise to her feet. She wanted to take him in her mouth, to thrill him in every way possible. Now she truly was the teacher and she was going to make sure her student passed with honours. Using one hand to cup his testicles she grasped the base of his penis with the other, aiming the glans toward her lips.

The water from the shower kept him moist as she ran her

tongue up his shaft, encircled the ridge around his glans a couple of times and then snaked her tongue down the other side of his solid erection. As her tongue continued to tease him, she realised he wouldn't be able to hold out for very long. Eventually, as she licked and kissed and caressed his sex, he gripped her hair tightly between his fingers, his rising passion evident in more ways than one. For a brief moment the simple act reminded her of another time and another man.

Swiftly she banished the memory, smiling up at Torran instead. To her surprise she saw that he looked a little disappointed and she hastened to reassure him. 'That's not it, Torran.' She smiled and tantalised his flaccid cock with her tongue until it sprang back to life.

With a sigh of relief he released her slick, wet hair and stroked it for a few minutes, his expression blissful. Then she rose slowly to her feet, running her hands lightly up the enticing musculature of his thighs and buttocks as she did so. She was particularly pleased with his body. Despite looking thin and gaunt in his clothes, his muscles were surprisingly well toned, although his body was nowhere near as hard or impressively defined as Haldane – her Norwegian lover's. She gave herself another mental shake, this was no time to be thinking about past conquests and, until there was a next time, that's all Haldane was.

She came back swiftly to reality. Torran was stroking her breasts, teasing her nipples with a childlike fascination, his fingers circulating her areolae again and again then skimming lightly across the hard pink buds, smiling as they tightened even more.

'Do you like my breasts, Torran?'

For an answer he bent his head and kissed first one rosy tip then the other.

A thrill of excitement ran through her each time he touched her there and she moaned softly, 'That's wonderful.'

Sighing with pleasure, she ran her fingers lazily through his thick dark hair – now that it was wet it had gone quite curly. She kissed the top of his head then placed a hand under his chin and gently raised his face to hers. Wrapping her arms around his neck and body she kissed him deeply, enjoying his initial resistance as she probed his mouth with her tongue. She felt his hardened cock brushing against her belly and suddenly felt weak with desire.

Sensing that he needed more guidance, she took his right hand and placed it on her sex, using her own fingers to gently part her labia and urge his exploring fingertips to the core of her excitement. He was a willing pupil and a gratifyingly quick learner. Within seconds he began to alternately rub and stroke the demanding bud of her clitoris until she reached the brink of her own climax. Then to her frustration he moved his fingers away, returning his hand to cup her breasts once again.

She was enjoying the novelty of the shower but soon realised that it was not the best of locations for his first time – if it was his first time. She still wasn't sure he was a virgin.

'Let's go into the bedroom,' she murmured softly in his ear.

They kissed under the powerful spray for a few more minutes then, with a slight feeling of reluctance, Hillary turned it off and pulled back the cubicle door.

Hillary and Torran padded hand in hand across the thickly carpeted bedroom, stopping to rub each other's bodies dry with thick, white monogrammed towels before collapsing onto the comfortable bed together. This time Torran controlled the action.

Perhaps he just wasn't used to vertical love-making, Hillary mused as he teased and stroked every part of her body, his tormenting hands sliding lower and lower down her torso until she was almost begging him to touch her between her legs. Opening her thighs wide she urged her pelvis upward, almost brushing his chin with the glossy curls of her pubic hair.

Steadfastly ignoring her encouragement he continued to lick her navel and the taut expanse of her belly, his tongue going around and around frustratingly in concentric circles. She tried to sit up so that she could at least caress him in return but he pushed her gently back against the pillow.

'I am exploring you, leave me be,' he commanded softly.

So she lay, moaning and writhing in mounting ecstasy as he discovered every part of her, front and back. When he'd finished, and only when he'd finished, he allowed his fingertips to drift across her lower belly, to create a path that divided the curls on her pubis to the natural division between the soft pink lips of her sex. Then he knelt on the floor, spread her thighs wide and slid his hands under her buttocks, pulling her toward him so that her lower body was level with the edge of the bed and his view of her was perfect.

She held her breath and waited, knowing that he was feasting his eyes upon her sex as she lay wide open to his view and desperate for his touch. As the minutes ticked by agonisingly slowly she toyed with her own nipples, desperate for a release that would not come.

Then, so lightly that at first she thought it was a slight breeze through the open window, she felt something caress the outer edge of her vagina. She tensed her thighs until they trembled, her whole body was aflame. She wanted to scream the words, 'Touch me, damn it!' But he was young and had all the time in the world.

Then she felt a fingertip inside her and another. Gradually she felt herself being filled up by him and ground herself against his palm as he probed inside her. She could feel her vagina moistening and expanding to accommodate him and, close by, the burning, urgent flesh of her clitoris swelled and throbbed. He had not touched her there since the shower and she felt she would scream aloud if he didn't offer her some release from the lust that had been building within her for the past few hours.

Strangely enough she didn't quite know the best way to communicate this need to him. She seriously doubted that he had ever performed cunnilingus before. Then she remembered that she was the teacher and it was up to her to show him how to please a woman. With a little difficulty she sat up and gently removed his hand from between her legs.

Torran looked hurt. 'Wasn't I doing it right?'

She smiled weakly. Between her legs she could still feel the legacy of his fingers. 'Good God, yes. But there are other ways to excite a woman, you know.'

He shook his head. 'No I don't. Tell me.'

She patted the bed next to her, then when he was seated beside her she pushed him gently backwards until he was laying flat on his back, his cock pointing at the ceiling.

'Do you remember when I did this in the shower?' She took his penis between her lips again, sucking and lapping it with her tongue as though it were an oversized lollipop.

He nodded, his eyes slightly glazed.

'Well,' she continued, 'you can do the same thing to a woman.' With uncharacteristic boldness she straddled him, her sex

197

directly in front of his face, and then she delicately parted her labia. 'Lick me here,' she ordered softly. 'That's it, nice and slowly, up and down, around and around. Ahh! Ooh!' She could feel her climax building very fast – there was something very beneficial about telling a man exactly what you wanted him to do, she decided.

He stopped and looked up at her as she was about to mount the first wave of ecstasy. 'Am I doing okay? You seem a little uncomfortable.'

She shook her head vehemently. 'Oh, no, Torran, you're doing absolutely great, just don't stop again until I tell you. Whatever you do, don't stop.'

She couldn't believe her good fortune. Here was a young man fresh and untrammelled, ready and eager to satisfy her every desire. Of course, no sooner had he discovered how to really arouse her than he began to caress her over and over and over. Finally, she had to stop him for a moment. 'Torran, this is great, it really is – but it's getting late. My sister and her friends will be home soon and they may come here looking for me.'

In all honesty she seriously doubted it, but she couldn't be sure; sometimes Alicia could surprise her with sudden inexplicable bouts of sisterly concern. He propped his head on one hand and regarded her with a serious expression, his dark hair flopping into his eyes.

'Do you want to go, is that it?' he asked.

'No, Torran, far from it, I just . . .' she hesitated and gazed out of the window at the darkening sky for a few minutes, then she looked him squarely in the eye and said, 'I want you to fuck me.'

He looked bewildered. 'But isn't that just what we've been doing all the while?'

She couldn't believe he was so naïve. 'Do you have any condoms, Torran?'

He nodded. 'A friend gave some to me before I came down here this time. He couldn't believe I hadn't scored yet. He said southern girls were much more forward. I think he was right.' He grinned, opened the cupboard next to the bed and rummaged around until he found a pack. 'I don't know how to put them on properly or anything.' He smiled at her apologetically but somehow she got the impression he had just overstepped the bounds of credulity.

'If I find out this innocence is all an act I'll, I'll . . .' She could hardly open the packet for laughing.

'You'll what?' he said, 'Withhold your favours? Fat chance.' Before she could think of a suitable retort he rolled her over, slipped on the condom and plunged into her. Each time he penetrated her a little deeper, all the time mumbling into her hair. 'You loved every minute of being the teacher. I've been playing hard to get. Did you honestly expect me to be a virgin at my age?'

And so it went on. Hillary didn't know whether to laugh or scream, he was so full of himself – so aggravating, so cocksure. One thing was for certain though, she thought to herself as he sent her senses soaring on the crest of a monumental orgasm, he certainly knew how to fuck.

Hours later, Hillary left Torran reluctantly to go back to her own quarters, making it with about five minutes to spare. No sooner had she shut the bedroom door behind her than she heard the screech of tyres on the gravel driveway and soon the heavy blanket of silence that hung over the house was shattered by Alicia and Chloe's piercing voices. Quickly, Hillary dived into bed and pretended to be fast asleep when they came in. As she expected there was a lot of giggling and the sound of someone stumbling about in the passageway, then her bedroom door opened a fraction and she heard Alicia's voice. 'Shh, everyone, Hillary's fast asleep.'

As soon as the door clicked shut again she smiled a secret smile and snuggled further into the warmth of her bed; compared with every other night for the past couple of weeks the air held quite a chill. She imagined Torran as he lay in his own bed, the sheets tangled and drenched with perspiration from their intense session of lovemaking.

Carefully she slid a hand between her legs, wincing slightly as she gently probed the tender, throbbing flesh. She still wasn't sure how much he had already known about sex but the outcome was what mattered most and she was certain that they had both benefited from her instruction. She lay awake for ages simply thinking and remembering, waiting for the sounds in the house to gradually die down, and when they did, she drifted off to sleep with a smile on her face.

The following morning started off pretty much like all the

others. Odile and Hillary were the first ones to wake with Chloe and Alicia less quick to put in an appearance. Eventually they all drifted together and sat convivially around the kitchen table, drinking coffee and discussing their plans for the forthcoming day.

'Well, after yesterday I certainly don't want to do anything too energetic,' Chloe declared, assuming an air of exhaustion.

'All shopped out are we?' Hillary murmured drily, adding, 'Where did you guys get to in the end?'

'Believe it or not only as far as King's Lynn,' said Odile. 'As you say we shopped, took in some local sights, had a meal, a drink, another drink . . .'

'I get the picture.' Hillary smiled. 'That's pretty tiring stuff. In that case why don't we all go down to the beach.'

Alicia groaned. 'I never thought I'd say it but I'm getting a bit tired of the beach.'

As if on cue, the other three women reeled back in mock horror.

'You cannot be serious!' exclaimed Odile.

'Well it's all right for you,' Chloe complained. 'You've spent most of the past few days locked in your room with Mr Universe, no wonder you fancy getting out in the open air.'

Odile pouted. 'That's not fair, we went ballooning.'

Chloe leaned across the table toward her. 'Tell me honestly that you didn't do it in the balloon.'

The young woman was silent, Chloe looked around at the others, a triumphant expression on her face.

'Okay, we did,' Odile admitted, a small gurgle of laughter catching in her throat. 'But only the once.'

'To quote your boyfriend dear, "Quelle horreur!"'

Hillary snorted and Alicia frowned at her friend.

'Oh, Chloe leave the poor girl alone for goodness' sake, you're only jealous,' she said.

'Too right I am.' Chloe picked at a piece of varnish flaking from her fingernail. 'Gus and I only did it once all the time he was here, can you believe it?'

Odile tutted and Hillary looked sympathetic but Alicia dismissed her complaint with a disdainful wave of her hand. 'Clive and I managed it twice, but . . .' She held up her hand to silence her friend who had opened her mouth to protest. 'But both times were so quick I hardly had time to put down the book I was reading.'

Hillary looked incredulous. 'You don't mean you read during foreplay?'

Alicia nodded, looking perfectly serious. 'Oh yes. At least if you can call it foreplay. If Clive ever learns to turn me on properly I'll buy a bookmark.'

Odile caught Hillary's eye and shook her head surreptitiously. Obviously, Hillary thought, she and Odile were the lucky ones. What bothered her the most was that both Alicia and Chloe seemed to take a rotten sex life for granted, as though sex with their husbands was something to be endured rather than enjoyed. Odile explained to Hillary later that she had given up trying to talk to Chloe about it, she simply didn't understand why she owed it to herself to make sure Gus knew how to please her in bed as well as out of it.

'And here I am with more sex than I can handle,' Hillary pronounced gravely.

'Oh, yes, tell me more.' Odile looked interested but just then they were interrupted by Alicia.

'Chloe and I are ready when you are.'

They had finally agreed to go to the beach again but this time they would take a detour to the naturist beach. This was Chloe's suggestion. They also decided to travel by taxi for a change as Alicia complained that she always ended up being the driver and so had to stay sober. None of the others were keen to volunteer so they called a local firm who dropped them at their usual parking spot near the wooded area where the two paths converged. They arranged for the driver to pick them up again at three o'clock and, each loaded down with bags and towels, set off down the path leading to the left.

At first they were agog – everywhere they looked men and women of all ages were sunbathing and swimming entirely in the nude. Some of them were even playing games, or walking the dog. Despite their apparent sophistication, none of the women really knew where to look and averted their eyes hurriedly every time someone walked past them.

'I can't believe how well hung some of these old chaps are,' Chloe whispered incredulously from the corner of her mouth.

Hillary was shocked and looked at Odile who stifled a giggle.

She looked around them. 'This seems a good spot to me,' she said.

Alicia started spreading out the towels while Chloe, naturally, rummaged in the cool bag for a bottle of wine and a corkscrew. They took turns to cover each other with sun tan oil then Chloe poured the wine.

'Don't you feel a bit conspicuous sitting here wearing a bikini?' They all turned to look at Hillary who had spoken.

Alicia was the first to reply. 'Well, I suppose it does seem a bit prudish.' With an air of bravado she reached behind her and unhooked her bikini top.

Slowly, Chloe, Hillary and Odile followed suit. They looked at each other in silence for a few minutes then Chloe said. 'Who's going to be daring then?' The other three women stared back at her, blushing profusely.

Chloe wriggled out of her bikini bottoms and sat ramrod straight on the towel, her thighs clenched firmly together, staring directly ahead at the sea. After a few seconds she spoke between clenched teeth. 'Come on, I don't intend to be the only one to bare my all.'

Hillary glanced around. There was still no one within a hundred yards of them so she quickly removed her bikini bottoms too and, shortly afterward, Odile and Alicia did the same. If they had expected crowds of spectators to suddenly appear, or a film crew, they were able to breathe a sigh of relief. Even when the odd person did pass them by they gave no more than a fleeting glance, or a friendly nod. Gradually, the women relaxed and began to enjoy the unique sensation of the hot sun caressing their naked skin. Hillary rolled on to her stomach and shyly asked Alicia if she would mind coating her behind with suntan oil. Soon they were all anointing each other and, their inhibitions loosened by the wine, the sun, and the lack of clothing, they all admitted to feeling aroused.

'What wouldn't I give for a group of nice hunky guys to come up to us now,' wailed Alicia.

Chloe blushed. 'Do you know who I can't stop thinking about?'

'No, go on,' Odile urged.

'That boy, Fearn's brother, Torran. Have you seen him in jeans? He's got a divine bottom.'

As she lay back on her towel and stared at the sky, Hillary couldn't help noticing that her nipples had become erect. She felt excitement bubbling up within her at the thought of him; she knew just how Chloe felt.

'I could teach that boy a thing or two,' Alicia asserted smugly, adjusting her sunglasses as she turned to face the opposite direction.

'I doubt it,' Hillary blurted out. She instantly regretted her slip of the tongue as all three women sat up and stared at her.

'Is there something we should know about, Hillary?' Alicia's voice was quiet and controlled.

Hillary trembled. This was a sure sign her sister was about to exert her authority but none of the women were going to let her remark pass.

'Okay, I'll tell you. But promise not to tell Torran I said anything,' she protested feebly. At that moment she felt about six years old again.

'Yes, yes, we promise.' Chloe was impatient. 'Just tell us what happened between you and Torran. I take it something has happened?'

Hillary nodded, failing to conceal a grin. 'Yes, yesterday, when you were all out. Our showers weren't working so I went to the main house. Darius and Fearn were out but . . .'

'But Torran was there, eager for someone to play with,' Alicia finished for her, unable to hide the wistful tone in her voice.

Hillary nodded, wondering what the hell she had to feel guilty about. Suddenly she faced them all, her expression defiant. 'We had sex for hours and it was really fantastic and I hope we get to do it all over again.'

'Well,' Alicia said, pausing to allow her sister's admission to sink in, 'I just hope I get to do it with him too.' At that she threw back her head laughing and soon they were all falling about helplessly. Of course they wouldn't give up until Hillary had told them every single detail and then they wanted to know about Haldane as well.

'Is there anyone else?' Chloe asked.

'Not yet,' Hillary admitted.

Chloe squealed. 'Did you hear what she said? Not yet. Oh, my God, I feel like a nun!'

'Sorry, can't see any around,' Odile quipped, sending them all into fresh gales of laughter.

'Are you ladies having a good time?'

The deep voice was unexpected. Thinking it sounded slightly

familiar Hillary looked up. It was Haldane. He too was naked and looking even more magnificent than she remembered.

Chloe and Alicia went bright pink with embarrassment when they saw him, but Odile grinned openly and waved a bottle of wine in the air. 'Would you like some?'

He nodded and sat down on the edge of Hillary's towel. Hillary noticed that Chloe couldn't take her eyes off his penis so after a few minutes she kicked her in the ankle.

'Ouch! Oh, sorry, Hilly.' Chloe pouted and rubbed her leg.

'What have you been up to?' Haldane asked.

It was a rhetorical question but Hillary blushed guiltily and stammered a reply. 'Just hanging around the Hall, sunbathing and so forth.'

Chloe snorted when Hillary said this, only blushing when Hillary flashed her a warning look.

Haldane sipped his wine and smiled openly at Hillary who was still red faced. 'I'm not checking up on you.'

They all sat around talking and drinking wine for a little while, then Haldane suggested a walk. Much as they fancied him, Alicia and Chloe shook their heads. They weren't mentally prepared to parade down the beach stark naked.

Odile was not embarrassed but sensed that Hillary would prefer to be alone with him. 'You two go, we'll just stay here and soak up some rays.'

Haldane took Hillary's hand and they walked for about half a mile in silence when suddenly he stopped and stared down into her face, his expression serious. 'Do you wish that we didn't meet any more, Hillary?'

'No.' She shook her head vehemently. 'Far from it. I just didn't want you to think that I was chasing you, or putting pressure on you.'

He nodded gravely. 'That's very perceptive of you, Hillary.' He stared out to sea for a moment or two, shielding his eyes from the sun with his free hand. Then he spoke, his words travelling out to sea on the ozone-laden air. 'It's true I don't like to feel tied down. I am a free man, a free spirit.'

'I know that, Haldane, and I'm not looking for any ties either, just some fun.'

'I know what sort of fun you like best, Hillary, remember?'

He ran his finger lightly down her spine and she shivered, her clitoris starting to tingle as though it had not been touched in

204

ages. She looked around but the beach where they were standing seemed quite crowded.

'Come on!' Haldane took her hand again and started to run towards the dunes.

They slowed down and walked by the side of the high banks of dunes for a few hundred yards until they came to a place where they could climb up. Haldane pushed his large hand against the underside of her bottom, helping her upward.

Hillary smiled to herself. He was such a gentleman; a gentleman who never passed up an opportunity to touch her.

As soon as they had both reached the top of the dunes, Haldane held her and they kissed deeply for several minutes, running their hands over each other in a feverish attempt to quell their growing lust. Hillary glanced around. The dunes were so high where they stood, in a low dip, that they were completely hidden from view. Suddenly, a dark cloud passed across the sun and she shivered, feeling her nipples harden. All at once she felt unaccountably primitive, like a child of nature, and couldn't deny an overwhelming urge to possess him there and then. One look at Haldane told her he felt the same way. They both knew there was no time for preamble; voices could be heard in the distance and the sound of children playing overlaid the rhythmic pounding of the surf against the shore.

He ran his hand over her belly and suddenly swooped between her legs, taking her unawares. His fingers were cool against her hot flesh and they soothed each desperate, throbbing part of her with deft strokes then hovered for a few seconds before plunging deep inside her, catching her breath from the inside.

While he caressed her, Hillary reached between their hot naked bodies, grasped his shaft in both hands and squeezed hard. She ran her fingers up and down the length of it, teasing the tip until the first drops of fluid appeared and coated her fingers. Then she held them up to her lips and sucked each one in turn, savouring the saline flavour before rubbing her lips across his chest. He tasted of the sea inside and out.

Behind her was a large, flat-topped dune about waist height. Haldane spun her around and pushed her forward unceremoniously. She gasped as her stomach and breasts came into contact with the hot sand, then cried aloud as he entered her. Holding her hips firmly he thrust into her eight or nine times, smiling with satisfaction at her cries of passion which were drowned out instantly by the squalls of the seagulls wheeling overhead.

She thought he would let her go as soon as they climaxed but she was wrong. Pinning her to the dune with one massive hand spanning her back, he slid the other between her legs. Gently he parted her labia, rubbing cool fingers over her burning clitoris. Then, using his pelvis, he forced her body forward, moving his hand at the last minute, so that her exposed bud was pressed against a tuft of marram grass, the spikes immediately prickling her delicate flesh.

Hillary moaned at the unexpected contact. Used only to the sensation of pliant flesh against the most sensitive parts of her body, she suddenly felt a primeval yearning for more of the same.

Haldane must have read her thoughts, she mused, as she saw him scan the area of sand around their feet. A few inches away, on top of another tuft of grass, lay a long smooth stone, its rough edges polished to a shine by years of tossing about in the tide. They both seemed to notice it at the same moment and Haldane swiftly bent and picked it up before returning immediately to his position as captor. For a few moments he weighed the stone in his hand, considering the possibilities. It had obviously been recently picked up by a seabird and dropped because it was still cold and salty wet from the sea.

The first thing Hillary felt was its cool slick dampness stroking her buttocks, occasionally sliding between the cleft and over her throbbing sex. Haldane's cock was no longer inside her and she wondered how he would use the stone – if he would use it to penetrate the place he had so recently vacated. The thought excited her but, at the same time, she realised that the dimensions of the inanimate object were nowhere near as impressive as the Norwegian's own member.

Haldane seemed in no rush to make a decision. He extended the path of the stone, trailing it up and down the length of her spine as he continued to stimulate her sex with his hand.

All movement ceased for a moment, then he spoke. 'If I let you go you will stay in that position.' His words were a command that Hillary wanted to obey. She nodded, her stomach tightening with fresh excitement.

As Haldane took his hand from her back, she pressed herself further forward over the sand dune and clasped it with both arms. A wisp of chill air whipped her exposed sex and she moaned with renewed desire, rubbing her swollen nipples against the hot grains of sand. She could sense him looking at her, considering what to do next.

Suddenly she felt his massive hands on her buttocks, spreading her wider and wider as his fingers teased the pink, puckered skin. Despite her embarrassment she squirmed under his touch, then jumped as the tip of the long smooth stone nudged the rosy opening inside her cleft. 'Haldane?' she murmured. Her voice was tremulous. He was going to do what she dreaded and desired the most.

'I won't hurt you, Hillary,' he replied, his tone reassuring.

Carefully he pressed the stone against the tight muscles surrounding her opening, using the fingers of his other hand to probe her vagina and arousing her to such an extent that her body automatically yielded to the new invader. With great delicacy he used the stone to mirror the actions of his fingers: probing, turning, withdrawing a little.

Gradually she relaxed into the rhythm, her mind and body totally consumed by the unprecedented sensations invoked within her. As her moans turned to screams of ecstasy, Haldane was forced to urge her into silence. The sounds that reverberated around them were approaching a crescendo that was sure to attract the attention of others.

After a few more minutes he withdrew the stone, replacing his fingers with his rock-hard shaft. Once more they took delight in each other's bodies, until they both exploded in a final, glorious climax.

Afterwards, Hillary sank to the ground, as limp as a rag doll, her breathing laboured. Using every ounce of her remaining strength, she turned her head to smile at Haldane who also sat on the sand, his back to a high dune. 'I've realised what's different about you, Haldane,' she said, when she had recovered her breath a little.

'Yes?' He smiled contentedly.

'Every time I think it can't get any better between us, it does.'

Led on by Compulsion

Leila James

Led on by Compulsion by Leila James is a story of chance and fortuitous encounters. When Karen shelters from the rain at an English country pub, she finds the attractive barman, Andreas, is unusually accommodating. In fact he is the wealthy owner and he wastes no time in seducing her into the ways of fast living and debauchery. Karen is introduced to Marieka, Andreas's partner in decadence, and together they indulge in unbridled hedonism. In this scene, Karen is being led to one of Marieka and Andreas's orgies and is due to be 'auctioned' for the night to the highest bidder. At first Karen is naturally hesitant, but soon comes to quite like the attentions of her wealthy and generous suitors.

Led on by Compulsion

Karen stood by the banister with Marieka and Andreas. Her eyes swept down the red-carpeted stairs into the hall below. Dinner-jacketed men and ladies in colourful evening dress deposited coats or wraps with several waiting slaves. The male slaves were dressed in white loin cloths that looked more like short skirts. The female slaves were dressed in very short, low-cut, sleeveless linen dresses. One woman ran a finger down the bare chest of one of the male slaves. He stood, impassive and muscular, holding a pile of coats. Karen could feel the cold air from the open door even where she was, so she wondered how cold the slaves must be feeling. The noise in the entrance hall was rising but Karen's mind seemed to be distancing her from everything. What had Marieka said? Were they really going to auction her? She snapped herself out of the daze she seemed to be sinking into and grappled hastily for one of the bolt rings. Andreas's hand went instantly to her wrist and held it.

'What are you doing?' he hissed.

'I'm not sure I want to be auctioned, thank you,' Karen told him, struggling in his grip.

'It's only for the evening,' protested Andreas.

Karen stared at him in disbelief. 'So I'm going to have to do whatever some gross lech wants me to so you can make as much money as possible?' Karen's voice was rising excitedly.

'Sssshh!' Andreas ordered angrily. 'It's just like a game. We auction you for presents for you, not money for us. You get to choose whose offer you accept.'

'What if I don't want to accept any?'

Andreas's expression seemed to say that he was running out of patience with her. 'I've already told you, you don't have to do anything you don't want to. You can say no to everyone who bids for you. You can say no to anything anyone wants you to do if you go with them. Will you stop ruining everything? This whole party's for you, anyway.'

Andreas's anger scared her. She was not sure how deep she wanted to let herself get into this. Faces had turned upwards to see the source of the noise. Andreas released his painful grip on her wrist and stood up tall and straight. 'Make a decent entrance,' he hissed at her.

Marieka was already gliding, tall and beautiful, towards the top of the stairs. Andreas pushed Karen roughly, making her stumble slightly. She recovered herself and walked as straight-backed and gracefully as she could behind Marieka, whose slow descent of the stairs was as grand an entrance as Karen had expected from her. Marieka commanded attention with every movement. Karen could not see Andreas, stepping softly behind her. She hated him for hurting her wrist, she hated him for his anger and his sudden lack of understanding, but most of all she hated him for giving her away instead of wanting her himself.

The male slaves cleared a pathway in the hall for them, so that they filed through a corridor of loin-clothed men to grand, arched, open double doors. Marieka swept through the doors, and Karen followed her into a huge high-ceilinged banquet hall. The walls were startlingly white, hung with foliage to give a loose impression of either a Roman or Greek setting. White pillars were scattered among what seemed to the frightened Karen like crowds of people in evening dress. More orderly white pillars framed a large platform at one end of the hall. As Marieka set foot inside the doors, bare-chested loin-clothed young men sprang forward to make another clear corridor to the platform. In spite of her collar and chains, Karen felt like a princess protected from a curious public. She wished they were an adoring public, but she was too frightened to believe that.

More muscular slaves darted forward to lift two throne-like chairs on to the platform as the trio approached slowly. Karen noticed the change from luxurious red carpet to cold polished boards under her bare feet as she mounted the steps with Andreas and Marieka, who stood in front of the chairs. Marieka pulled Karen beside her so that she did not obscure the audience's view of her. A slave darted forward and attached a tiny microphone to Andreas's lapel. Andreas moved to the front of the platform and held up his hands for silence. There was a gradual quietening until the noise finally stopped.

'May I call your attention to this beautiful slave,' announced Andreas. Several eyes turned to Andreas, although other members of the audience continued with their sexual activities while becoming politely quieter.

'This lady has only been with one man,' Andreas announced. 'Bids will be invited shortly from anyone wishing to widen her experience. She will remain on view here until then.'

Karen was aware of Andreas's fingers reaching to his microphone. That was it. That was her introduction to this audience. She looked out at what seemed like a sea of indifferent faces. Andreas went back to his seat and left her, open and scared, at the front of the platform.

Then there was a flutter in the audience, caused by a few men leaving their seats to come closer. A small procession filed up to her, the owners of faces she could only see as characterless, peering and squinting, eyeing her up and down. Andreas seemed amused by the procession. 'You can examine her more closely if you want to,' he called out, laughing at Karen's horrified expression.

Only one adventurous man climbed on to the platform, acquiring white dust on his dinner suit in the effort. Karen got a vague impression of brown hair and a snub nose before she closed her eyes to shut him out. She opened them wide again very quickly in shock. His hand went straight between her legs, slipping a finger into her vagina to explore her warmth. 'It's soaking,' he informed the interested onlookers, and they laughed raucously.

Karen pushed him away and kicked at his legs until he withdrew his hand. 'Is she meant to be submissive?' the man asked Andreas, and they all laughed again while the man jumped down.

'I want to see her walk,' called a deep voice from the front. Karen looked across in time to see the twinkle in the man's eyes. She glared at him angrily while Craig pulled at her chain so that she walked behind him across the platform.

213

'Don't we get to see all of her?' shouted one of the anonymous crowd.

'No!' Karen shouted emphatically. Her hands went defensively to her dress fastenings as Craig's free hand moved towards them. He let his hand drop at her protest.

'Why are you letting them do this?' she shouted angrily at Andreas.

'Because it amuses me,' Andreas answered coolly.

He sat draped across the chair, his chin resting on one hand, his eyes levelled at Karen.

'Well, I don't want them to so they have to stop,' Karen asserted. 'That's the rule here, isn't it?'

'Yes, that's the rule here.' Andreas grinned.

The small procession made their way slowly back to their seats, cracking jokes between themselves, which Karen had no doubt that she was the butt of. Andreas seemed the most amused of any of them even though he was apart from their joviality. The more angry or scared she got the more amusing he seemed to find it, which made her angrier and him more amused.

She turned away from him, trying to hide her feelings. She hoped he did not know that his presence made her skin tingle, but she felt that her feelings and sensations were open and obvious to everyone, particularly Andreas. As open and obvious as they had been when she had met him at lunchtime.

She let her eyes stray around the vast hall. The only people she knew were Andreas, Marieka and Craig. She had only known them a few hours, and they scared her. She felt very, very alone. The laughter at her expense highlighted her loneliness. She was cut out of all their talk and laughter, ridiculed, and cut out even from the sexual play in the hall. If she ran out now, who would she run to? Her eyes were drawn again to the owner of the twinkling eyes. His interest in her made him seem like the closest thing she had to a friend in the audience, but he scared and angered her too. How could she think of him as a friend when his interactions with her were deliberately provocative and even cruel? Now he wasn't even looking at her. He was involved in a joke with a neighbouring man. Was he laughing at her too? She let herself become aware of the closeness of Craig's tanned skin. It was smooth and shiny, and she imagined him standing behind her, his strong arms around her waist, his lips gently brushing her hair. She was alarmed to find herself imagining that he was bending her forward as he had done to one of the girls, slipping his large erect penis into the warm wet space waiting for him. The tingling in her vagina began again at the thought of feeling a penis inside her, which could be happening soon. She realised that she was now standing with her legs slightly apart, as if she was waiting for the ultimate moment. She closed her eyes and imagined the sensation of it flooding through her.

'I'm getting bored,' Marieka announced, bringing Karen abruptly back from her dreaming. 'When are we going to auction Karina so I can go and play?'

'In a while,' Andreas answered.

'What are you waiting for?' Marieka asked, agitated. 'Are you planning some other entertainment first?'

'Why don't you go away and play if you're that bored?' asked Andreas.

Marieka rose and trounced to the front of the platform, stopping behind Karen. Her hands slid into the slits at the side of Karen's skirt to massage her buttocks. Her fingers slid further down, straying towards the middle, catching at Karen's chains and pulling them tight between her legs. Marieka's fingers began massaging and parting the lips of Karen's vagina. Karen fought not to let her eyelids flutter closed. Her body ached in expectation each time Marieka's fingers neared the edge, only to feel the fingers tease and move away again. It was only the sight of the audience that kept Karen from begging Marieka to push her fingers in.

Marieka's fingers slid between Karen's legs to find her clitoris. She rubbed at it gently, then slightly harder. Karen's eyes closed and the audience was forgotten.

'Not that, Marieka, please,' Karen breathed. 'I can't take that. Please, Marieka.' Marieka's arm circled Karen's waist to hold her firm as Karen tried to wriggle free. Karen did not see that Andreas and the owner of the twinkling eyes were absorbed in watching her. She was too busy struggling against Marieka's strong grip, moving her clitoris away from Marieka's fingers but finding that they could follow every move.

Marieka held the front flap of Karen's skirt aside with her hand round her waist, so that her pubic area and Marieka's moving fingers were clearly visible to those in the audience who were close enough to see. Karen's breasts heaved with her frantic breathing. She was leaning heavily and helplessly against Marieka now, who continued to rub until Karen's groans were audible to those sitting near the front. Marieka stopped, keeping her arm round Karen's waist to support her.

Karen opened her eyes and remembered the watching people in horror. Marieka laughed at Karen's shocked expression before pulling Craig to face sideways to the audience. Marieka stroked his penis, turning the stroke to a grasp until it stood erect. She pulled a condom neatly and swiftly over it, then opened her legs on to him as he bent his knees slightly for her. Holding his penis firm against the silk pulled tight between her legs she rubbed herself up and down on him. Karen could see how much this teased Marieka, and waited for her to plunge the cock into herself. Marieka's juice darkened the silk before she pulled it aside and pushed Craig's hard penis into her with difficulty. She ground herself on to it before allowing herself to move up and down. Craig responded, pushing into her in spite of the taut silk rubbing against him. He was breathing heavily, approaching climax, when she pulled herself off him suddenly. Karen wondered how Marieka could do that, when her breathing had sounded so desperate. Karen's own need was dreadful enough just from watching.

Marieka flounced back to her chair and sat down. 'Now Karina's definitely as ready as she'll ever be,' she announced to Andreas.

'Maybe almost as worked up as you,' he teased.

Marieka pulled the silk back between her legs.

'You don't have to stay here,' Andreas reminded her.

'I don't want to miss it,' she said.

Karen's need was taking over all her thoughts and senses. She longed to ask Andreas to get on with it, but she knew he would delay it further if she did. She stood with her legs slightly apart, trying to absorb her sensations into herself so that nobody would see how intense she felt.

Andreas sat for a few moments to annoy Marieka, but was becoming impatient himself. At last he rose, switched on the microphone, and stepped forward to stand behind Karen, slightly to the right of her. His closeness heightened her sensations as always.

'Would anyone like to start the bidding?' he asked.

A hush crept from the front of the audience to the back. No

one spoke up for a terrifying moment, and Karen did not feel as confident as Andreas seemed to that anyone would want her.

'A gold bracelet,' stated the owner of the twinkling eyes.

'Hardly realistic, Owen,' Andreas said to him.

'I'm just starting the bidding off,' Owen countered.

Karen was taken aback by Andreas's reaction. A gold bracelet seemed a lot to her and she was grateful to Owen for breaking the silence.

'Matching gold earrings and a bracelet,' came a voice near the front.

'I think we can do better than that,' Andreas announced. Karen wondered what on earth he was expecting.

'A solitaire ring,' said a voice quite far back. It was the plump dark-haired man with whom Karen had made eye contact earlier. She felt neither happy nor alarmed that it was him.

'Earrings and necklace with a solitaire diamond each,' said a voice from the back.

The voices began to float into the background for Karen. She tried to tell herself that she would be going off with one of them – or would she be staying here? – and letting whoever it was fill her desperate wanting, but she could not quite believe it.

A ruby tiara was the bid they seemed to have reached so far. She would hate that, she thought, but so what? She could sell it. She looked towards Owen. He had not joined the bidding since he had started it off. She must be a joke to him then. She thought he had been interested in her and now it seemed he had just been amusing himself after all.

'You should be listening,' Andreas hissed. 'How can you choose if you don't hear what they're offering?'

She forced herself to concentrate. The eye contact man was bidding for the fourth time. 'A ruby necklace and a silk dress to match,' he was saying.

'I don't like rubies,' Karen said rudely. She looked at Andreas, expecting him to be angry, but he was laughing. A low laugh reached her ears from the front. It was Owen.

'Do you like cars?' Owen asked as he saw her turn towards him.

'What sort?' she retorted.

'How about a Golf GTI convertible?'

'Actually I can't drive, but then you could always throw in

some driving lessons while you're at it.' She stared him out, proudly defying his ridicule of her.

'That's my offer then,' Owen concluded. 'The car and driving lessons. Will you accept it?'

'Andreas, he's serious,' Karen whispered, turning to Andreas in a panic.

'Of course he is,' Andreas replied.

'What's he going to expect me to do for a car?'

'Nothing. The car's a present. You do what you like.' Karen looked very uncomfortable. 'Don't feel so bad about it,' Andreas laughed. 'He could have bought you a Porsche without blinking. That's what he should have done, the skinflint. Do you want to hold out a bit longer and see if he will?'

'No!' Karen was alarmed that Andreas could even think of pushing for more. 'I wouldn't have asked for driving lessons if I'd thought he was serious.'

'The car wouldn't have been much use then,' Andreas laughed. 'Do you want him or not?'

Karen let her eyes rest on Owen. His blue eyes still twinkled, the skin around them wrinkled slightly with the laid-back teasing smile across his handsome face. He scared and infuriated her. She wanted to cling to Andreas like an old friend. She let her mind wander over the other possibilities – the raucous laughing crowd that had looked her over, the plump dark-haired man who had offered her rubies and a dress. She thought again about Andreas, imagining his fingers reaching into her body, imagining his penis, erect and ready, pushing inside her. That offer was not there, and Owen was extremely attractive.

'Yes,' she answered quietly. The word almost stuck in her throat.

'She accepts you,' Andreas said loudly.

The audience lost interest instantly and the noise resumed. Andreas placed his hands on Karen's shoulders and leant down to her ear. 'Get used to how beautiful you are,' he whispered softly. 'You're worth anything anyone gives you, just because you're you.'

The softness of his voice melted her; the compliment lit her eyes. Andreas nodded to Craig, who began to lead her towards Owen. 'She's really new to this, Owen,' Andreas called in a voice filled with concern.

Craig reached Owen and handed him Karen's chain. Owen

stood, holding it firmly a short way from Karen's neck. His firmness sent a flutter of fear and excitement through Karen's stomach. He was tall beside Karen, quite broad shouldered and solid. He gave off a feeling of strength that had not been apparent when he had been sitting. Her legs felt jelly-like as she breathed in his closeness. She felt small and frail and even more helpless than usual.

'Let's go,' he said in a soft, deep voice. He pulled, and her feet moved in spite of herself, one in front of the other towards whatever he had in store for her. She glanced one last time at Andreas. He was draped across his chair again, relaxed and unconcerned. She took a deep breath and resigned herself to forget him and enjoy Owen – if whatever he had in mind would be enjoyable.

Andreas waited a long minute after Karen's back had disappeared through the doorway before leaving his chair and following her silently.

Karen watched her feet move automatically down the polished steps and along the red carpet behind Owen. She did not lift her eyes and had only a vague impression of Owen's powerful frame leading her. The red carpet did not change under her cold feet as they climbed the grand staircase and turned left. She walked close to the cream textured wall, running her fingers along the mahogany dado rail as if she could grip it for safety if she needed to. The mahogany banister at the other side seemed too open and unprotected. She shrank further towards the wall as she walked.

Owen turned in front of her and pushed open a door. She followed meekly to the doorway, then froze. He stopped and turned to see what the problem was.

'I can't do this,' Karen said. Her voice came out as a frightened whisper.

Owen looked into her panic-stricken eyes. His blue eyes had become gentle. 'I won't hurt you,' he promised. His eyes twinkled. 'Unless you want me to, of course.'

Karen shook her head rapidly, her eyes wide.

'Then I won't,' he promised again.

Karen did not move. He gripped the tops of her arms gently but very firmly, pulling her towards him as he walked slowly backwards into the room.

Karen's eyes roved nervously around the room, trying not to

look at Owen. The bed was a grand four-poster, made up with a black silk sheet, duvet cover and pillow cases. The canopy was matching black silk. The furniture was all dark mahogany, including a full-length, oval, free-standing mirror. Black silk curtains with red edgings were drawn across the large windows. Karen thought wistfully of the wild coastline in the darkness beyond.

Owen stopped with his back to the bed and released her arms. He pulled downwards on her neck chain until she knelt before him, her eyes facing the zip in his well-tailored black trousers. He undid the hook and zip in front of her to let his large penis spring out, half erect. He cupped his strong hand behind her head and pushed her towards his manhood. She opened her mouth in an almost automatic response and enveloped it, moving her lips gently up and down. He kept his eyes on the movement of her lips while removing his black dinner jacket and formal white shirt. Karen's eyes were drawn instantly upwards to his lightly-tanned muscular pectorals and upper arms. She pressed her tongue and mouth hard on to his penis, excited by the sight of him. She pressed more and more urgently while still moving her mouth up and down, listening to the changes in his breathing. She was surprised and ecstatic that she could have such an effect on this tremendously attractive man.

Owen tugged at Karen's neck chain suddenly, pulling her off and upward. She felt awkward having to use her arms to stand from kneeling. He pulled her to the bedpost, turned her back to it so that she faced outward, and tied her neck chain to it. He stood back for several seconds just to look at her. Then he walked to the mirror and carried it easily to stand in front of Karen, positioning it far enough away so she could see all of herself and a bit higher reflected in it.

He knelt on the bed behind Karen and held her head between his large hands to view her reflection. She could see his broad shoulders and strong arms on either side of her, as well as his twinkling eyes and greying hair. 'Let's watch this together,' he said, his mouth close to her ear.

He moved his hands and tugged once at the sides of her dress. The dress came apart at the shoulders, as it had been designed to do, and slid gracefully to the floor, revealing first her firm breasts, then her smooth stomach, then her dark tussle of hair with the bright contrasting gold nestling in it. Owen stared at Karen's body in the mirror.

Karen felt a little pride as her body revealed itself slowly. The gold chains looked flattering and effective on her milky skin as well as entwined in her dark down. She was pleased at Owen's appreciative expression.

Owen grasped her right hand in his and pulled it to her sex. She was fighting against him, but he was so strong that her struggle made no impression. The sight of his large dark hands in the mirror covering her slender pale ones excited her. He pushed her fingers into the entrance of her vagina. Her fingers were soaked.

'Isn't that a beautiful sight?' he said, pushing her fingers in and out at the edge.

Karen wanted him inside her. The feel of her own fingers touching the edge just teased and even annoyed her.

'No,' she answered angrily.

'Well, if you don't like the sight of your hands . . .' he said.

He unhooked one end of the chain between her manacles, and wound it swiftly round the bedpost, securing one hand. Karen turned to face him, trying to pull herself free, but his arms were long and his movements quick. He caught her shoulder, then her wrist, and pulled her so that she had her back to the post again, with both hands behind it, her wrists crossed over each other. He wound the rest of the chain round the post and the manacles and fixed it tightly. She struggled, but the chain held her, and her movements caused her collar to tighten.

'That can go now,' Owen said, and unbuckled her collar gently, throwing it to the floor.

The loss of the firmness round her neck made her feel more naked and vulnerable than her lack of clothes. The tickle of Owen's fingers as she watched them move slowly across her neck and down between her breasts drew her skin into a shiver. The fingers of both Owen's hands moved lightly around each areola without touching her nipples. Her breath sucked in and out with expectation and disappointment as he circled them lightly. Her nipples went cold as though a breeze had crossed them, and then stiffened, tingling unbearably in their need for his touch or his teeth on them, making her shudder with desperation. Her eyes could not leave the sight of his hands in the mirror, which moved lightly away from her breasts and

221

down her skin. Owen's long fingers reached down slowly into Karen's black patch of hair, running fondly through the curls. Her breath held itself each time they approached her opening, and released itself as he moved away. She could see his striking face, his rippling arms and his roving fingers all at once in the mirror. Her cheeks were flushing hot at the sight of him, a light sweat breaking out over her body. She was leaning against the post now, desperate to rub against his firm body instead of the cold hard wood. His fingers circled the edge of her entrance and her breathing became deep. Her body moved up and down slightly against the post.

Owen removed his hands and stood up from the bed. He moved round to face Karen, and crouched in front of her. He parted the folds of skin gently from her clitoris with his fingers, then pressed his tongue against it to rub over it. She squirmed in an effort to get away from him, breathing noisily, but she could hardly move because of the chain round the post. Her eyes closed helplessly as she leant even more weakly against the wood. He lapped with his tongue until her breathing was almost a shriek, then darted it inside her. He could almost drink her wetness. Her eyes opened in surprise as he licked against her tingling. As she looked down to watch him, she noticed his erect penis above his open zip, moving as he did. She swallowed, longing for the strength of that penis pushing against her vaginal walls. She watched his fingers grasping the tops of her legs to keep his balance. Even they would be less teasing inside her than his soft licking tongue.

Owen stood and moved back from her. Karen moved the tops of her legs together and drew in her vaginal muscles in an effort to create the feeling she so desperately needed inside her. Each effort worsened the need. Owen watched each of her movements greedily, hungry for each sign of her aroused distress. Her wrists twisted against the manacles. Her tongue licked her lower lip before she bit it lightly, trying to ease the need to close her mouth on to something, or for Owen to close his mouth passionately on to hers. Her eyes pleaded with him, but he answered with a cold hungry stare. More long seconds passed while he left her to her agony.

A flutter of excitement swept from her throat through her stomach to her vagina as Owen approached her. He stood close enough to cause a flush of desire as he unwound the chain from the post and fastened it loosely back to the manacles so that Karen's hands were now in front of her. She breathed his smell deeply into her, her eyes fixed on his firm chest. He moved to kneel behind her on the bed again, moving her sideways so that the bedpost no longer came between them. The touch of his skin against hers and the strength she felt he exuded made her feel dizzy. His arms circled her, reaching for her hands. This time when he pushed her own fingers inside her she could not help pushing them desperately up and down. She felt his penis twitch excitedly against her back as he watched them moving in the mirror. Her urgency did not ease, but became worse with each push of her fingers. They were not large or strong enough to fill her. Her gasping breaths filled the tense silence.

'Louder,' he ordered.

Karen was already embarrassed by the noise she was making.

'Louder!' he repeated.

She did not have to try for him. The gasping was becoming helplessly louder as she pushed harder in and out of herself.

'That's enough.'

Her fingers obeyed his voice without question. Her gasping subsided to deep breaths.

Owen moved to stand at the other side of the bed, turning his back on Karen. His trousers slid to the floor, and he stepped out of them. His legs were long, firm and muscular without being muscle-bound.

'Come here,' he ordered.

She scuttled hastily round the bed to stand in front of him. His erect penis was sheathed in rubber. Her skin shivered again as his fingers brushed lightly but deliberately down her skin. He brought his hands up to rub both nipples at once between his thumbs and fingers. Her breathing deepened. He grabbed her suddenly, turned her towards the bed in front of him, and pushed her face down on to it. She pulled her arms out from under her, where they had been squashed uncomfortably. Her hands grasped at the slippery black silk on the duvet. He opened her up with his fingers to force his large strength into her. She sighed with the relief of it. He held himself over her with his arms on the bed and pushed again, and again. Then he held himself at the edge of her, feeling her body shudder, waiting.

His own need overtook him. He pushed forcefully and frantically, hard and fast, the rubber slipping in her juices. She gripped the silk harder, pulling her hands apart so that the pull of the chain made the manacles rub against her wrists. She needed sensation. She wanted the firmness of the metal against her skin. Her body rubbed up and down on the silk with his forceful pumping. Inside she felt an itch that could not be scratched enough. She bit hard into the silk, her eyes closed, as his thrusting grew harder and faster, ramming her into the bed. His last push ground into her, and she cried out as she came. She looked up into the mirror to see his body raised on straight arms above her, his face unclenching itself from its expression of orgasm.

He rolled from her to sit upright on the bed. She tried to stand but her legs gave way. He crouched and gathered her up, then stood and placed her on the bed as if she was made of feathers.

Owen walked into the en suite bathroom while she lay, tired out, watching him, listening to the sound of the shower as he turned it on.

'You certainly weren't disappointing,' came a voice from the outside door. Karen rolled over to see Andreas leaning on his arm against the doorpost. She closed her eyes, too tired to say anything. Andreas walked over to her and sat beside her on the bed. 'I think these can go now,' he said.

He pulled each of her wrists to him and released the manacles. A voice in Karen's head told her she should be watching how to do it in case he put them on her again, but her eyes refused to open.

'You caught the end then,' she mumbled sleepily.

'I made a point of watching all of it,' Andreas answered.

The voice in Karen's head told her to be angry, or pleased, or something. Tomorrow, she told the voice as she slipped into sleep.

Andreas was looking at Karen's eyelashes, and watching her body move as she breathed when Owen walked back into the room. Owen picked up his clothes and started dressing.

'It should have been at least a Porsche,' Andreas told him.

'I know, but I'm scared she'll smash it up while she's learning,' Owen answered. He looked up at Andreas. 'Nothing to stop you buying her one, anyway.'

'Maybe some other time,' Andreas answered, and left Owen to his dressing.

Now no one could see him, Owen allowed himself to look

lingeringly at Karen on the bed. When he had pulled on his trousers, he sat close beside her to dress himself in his shirt and jacket. He eased the duvet from under her, lifting parts of her when necessary, ready to cover her with it. He could not resist stroking between her legs. She sighed and opened herself to him in her sleep. His fingers slipped into the edge of her. Her body sighed again. He smiled, covered her with the duvet and left to rejoin the party.

The House in
New Orleans

Fleur Reynolds

In *The House in New Orleans*, the central character, Ottilie, is fighting for her right to just that: the property she has jointly inherited with her scheming half-brother, Elmer. Elmer has leased the house to the cunning and lustful Count Helmut von Straffen, who is using Ottilie's future dream home to throw outrageously decadent Mardi Gras parties. She is appalled. Soon after meeting the Count, she is lured into some strange games in steamy locations and soon realises that not all dangerous animals live in the swamp! In the following extract, a picnic on the river with von Straffen results in a curious and very arousing turn of events for young Ottilie.

Fleur Reynolds has written a number of Black Lace books. *Odalisque*, her first novel, deals with family feuding and jet-set sex; *Handmaiden of Palmyra* is set in third-century Syria; *Conquered* tells the story of an Inca princess in sixteenth-century Peru, and *Bonded*, which is due for publication later this year, is the sequel to *Odalisque*.

The House in New Orleans

*O*ttilie turned quickly and received a shock. A shock that was like an earthquake trembling through her own private fissure. There was her man. Her handsome stranger. Her fantasy man. And the same thing happened to her as had happened in the restaurant in Paris. A shiver of excitement enveloped her. Her heart fluttered and her womb tightened. Her nipples hardened and a tingling rushed through the softness of her hidden self leaving a moistness between her legs. Ottilie immediately stopped rocking, put her knees together and her hands neatly in her lap and, though she tried not to, she gulped.

Helmut was composed and controlled. He knew he was meeting her. Ottilie didn't and she began to shake nervously, even more so when she felt her erect nipples straining against the silk of her dress, betraying her sudden inner turbulence. As he advanced into the room, Helmut looked from her shining hazel-green cat's eyes to her wide luscious red mouth, from her hard nipples piercing the smooth outline of her frock to her knees held fast together and her hands clasped with white knuckles in her lap, and then back to her red mouth. He was aware of the telltale signs of her sexual stimulation and enjoyed it.

Helmut had watched Ottilie arrive from an upstairs window. He had been enchanted by her bearing, her upright carriage and her air of self-containment, also by her beauty. Whatever it took, however much he had to lie, twist and turn, manipulate his diary, he was utterly determined to have her – and have her in every possible way. Ways he didn't think she had ever dreamed of. The Count found himself excited at the thought of licking her fine body, her neck, her breasts, her thighs, between her thighs, opening up her secret hidden lips and allowing his tongue to travel up, supping at her juices. He thought of the constraints he would put about her body and caressing her under those constraints; exciting her, taking her higher, inducing in her erotic thoughts and ideas that he would play out.

When she turned to see him Ottilie was surprised to find him dressed for the country rather than a formal business meeting. He was wearing white riding breeches, a white short-sleeved polo shirt and shining brown riding boots. In these sports clothes she could see that though he was as tall as she had remembered, was still as blond with a sense of power, and his ice-blue eyes were icy blue and cold as ever – though now she noticed they were fringed with long black lashes – his chest was broader and deeper, and his legs were longer than before. He was far more athletic; the tight breeches allowed her to see his rippling thigh muscles. Once again she had the feeling of danger, as if faced with a jungle animal. Only this was the king of the jungle. The lion. And he was on the prowl. Ottilie had the distinct feeling she was the prey.

That insight forewarned her. She must remember why she was here: that he had something that was hers. She wanted it returned and had every intention of reclaiming it. She was not going to fall for his charm. His very sexual charm. She smiled at that thought. What an anomaly: that this man, who provoked such an incredible sexual fever within her, should have a collection of Shaker furniture, from the sect that denied sexual intercourse to its members.

'Miss Duvier,' said Count Helmut, with that slight foreign accent she had noticed on the plane. He bowed, picked up her hand and brushed his lips over her fingertips. His touch seared her. Momentarily, electricity fused their flesh.

'Forgive me for keeping you waiting.'

Ottilie inclined her head, anything to get away from that stare and those eyes that could see into her soul; and quickly, with a sharp jerk, she pulled her hand away from his.

'Ottilie, this is Count Helmut von Straffen,' said Elmer, jumping up to meet him.

'I thought you might be,' said Ottilie.

'Did you?' said Helmut, smiling straight at her then turning to greet her step-brother. 'Elmer, good morning.'

Ottilie found herself staring at the Count's rear, thinking how neat and high and well shaped his bottom was. She noticed it had hollows in it where other men's filled out. It was a trait in the opposite sex that, combined with a barrel chest, Ottilie had always found particularly attractive. She had the strongest desire to trace that curve and hollow with her fingers. She pursed her lips, drew in a sharp breath and told herself to stop her ridiculous thoughts.

'Oh, Miss Duvier . . .'

'Please call me Ottilie,' she said.

'And I'm Helmut. Ottilie, I would like to talk to you, perhaps show you the house'. Helmut turned to Ottilie who was gently rocking in the chair.

Every bone, every fibre of her body told her to get up and run. Don't stay. If you stay you're lost. But she was fascinated, not only by the Count but also by her reaction to him, and the fascination was stronger than the warning. There was a desire to find out how far she would travel with the danger. She was quite certain he was as attracted to her as she to him. She could feel the intensity of that attraction in his glance. The thought that he would touch her gave her goose pimples. When would he touch her? Ottilie squirmed slightly in the chair; her hiddenness was swollen and damp but her mouth had gone completely dry. She decided discretion was the better part of valour. She would give the house a quick once over and then go to the concert all and meet Beau. And sing.

'I don't know what you have planned for the rest of the day,' said Count Helmut, sitting back in the swivel chair, 'but as you can see I am not dressed for the city. I have to go out to the country. There's some business I need to attend to. It won't take long. If you'd care to come for the drive I'd be delighted for you to accompany me.'

'I'd like that,' Ottilie heard herself say. Every intention had gone, overtaken by her desire, her curiosity. Her wild sexual curiosity. Her virginal body screamed go with him. Take him and everything on the wing. To hell with the consequences.

When they arrived in the state capital Ottilie stayed in the car whilst Helmut quickly dealt with the lawyer, then they proceeded out to swamp country. Ottilie hugged herself with joy.

Since childhood she had loved the earthy lushness of Louisiana. She was driving through the primeval landscape she adored with a man she fancied like crazy; and she didn't know exactly where she was heading. It was exciting. And everywhere she looked the sky, the trees, their branches, their leaves, even the man beside her, had a sharp clarity; outlines and colours were heightened as if during her absence they had grown in intensity.

Helmut turned from minor roads on to dirt tracks, then parked the car on a small landing stage at the edge of a creek.

'It's by boat from here,' he said, pointing to a small craft.

'That?' she queried, looking from it to the greeny brown water and wondering how many alligators were lurking in its depths.

'Yes,' he said, 'and you're to put some of this on.' He gave Ottilie a small jar of oil. 'Oil and lemon juice, a sort of vinaigrette sauce. Mosquitoes hate lemon, but I'm sure you know that. Don't forget your ankles.'

Whilst Ottilie coated herself with the coil, Helmut climbed out of the car, opened the boot, and retrieved a couple of ice boxes.

'Lunch,' he said, 'prepared by Missy Lee.'

'Who's Missy Lee?' Ottilie asked.

'My housekeeper,' he said. 'She's many things, including a marvellous cook.'

Helmut lowered the ice boxes carefully into the boat, then stepped in himself.

'Come on, get in,' he said, holding out his hand for her. She hesitated. He reached out, put his hands around her waist and lifted her lightly up. His touch made her tremble. She laughed, nervously. He placed her carefully on a seat, then undid the rope holding the boat, pulled the throttle of the outboard motor and they were away.

In the steamy heat Count Helmut aimed the boat upstream, away from the dark green stagnant pools where serpents and alligators lay basking in the dappled sun, and towards his hideaway on Bayou l'Extase.

Ottilie felt as if she was in an enchanted land. And enchanted lands are always dangerous. Birds flew overhead, there was the swish of tails in the water and the drone of the outboard motor, and the smell of the bayou mingled with her own smell, of French perfume and lemon juice and oil. She lay back in her seat and sighed, a happy, lazy, erotic sigh. She was floating between dreams and reality.

Helmut steered through the brown swampy water. Speckles of sunlight beamed through the canopy of black interlocking branches, exposing the glistening damp contours of Ottilie's sensual body. Sunbeams emphasised her hard, erect nipples, and Helmut's desire for her deepened.

He wanted her soft smooth body. He wanted it yielding to his passionate embrace. He wanted her lips on his lips. He wanted her breasts crushed against his chest. He wanted her crouching over his mouth. But Helmut knew the power of anticipation and kept the boat on course.

Some twenty minutes later he brought it in beside a broad landing stage. Ottilie gazed up at the precarious muddy and green-slimed wooden steps. In her high heels getting out of the boat was going to be difficult. Seeing her hesitate, Helmut lifted her high on his shoulders and carried her up the steps over the porch and into the rough log cabin with its roof covered with palmetto leaves.

Inside the dark room Ottilie felt his hot breath on her neck as he put her down. Leaving her trembling from his touch, he went back to the boat for the ice boxes. Her mind reeled off into a whirr of lascivious fantasy. Every part of her, every nerve ending, was aching and waiting to be caressed. Helmut came back and lit an oil lamp and candles. Immediately the cabin, so crude on the outside, was transformed into a wonderland of exotic drapes, cushions and carpets.

'Please sit down and be comfortable,' said Helmut, indicating a large cushion covered in slippery maroon satin close to the wall. There were no chairs in the room, just cushions of every size and shape. Ottilie curled up, with one foot sticking out and one under her, and the cushion moulded to her body.

Helmut opened up the largest of the two ice boxes, taking out two crystal flutes and a bottle of her favourite champagne. He then sat languidly opposite Ottilie and held out a glass of the light corn-coloured fizzing liquid he had just poured. With a shaking hand and her heart thumping she took it.

'To us,' he said, and leaned across a low table between them so they could clink glasses.

'To us,' she repeated, thinking to herself – oh my God, now what? And every portion of her body screamed out to be touched but was frightened of him doing it. Frightened because she wanted it but couldn't escape. She didn't want to escape; she wanted him. Ottilie was a turmoil of emotions. She avoided his eyes. She sipped at the wine, then not knowing what to do with herself she sipped again and again, faster and faster until the glass was empty.

'The heat has made you thirsty,' he said, reaching for the bottle and re-filling her flute.

'Yes,' she said hoarsely.

His voice had that special timbre, that slight accent that conveyed the danger she found so exciting.

'Perhaps you are hungry, too?' he asked.

'No . . . I mean yes . . .' she said.

'Let's see what Missy has prepared,' he said, opening the other ice box. First he removed a white table-cloth and two napkins. Then he took the vase that stood on the table with a fine display of feathers in it and put it on the floor beside him. Then he covered the low table with the table-cloth and gave Ottilie one napkin, putting the other on his own lap. Then he peered into the ice box again. 'Ah, caviare, and smoked salmon. Do you like that?'

'Yes,' she whispered, sipping at the wine again, telling herself to go slowly, not so fast, or she'd be drunk.

'And home-made brown bread. Missy makes it. There's cheese here too . . . and cucumber.' Helmut held up the large hard stiff green vegetable and stroked it lovingly before placing it on the table. 'And carrots, and bananas . . . and lettuce, tomatoes, and here we have a jar of mushrooms *à la grec* . . . what would you like?'

'Smoked salmon,' she answered, moving her body towards his hand holding out a plate.

As Helmut took her plate their fingers met. Shaking with anticipation Ottilie gave a slight gasp. Helmut pretended he hadn't heard and served her with the pink smoked fish. He knew exactly what he was doing. He wanted Ottilie at a fever pitch and his not touching her increased her frustration and desire. She would have to make the first move towards him. Only then would he know she was ready – for anything.

Helmut opened the small jar of mushrooms, and began to spoon them on to her plate. Ottilie realised she had pins and needles in the leg that was curled under her. She moved the leg. Helmut dropped some of the mushrooms and the sauce on her ankle.

'Oh, I'm so sorry,' he said, taking a sparkling white damask napkin, removing her shoe and dabbing at her ankle.

Ottilie held her breath and swallowed hard. His touch sent exciting, tingling messages along every part of her skin.

'There, that's better,' he said, lay back on his cushion and finished his glass of champagne.

But it wasn't better for Ottilie. Her sexual desire was heightened: she was aware of every nuance in her body, every movement, every tremble – and he appeared oblivious to her feelings. Ottilie decided she would give herself some caviare. She stretched across his legs and her breasts pressed into his thighs and knees as she scooped out the sturgeon eggs.

'More wine, I think,' said Helmut, leaning over her and retrieving her glass.

Ottilie moved her head, knocking Helmut's hand. A couple of cool drops hit the back of her neck. His fingers stroked where the liquid had spilled. She froze, suspended between desire and fear.

'Would you give me some caviare?' he asked, standing up.

Ottilie did as he asked then turned towards him holding out the plate. He took it and her hand, and their eyes met. Never letting his eyes leave hers Helmut put his glass down, and pulled her up towards him. In one swift movement he had clasped her fast to his body. She could feel his strength, the exciting hardness of his penis erect and pushing against her belly. Ottilie held her breath. His lips came down on hers. She closed her eyes.

Every dream she had ever had of this moment sprang to life as the red, wide softness of his yielding mouth touched hers, his tongue and his taste exciting her. With the heat and damp of the day and of their bodies they were locked together in a languorous embrace. His tongue pushed past her lips, entering into the tiny cavern beyond her teeth with controlled pressure. His lips travelled from her mouth to her cheeks to her earlobes and back again to her mouth. Then he nuzzled her neck and a quick spasm, a rash of goose pimples, broke out where his lips met her flesh. Erotic desire flushed through her.

When his tender kisses touched her vibrant skin the whole of her body quivered with pent-up longing. Each kiss found her more heady, as if she had taken the most potent drug. The wet heat of his lightly clothed body melded with hers. Leisurely, his lips started their journey again, brushing her ear, her throat, then the delicious curve of her neck. Exquisite sensations flooded into and out of her womb. Her mind ceased to think, to plan, to observe. It no longer functioned as a rational instrument. Emotion and desire were paramount. Respond. Respond, cried her tongue, her mouth, her breasts, her arms, her legs and her opening, ripe sex.

Ottilie wound her arms around Helmut's neck.

'I want you,' Helmut whispered in her ear.

His potent words let loose her womb, as she felt the swelling and the moistness of her inner self increase with her desire to have him lay her down, fondle her breasts and lie between her legs.

His hands moved down from her neck to hover over the buttons covering her cleavage. He made no attempt to undo them or remove her frock; instead with infinite delicacy, the tips of his fingers touched her hard erect nipples. Ottilie gasped: the sensation was extreme.

It was as if he had turned a key in the core of her body. Ottilie lay back taking his tongue, entwining hers with his, giving it affirmative answering messages. His fingers gradually increased the pressure on her nipples so that from gentleness the feeling progressed to heightened pleasure, then to pain, then to a combination of the two. And Ottilie could not tell where one sensation ended and the other began.

Helmut bent her back, down amongst the cushions.

'Open your legs,' commanded the Count, pulling at the hem of her frock.

Ottilie did as she was told. Helmut eased the soft floaty silk up along her thighs.

'Spread them wider,' he said, his fingers winding under the elastic of her panties, lingering with the lightest of touches on the swollen moistness of her wet labia. Tiny currents of torment rushed through her as he squeezed her sex lips together, not entering, just a pressure and a squeezing. The yearning within her to be taken and ravished by him grew stronger. Her breasts were aching to be fondled, and her own hands wanted and needed to caress him. He was playing her as if she were a musical instrument. He was the master player tuning her up, tuning her way above her known capacity. The candles slowly going out, leaving them in increasing darkness, helped Ottilie discover her innate licentiousness. Very slowly Helmut's fingers

began pushing into her juicy wet folds. Ottilie's body moved this
way and that, dancing to the incessant tune of his fingers inside
her. She found her own natural rhythm, her lips rising and
lowering and the muscles within her opening and closing about
his exploring fingers.

'Put your hands above your head,' Helmut commanded.

Ottilie lifted her hands up and back beyond the cushion and
found her flesh touching iron.

'It's a ring, hold it,' said Helmut.

Ottilie clasped it.

'Grip it hard, and don't move,' he said. Then he poured some
more champagne into a glass and lifted it to her lips.

'Drink,' he commanded. Ottilie drank the fizzy liquid, becoming even more heady and abandoned than she was before.

'I want to make love to you,' he said, nibbling at her ear lobes.
'I want to pleasure you. Would you like me to do that?' He
delicately pressed her nipples between his thumbs and fore-
fingers. 'I want an answer from you, Ottilie. Say yes or no. Do
you want me to pleasure you?'

'Yes,' she whispered.

'Yes, is that all you can say? Tell me what you want me to do
to you.'

'I . . . I don't know . . .' she said, confused.

'Would you like me to kiss your breasts, suck your nipples, or
go down between your legs . . .' Ottilie drew in a sharp breath as
he said that. 'I see, so you want me between your legs. But
Ottilie, do you want my tongue or my cock?'

Ottilie was silent.

'My dear, if you cannot choose I must choose for you, but I
must do it my way. And that means you submit to my every
whim. Whatever I want to do to you I'll do. Do you agree to
that?'

'Yes,' said Ottilie, who had no real idea what he meant but
wanted him to caress her more, fondle her breasts; she wanted
him between her legs. And she wanted to touch his penis, to feel
its strength and erect hardness.

Helmut reached into his pocket and drew out a long piece of
black silk fabric.

'Lift up your head. I am going to blindfold you.'

'Blindfold me!' she exclaimed.

'Your sense of touch will be heightened by the deprivation of your sight. Also you will not know which part of your body I will touch next and I think you'll find that exciting. If you don't you will tell me and I will stop and remove the blindfold.'

Helmut gently kissed her lips then tied the dark material around Ottilie's eyes. He knelt beside her, swiftly unzipped his trousers and took one of her hands from the iron ring.

'Hold it,' ordered Helmut, placing her hand over his penis.

Ottilie's hand had been aching to hold the stiff warmth of his prick. She encircled it then let her hand trail its length, finding his balls and letting her fingers glide over his testes, then took her hand back up again, under the hood and played up and down between the rim of the cap and the head. Each stroke she gave him gave her pleasure. She had a wild desire to take its erect fullness into her mouth.

'Suck me,' Count Helmut demanded.

Ottilie turned and put her head down to meet his prick. She opened her mouth and took its urgent roundness in between her soft red lips.

Helmut took hold of her hands and put them back on the ring. With the blindfold about her eyes Ottilie could not see the strips of leather hanging down from the ring. Firmly, but giving her plenty of leeway, he tied Ottilie's wrists. then slowly, one by one, he undid the buttons on the front of her frock. When each button was undone, he sensuously stroked her skin, laying bare her breasts, then bending and licking them. Then, taking a feather from the vase he caressed her erect nipples. She kept his prick in her mouth, and with a natural inborn rhythm she stayed sucking his cock.

Helmut undid every button on her frock and let the fabulous soft fabric fall to one side. He pulled off her silk half slip. Without undoing her brassière he lifted her breasts from their enveloping silk and lace, revealing their beautiful white swell and contours. Deftly he massaged her nipples, enjoying the sweet sound of her sexual whimpering. Then he took the feather and swept it down over her belly to her panties. Snakelike he eased his hand under the waistband, and with his middle finger the advance guard, found her hidden but aroused clitoris. In one fast movement he spread his whole hand over her sex, gripped and held her hard, only the middle finger continuing its salacious work. The slowness of the feather and the swiftness of his action caught Ottilie unawares. She gasped and felt the moisture and dampness increase between her legs. His fingers slid inside her. They skimmed on her silken wet sheen that was lightly covering her palpitating and swollen inner flesh. The sensation Ottilie experienced with his fingers gliding inside her was beyond anything she had ever imagined. She was completely lost to all reality except the fever his fingers wrought within her.

Helmut changed his position, so that his knees were either side of Ottilie's head. His cock remained in her mouth, where she was busy practising her newly acquired skill. Helmut pushed the leg of her pantie elastic to one side and she felt his tongue licking her thighs and then the swollen outer lips of her sex.

Her entire body was trembling. Tiny tremors of pure excitement shuddered through every nerve ending and every part of her body, whether she had ever considered it sexually erotic and arousable or not. Ottilie was amazed by this discovery. Sex did not stop in and around the top of her legs but was made up and heightened in each particle of her living being.

Helmut slid her panties down her legs and removed them.

'Spread your legs wide,' he commanded.

Submissively Ottilie did as he ordered. Helmut smiled a secret smile, delighted by her instant and total acquiescence to his every command. He was pleased, very pleased. Everything he had thought about her from the first moment he saw her was coming true. She had a pure and natural love of sex that was so far unsatisfied, certainly untapped and definitely unknown. He put his head between her legs and the next moment Ottilie felt the most delicious sensation fire through her taut body as his tongue enjoyed the soft sweet sea-smelling tissue of her inner body, probing its way further inside her soft, warm, wet folds. But it was when his tongue came up and flicked at her clitoris that her mind and body exploded simultaneously, not with an orgasm but with uncontrolled sexual abandonment. She writhed and squirmed and gasped and sighed and visions of total erotica flooded into her brain. She didn't care what he did as long as his tongue didn't stop its extraordinary work. And she stayed sucking his prick.

Helmut slithered away from her mouth, down the length of her body and took hold of her feet. He removed carefully positioned cushions hiding ankle fetters in the floor, put her feet into the shackles and quickly snapped them shut. Ottilie now lay blindfolded and spreadeagled; her arms tied above her head, her legs apart and manacled, her sex bare, her breasts billowing over her brassière, and her nipples erect. She was longing to be fondled and fucked.

'Lift your bottom up high,' he said.

Ottilie raised her hips. Helmut put three cushions under her buttocks. Then he removed all his own clothes and stood in front of her, naked with his penis erect and throbbing, admiring the beauty of the Titian-haired girl he now had at his sexual mercy. He sat down beside her, and while with one hand he began caressing her aching nipples, with the other he took an oily mushroom from the jar and trailed it through her sex before eating it.

The cold wet squashy feel of the unknown object dipping into her sex was so unexpected that Ottilie tensed then opened wider, wanting more, wanting that strange feeling again. She rolled her hips and moaned with delight.

Helmut denied her wish. Instead he took hold of the cucumber and, with infinite care, began to insert it in her soft pink opening. He watched her sex clasp it like a sea anemone, her muscles gently accepting its hard coldness. When he had thrust the tip in he left it hanging lasciviously from her sex and took another mushroom and rubbed it up and down on her clitoris, stimulating her hard little bud. Then he fastened his lips on Ottilie's warm erect nipples.

The lascivious pleasure of his assaults on the aroused membranes of her sex and on her body was bringing Ottilie to the point of climax, but Helmut wasn't ready for her to come. She had to know more, experience more, before she would be allowed her release.

Starting at her toes Helmut slowly sucked and licked his way along her body. Ottilie felt his prick pressing against her legs, her thighs, and then as his hands and his tongue went higher and higher, his cock stayed at the top of her legs. She could feel the hardness of the unknown something just inside her hidden wet entrance and the urgent warmth of Helmut's penis on her inner thighs. The whole of her was crying out for him, his cock, his prick, his penis, to enter her, penetrate her, dominate her.

'Please,' she moaned, 'please take me.'

'Take you?' he asked. 'What do you mean take you?'

Ottilie hesitated. Could she say what she meant? Could she say the word?

'You must tell me what you want?'

'I want . . . please will . . . please fuck me,' she whispered.

Helmut smiled and watched her tongue licking her lips, flicking in and out like a snake's. He leant his body over hers. Ottilie gasped. She had been longing to feel the strength of him against the yielding rounded softness of herself. Helmut took the cucumber from her ripe wet folds. Then he positioned himself carefully between her open legs and his cock at the entrance to her love channel. With his outstretched arms taking his weight, slowly he drove forward into the dark pink depths of her wanton sex.

There was an agony in his taking her. She had waited so long that her bladder had filled up and each time Helmut's pelvis met hers the pressure sent an exquisite piercing through her vulva and her womb. Helmut edged his body to one side, put his hand down between their sticky damp bodies and touched her clitoris.

Then Ottilie knew she was on fire. His touch seared her. He pounded into her inner depths with two fingers massaging her hard over-excited little point and she felt she would burst, not only with love juices flowing down from her womb but with water needing to flow out from her bladder. She tensed in order to stop it happening. Helmut knew full well what she was doing and increased his pressure on every part of her that was affected. She could only moan and sway.

Then he put his other hand under her bottom and gripped it hard. He dug his nails into her rounded flesh and continued to pound into her. Ottilie was twisting and turning on her bindings like a woman possessed.

Then she felt other hands take hold of her hair and push her head back so that her mouth was opened. A glass was held to her lips.

'Drink,' said Helmut. And she sipped but her head was tipped back and she was made to take the glassful of champagne. Now she was heady with the wine, heady with the pounding she was taking, and heady with her own ribald and erotic thoughts. She thought she must be so drunk that she had lost all sense. Nobody else could be in the room with them. Nobody. Nobody. Nobody knew they were there.

She was dreaming wild and fantastic dreams, of men holding

241

her down, licking her, sucking her, screwing her back and front. All inhibitions had evaporated.

When another cock was placed on her lips, Ottilie opened her mouth willingly and slowly took its great length in and sucked.

Helmut's fingers continued to play with her clitoris and her buttocks. The other hands reached for her breasts, oiling them encircling them, tweaking their rosebud nipples. She was powerless to do anything except let her body go with its outrageous desires.

The shackles on her ankles were sufficiently loose to allow her to put her feet flat on the floor, raise her hips higher, and take the pounding penis deeper within her.

Without warning both cocks stopped moving and were removed. Ottilie was left a vibrant shudder of emotions with an awakened, sensitised body. Hands rolled her over. She lay on her stomach. Now her bottom was raised high. Hands oiled her buttocks. The same hands occasionally slipped round and entered her sex. Then she felt something long, thin and supple – she was reminded of a leather belt she sometimes wore – and this was trailing along the soft tingling flesh of her vulva and her arse. Hands came up and gripped her bottom, holding it open. Ottilie had little time to register her sense of mortification as she realised her tiny hidden puckered place was on view. Suddenly and without warning that same small forbidden hole was being flicked with the leather strip. Flick and then her sex was stroked. Flick and her sex stroked again. She was opening and closing – the flicks were strange but oddly pleasurable. Then the strength of each tiny lash stroke was increased. Pleasure became pain. In between the pain there was a sudden stab of pleasure as fingers searched inside her sex, playing with her. She was wet and open and could do nothing except sway and moan and cry out with the unexpectedness of the extreme desire she was experiencing.

More oil was poured on her buttocks. Two sets of hands rubbed it into her naked rounded flanks. She could feel the hardness of two warm cocks either side of her digging into her waist. One set of hands travelled along her back. Massaging, massaging. The other set of hands had stopped. Then all hands stopped. That cold hard something, which she thought could possibly be the cucumber, was inserted into her moistness and thrust backwards and forwards, backwards and forwards, loosening her, sending wafts of licentiousness surging through her body. And the next moment she felt the fire across her oiled bottom as thin leather scorched her bare buttocks.

Ottilie cried out. She did not know whether she was crying with pleasure or pain or whether it was a mixture of the two that led her to yell.

Soft hands immediately came down on her buttocks and more oil was massaged into her rounded raised bottom. The massage eased the pain of the stripe. But then she was turned over and those same hands began to press on her belly, on her full bladder, and the cold hard elongated thing within her was moved up and down, up and down.

'Please,' she moaned. 'No, please don't do that.'

'Why not?' asked Count Helmut, increasing the pressure so that she was almost at the point of spilling out her water.

'I might . . . I might . . .' Ottilie faltered.

Unexpectedly Helmut kissed her lips.

'You might what?' he asked.

'I might not be able to hold my water,' she said.

'Oh but you must,' he said, and began to play with her sex, stimulating her again. 'If you don't I will have to lash you once more. I must say, your bottom looks very pretty, a neat red line across just waiting for others to join it.'

Ottilie was completely bemused. Who was this man who had her at his mercy? She recognised the voice but not his intentions. She shivered, partially with fear and partially with the pleasure of expectation and excitement.

Once more she was subjected to the twin sensations of the acute pain of the hand pressing on her belly while the thin leather strip was trawled through her sex. A mouth began to work along the lips of her labia. A tongue licked and flicked at her clitoris. She raised her hips to take that tongue deeper. And a cock was put beside her mouth. Hands pulled back her head and the cock pushed through her open lips. She sucked. Enjoying the motion and the feel of the prick in her mouth she relaxed and the pressure was increased on her belly. She forgot the discomfort and her water eased out, marking the maroon satin with a dark stain. Once she started she couldn't stop, and she felt herself flush with shame.

'Ottilie,' she heard the Count's voice. 'You disobeyed me.'

The prick in her mouth was removed and hands turned her over once more and oils were rubbed into her buttocks.

243

'I will have to punish you,' he said, and she felt the quick hard flicks of the thin leather on her bare rump.

'No,' she whispered. 'No.'

'Ottilie, it is my pleasure to whip you. And you will say, "Thank you, master." Do you understand?' Helmut touched her hard, aroused clitoris with his tongue and wiggled the cucumber inside her. 'Do you understand?'

'Yes, master,' she said.

'I shall give you six lashes and when I've finished you will thank me. Do you understand that too?' He licked her clitoris again. Ottilie writhed with the sensual pleasure of his tongue.

'Yes, master,' she said.

Helmut put another couple of cushions under her bottom.

'Let your buttocks go loose,' he said, wobbling them with his hand while massaging more oil into her skin.

'And you will not make a sound. If you do I will give you another six.'

He brought the lash down with swiftness and expertise, criss-crossing her white flanks with bright red weals.

She moaned but did not cry out as the sharp piercing blows left her with a greater sense of abandonment and opened her up to the pleasure of humiliation and unabashed wantonness.

And then Helmut took her again. He thrust into her hard, and she responded with a glorious wildness. Her yoked hands and feet twisting and turning, her arms and legs shuddering, her head moving with a fluency of motion as he obsessively and urgently immersed himself in her, blending her body with his. They were completely one.

They slept. Helmut curled himself around her marked and shackled body and they drifted into a deep and satisfying sleep. Helmut awoke first. He re-lit the candles then untied her wrists and unlocked her ankle fetters. He kissed her warm bruised lips.

'You did well,' he said, smiling.

Ottilie stared at him slightly bemused. She was still half-dressed. He was naked. It was the first time she had seen him without clothes. His thick broad chest, his slim hips, long legs and his penis, which even in repose she noticed was large. She looked around the room. Had there been someone else there or had that been her overactive imagination?

'What's the matter,' Helmut asked, stroking her hair, and her neck. 'Are you hungry or thirsty?'

244

'Thirsty,' she said.

'Wine, water or orange juice?' he asked.

'Orange juice,' she replied.

Whilst Helmut poured her drink Ottilie looked around the cabin. There was no evidence of anyone else having been in the room.

'You're an extremely sexual woman with a wonderful body,' said Helmut, handing her the orange juice. 'Turn round, let me see your bottom.'

She turned and he lifted her silk frock and gazed at the weals.

'They'll be gone by the morning,' he said, fondling her buttocks. 'But they look very pretty.'

He pulled her down beside him and kissed her mouth. His hands began to roam over her body. She reacted instantly. Her nipples hardened. He caught them and squeezed them. She gave a sharp sigh.

'Lie down and open your legs,' he commanded. 'I want to fuck you again.'

Ottilie, excited by his choice of words, did exactly as he ordered. She wanted to watch. She wanted to see him entering her. He climbed on top of her and positioned his prick at her entrance. She gave a series of short gasps as she felt his throbbing member push past her folds. Slowly, slowly he pushed inwards. She lifted her head so that she could see his cock penetrate and dominate her. Then he put his lips over her lips and suddenly rammed into her, fast and furiously. She raised her hips to meet every thrust. She twisted and turned beneath his sweating body. She ran her hands up and down his back then clasped her ankles over the small of his back and he kept thrusting until all their energy was spent.

Later, after they had eaten and made sure all the candles were out, and the oil lamp was made safe, he drove her home.

It was a pleasant drive. They didn't talk much. Neither of them said anything about the sex they'd enjoyed together. It was as if it was a secret not to be shared in the open air.

Wicked Work

Pamela Kyle

In Pamela Kyle's *Wicked Work*, her central character Suzie Carlton has status, money and power. What she doesn't have is a masterful partner who will allow her to realise the true extent of her submissive sexuality. At work Suzie is assertive and in control; in the bedroom she delights in the thrill of total surrender but cannot find anyone who understands her fantasies. After taking advice from a girlfriend, Suzie contacts a male escort agency and so begins a process of discovery without complications, until, that is, Suzie meets Michael. Here, Suzie and Michael meet for the first time and they launch into games of sexual power play.

Pamela has written one other Black Lace book. It's called *Rude Awakening* and, like *Wicked Work*, explores the sometimes controversial theme of erotic domination.

Wicked Work

The moment Suzie saw him, she knew Michael was different. There was something about his confident air as he strolled in the bar, his eyes casting casually about; there was an almost tangible aura about him that seemed to glow with his presence. All the Benson Agency men were self-assured and socially at ease – it would have been a prerequisite of the job, naturally. One of them anyway. But this man fairly oozed confidence, and wore it like a comfortable suit. His charisma was phenomenal.

She recognised him at once, of course, from Grace Cummings's description, but Grace had not done him justice. Tall and slim without being rangey, he had a neat crop of curly black hair, and a face that was ruggedly good-looking rather than handsome. But it was a face she instantly fancied.

A young woman, not unattractive, was sitting at a nearby table, and Michael's eyes went to her. Suzie felt a momentary stab of what might have been jealousy, but which couldn't have been. Could it?

Michael nodded to the woman politely, but seemed to know she wasn't the one.

And then his eyes found Suzie.

Suzie's heart missed several beats and began suddenly to flutter as she smiled and started towards her. Silly bitch, she told herself, what are you suddenly so nervous about? He's just a man, like the others. Your meat on the hoof for the night. But she couldn't help it; she felt like a schoolgirl on her first date.

He reached her table. 'Miss Carlton,' he said. It was a statement, not a question. He was in no doubt.

'Er, yes,' Suzie squeaked. She cleared her throat, both surprised and abashed at the sound she had made, and managed to regain some composure. 'Suzie. And you're Michael.'

Michael inclined his head. 'At your service.'

'Would you, er ... would you like a drink?' She could suddenly use another herself.

'Sure, but let me. What'll it be?'

'Martini. Thank you.'

Michael went to the bar. And her eyes followed him every step of the way, mesmerised. He moves with the grace of a cat, she thought. No, not a cat – a panther: yes, that was it. Powerful, yet light, supple. Though not at all like the black girl she had watched pose in the studio, who had also brought a panther to mind. Michael was as masculine as she had been feminine; like a prowling, male panther – a panther in search of a mate; feline and overtly sexual.

As he stood at the bar Suzie studied his buttocks: they were small and tight, deliciously delineated by the tailored cut of his slacks. (Suzie was definitely a bottom girl.) She imagined them naked, her hands on them gripping those hard, muscular nates as she pulled him inside her. She savoured the image with a lick of her lips; felt a familiar heat spread out from her groin to warm her all over.

He returned with their drinks; Suzie's Martini and a glass of white wine for himself – which he had paid for – and sat down beside her.

'A pleasant evening,' he said.

'What? Oh. Oh, yes, pleasant,' she muttered distractedly.

It was quite usual for her to be feeling nicely sexy by this time on a Friday evening, her thoughts of the night ahead readying her for what was to come. But tonight her need was suddenly desperate; she couldn't wait to get this Michael up to her room.

She swigged at her Martini to steady her nerves, and said, 'Look, would you mind if we took our drinks upstairs?'

She had taken several of the others aback with her forthrightness, her keenness to get on with the action, but if Michael was fazed in the least he didn't show it. 'But of course,' he said smoothly, immediately standing and gathering their glasses. 'Why don't you lead the way?'

In her room, Michael set their glasses down on a table and turned to face her.

'Look, I'm sorry to bring up the subject of money,' he said, without embarrassment, but with a look of genuine regret. And with none of the businesslike coldness there had been with the others, and that she had come to expect. 'But – '

Suzie stopped him with a shake of her head. 'No, really, it's all right.' She found her purse and took out the seventy-five pounds that seemed to have become the standard fee. 'I expect this will cover it, yes?'

Michael raised an eyebrow at the fanned-out notes. 'Oh, but that's really more than – '

'Please, take it,' Suzie insisted. 'Really.'

She had a feeling it would be worth every penny; she just knew it. She could feel it in her bones; in the surges of excitement that even now were tugging at the pit of her stomach. And that made her hand shake as she held out the notes.

Michael thanked her and accepted the money.

'But,' she added, 'I do expect . . . I mean, I would like a full hour for it.'

'I understand,' said Michael, sitting himself comfortably on the edge of the bed. 'Is there anything else?'

'Yes, I . . . er . . . no . . .'

Earlier, she had known exactly what she would say; what her list of instructions for that evening would be. Despite her resolve not to, she had spent a delicious hour in the bath mapping it out as usual. But now it was suddenly all gone; her mind a blank.

She shook her head dumbly.

'Then, come here.'

It was practically a command – it was a command – and the sound of it turned Suzie's belly to sudden jelly, sending an erotic shiver tingling along her spine. And on legs that were suddenly weak, she went to him, stood before him (as she instinctively knew he had meant she should do), and waited.

A moment passed. Another. And still she waited, standing passively before him and feeling his presence through every nerve of her body; expectant and tense. Then, at last, he reached up and cupped his hands to her breasts, squeezed with strong but gentle fingers. She gasped at the sudden assault, but remained still, her hands by her sides.

'You're wearing no bra,' he said.

'No,' she replied breathlessly. It was almost a struggle not to add sir, or master. 'I ... I rarely do.'

Michael trapped her nipples between fingers and thumbs, and applied a firm pressure that again made her gasp.

'I see. And I'll bet you're not wearing knickers either.'

How did he know?

'Are you?' he pressed.

He was looking up into her face, his eyes locked on hers. They were striking, grey eyes, which seemed unfathomable – as if they were hiding a million secrets. And there was something in them that made butterflies dance (or spiders crawl) in her belly. But she couldn't have looked away if she'd tried.

They were demanding an answer.

'No,' she admitted, blushing down to her neck.

'No. You are a dirty girl, aren't you?'

She swallowed thickly. 'Yes,' she muttered. It was a barely audible whisper.

As if in just punishment for her brazenness he gave her nipples a sharp tweak, and she sucked in a breath through teeth clenched in sudden pain. He watched the distress that appeared in her eyes and smiled. An enigmatic smile; a smile almost of sympathy, yet which seemed to conceal a deep understanding.

'A very dirty girl,' he said, tweaking again. Harder.

Suzie's blush deepened, and her nipples hurt. She wanted to twist away; to free the tender buds from his dreadful grip on them. But she didn't.

'Tell me, Suzie,' he said, his eyes still holding hers; his voice soft. 'Are you going to do everything I say this evening?'

The question was a shock, yet wasn't. It was as if she had known it would come.

'I ... Yes,' she muttered weakly.

'Everything – anything – I tell you to do?'

Her senses swam dizzily. His grip on her nipples was tacitly threatening, daring her to refuse him. But there was much more than that: he seemed to exude a certain power, a sexual energy that demanded obedience and which she could not resist. What could she say?

'Yes,' she breathed on a rush of air, the thrill of total surrender preventing the word from properly forming.

'Good. Then open your legs.'

The simple command sent a shockwave through her. A shock she found difficult to construe. After all, she had opened her legs for other men; what was suddenly the big deal? But she had never before been ordered to, and that, somehow, was intensely erotic; thrilling in a way she had never experienced. However, there wasn't the time to consider it further.

Abruptly, Michael released her anguished nipples from his grip on them and they flared with sudden fire. She winced, but resisted the urge to rub them, to soothe the fire away, and kept her hands where they were, sensing she should. Sensing she must, as she set her feet a little apart just as he'd told her.

The backs of Michael's fingers stroked lightly for a moment across the now hardening buds, as if to explore the heat he had caused to burn within them, then he lowered a hand to the inside of her knee. Slowly, he ran his palm up her inner thigh, beneath her skirt, until his fingers reached the moist warmth at the top.

It was a fleeting caress, the briefest of touches; as though he had wished only to confirm that she had obeyed him, and had parted her thighs to allow it. Or, perhaps, to confirm for himself that she was not wearing panties. Whichever it was, his hand was there for just a tantalising moment before it withdrew. Nevertheless, it was enough to leave Suzie's thighs quivering with need, her abdomen taut; excitement mounting in her lower belly as it gathered in search of release.

Michael reached back up, to the buttons of her blouse now. Deftly, he plucked them undone and pushed the material aside to expose her breasts.

Then he sat back to regard them.

Suzie's legs turned to water and she started to tremble. 'Oh, please . . .' she whispered hoarsely.

'What?' Capricious eyes flicked up to meet hers just for a moment, then deliberately returned to her breasts. 'You have nice breasts. I'm admiring them, that's all.'

'Em . . . Embarrassing,' she breathed.

'What's that you say?'

He made her repeat it. 'It . . . it's embarrassing.'

Michael smiled a knowing smile.

'Is it now? Then we'd better look at the rest of you, hadn't we?'

In a single fluid movement he sat forward again and pushed the blouse from her shoulders, laying them bare and now fully exposing the swell of her breasts. Then he reached for the clasp at the waist of her skirt. Unhooking it, he slipped the zipper and let the skirt drop down to her ankles.

Apart from her stockings and shoes, Suzie was now standing naked.

And when Michael sat back to look at her, she shuddered hugely and came.

Her thighs trembled and her belly shook. Her jaws were clenched in a struggle to keep herself silent. But she couldn't prevent the nasal grunt that sounded loud in her ears; that betrayed she was wracked in the shaming throes of orgasm. Her eyes were squeezed tightly shut, but she remained acutely conscious of Michael's gaze upon her, watching her. Watching her come right there in front of him. God, what a wanton slut he must think her. But she could do nothing to help it; only let herself finish.

And then, mercifully, her orgasm at last began to subside, through dying spasms of lesser intensity, to finally release her from its fervid grip. She wanted to open her eyes, but didn't dare. And then she couldn't help herself but, knowing the shame that awaited her, that would be reflected in Michael's eyes. And craving it.

Her eyes came slowly open to remind her poignantly that Michael was still fully clothed, sitting on the edge of the bed while she stood naked before him. Naked and vulnerable, her breasts rising and falling on the small juddering breaths she was still heaving; her thighs shaking; her blonde bush a scream of immodesty that begged to be covered. But cover it she dared not; he had not said that she could.

A small smile was playing on Michael's lips as his eyes drank in her nudity. It was a smile of amusement; amused, she knew, by the fact she had come so readily, with so little provocation. Right there, as she stood before him, the only stimulus that of his watching eyes. What a wanton slut indeed.

But seething tendrils of desire were already beginning to arouse her again, that very thought exciting her. An excitement that surged when Michael reached out a hand to her; slid a searching middle finger between her legs in quest of her hidden furrow and began to slide along it, teasing her lips apart to reach the pink inner sanctum.

His eyes came up to meet hers and commanded her to look into them while his finger continued to delve, bathing in the liquid, undeniable proof of her wantonness. And things squirmed in her belly as she read his knowing eyes, exciting her further.

'Was that a good come?' he asked.

His tone was teasing and her cheeks burned.

'Well?' he pressed when she didn't answer.

He was making her say it. 'Yes,' she whispered at last, the word catching on a ragged breath.

His finger continued to work.

'So I can feel. You're soaking down here.'

He withdrew his hand and held up his finger to where they both could see it.

'Look,' he told her, 'my finger's covered with your come.'

And so it was. It glistened with her juices and, seeing it, her cheeks burned hotter. Burned hotter still when he slipped his finger slowly into his mouth. She cringed with embarrassment and wished desperately to look away. But his eyes forbade it. They held hers and insisted she watch.

'Mmmm . . . You taste good,' he teased; his tone calculated, it seemed, to cause her the maximum embarrassment. It worked.

He gave his finger a final long lick, and then it was back in her pussy, probing deeply.

But not for long.

As soon as it had buried itself up to its hilt he withdrew it and raised it again, this time up to her face. It was fully re-charged with her juices, and she caught the faint tang of her feminine fragrance as she waited for what she knew, with dread certainty, was to come.

And come it did: 'Here, you taste.'

It was a command, not an invitation, and she slowly opened her mouth. He slipped his finger inside, rolling it on her tongue as her lips closed upon it.

The taste of a woman's sex was not of course new to her. Nor even her own; she had tasted it before on the lips of others, on her ex-boyfriend Geoff's cock when she had fellated him hard again following intercourse. But this was in a different dimension: having to suck her own sexy juices from Michael's finger,

at his command and while he watched, was acutely humiliating. And once again a part of her wished desperately she could look away to avoid the look of almost mocking amusement she saw in the mysterious depths of Michael's grey eyes, and on the small curl of his lips. Yet that other part of her, that darker part, thrilled to the shame of it, and she could not look away. Not even were those compelling eyes to allow it.

'Tastes good, doesn't it?' Michael said. 'Sexy.'

After a while he withdrew his finger, leaving only its lingering aftertaste on Suzie's tongue, and returned it to her now aching pussy – aching, reach to come again. All that was being done to her: the humiliations, her very submission to this man, the direct stimulus of his fingers, had re-aroused her to that peak of desire which refuses to be contained any longer – she was close, very close, to a second climax.

'Now, stand quite still,' Michael told her, as his clever finger slid back and forth, finding a rhythm. Teasing her slippery outer lips, tantalising the inner flesh with delicate, fluttering touches. Occasionally probing deeper but always, it seemed, maddeningly missing her clitoris – that very part of her which yearned for its touch most of all.

She tried to catch it, to rasp her frustrated nub against his moving knuckle, knowing that just one touch would be all it would take. But she had been told to stand still and so dared allow herself no more than the most imperceptible shift of her hips, the barest squeeze of her thighs, and it wasn't enough. She failed, and only ached all the more for her efforts.

'You're not to come again yet,' Michael warned, as if reading her thoughts. And that explained it. He was purposely avoiding her clitoris, deliberately teasing her. 'There'll be time enough for that. But first I want to see all of you.

He withdrew his hand.

'Turn around.'

Her heart was already a thing that pounded in her chest, but it suddenly leapt to her throat thudding harder. See all of her? Just where did he mean?

'T-turn around?' she muttered thickly.

The saliva in her mouth cloyed and was something she couldn't swallow.

Michael's face didn't change.

'I think you heard me, Suzie. Yes, turn around.'

Did he have any idea what he was doing to her? The torment, physical and mental, he was putting her through? Yes, of course he did; he knew exactly what he was doing.

But it seemed there was nothing she could refuse this man; he could do with her just as he pleased. And with that daunting yet thrilling thought, her legs like jelly, she slowly obeyed his command.

Standing with her back to him, she fancied she could feel his eyes on her skin, travelling down her back, to her buttocks, settling there; eyeing the lush firmness of her rounded nates, the dark crevice between them.

That crevice which held secret her most inviolate place: the forbidden entrance that was the source of her most inhibiting hang-up of all. That place she had permitted no one – not Hilary, not Geoff; no one, ever – to openly view before. Under this man's dominance, was that about to change?

Long seconds took hours to pass. She was trembling all over now, her heart thudding adrenalin through her veins, yet it seemed to weaken rather than strengthen her. A thundering waterfall rushed past her ears as blood throbbed at her temples, and she felt light-headed. She feared she would faint as the tension mounted and she waited for something to happen.

And then it did.

She jumped and almost cried out at the sudden shock of it when it came; the sudden touch of Michael's hand on the underswell of her buttock. And then the hand was between her legs once again, sliding upwards between her lightly-closed thighs towards her longing sex. Reaching there, gentle fingers stroked for a while, teasing her back up to the peak from which she had only slightly subsided. They were soon driving her wild, and she squeezed her thighs against them in an attempt to trigger her climax (the reason she had been ordered to turn around for the moment forgotten as her sexual tension rose to a heady summit and orgasm grew ever nearer).

But then, just as she felt she was almost there, the firm pressure of fingertips against her inner thigh was a silent command telling her to open her legs. She groaned in frustration, knowing this would deny her any hope of the self-help she had sought; that she had once again been thwarted. Aching with ungratified arousal, she obeyed the unspoken command and took a small step to the side, parting her thighs and regretting she could no longer use them to find additional friction against Michael's teasing fingers.

But those same fingers, pressed to her thigh, told her it wasn't enough and made her step out further, opening her legs wide.

And still, for Michael, this wasn't enough.

'Now bend your knees a little, Suzie,' he told her. 'Bear down slightly to open yourself wide for me.'

Her breathing shallow, her pulse racing, she did as he said.

The slight crouch opened her thighs obscenely, forcing her mound forward and her sex to gape, and Michael's fingers – the backs of them, she sensed – began gliding back and forth right inside the wide open slit, his knuckles grazing the delicate pink petals of her soft inner sex. She was aware, too, acutely aware, that it had opened that very crevice she had sought to keep closed.

It went on for a while, until the muscles of her thighs began to ache dully from the strain of holding the awkward posture. Until that ache became more acute, her muscles burned in protest, her thighs beginning to tremble as the strain grew worse. But it was a pain she tried to ignore. She was so close to coming, and just a few more stokes of Michael's ministering fingers would be bound to take her over the brink, and send her exploding to climax. With that in prospect she had no wish to move; the pain she would bear.

But then, as Michael's finger slid backwards, away from the nub it had all-too-fleetingly pleasured, she felt it go further, its nail scratching lightly at the delicate membrane beyond the join of the lips. And this time it didn't stop to return, but instead travelled on... Oh, God, no, ... to draw right across the puckered ring of her anus. She groaned anew, Michael's hand sliding licentiously between the opened cheeks of her bottom a sudden and sharp reminder of why he had turned her around.

Sweat sprang to her brow and she began to shake uncontrollably; her secret opening snatching tight on itself in guard against threatened intrusion. Even the frustration of Michael's hand leaving her pussy, denying her the orgasm that had been so maddeningly close, was of small consequence against that which she feared was to come. He wanted to see all of her, he had said.

Michael's hand withdrew.

And she waited with bated breath. Making her wait was something Michael liked doing, it seemed.

'You know, Suzie,' he said at last, 'just looking can be so incredibly erotic, can't it?' Oh, God, thought Suzie, her heart in her mouth; here it comes. 'Oh, touching of course. Touching, feeling; the scents, the tastes, even the sounds of sex can all be erotic. But none more so than just looking. Or being looked at, eh?

'And especially a body like yours, Suzie. A terrific body. A body I want to see every part of. And you'd let me, wouldn't you, Suzie? Let me see all of you?'

This was it; the brink from which there would be no return.

Suzie could barely speak. A part of her quailed. Yearned only for his resumed caress, a swift and natural path to much-needed climax. And why not? After all, she was paying the piper; she could have whatever she wanted. She could put a stop to this at any time: just the one word was all it would take. The one word: no.

She steeled herself. 'Yes,' she whispered.

The other, darker side of herself had answered the question: the part that yearned for the command to bend over.

But then his hands were on her hips, gently turning her round, and a surge of relief swept through her that almost – though not quite – compensated for perverse dismay!

But any dismay was instantly forgotten as Michael issued his next command: 'Keep your legs wide apart,' he ordered as he turned her to face him.

For somehow, even this – just being made to stand with her legs apart, submissively offering her sex – was humiliating enough. Enough to set delicious tendrils of erotic desire writhing within her as she watched Michael's eyes on her bush.

Michael slid down from the bed, and shuffled himself close on his knees. Reaching behind her he took her buttocks in his powerful hands, holding on to them tightly while he leant in with his face, his lips brushing damp hair aside in search of her throbbing sex.

Suzie moaned in agonised delight. His tongue probed into her, making white-hot spears stab at her loins. His lips found her clitoris, exposed in its need, and brushed against it. So did his tongue, making a single rapid swirl around its aching stem. Her belly juddered at the longed-for touch and her climax reared yet again; was again just a moment, just a touch away. Dizzy with tension she thrust out her hips, pressing her mound to Michael's face, her clitoris harder against his lips in urgent need of release. Of relief.

But just as she felt the melt-down begin – that reaction in her sexual core that could not be reversed and would, inevitably, lead to explosion – he suddenly pulled away. Suzie cried out in shock, hardly believing it. He couldn't stop now; not now for God's sake!

Michael looked up at her. 'I thought I said you were not to come again yet. Not until I'd seen all of you.'

Suzie's knees almost buckled and her thighs shook. A groan erupted from deep in her throat, and the dull ache in the pit of her stomach was almost unbearable.

'Oh God, Michael. I don't think I can hold myself back any – '

Michael put a silencing fingertip up to his lips. 'Shhh,' he said gently. 'Of course you can. You must.' He pushed himself back and returned to the edge of the bed. 'Self-control is a virtue, Suzie; pleasure all the sweeter for having to wait . . . But perhaps my tongue is a bit too testing. I'll let you off with that for now. So, now, I think it's time you should show me what I haven't yet seen.'

Suzie groaned inwardly. Knowing she must make herself wait. Knowing she must now display herself in some no doubt lewd and humiliating posture for this man; for this virtual stranger. For this wonderful, exciting, irresistible stranger. Knowing it would turn her on further, and that her desperate ache, the waiting, would be all the harder to bear.

'Now, Suzie, sit down on the floor,' Michael told her. 'Yes, there where you are, directly facing me. Now, bring your knees together and bring them up to your chest. Yes, that's right.'

Suzie was surprised to say the least. She would have thought that bringing her knees together would have been the last thing Michael would want. But she wasn't complaining; she was glad to take a moment's comfort in the sense of modesty the position afforded – her legs had been apart for such a long time, it seemed, her sex open and available. And it came as some relief to now be sitting with her knees drawn up and together, that part of her which pouted sexily from between her thighs shielded from Michael's eyes by her shins. Even her breasts were covered, her nipples hiding coyly behind the tops of her knees. She still wore her shoes and her heels were now tight to her buttocks, and as she wrapped her arms around her legs for balance, it put her in the classic posture of modesty; that which any naked female will instinctively adopt in the presence of male eyes. It afforded her some respite from the excruciating tension that was quivering inside her.

But, as she might have known, it wasn't to last.

'Now, Suzie,' Michael told her. 'Lie back, your arms by your sides. Good. Now, keeping your heels together, let your knees drop apart.'

The sudden realisation of it hit Suzie like a thunderbolt; what a naïve innocent she had been not to have seen it coming! Not that it would have made any difference of course; she could refuse Michael nothing. Yet, still, she hesitated. For the position, she knew, would be staggeringly effective. Both for her and for him. For him, because it would give him a totally unimpeded view of her wide open sex – no position could have opened her wider. For her, because not even her fair bush would any longer provide her with even the meagrest refuge from his gaze. She could hardly conceive of a more humiliating position. Well, perhaps one.

But finally, knowing she could do no other, slowly, very slowly, she let her knees fall apart.

'Oh, wider than that, Suzie,' Michael chided her when she tried to hold back. 'Much wider than that.'

He was allowing her nothing; nothing short of total surrender. And, resigning herself to that fact, she suddenly let go; let her knees drop all the way open, until they were almost touching the floor either side.

Her groin screamed in protest at the sudden strain put on it. But physical discomfort was the least of her worries.

Never had she felt so utterly naked. Her sex was obscenely, disgracefully displayed, and it was as if Michael's eyes bored into her, ravishing her, taking her. The strain on her upper thighs forced the indentations on the insides of them into deep hollows, from which her pubic mound stood high and alone as if profering itself; abasing itself in its pride. Her sex-flesh pulsed in a wanton display of its hunger, her juices flowed freely, and things crawled in the pit of her stomach to know that Michael was watching it all.

'Good. Suzie, good,' Michael praised. 'Now, put your hands to your pussy; hold yourself wide for me. Let me look right inside you.'

God, was there no end to this? Was she to be allowed no dignity at all?

It seemed not. Swallowing hard, she tentatively slid her hands down her sides, then inwards, across her lower belly; pressing trembling fingertips either side of her prominent mound to spread herself wider still, aware that the pressure forced her clitoris free of its fleshy hood to beg with profligate boldness.

She almost cried out with the shame of it. It was no more, no less, than Hilary had once made her do. But with Michael it was a million times worse. A million times better; a million times more thrilling. For one thing, with Hilary, the humiliation of it had brought about the rapid onset of orgasm; the ordeal had lasted but seconds. But Michael had forbidden her from coming; this could go on for as long as he chose. And though a part of her cringed at the thought of him watching the inner core of her sex pulsing wantonly in the uncontrollable throes of climax – an embarrassment she was thus being spared – that other part of her thrilled to the notion, making resistance to it all the harder to bear. She was aching to come, was right on the verge, yet she was forced to contain it within her. Her sexual strings pulled taut, almost to snapping, she was only glad of her earlier climax. But for that she doubted she could have borne it at all.

Michael slid himself down from the bed and came to kneel by her heels. Placing his palms on the floor by her hips he lowered his face to her groin. He flicked his tongue at her clitoris, making her jerk in sudden spasm and bringing a gasp from her throat. It was a single flick, and then he raised his head again, his eyes finding hers.

'Are you close to coming?' he asked.

'Oh, yesss!' she said, tension forcing the air from her lungs to make it a sibilant hiss.

He flicked her clitoris again. Again just the once, a single swirl of his tongue, before he again found her eyes.

'How close?'

Her belly quivered then tautened at the flicking caress. 'Very,' she gasped.

He smiled then, and again dipped his head. His tongue lapped at her aching nub. Not once now, but twice. Then three times.

Was this it? Suzie thought desperately. Was he finally about to relent and trigger her climax? Tension clutched at the pit of her stomach, and she held her breath, her every muscle straining in expectancy of the final touch.

But . . .

Was she allowed? Sudden horror snatched at her gut. He hadn't said she could come.

Yet surely he couldn't expect her to endure this and not. Surely he now meant her to let herself go, to avail heself of his tongue and erupt in the orgasm he had already denied her for so unbearably long. But she just didn't know; she was impaled on the horns of a cruel dilemma. To come or not to come, that was the question: to surrender to orgasm or to continue, somehow, to hold herself back. Finally, in the split second it took for these thoughts to race through her mind, the decision was made. She would wait for the very next swirl of his tongue, and would allow it to burst the swollen dam, to snap her sexual tension and send her flooding in the relief of climax.

It was a long second before she realised that that next caress wasn't to come.

Michael had lifted his head again, was again searching her eyes.

A long groan issued from deep in her being, exhaled on a rush of anguished breath; breath she had held in expectancy, but which now gushed from her in a long shudder of bitter frustration. 'Oh, God, n-o-o-o,' she cried, close to sobbing.

'You weren't about to let yourself come, were you?' Michael's voice was teasing.

'N-no,' she lied. Her belly heaved.

'Because you know you can't come yet, don't you?'

Her voice was barely audible. 'Yes.'

'And you know why?'

Her mind raced. *Why?* She had said yes, but she couldn't think of the reason. Her mind was reeling and she couldn't muster her thoughts, couldn't think anything straight. *Why?*

Michael reminded her. 'Because I haven't seen all of you yet, have I?'

Suzie's heart almost stopped, then thudded all the more fiercely. When Michael had turned her to face him again, after she had stood with her back to him, she had dared to hope he had spared her that final ordeal; that final, utter, invasion of her privacy.

263

'You promised to let me see all of you before you came,' Michael went on. He chuckled softly. 'Why, you didn't think I'd forgotten, did you?'

Suzie could only roll her head slowly from side to side, not daring to trust her voice, knowing now, from his chuckle, that Michael had done it deliberately. Had deliberately allowed her to believe she'd escaped, only for the blow to be more cutting, now, when it came.

'So, then, how do you intend to show me that final place?'

Suzie gulped hard, seeing no way out. She saw herself kneeling on all fours while Michael spread the cheeks of her bottom – or made her do it herself, she couldn't think which would be worse – to expose her secret opening. Resigned, she slowly went to turn over.

But Michael stopped her.

'No, no,' he said. 'Before you move, I want you to tell me how you intend to show me.'

Suzie's tummy turned, squirming impossibly. 'I ... I ...' She could barely speak. Was she to be allowed not a single shred of dignity? Was it not humiliating enough that she would have to do it, without her having to describe the act in advance? It was mortifying, but finally she found a small voice. 'On ... On all f-fours?' she ventured.

Michael smiled, but shook his head. 'No,' he told her. 'Interesting, but no; I've a better idea.'

He reached his hands under the crooks of her knees and raised them a little.

'Here,' he said. 'Hold your legs here. Hold them wide, then roll yourself back on your shoulders.'

Her shame was complete. As she rolled herself back as Michael had told her, holding her legs wide, she knew she could not have displayed her bottom more lewdly; more obscenely. It was utterly demeaning. Utterly degrading. And utterly, utterly thrilling. Her worst nightmare, her wildest dream, had come true.

For how long Michael had her remain so, feasting his eyes on her most secret place, she had no idea; time lost all significance and no longer mattered, washed away on a tide of erotic sensation. If his eyes had ravished her before, they were buggering her now, and it was all she could do not to pass out with the thrilling shame of it.

But then, at last, he was telling her to sit up. And then to kneel.

'You can sit back on your haunches,' he told her as she hurriedly shifted position, not needing to be told twice. 'But you're to keep your legs wide apart. I want you available to me, to look at or to touch, at all times. And now, it's your turn to look.'

With that, he stood and quickly stripped naked; sat down again on the edge of the bed, his thighs apart.

'You can look,' he said. 'But not touch.'

Suzie stared entranced at his crotch. While she remained acutely aware of her wide open thighs – of the submissiveness of her position – Michael displayed himself without any shame; with pride, even. And a pride he had every reason to feel: he was superbly endowed, his penis long as it hung before his pendulous balls. And even as she watched, it began to erect. She had never seen a cock harden of its own volition before, with no direct stimulation. (At least, none other than that provided by his eyes, which were locked, she knew, on the V of her wide-spread thighs.) Yet as she watched, it thickened and swelled; began to stand upright and finally sculpted itself into a magnificent phallus. The shaft was thick and strong, its head large and bulbous, deeply clefted by the dewy eye at its tip.

And it was tempting, oh so tempting. She yearned to reach out to it, to grip it, to take it into her mouth and suck it until it throbbed. To straddle him, then, and force it deep inside her; ride it to the orgasm that was tugging unbearably at the pit of her stomach.

Even as she thought it she felt her climax, yet again, gather within her and she almost came. She fought for control and found just enough to contain herself. God, how she longed for climax.

'And now,' Michael said, as if prompted by her thought. 'I think it's time you came.'

Suzie breathed a sigh of relief. And Michael reached down and dipped a long middle finger into her splayed-open sex. He withdrew it, now glistening, and held it poised.

'There,' he said, 'use my finger to get yourself off.'

Suzie stared at the rigid finger for a moment, slightly puzzled. She had no need of such stimulus: now she had permission, she could come merely by allowing herself to, no longer in need of a physical trigger. And having watched her come earlier, Michael must know that. Yet he wasn't suggesting; he was, as usual, commanding. But why? And then a little groan rose in her throat as the answer became patently obvious: at the position he was holding his finger, she would have to kneel up and thrust herself forward to reach it; put on a lewd and ignominious display as she strained for the offered stimulus – even in this, in finally allowing her the relief she craved, he sought to make it as humiliating for her as possible; an act of self-debasement.

Blushing scarlet, she kneeled up, pushed forward her wide-spread thighs and strained for Michael's finger. Found it, just, and began writhing her hips in an undignified display as she ground her aching nub against it.

Orgasm gathered, was about to trigger. Then suddenly, impossibly – oh, God, no – it began to recede.

Suzie groaned aloud, suddenly seeing the wizened face of Sister Marianna leaning in towards her, her finger wagging.

'Sex is sinful,' the old nun was warning, the terrified child cowering before her. 'Wantonness will see you in the fire of Hell.'

It was a face that appeared to her all too often; always, when it did, just at the point of orgasm. It would instantly set up a mental block – try as she might she couldn't come – leaving her frustrated and angry.

Oh but, God, now now. Please, not now.

But orgasm continued to recede; her bucking hips, her writhing sex, the friction of Michael's finger, the humiliating thrill of it all, none of it making the slightest difference. She was about to be left frustrated again.

But then, just as all seemed hopelessly lost, the mental block set firmly in place, Hilary's words came back to her.

Desperately, she clutched at the straw they offered: 'It isn't me,' she screamed at the black-swathed ghost in her mind, new hope rearing within her. 'This man's making me do it.'

No culpability, no guilt.

And the moment the words fully formed, the nun's image, miraculously, began to shimmer. Faded, then went altogether. And a sense of release swept over her the like of which she had never before felt.

And she knew, then, that thanks to Hilary and Michael, to the wonderful liberation of sexual submission, Sister Marianna was gone for good and would never trouble her again.

And it was then she came, shuddering to a massive second climax that was made all the sweeter for her victory over the Merciful Sisters; banished from her life for ever.

BLACK LACE NEW BOOKS

Published in January

NADYA'S QUEST
Lisette Allen

Nadya's personal quest leads her to St Petersburg in the summer of 1788. The beautiful city is in a rapturous state of decadence and its Empress, well known for her lascivious appetite, is hungry for a new lover who must be young, handsome and virile. When Nadya brings a Swedish seafarer, the magnificently-proportioned Axel, to the Imperial court, he is soon made the Empress's favourite. Nadya, determined to keep Axel for herself, is drawn into an intrigue of treachery and sedition as hostilities develop between Russia and Sweden.

ISBN 0 352 33135 6

DESIRE UNDER CAPRICORN
Louisa Francis

A shipwreck rips Dita Jones from the polite society of Sydney in the 1870s and throws her into an untamed world where Matt Warrender, a fellow castaway, develops a passion for her he will never forget. Separated after their eventual rescue, Dita is taken back into civilised life where a wealthy stud farmer, Jas McGrady, claims her for his bride. Taken to the rugged terrain of outback Australia, and a new life as Mrs McGrady, Dita realises her husband has a dark secret.

ISBN 0 352 33136 4

Published in February

PULLING POWER
Cheryl Mildenhall

Amber Barclay is a top motor racing driver whose career is sponsored by Portia Lombardi, a professional dominatrix with a taste for control as forceful as Amber's driving. In the run-up to an important race, competition is fierce as Marie Gifford, Portia's financial dependent, sparks a passionate sexual liaison with the dashing Lawrie Samson, Amber's only rival. But what will happen when Lawrie discovers an astonishing link between the three women?

ISBN 0 352 33139 9

THE MASTER OF SHILDEN
Lucinda Carrington

Trapped in a web of sexual and emotional entanglement, interior designer Elise St John grabs at the chance to redecorate a remote castle. As she sets about creating rooms in which guests will be able to realise their most erotic fantasies, her own dreams and desires ripen. Caught between Max Lannsen, the dark, broody Master of Shilden, and Blair Devlin, the sexy, debonair riding instructor, Elise realises that her dreams are becoming reality and that the future of these two men suddenly depends on a decision she will be forced to make.

ISBN 0 352 33140 2

MODERN LOVE
An Anthology of Erotic Writing by Women
Edited by Kerri Sharp

For nearly four years Black Lace has dominated the erotic fiction market in the UK and revolutionised the way people think about and write erotica. Black Lace is now a generic term for erotic fiction by and for women. Following the success of *Pandora's Box*, the first Black Lace anthology, *Modern Love* is a collection of extracts from our bestselling contemporary novels. Seduction and mystery and darkly sensual behaviour are the key words to this unique collection of erotic writings from the female imagination.

ISBN 0 352 33158 5

To be published in March

SILKEN CHAINS
Jodi Nicol

Fleeing her scheming guardian and an arranged marriage, Abbie, an innocent young Victorian woman, is thrown from her horse. She awakens in a lavish interior filled with heavenly perfumes to find that Leon Villiers, the wealthy and attractive master of the house, has virtually imprisoned her with sensual pleasures. Using his knowledge of Eastern philosophy and tantric arts, he introduces her to experiences beyond her imagination. But will her guardian's unerring search for her ruin this taste of liberty?

ISBN 0 352 33143 7

THE HAND OF AMUN
Juliet Hastings

Marked from birth, Naunakhte – daughter of a humble scribe – must enter a life of dark eroticism as the servant of the Egyptian god Amun. She becomes the favourite of the high priestess but is accused of an act of lascivious sacrilege and is forced to flee the temple for the murky labyrinth of the city. There she meets Khonsu, a prince of the underworld, but fate draws her back to the temple and she is forced to choose between two lovers – one mortal and the other a god.

ISBN 0 352 33144 5

If you would like a complete list of plot summaries of Black Lace titles, please fill out the questionnaire overleaf or send a stamped addressed envelope to:-

Black Lace, 332 Ladbroke Grove, London W10 5AH

BLACK LACE BACKLIST

All books are priced £4.99 unless another price is given.

BLUE HOTEL	Cherri Pickford ISBN 0 352 32858 4	☐
CASSANDRA'S CONFLICT	Fredrica Alleyn ISBN 0 352 32859 2	☐
THE CAPTIVE FLESH	Cleo Cordell ISBN 0 352 32872 X	☐
PLEASURE HUNT	Sophie Danson ISBN 0 352 32880 0	☐
OUTLANDIA	Georgia Angelis ISBN 0 352 32883 5	☐
BLACK ORCHID	Roxanne Carr ISBN 0 352 32888 6	☐
ODALISQUE	Fleur Reynolds ISBN 0 352 32887 8	☐
THE SENSES BEJEWELLED	Cleo Cordell ISBN 0 352 32904 1	☐
VIRTUOSO	Katrina Vincenzi ISBN 0 352 32907 6	☐
FIONA'S FATE	Fredrica Alleyn ISBN 0 352 32913 0	☐
HANDMAIDEN OF PALMYRA	Fleur Reynolds ISBN 0 352 32919 X	☐
THE SILKEN CAGE	Sophie Danson ISBN 0 352 32928 9	☐
THE GIFT OF SHAME	Sarah Hope-Walker ISBN 0 352 32935 1	☐
SUMMER OF ENLIGHTENMENT	Cheryl Mildenhall ISBN 0 352 32937 8	☐
A BOUQUET OF BLACK ORCHIDS	Roxanne Carr ISBN 0 352 32939 4	☐
JULIET RISING	Cleo Cordell ISBN 0 352 32938 6	☐

------ ✂ ------------------

Please send me the books I have ticked above.

Name ....

Address ....

....

....

.... Post Code ....

Send to: **Cash Sales, Black Lace Books, 332 Ladbroke Grove, London W10 5AH.**

Please enclose a cheque or postal order, made payable to **Virgin Publishing Ltd**, to the value of the books you have ordered plus postage and packing costs as follows:

UK and BFPO – £1.00 for the first book, 50p for each subsequent book.

Overseas (including Republic of Ireland) – £2.00 for the first book, £1.00 each subsequent book.

If you would prefer to pay by VISA or ACCESS/ MASTERCARD, please write your card number and expiry date here:

....

Please allow up to 28 days for delivery.

Signature ....

------ ✂ ------------------

BLACK
lace

WE NEED YOUR HELP ...
to plan the future of women's erotic fiction –

– and no stamp required!

Yours are the only opinions that matter.

Black Lace is the first series of books devoted to erotic fiction by women for women.

We intend to keep providing the best-written, sexiest books you can buy. And we'd appreciate your help and valued opinion of the books so far. Tell us what you want to read.

THE BLACK LACE QUESTIONNAIRE

SECTION ONE: ABOUT YOU

1.1 Sex (*we presume you are female, but so as not to discriminate*)
Are you?
Male ☐
Female ☐

1.2 Age
under 21 ☐ 21–30 ☐
31–40 ☐ 41–50 ☐
51–60 ☐ over 60 ☐

1.3 At what age did you leave full-time education?
still in education ☐ 16 or younger ☐
17–19 ☐ 20 or older ☐

1.4 Occupation _____

1.5 Annual household income

       under £10,000 ☐   £10–£20,000 ☐

       £20–£30,000 ☐   £30–£40,000 ☐

       over £40,000 ☐

1.6 We are perfectly happy for you to remain anonymous; but if you would like to receive information on other publications available, please insert your name and address

    —————————————————————————

    —————————————————————————

    —————————————————————————

    —————————————————————————

SECTION TWO: ABOUT BUYING BLACK LACE BOOKS

2.1 How did you acquire this copy of *Modern Love*?

    I bought it myself ☐   My partner bought it ☐

    I borrowed/found it ☐

2.2 How did you find out about Black Lace books?

    I saw them in a shop ☐

    I saw them advertised in a magazine ☐

    I saw the London Underground posters ☐

    I read about them in ————————————

    Other ——————————————————

2.3 Please tick the following statements you agree with:

    I would be less embarrassed about buying Black
Lace books if the cover pictures were less explicit ☐

    I think that in general the pictures on Black
Lace books are about right ☐

    I think Black Lace cover pictures should be as
explicit as possible ☐

2.4 Would you read a Black Lace book in a public place – on a train for instance?

    Yes ☐   No ☐

SECTION THREE: ABOUT THIS BLACK LACE BOOK

3.1 Do you think the sex content in this book is:
    Too much   ☐   About right   ☐
    Not enough   ☐

3.2 Do you think the writing style in this book is:
    Too unreal/escapist   ☐   About right   ☐
    Too down to earth   ☐

3.3 Do you think the story in this book is:
    Too complicated   ☐   About right   ☐
    Too boring/simple   ☐

3.4 Do you think the cover of this book is:
    Too explicit   ☐   About right   ☐
    Not explicit enough   ☐

Here's a space for any other comments:

SECTION FOUR: ABOUT OTHER BLACK LACE BOOKS

4.1 How many Black Lace books have you read?   ☐

4.2 If more than one, which one did you prefer?

4.3 Why?

SECTION FIVE: ABOUT YOUR IDEAL EROTIC NOVEL

We want to publish the books you want to read – so this is your chance to tell us exactly what your ideal erotic novel would be like.

5.1 Using a scale of 1 to 5 (1 = no interest at all, 5 = your ideal), please rate the following possible settings for an erotic novel:

Medieval/barbarian/sword 'n' sorcery	☐
Renaissance/Elizabethan/Restoration	☐
Victorian/Edwardian	☐
1920s & 1930s – the Jazz Age	☐
Present day	☐
Future/Science Fiction	☐

5.2 Using the same scale of 1 to 5, please rate the following themes you may find in an erotic novel:

Submissive male/dominant female	☐
Submissive female/dominant male	☐
Lesbianism	☐
Bondage/fetishism	☐
Romantic love	☐
Experimental sex e.g. anal/watersports/sex toys	☐
Gay male sex	☐
Group sex	☐

Using the same scale of 1 to 5, please rate the following styles in which an erotic novel could be written:

Realistic, down to earth, set in real life	☐
Escapist fantasy, but just about believable	☐
Completely unreal, impressionistic, dreamlike	☐

5.3 Would you prefer your ideal erotic novel to be written from the viewpoint of the main male characters or the main female characters?

Male	☐	Female	☐
Both	☐		

5.4 What would your ideal Black Lace heroine be like? Tick as many as you like:

Dominant	☐	Glamorous	☐
Extroverted	☐	Contemporary	☐
Independent	☐	Bisexual	☐
Adventurous	☐	Naïve	☐
Intellectual	☐	Introverted	☐
Professional	☐	Kinky	☐
Submissive	☐	Anything else?	☐
Ordinary	☐	_____	

5.5 What would your ideal male lead character be like? Again, tick as many as you like:

Rugged	☐		
Athletic	☐	Caring	☐
Sophisticated	☐	Cruel	☐
Retiring	☐	Debonair	☐
Outdoor-type	☐	Naïve	☐
Executive-type	☐	Intellectual	☐
Ordinary	☐	Professional	☐
Kinky	☐	Romantic	☐
Hunky	☐		
Sexually dominant	☐	Anything else?	☐
Sexually submissive	☐	_____	

5.6 Is there one particular setting or subject matter that your ideal erotic novel would contain?

_____

SECTION SIX: LAST WORDS

6.1 What do you like best about Black Lace books?

_____

6.2 What do you most dislike about Black Lace books?

_____

6.3 In what way, if any, would you like to change Black Lace covers?

_____

6.4 Here's a space for any other comments:

_____

_____

_____

_____

_____

Thank you for completing this questionnaire. Now tear it out of the book – carefully! – put it in an envelope and send it to:

Black Lace
FREEPOST
London
W10 5BR

No stamp is required if you are resident in the U.K.